Summa Totalis

Keith Allan Noback

Summa Totalis

Keith Allan Noback

For Janice and Marshall

Contents

Prologue

In a neglected quarter of the dendritic event radiation, Laplace brooded on the day's poor prospects. He was on track to complete a major project, which usually put him in a good mood. Before he could get to the happy part, however, he would have to commit three murders. He was unlikely to face any consequences for the killings besides the consequences that came with the act. Despite the look of nonchalance men like him cultivated in their approach to violence, none of it was easy. All of it left a mark.

In this case, it would be worse, since he knew two of the victims, who had been his slaves for several years prior. At least he would not have to pursue them. He had set them up to think that they were coming for him. After all the work he put into their training, they fell for the ruse so easily. They trusted Thomas when he volunteered the time and location of Laplace's next excursion in the event radiation.

They knew the man worked at once for Laplace and Augustine, Laplace's sworn enemy. Yet when he knocked on their door with a gift, they let him in like he was one of the family. It made Laplace angry, and he estimated the anger would be enough to get him through. He stood up, put on his hat, and set things in motion.

One

The Fate of Runaway Slaves

ONE

Two frightened creatures drifted through a sea of shifting, interwoven shapes. The Koch curves, Julia sets, Apollonian gaskets, and pyramid surfaces were translucent and stained with the entire spectrum of colors. A dim light permeated the space without shadows or gradients to indicate a source. Close examination revealed the larger shapes as constructs of smaller, similar shapes, each building on the other up a scale that must culminate in structures too monstrous to apprehend.

The coloration of larger shapes was a blend of the tints that their building blocks gave to the ambient light. At regular intervals, eddies of warped and compressed geometry formed long, parallel columns that curled and uncurled as they circled an invisible axis, always in a counterclockwise rota-tion. The eddies were the only landmarks in the sweeping impermanence.

The kaleidoscopic ocean shifted

seamlessly around a bubble of clear space containing the two figures.

Anyone entering this venue played at only one game, and anyone marginally familiar with that game could have taken one look at the pair in the middle of the dizzyingly complex structure and told them that they were in trouble.

Their equipment was a bargain-basement kit, not suited for grand calculations. They bore the markings of their culture's middle class, a demographic without the requisite sense of self-importance to thrive on violent competition.

They had accentuating marks around their eyelids and eyebrows, but nothing fancy or extravagant like scalp tattoos. Their eyes were relatively small, with brown irises that obscured the sclera. The smaller of the two had a ring fitted through her right nasal flap. They had thin lips and small mouths, drawn into tight lines by the tension in their jaws.

Their limbs had the sculpted look of generic bio prosthetics. They wore gray robes in a style reserved for slaves. If anyone spotted them on their own in the dendritic event radiation, they were subject to arrest or worse.

The fronts of their torsos bore the distinguishing characteristics of their race. Across the chest and abdomen, four sets of four filamentary tufts sprouted clumps of fine, densely packed fibers. The fibers protruded three handbreadths from the structure's base, covering the chest and abdomen at rest.

The rows of tufts were situated, with each row above a pair of narrow flaps of tissue covered with skin and inlaid with a weave of wires and beads. When relaxed, the flaps rested against the skin of the abdomen and thorax, hidden by the tufts. Under the current circumstances, the tissue flaps extended fully. On the larger individual, all the flaps worked together to support a mechanism made of four cylindrical arrays of metal beads

strung on wires around a central axis and anchored to a metal disk on each end. The cylinders were fixed to a thin, unmarked frame. The polished wooden rectangle also contained compartments on either side, each covered by a sliding door.

The appendages on the smaller individual's chest and abdomen supported a loop of wire strung with beads woven between the extended tissue flaps. Tuft filaments worked feverishly on the beads suspended on the frame device and the loop of beads alike, but the difference between the two operators was blatant.

The bead loop rested too loosely on the flaps. It slipped frequently and required awkward pauses to readjust its position, further complicated by the tremor affecting the operator's hands during the reset.

By contrast, the flaps and filaments moved over the beads on the frame device's cylinders with smooth competence. The rest of her body grew still as the intensity increased.

A distortion wave shook the excluded space surrounding the pair. In the time it took to recover, the leader turned her head briefly to address her compatriot, who had dropped the loop of beads entirely in response to the

twitch.

"Get the 2nd nachinak deployed right now!" she said.

"No, Shelley," said Carmella," It's too soon. It's going to give us away."

"God dammit Carmella! You do what I say, and you do it right now," Shelley said, "Those are the rules. I'm already further behind on my calculations. He is solving fast. This was a mistake. What made me think I could turn the tables on him? We should have listened to Anisa."

Carmella let out a tremulous whine, a sound that she typically followed up with a full-scale breakdown. "Don't you dare," said Shelley.

Carmella hesitated for a heartbeat and then rallied. She fished around in her hip pocket and finally produced the second nachinak. The first nachinak was already in action, suspended just above their heads.

Both devices were small, about half again the size of a mouse. They had the body shape of a thick, tailless lizard, but the head was square at the base, without any suggestion of ears. A pair of frog-like eyes perched just in front of the blocky base of the skull.

A small trunk led to a circular mouth lined with a ring of short, pointed metal teeth. Their base color was white, marked with oval blotches of red pigmentation within thin borders of yellow. The square portion of the head was black. Twelve delicate pairs of legs protruded from its sides; each tipped with a three-toed foot. Carmella stroked the most prominent of the little blotches on its back. A ripple spread down its body, and it squinted its eyes as its mouth opened wide. It shook one more time and then stood quietly on her palm. She touched a second red blotch on its back, and it shot up to float next to the other nachinak. Its legs began to move as if they were gathering some invisible substance to its underbelly.

The legs moved faster and faster until they were just a blur, and a small whirl-pool of shifting colors began to form between them. The whirlpool lengthened over a few seconds and developed an area of distortion surrounding the vortex as if the swirl were viewed through a concave lens.

Carmella picked up the loop of beads and began a new series of con-

figurations. Shelley redoubled her efforts. Very slowly, the Byzantine polychro-matic structure surrounding them shifted in unison.

The small, complex shapes slipped, rotated, and flowed away from them while larger structures blossomed to occupy the area surrounding the two calculators. As the mosaic grew less complex, the colors became monotonous, and their boundaries grew sharper.

Without warning, another wave swept through the local structure. Before it contacted their exclusion sphere, the first nachinak's vortex turned slightly to in-tercept it. The wave deflected from the point of contact and passed by. Shelley and Carmela exchanged glances.

4

Shelley squinted in the direction of the wave's origin. Like clouds parting to reveal the sun, a dark purple ellipsoid pirouetted while it joined with a Levy C curve of gold and pink, revealing her target for an instant. She flinched, and a trickle of urine ran down her leg. She looked over to assess Carmella's readiness.

Carmella knelt curled over in the bottom of their exclusion sphere, her eyes shut and her head in her hands, rocking slowly back and forth. The collection of shapes and the wash of light across the surrounding expanse continued to rarify at an increasing pace.

Shelley forced herself to face the enemy, now clearly visible. He stood about twenty meters in front of her. She had recognized him at the first glimpse of his silhouette. He meant for people to recognize him.

His shape, overall, was quite like hers. He had undertaken a few modifications, however, some via wardrobe, others by means of interventional cosmetics. A wide-brimmed hat perched lightly atop his narrow head. It was made of felt and stained deep red. A leather band encircled the crown, which held a radiation of eagle feathers set in a beadwork plaque of nested arches, with a peacock feather angled back on each side.

He had opted to change the opacity of tissues in his face and neck. The eyes, elements of the central nervous system, and blood vessels

were wholly opaque and matched his hat. The other tissues were transparent and tinted red, including his eyelids.

He had intricate tattoos on his bioprosthetic limbs. His hands were delicate and sharp, slender claws tipped the fingers. He put a finger to his lips, requesting silence. With his other hand, he pointed up and over his left shoulder. As she transferred her gaze to whatever horror he had in store for them, Shelley broke from her paralysis with a shiver.

She followed the aim of his finger to its target. A woman stood with her back to them and worked an abacus with furious precision. Given her skill and focus, she undoubtedly attempted a complete calculation.

The man, Shelly's former master, Laplace, was stalking the aspirant. He would jump when her attempt failed. Shelley turned her attention back to the perimeter of the exclusion sphere across from her own. A count of the nachinaks surrounding it came to ten versus her two humble units. She glanced back at Carmella, still lying in a heap, whimpering. The lapse of attention was her last mistake.

When she looked back towards the threat, two waves of kaleidoscopic distortion washed over her. The abacus she clutched to her body delivered a jolt with the second wave's passage. She got a flash of both of her nachinaks tumbling in a violent maelstrom, and then he stood before her.

Before she could move, he leaned in and whispered in her ear. At the touch of his breath, the neurotoxic dart she had prepared for this moment, dropped from her hand.

"Look at her. Such skill. She is so close! But she is not getting there today, and it turns out today was her last chance. Express my condolences."

As he spoke, she did everything she could to avoid looking

into his lidless eyes. Two claws hovered over a major vessel in her right neck and pricked her skin with every heartbeat. Laplace brandished a nachinak as big as a rat in his right hand, with a head at either end of a body covered in spiraling black stripes.

"You're so scared. You needn't say anything. You recognize this little treasure, don't you? It is the only instance of the genus

that a person of your means and level of achievement would likely ever encounter. You should feel honored that I'm wasting it on you. You know, I did not hold it against you – the escape, the conniving with Anisa – I expect my slaves to try to escape. What infuriates me are the recaptures. I can't abide the stupidity."

With that, he slapped one end of the nachinak down on Shelly's forehead where the round mouth ringed with teeth puckered up and dug into the skin. Shelly's second nachinak stopped being in the vortex over their heads and started being just above the head of Laplace's quarry, who was working frantically at an abacus nearly as impressive as the one her nemesis wielded. Shelley had shifted with her nachinak. She stuck to the wall of the sphere above and behind the woman. Laplace turned away from his first two victims.

He did what his face would allow in the form of a frown as he shifted his attention to Carmella.

Carmella tried to scramble to her feet but stood too fast and dropped back to her hands and knees, looking like she might faint. She hit the sphere's surface and pushed off toward Laplace with her arms outstretched. The move surprised him, so he failed to sidestep or activate the security measures on his heirloom abacus, whose delicate wires were now wrapped in her fingers. He disengaged from the abacus to avoid damaging it in a tug of war.

"Yikes!" he said.

She still had a lead on him and got the next word in before he could elaborate.

"Laplace! Please let me come back. I am not the kind that can make it out there on my own. Can you imagine

how easily they pressured me into the vicious betrayal they had planned for all those months? I accept my fate.

"I need guidance and help with my humble and affordable basic needs. I can be of use! Here: Anisa. She made contact with us. She separated from her skin, and it got displaced. I'll help you get Anisa back if you want. She

told us she was looking for a nachinak to pull the amalgam apart. Why would she want to do that? Oh God, oh God! This is what I mean! I can't keep things straight out there! Please!"

Laplace stepped back to regain his composure.

"Carmella," he said, "I don't doubt the truth of your confession or its sincerity.

"I'll admit that I have been remiss on several accounts in my duty to you. It is true, and I will admit it, I have not been a good master. The trouble is: you lack the competence to be a slave of mine."

She threw her head back and started a scream that broke into a cough as a small packet of dust smacked her between the eyes. After a pause to be sure that she had inhaled a good portion of the powder, Laplace knelt to pluck the nachinak that had attached itself to the back of her calf during the crawl. "You didn't catch me completely by surprise after all, it would appear. Off to richer harvests, I go."

"No!" she wailed," Put it back on!"

When she raised her head again, he had gone. She looked at the shrinking exclusion sphere; despite her situation, her tears stopped, and her breathing slowed as the tension in her shoulders melted away.

She was illuminated from within by a faint, reddish glow. "What a beautiful color. It isn't red, is it?"

"Wait, who am I?"

"Did somebody pee on the floor?"

Laplace watched the image in the relief carved from the swirls and ripples of the Nachinak's vortex. The figure slumped in the exclusion sphere, and the body began to sublimate. The deterioration already rendered it unrecognizable.

"No loose ends, ever," he said to himself.

In a ring around him in the vertical plane, his nachinaks churned their legs fast enough to shake the sphere. The sea of shapes surrounding him had consolidated into just a few dozen gigantic constructs in the visible

portion, and the light carrying the sparse assortment of colors remaining in calculation's palette so close to completion barely lit the area out to three radii beyond his sphere.

"Good work, boys," said Laplace," How about some help now?"

He readjusted the abacus and took a deep breath. His filaments whipped through the mechanism fast enough to outpace the cooling system. Small tendrils of smoke drifted around the edges of the frame. Around him, the stark simplicity of the obscure shapes, now fading further in the waning light, grew towards unity with uncertain implications. He could have touched his primary target had he extended his arm.

His tactics succeeded. She hadn't noticed him yet, or Shelly, who was practically sitting on her head, motionless. A filament flicked away from the beads to open a compartment in the abacus. Above him, the nachinak with the black whorls on its skin dropped out of the spinning hoops around the sphere's circumference and dove into the open compartment. Laplace quickly slowed his abacus, and the outside conditions solidified. His victim carried on.

Meanwhile, Shelly began to move, setting her abacus in motion and speeding up its lines of spinning beads until she threatened to match the efforts of the stranger standing just below her.

Laplace watched them intensely as he kept pace, now at a safer distance.

Two

Prospecting

The chase continued until Shelly's second nachinak began to oscillate in the spinning ring it rode. The amplitude of the wave exploded. It bounced off another vortex, this one belonging to one of the victim's devices, and crashed into the side of her abacus, a crumpled mess. Everything stopped except for the victim's abacus and Shelly's. Shelly screamed and thrashed but could not force any change in her position. The other calculator spun around to glare at Laplace. She began to say something, but it was too late. A flat grey surface ballooned in front of her. It drew the diffuse light to itself, and darkness shrank toward it all around. Then, the surface expanded past the doomed pair. Light diffused back into the periphery while the interlocked geometry shifted and flowed around the rim of the shrinking grey surface. Laplace stood frozen for a moment.

The expansion nearly got him this time. Without further indication of distress, he set his abacus to one side and pulled a pair of large nachinaks from their compartment.

For this mission, the abacus packed a dozen nachinaks with a variety of sizes and functions. Superficially, his instrument resembled Shelley's. The layout was the same. There were pairs of cylinders supporting rows of beads strung on wires. The wires connected a pair of discs forming the base of the cylinder on each end. The frame was similar in shape and proportion.

The similarities went no further, though. The beads on his device's cylinders were much smaller and more ornate in their surface carvings and features.

The incredible number of wires packed into the space around the axle of each cylinder and the density of beads that those wires supported jumped the line between quantitative and qualitative differences in the comparison. Compartments secured with numbered sliding doors covered the deep brown wooden frame. Ornate gold end covers capped the cylinders set inside the housing. Laplace lined up the pair of nachinaks on the abacus frame.

One device had overdeveloped final pairs of legs on each end, and tufts quite similar to those of its makers, but with only one pair on its upper body. The second nachinak was slightly smaller, the size of a rat, with a transparent skull base and rows of rust-colored spots over its entire body and head. He activated both and produced a spray bottle from an adjacent box.

Laplace pulled the trigger on the spray bottle without looking, sending a narrow stream of clear liquid toward the receding surface. With his other hand, he released the gold cap on the upper right cylinder of his abacus. Peering into the nest of wires underneath, he selected a black wire with a numbered tab and unplugged the end from its connection on the cylinder end plate. The wire's connector fitted perfectly into the mouth of the larger nachinak. As soon as its mouth closed on the end of the wire, it backed up until it could grasp the back end of its partner with the exaggerated first pair of legs.

The small legs on both nachinaks began to beat in the gathering motion they used to generate a vortex, but at a slower rate. Just as Laplace completed the activation process, the liquid from the spray bottle passed through the shifting landscape, creating a slight distortion as it flew. It reached the grey surface and disappeared without any reaction from the target. The pair then set off towards the patch of gray, moving backward steadily, joined to

Laplace's abacus by the wire and the thin vortex surrounding it.

Laplace focused on their movement, leaning forward while adjusting the wires under the cap with the clawed fingers of his left hand. As the pair of nachinaks reached the flat patch of gray, they turned to move parallel to the surface and made for the shrinking edge. The larger device gently lowered its passenger onto the surface as they intercepted the border. The gray disc flickered as the tiny legs made contact, followed by the upper half of

11

the body. Laplace tensed. His gaze swept over the area where the devices had made contact.

He slouched in relief when he got a fix on them once more, but his eyes remained locked on the movements of his nachinaks. His surroundings accumulated shapes like precipitate settling in a puddle, while the shrinkage rate of the gray surface accelerated. He had trouble keeping track of the nachinaks' activity. The situation's precarious nature showed in the recurrent flickers and tugs from the gray space, now becoming more frequent and persistent.

Laplace took his hand off the wire plugged into the cylinder and, from a slot beside the open nachinak compartment, grabbed a small, thin rectangle of glass with a handle attached to the edge of its long side.

"No," he said to the wild scramble at the other end of the wire he held. "You can't have them."

He held the glass before his eyes. It showed static, like a colorized version of the cosmic background radiation seen on a cathode ray tube. He watched patiently despite yanks on the wire strong enough to pull it from his grasp if the timing were right. A small green dot appeared in the right upper quadrant of the screen.

"There you go!" he said in a hoarse whisper. "Come on, boys, grab that ammonium, and let's get out of here."

Now less than 2 meters in diameter, the disc flipped on its vertical and horizontal axes several times, briefly expanded, and then flipped over one

more time and began to curl in on itself. The screen in his hand flashed gold, and then it played a cartoon depicting a flood of coins spewing out of a slot machine, with triple cherries flashing on top. Laplace jerked the wire as the involuting disc flipped on end to present as a

cylinder with razor-thin walls closing in on the nachinaks in the middle.

The wire came screaming back, towing both nachinaks to a rough homecoming. Laplace ripped another cylinder wire out of its clip as the tow cord piled in a tangle at his feet, and the two prodigal devices slammed against the side of the abacus.

Only a horizontal line remained where the gray disc had been; both ends contracting towards the middle and bending the surrounding shaped layers toward the central conjunction. Bolts of gray, like pencil markings on the background of shapes, shot through various standing wave patterns, lashing out tens of meters from the dying line until they blinked out of existence, taking with them any influence they had exerted on their surroundings.

Laplace impatiently squashed the wire tangle into a ball beside the abacus, then checked on the nachinaks still deployed around the excluded area. He moved quickly but purposefully, taking no shortcuts in his evaluation. When he was convinced that all was in order, he picked up the pair of expeditionary nachinaks and started his examination.

There was no visible damage on either one. He pulled the wire plug from the mouth of the carrier machine and gently disengaged the front limbs from the tail end of the other. He carefully identified a small slit in the dorsal surface of the passenger's tail end, just beyond the last pair of legs' attachment. Within the slit, there was a small, clear cylinder with a drop of liquid inside that gave off a pale green glow.

Laplace stowed the carrier nachinak and then very slowly, very gently inserted the cylinder into the passenger Nachinak's mouth. The ring of teeth closed over it, and the device arched backward. It convulsed violently for several long

moments. Its eyes deviated to opposing upper quadrants of their gaze. The convulsions passed, and it shivered for a few moments longer before growing still. Laplace removed his hat and ran his hand over his scalp. He sighed deeply before setting himself to straightening up the wires piled next to his abacus. He watched the nachinak while he went about the chore but restrained himself from touching the device again before the wire was in good order and stowed in its proper place.

The nachinak had not shown any signs of life since he set it down. He picked it up again when he was finished straightening up. All was as it had been before the conflict, except for one wire that remained unplugged from its connection on the end of its cylinder. He activated the nachinak once again, this time without any fireworks. He inserted the plug into its mouth and held his breath. It stirred and stretched its legs as any other functional nachinak would do upon

13

activation. The eyes blinked rapidly and then steadied. It shivered once before it assumed a ready posture.

Laplace picked up the little screen. He blazed through the diagnostic report on display and nodded his approval. After removing the plug from the nachinak's mouth with exaggerated care, he held the device at eye level for inspection.

He saw no evidence of damage and no twitches or other behaviors to suggest a heretofore undetectable problem.

The exemplary data fitted the hardwired programming.

When asked, the nachinak would manipulate the data source flawlessly. Laplace threw his hands in the air as he let out a celebratory "Whoop!" He took a deep breath and calmed himself before things went any further. He looked down again at the day's accomplishment.

"My new treasure of treasures. What shall we

do now?" he asked," Right back to the gates of hell, eh? We just came from there. There's no use in waiting, though. I would hate for anything to happen before we arrive. We've got them where we want them, all of them. Ad Majorem Dei Gloriam, indeed. They will be eating those words."

Three

Glamping Ain't Easy

The stars shed enough light to set up the tent, but the camper had not finished the assembly. He had barely made it off the freeway and up the fire road to the dispersed camping area. The weather app on his phone promised clear skies for the rest of the week, so he left the rain fly off. No rain and stable temperatures meant light winds as well. He did not stake the tent down either.

Despite the progressive stiffness and incoordination, he managed to set up the sleeping bag and cot. He had taken his pills as the spell was coming on, but it would be some time before the medication crossed the intestinal membranes to the bloodstream and then the brain. Overall, his problems didn't look any better lying down, but it was more comfortable.

He parked his station wagon on the downhill side of the hairpin turn at the road's crest. The extra space at the turn protected him from traffic and had a view across the small valley below the ridge to the freeway. Even during settled weather, the geography usually produced a nighttime breeze. Nothing stirred, however.

One cricket chirping contributed the only sound for miles.

The little insect was clever enough to begin singing at a distance from the

activity surrounding the car and the tent, so his song seemed to come from all directions. A shadow filled the valley. The faint, jaundiced sodium glow from streetlights in the tourist town over the next ridge defined the shade's border. Not a single vehicle passed on any of the roadways below. He squeezed the handle of the cheap machete that lay across his chest.

He looked like he was expecting something, but it was hard to tell what that might be. The machete was neither a weapon nor a tool. Over the blades' black undercoat, several paragraphs in white print warned against using the blade for the very purposes suggested in the packaging. He had seen to the edge, however, and it would cut at least once, if not twice. Its solidity reassured him. He woke once in the night for a dose of medication, with the quiet still looming.

He woke for the day at midmorning. He lay exactly as he had when he stretched out on the cot the night before. He lifted his head off the pillow and looked down as far as he could. The machete was still there. He let his head drop, and he sat up after stiffening his back and neck. He winced slightly during the transition.

He recovered to a reasonable approximation of good sitting posture, then rummaged around the tent floor for his medication and water bottle. He found both of them under the down bag he had used as a blanket the night before. When he stood up, he stayed up and gathered his clothing off the floor. He checked the tent's door. He had managed to close the mesh completely last night. He shook the clothing out anyway before putting it on. The area was a good scorpion habitat. He pulled on a pair of relatively new jeans, with just a few white threads showing on each leg's medial cuff. As he was about to slip his orange plaid button-down shirt over his head, he noticed a mark on the collar. It was the letter "J," written on the lapel. He was not sure why it caught his attention. He assumed that it stood for something, probably his name, but he could not remember either the name or the reason for the mark's odd location. Whatever the problem was, two

strokes from an indelible marker had solved it, so it mustn't have been too important.

He put on a wide-brim sun hat to cover the short, dark hair on his scalp and to protect his ears.

He stuffed a rain shell with a hood, his medication, water bottle, and a pair of lightweight running shoes designed for "barefoot" running, into the day pack that sat in the front corner of the tent. He laid a large candy bar and a bag of dried fruit on top of everything and zipped the bag shut. It sagged on his shoulders due to the excess space. He folded up the cot and double-checked his pockets for keys and wallet. Both were there. However, his mobile phone was nowhere to be found. He unzipped the tent door and slipped his feet into the sandals sitting just outside the entrance. After searching the area around the tent, he opened the front of the car and found his phone charging in the middle console. When he unplugged it, he noticed a new text message. He locked the car door and zipped the tent shut. He took the time to stake out the four corners before reading the text.

"Hope everything is well. See you soon. Take some pictures!" He frowned. The ID said, "private." He shook his head slightly and tucked the phone in his pack. He did a brief assessment in the driver's side mirror to ensure he didn't look too scary should he run into anyone else on the trails that morning. His hair was a little bristly but naturally in good order as long as it stayed reasonably short. His face was relatively narrow for his body habitus. His nose looked like it had been broken several times. It was hard to tell what it might have looked like before that. His beard was sparse and had not grown out much since the last shave two days ago. His eyes were grayish-blue and slightly sad, with a small wrinkle at the outer corner of each lid. It would've been hard to guess his age based on his appearance. He looked older than thirty and younger than fifty-five.

He turned and looked up and down the road once to be sure nothing had

passed in the night, then went to seal the tent. He partially zipped up the tent door, then stopped, shook his head in a gesture of self-disgust, and reached back inside to retrieve the machete. It barely fit inside the day pack diagonally, but he could close the zipper.

As he set off for the small valley at the base of the primary ridge line, he chose to stay on the crest of the subsidiary ridge. It was not ridiculously steep, and the soil was thin enough that it did not support a heavy growth of underbrush. He also had an unobstructed view down into the valley, including a clear line of sight to the national forest road and the freeway beyond.

He had concluded that something was wrong and of a serious nature by the time he got to the forest service road. There was no traffic at all on the freeway.

He crossed under it on the state road, which he would follow for the 6-mile trudge to town. The wind never showed up. There was no evidence of a developing wildfire or war. When he reached the convenience store near a bridge over the wash marking the last mile to town, he was jumping at every shadow and rustle in the bushes.

A look inside the abandoned store only confirmed the gravity of the situation. The lights inside were on, but it appeared that the power to the coolers had been off since at least the previous day, if not longer. They contained pools of room-temperature

water and melted ice cream. He tried to get into the back where the owners kept their security camera monitors and recordings, on the off chance that he could access the system. He could not get past the door and repeatedly checked the road and the area behind the convenience store during the investigation. He worked on the lock until his nerves got the better of him. After abandoning his efforts at breaking and entering, he ran for a bit until he reached the last forest service road on the main highway into town.

He knew that road. It meandered up into the hills and canyons on the undeveloped side of the wash.

After walking the road into the Juniper Forest for a few minutes, he

stopped to look back. He didn't see any recent tire tracks in the red sand. He had a difficult decision to make. Something was wrong.

If he had strayed into a metaphorical werewolf movie somehow, sometime during his drive last night, then he should seek out other survivors and the common defense. If he somehow drove into a zombie film, he should get as far away from other people as fast as he could. Since he had not heard howling, he continued moving away from town.

After half an hour of walking, he arrived at a familiar trailhead. It was midday, and he still had not heard any birds singing from the woods. The fenced lot was unoccupied. Between this visit and the last, the Forest Service continued its repair and trail-building cycle. A flyer in the trailhead kiosk described new trail construction on a route that led up into the canyon northwest of the trailhead, following the small perennial water flow in the creek. The trail he had walked before was under repair, and sawhorses blocked the exit from the wooden fencing. The trail beyond was churned up where the crews had worked on it.

They had completed a new cut to about a quarter mile from the trailhead. After that, it looked like the trail had washed out. Judging by the rubble and mounds of dirt on the trail, it may have even suffered a landslide. In any event, it was impassable. After a few minutes of struggling on the loose dirt and unstable talus, he returned to the trailhead and started up the new route. The trail proved to be a tourist's path. The trail crews had cut the track smooth, double wide, and level. All it lacked was asphalt.

He made good time and covered several miles by early after

noon, traveling up the gently rising canyon floor that sheltered the creek in its upper reaches. The vegetation consisted of juniper, with occasional yucca plants and cacti. The trail switched back up a steeper slope at the head of the canyon and then ended in a 75-meter wall of steep sandstone. He looked at the wall and shrugged. After a quick drink from his water bottle, he explored the ground beyond the end of the trail and, finding no good way forward, turned around to head back to his car and tent. Hopefully, the

zombies were still busy with the town folk.

He took one more look at the wall. In the late afternoon light coming over the canyon's rim, he had not noticed what he could now see when facing the sun. He shaded his eyes to look up to the top of the wall without being blinded by the glare. A staggered row of divots followed a weakness in the slab to a ledge near the top of the formation. The span of the two sets of marks was about two and a half feet, while the vertical distance between divots was somewhat greater than that. As he followed them up, squinting against the sun, he could make out a patch of dried mud where the wall flattened out into the ledge.

The ledge ran the width of the slick rock patch and intersected with vegetation on the far side. As he focused on the mud, he shifted around from side to side and up and down the slick rock for a few steps. He thought he could make out a larger structure associated with the vertical mud. He shrugged again and walked over to the lowest divot in the rock. It was just deeper than the distance

19

from the ball of his foot to the end of his big toe. It appeared to have been worn into the rock rather than chiseled. The hold had an indistinct lip and curved bottom, like a bowl. He took a deep breath, set his foot in the bowl, and started climbing. Although the arrangement of the steps allowed a climber to use the divots for handholds, they were of

little use. The footing was sandy and insecure. Before he

thought about it too hard, he found himself about sixty meters up and faced with a few slightly steeper steps.

A check to each side confirmed that the people who carved the path into the stone had indeed found the best route. He placed his foot in the next divot and hesitated. It was a high step. He forced himself to straighten his back and bend his knee slightly deeper. He rested his fingertips against the wall instead of grabbing for the next obvious handhold. He rocked back and forth on the ball of his foot a couple of times and then committed to stepping up. All went well. He took the next two steps quickly. An easier section brought him up to the level of the flat ledge stretching across the

entire formation.

He saw the mouth of a cave where the ledge curved back toward the canyon's left wall. A wall of adobe bricks covered with daub partially blocked the hole in the cliff. He walked along the ledge until he could step around the end of the brick wall and look into the space behind it. The remnants of a large Adobe building filled the near side of the cavern. The intact ruins consisted of several smaller, single-level houses on the right, with a pair of two-level structures occupying the left side of the cavern, where the roof was higher. Between them, a single square opening accessed a large sunken room.

He looked around, being careful not to damage any of the structures. There were a few shards of pottery here and there. He left them. The rooms were cozy but more spacious than they looked from the outside. He cautiously stepped out onto the top of the building in the middle and knelt to examine the ground. The dust held footprints; someone walked there within the last few days.

The rim of the prints was still sharp. He couldn't identify the footwear based on the tread pattern. When he got to the opening, several strips of clean wood stood out on the otherwise dusty frame. He pulled out his mobile phone and activated the flashlight. The chamber below had a low ceiling but would be navigable if he crouched.

There were more footprints in the dust. Many dry corncobs lay scattered across the floor. In the back of the chamber, a wooden ladder protruded above a hole in the floor. He lowered himself through the opening into the room. Prints on the floor confirmed the other explorer's access via the same route. He made his way over to the ladder propped on the hole's edge. Looking over the lip, he saw that the shaft dropped for a surprising distance. The builders had chiseled the shaft out of the rock rather than building it down through a pre-existing void in the formation.

After about twelve feet, the shaft became choked with brush and leaves.

Something had forced its way into the plug of detritus, leaving a burrow through the top of the far side.

At the edge of the illuminated blockage, he could make out a hint of more solid objects, maybe even a floor. He sat and thought for a long time. He looked over the side one more time. With no new revelations forthcoming, he pulled the headlamp from its home in the pack's zipped inner pocket. Once he switched the lamp on and properly situated it on his forehead, with the hat on top and all secured with the chin loop pulled tight, he tucked his phone in the bottom of the pack. He tested the steps on the ladder before putting his full weight on it. They flexed slightly but seemed solid enough. He made his way down to the brush pile and the top of the burrow without incident. The mix of materials forming the plug contained significantly more dirt than the view from above suggested.

The portion consisting of vegetation was dry but not old enough to date back to the original occupants 'era. He worked to get one leg into the burrow so that he could transition off the ladder. He finally flopped over onto the pile of brush face down, sending a cascade of dirt and leaves farther down the shaft. Still lying on top of the brush pile, he managed to push an obscuring tangle of twigs aside without losing his hat and headlamp.

The light now penetrated to what appeared to be the bottom of the shaft, about eight feet below. He could see that the smaller bits of the plug had consolidated into a cone, with a covering of loose leaves.

Partially buried in that cone was a body.

He couldn't see much detail from his vantage point, but it appeared to be a person somewhat smaller than he was, with both arms extended above their head. The right leg was positioned next to the shaft wall, extending downwards and buried to the top of the thigh in the leaves and dirt that formed the cone. The left leg was flexed entirely at the knee and the hip. Some kind of metallic glove covered the hands. The body had no hair on its scalp. He looked over at the ladder and up to the opening of the shaft above, then back down at the body. After a painful internal debate, he decided that

he could not leave it for the coyotes.

He thrashed his way over to the burrow's opening and managed to swing his feet and lower legs over the indistinct edge of the passage through the brush pile. It was slightly too narrow to let him slip through effortlessly, but that worked to his advantage because it allowed him to push against the sides and let himself down to the floor in a controlled manner.

As he came even with the body, he panicked and struggled to gain some more distance between him and it.

It was not human.

Straight, coarse hair covered the front of the body from the collarbones down to the lower abdomen. What had looked like a glove from atop the plug now appeared to be an alteration of the skin itself involving all four limbs, giving their surfaces a silver/gray sheen.

The alarming thing, however, was the face. Its brow was angled backward slightly, with light eyebrows.

The eyes were open and staring straight ahead. There was no visible sclera, just a dark pupil and a yellow Iris. The orbits were shallow and slightly small for the face.

It had no nose to speak of, just a small central ridge running from the upper lip to the brows. About two-thirds of the way down the ridge, on either side, a checkmark in the skin formed a flap over the respiratory passages.

The mouth lay open slightly, revealing a uniform set of upper and lower teeth. The lips were thin and covered less of the mouth's aperture than a human's. A short, tilted groove spiraled into the skull on either side, right behind the angle of the jaw. It lacked any other external ear structure.

Its skin was smooth and the color of the deep ocean. He stared at it, panting and sweating. After it failed to move for several minutes, he shivered once and leaned over to examine the body closely. It certainly looked dead. He didn't detect any movement of the iris when the light swept across its eyes. He started to put a finger on the throat but retreated, eyeing the mouth suspiciously. He rubbed the back of his neck as he cast about the

tangle of brush in search of an idea.

He picked out three sizable branches and did his best to maneuver them

into a position where the end of the limb, which tapered to its clusters of twigs, rested against the body and the base of the limb, where it had been separated from the trunk, wedged against the junction of the wall and the floor. He managed to get two of them in place but couldn't force the issue with the third.

He put one foot and one hand on the ladder, did his best to extend his other foot to the side wall, where he could apply counterpressure, and began to clear the brush around the buried leg.

It was slow work. The dirt had settled and consolidated after it came down the shaft. He had to remove a lock blade knife from the pack's inner pocket to chisel away the hard dirt encasing the leg at several points. At last, he excavated the knee. The joint had no deformity or other findings suspicious for an injury. He continued digging with renewed vigor. As he swept dirt from the hollow of the knee, he felt a firm irregularity at the top of the calf. It was barely palpable, and he couldn't discern much about the shape, size, or extent of its involvement with other tissues. He worked his head around so that he could get a more direct view. All he could see was a small black cube about the size of a grape with smoothed-

23

over corners and the suggestion of more structures attached to its ends. He went back to digging but stopped to feel the lump's outlines every few minutes. Finally, he reached the halfway point, where he paused and maneuvered the headlamp back around to have

a look.

The skin was intact at the edges of the cleared area. The small cube at the top of the calf had some structure emerging from it, made of a flexible, white material that felt like leather. Two black dots, separated by about 1 cm, were visible just where the end of the object had entered the tissue, suggesting that additional embedded structures lay below. A clean cut at the base suggested a skin incision at the attachment, but this was a simple incision and offered no clue to the surgeon's identity or the purpose of the implantation.

The parasite's body, for that's

what it surely was, had additional markings, at least two patches of dark red pigmentation in an oval shape, surrounded by a yellow border. Twelve pairs of delicate ceramic legs, each with a three-fingered foot, projected from the sides of the body. The body ended in a small tissue extension just behind the last pair of legs. The nubbin of tissue tapered rapidly to a dull end.

He worked to remove the parasite. He had the knife out briefly but decided against using it. After prying, pushing, pulling, twisting, and jiggling the little moocher without even loosening it, it was clear that he would not break the thing. He got a firm grasp around the middle of the little body, with the legs folded underneath. He pulled with both hands while pushing away with his legs. After a breathless 30 seconds of traction, he applied a last burst of force, and the parasite popped loose.

He flopped backward with the sudden release of resistance and slid down about four feet. As soon as he had straightened himself up in the tangle, he looked at the creature in his hands.

The front end, which had been firmly buried in the tissues of the upper calf, had a triangular head, with two frog-like eyes perched on top, just in front of the black cube that formed the base of the skull, and a short trunk with the ring of pointed teeth arrayed around the mouth at the end of the trunk.

He gripped the little creature in his right hand, his elbow bent and shoulder back, as he intently watched for any sign of movement. It appeared quiescent.

He lowered his arm, maintaining a firm grip on the parasite, and pulled himself up with his other arm until he regained the ground lost in the slide. Once he was even with the body again, he grasped the outstretched left arm just past the junction with the shoulder and pulled to free the body from the remaining dirt cast. He smiled as the body moved slightly, and then he pushed back in the other direction.

The body bumped against the wall, and the left eye suddenly turned to glare at him.

"Whoa!" he shouted, jumping back.

The dead thing stuck in the dried mud plug crouched and tried to face him, twisting its right leg in the process. Torsion was the key because the mud cast popped off the imprisoned leg as a crack shot through the accretion binding the plug. The floor of the plug gave way with a thud. The entire interwoven mass took a slow fall down the rest of the shaft.

The erstwhile excavator somehow maintained his grip on the parasite as he did his best to carry on backpedaling. The effort spared him a longer fall. He kept pressure on the opposite wall as the raft of limbs fell into the larger shaft. The amount of force he could exert in that position was minimal, but it proved sufficient to propel the branches, with him on top of them, several feet past the edge of the shaft. As a result, he landed on a 3 x 3 platform at the top of a stairway leading down into a much larger rectangular extension of the hole.

As he struck the insecure platform, he flipped his legs around to keep his body parallel to the flight of stairs. He slid down a couple of feet and rocked towards the edge as the tree limbs decompressed. However, he had enough time to slap his palm down on the stairs and push the other side of his body firmly against the wall, preventing him from tumbling down the stairs. The resurrected and now free creature drew the short straw and dropped another fifteen feet to the landing at the next level of the stairs.

He heard it hit. It didn't sound like the wet slap that accompanies a bad landing. Instead, there was a thump, followed by a shout of pain, and a solid half minute of what he had to assume was heartfelt swearing in another language.

Miraculously, he retained his hat and his headlamp. His day pack suffered a tear at the top, and the end of the machete handle stuck out through the hole. One of his sandals was gone. He got to his feet and brushed himself off. He kicked the remaining sandal off his foot. He peered down the stairway, but his light would not reach the landing below unless he stepped over to the edge of the stairs, exposing himself in the process. It was too late to check his reanimated specimen for weapons.

He pulled the machete out of his pack. He turned sideways on to the stairway to hide the blade from the creature now approaching from below. It climbed the stairs at a leisurely pace, which did not falter. It did not stop either when it entered his line of sight. When it reached a stair high enough, he directed the headlight's beam at its face, but it just shaded its eyes and kept coming.

He took a step back when it drew within arm's reach, and the creature halted in response.

It looked him over in an obvious way that conveyed disdain. He put his left hand across his chest with a smile and a slight bow. The creature dropped the hand shading its eyes and leaned forward, pointing its index finger at his nose and speaking emphatically in its own language.

He shrugged and pointed to his ear. He shrugged again, more dramatically, with his palm raised, and began shaking his head back and forth. The creature looked down and frowned. It narrowed its eyes, pointed at his nose once again, turned the indicating digit back towards itself, and ended its exposition with the finger pointing directly at his left hand, which still held the parasitic creature he had plucked from the back of its trapped leg. "What?" he asked. "You want your giant tick–centipede back? Okay. No

problem at all. Here you go."

He extended his hand with the small body held lightly between

his thumb and index finger. The creature reached out slowly and took the parasite from him with surprising care. It examined the tiny body in detail. Then it turned its head once more to look at him. Its thumb drifted over one of the red markings on the back of the parasite, which began to move as its recently former host lowered its chin and almost imperceptibly flexed its knees.

"Hey now," he said, extending his left arm with the palm out while his right hand adjusted its grip on the machete. "Are you sure? This has all gone your way up till now. Do you really want to risk what you've got on a bet you don't need to take, at least that's what it looks like to me."

He sat down with his legs crossed. He never looked away from the creature as he moved. When he was settled into the position, he turned the machete over with the length of the blade across his knees, and his right hand still on the grip. The creature narrowed its eyes and cocked its head to the side. With the carefree tempo of someone off to the park for lunch, the creature turned away and descended the stairs into the dark. He listened for a few minutes without moving. Footsteps rang out in the narrow shaft, with a break in tempo at each of the four remaining landings. A shuffling sound followed the last interrupted cadence, and then the footsteps faded

altogether.

Allowing the silence to consolidate, he stared at the floor in front of him, passing enough time to be sure that the thing was either gone or waiting for him right outside the stairway's exit with a weapon of its own.

He stood slowly. The tightness in his back and legs reminded him that he was late for the next dose of medication. He unzipped the pack with a shaky hand and felt around for the pills. He let out the breath he had held during the search as he pulled the pills out to look at them and confirm that all

was well. The pills were in the bottle, the lid was tight, and the bottle was not cracked. He took two tablets and washed them down with half a mouthful of his critically depleted water supply.

He forced himself to eat the candy bar. Although it would intensify his thirst immediately, it would allow him to go longer without water and provide the energy needed to return to the creek. He checked the pack to ensure he had not lost any other items. Everything appeared to be there. He picked up the machete and walked slowly down the stairs. There was a doorway just beyond the end of the last flight.

It looked like it had been laser-cut into the sandstone, smooth and square. The occupants of the Cliff dwelling did not have the means to create such a passage. He stood as far back as he could, his back pressed against the wall opposite the doorway. He removed the hat and the headlamp. He leaned

forward and extended his arm as far as he could, holding the headlamp in his hand and angling the beam as far to the left and right of the doorway as possible. He saw that the area beyond opened like a natural cavern. On the left, he could see a jumble of branches and dried leaves piled on the floor near the edge of illumination. He couldn't see anything closer on either side, including the cavern walls. He quietly slipped the lamp's band around his head and secured the hat on it again.

Holding the machete behind him with the point directed downward, he walked quickly through the doorway, looking first to his left and then to his right.

He made two steps around the right-hand door post before tripping on something crunchy on the floor, which caught on his right foot as he fell. He hit the floor in a puff of dust. He blinked several times to clear the smudge of powder over his eyes, and when he opened them fully again, he confronted a dilemma. He was eye to eye with the delicate features of a

small skull still attached to its vertebral column and rib cage.

Several more skeletons were scattered across the right side of the room. One was attached to his right foot, where he had stepped through the rib cage.

Across the room, in the right corner of the junction between the doorway wall and the right wall of the cavern was a white cylindrical object, perched on three pairs of legs sticking out to the sides, a square structure with rounded edges set in front of the closest pair of legs, a trunk like appendage in front of that which tapered from the base down to a tube about the size of a garden hose, and in the middle of everything atop the base of the trunk, a blinking red orb like a Cyclopean eye.

He chose to address the skeleton problem first. He kicked frantically at the rib cage, pinching his right foot. It came off easily, with several more of the ribs shattering.

He jumped back to his feet, and with no sign of movement on the part of the skeletons, he raised the little machete and faced down the object in the corner. It didn't move either, though the light kept blinking steadily. He looked back down at the skeletons. They were adult based on the appearance of their arm bones, but relatively small, with most measuring between four and four and a half feet tall. All of the skulls had an odd mid-face deformity, distorting the nasal aperture. He walked carefully around them to approach the object in the corner. It was large. He estimated that the girth was close to what he could encompass with his two arms, and the length was approximately 6 ½ feet. The legs ended in three toes. Based on the legs' articulations, they were capable of movement rather than being mere supports.

The eye's transparent cover protected an optical sensor array. He gave the trunk in front a wide berth as he had noticed an unpleasant ring of teeth

Just behind its terminus, he tapped it here and there with the end of the machete. It sounded like it was made of metal, though nothing that was resonant—more like aluminum, based on the clunk it made when the blade hit it. He placed his hand on the object. There was no vibration, no warmth. He stepped away from the corner and panned the headlamp around the room.

A couple more skeletons lay scattered about, but nothing else. A passage with a carved doorway extended past the far wall of the cavern, leading deeper into the rock behind. Before the doorway, an irregular hole—about five feet high and six and a half feet wide—opened onto the cliff face at an angle, blocking the view from vantage points below.

The hole led to a narrow ledge, which was contiguous with the steep dirt slope on the canyon's side beyond the slick rock.

The ground was steeper than the hand-and-foot path that led from the trail's end up to the ledge with the cliff dwelling, but it was more uneven, making it a slightly easier way to reach the dwelling, as long as the small

trees, fractured rock steps, and boulders that served as holds remained stable.

He looked around, but the route back to the line of holds carved into the slick rock looked too sandy and steep to risk. Going down to reach the line of holds didn't seem any easier than going up. He began climbing cautiously. There were occasional loose rocks and poorly rooted trees, but he didn't encounter anything that forced him to stop.

He stepped onto the cavern's edge, sat down, and looked over the starlit canyon and the valley beyond. He checked his water bottle—it was just as empty as the last time he checked it. He pulled the wind shell jacket with the hood out of his pack and zipped it all the way up.

He looked around the ancient

structures. He stared down the portal to the underground rooms for several minutes but made no move to climb through it. In the end, he climbed up into the two-story building where he found a relatively comfortable patch of floor that seemed sturdy enough to last the night. He took two more pills, chewing them up and swallowing the powder without any water to help. He bunched the pack into a plausible imitation of a pillow, tucked his hand on top of it with the palm against his cheek, and curled his body into a fetal ball for the night.

Four

No returns

During every unplanned night out, time passes unevenly. He woke several times to switch sides, and twice shivering. Between awakenings, he slept in the shallows, with drowsy wakefulness instead of light sleep, and dreams that intruded into the drowsiness.

When he finally achieved adequate depth to really rest, it was because the air had begun to warm as a prelude to dawn. When he woke for the day, it was well after sunrise, with a ray of light from the window beating down on his face. He turned his head away from the light carefully.

As an experienced ground-sleeper, he knew the importance of rising gradually in the morning. Neck rotation didn't hurt, so he flexed his neck, straightened his legs, rolled slowly onto his back, and then to his hands and knees, where he could use his hands to climb up his own legs to an assisted stand. He curtailed the movement just in time to avoid a collision with the low ceiling. Still crouching, he stepped out of the building.

As he cleared the low roof and stood fully upright, he found himself nearly face-to-face with a man who was slightly shorter than him, standing in front of the building.

He jumped and would have screamed, but his throat was too parched, and

all that came out was a hoarse wheeze. The man didn't move.

The two of them stood looking at each other for a dozen heartbeats. The visitor had dark hair that came down to his shoulders and looked like it had not been combed for a week. He wore black-framed glasses, a black bomber jacket, baggy blue jeans, and tactical boots. His heritage was Asian, most likely Japanese, given the trio of kanji embroidered on a small patch adorning his jacket's collar. As the silence became uncomfortable, the man in the bomber jacket spoke.

"Oh, look! You have one too, "he said pointing at the "J" on the plaid shirt's collar while holding up his own jacket's patch, "'J,' Is that your name? Anyway, you should be careful hopping around these ruins. If you fall off, it isn't a clean drop, and then splat!" he said, emphasizing the "splat" with an overhand slap of his left palm against his right. "No, it is more like being beaten to death or tumbled to death in a clothes dryer. Did you sleep over there last night?"

J tried to respond but choked on the whisper. "You sound dry. Do you have any water?"

J reached into his pack for his water bottle. He fumbled as he pulled it out, and it landed on the cavern floor with a hollow thunk.

"And that was your only water for the trip, I would guess. Here," said the man in the bomber jacket, pulling a pair of collapsible water bags from a pack on the ledge hidden behind his right leg, "take these."

J took the water bags with a gracious nod, opened one, and began to drink. "What is your name. again?" asked the man in the bomber jacket.

The sound of gulping water stopped in a fit of coughing and spluttering. "Oh, pardon me. I should know better than to ask questions of a thirsty

man while he is drinking. Forget what I said.

I want to give you a name. You are lucky. I am the only one who comes down to these ruins, not to mention the canyon and the valley beyond.

The path is difficult going up and even more difficult going down.

I carry a rope to go down and for some security as I climb up. I wasn't planning to come this way today, but I thought I saw something on the path leading to this rock, so I followed.

Otherwise, it would have probably been two more days before I came down here again. Once you get to the top, you may have other problems. This is a secure area, so men who guard security are permitted to walk around and play with their weapons. So, you are lucky I was here to warn you.

And therefore, Lucky you are. That will be my name for you, with your permission. It is best anyway."

He looked around as if searching for something he had lost on the cliff dwelling's floor.

"You see, I have great trouble with names. Even my own name."

The coughing had stopped, and Lucky wrung a few phonemes out of his desiccated vocal cords.

"Well, I certainly owe you. Especially since I came unprepared. You're welcome to call me anything you want, but I know that others are often a little more particular than me, so I will ask. Do you have a name that you would rather I call you? If you don't want to say, it doesn't bother me, but it may take me a while to think one up for you."

"My name is Takezo. At least I'm pretty sure that's it."

"Thank you, Takezo, for the water. I'm sorry I ruined your trip."

"Don't worry, it wasn't going to be much of a trip anyway, I'm afraid," said Takezo, "chasing an illusion down the cliff."

"Do you know anything about this place?" asked Lucky. "I mean, this dwelling, the old bones, and whatever kind of machine is parked in the corner at the bottom of the stairs, and what's

been happening with the national forest, the trails, and the people?"

Takezo squinted at Lucky and leaned in a little closer, examining Lucky's

expression.

"All of those things are unfamiliar to me," said Takezo. "What I can tell you is this: I have walked very far, I have a habit of walking far, and I have not found a way out of the valley. I get lost despite my best efforts because the brush becomes very thick on the hillsides, and the paths end, while others appear to emerge from the low thorn bushes leading off in other directions, or, most often, back into the valley."

Lucky turned to look down the canyon. It was the same as it had been when he came up, at least as far as he could tell. It was still early to midmorning.

"Maybe I'm not so lucky. I have a car and a tent on the fire road just off the state highway. I would like to get home at some point. I have someone

waiting for me."

Takezo nodded. "No such attachments bind me, so I rarely suffer from the pressure of expectations' secret calendar. However, I understand its power. Please, you must go to your car and home, where your obligations await you, before you become delinquent."

Lucky smiled and looked back at Takezo. "I understand, too; there's a way to make all that sound bad. But I am a shell-bound crab by nature. If I don't have something to consider besides my own thoughts and worries, I'll stay in that shell and smother rather than mount the effort to squirm out of it."

Takezo chuckled, "Okay. If I do not see you again, I will assume that you have taken that name I gave you and gone home with it in the front seat of your car with your tent packed up in the back. If you cannot find your camp, you are welcome to return and stay with me if you wish. I am working on a project

under contract. I can't tell you what it is right now because

you wouldn't believe it, and I couldn't explain it to you. The important thing is that the job comes with very nice amenities. They are excessive, I would say. I suspect my employers hope that I will accept perks in place of money. If someone else were to use them as well, I would feel less swindled. I will

return in the evening, the day after tomorrow, to see if you have returned. I will bring my rope with me as well."

"Okay," said Lucky, "You certainly have a way of putting things that makes me feel better about them. A lot could happen – more than what you mentioned – but it all ends up out there on the fire road or back here.

Once more, I owe you. Forgive me if I hope I don't see you again, but if I do, I'd be happy to sop up the excess for you."

Takezo nodded in a curt bow. Lucky indicated that he should lead the way. Takezo picked up his pack and strolled along the ledge to its intersection with the small path leading into the forest. A rope hung down at the end of the path, anchored to a stout Juniper several feet back from the edge of the slick rock.

Lucky glanced at the knot that secured the rope to the tree. It was an older knot, a variation on a bowline, but it was tied correctly, backed up, and dressed. The rope was knotted every few feet to allow hand-over-hand progress.

"Very nice!" said Lucky. "Thanks again."

Takezo waved and bowed slightly again. He took a seat on the ledge where he could monitor Lucky's progress. The rope was hard on the hands, and Lucky had a couple of small blisters on his palms by the time he reached the bottom. Still, it was an improvement over the shallow, carved steps. Lucky waved in an exaggerated arc over his head to signal to Takezo that he was off the rope as well as to say goodbye. Takezo stood and returned the wave.

Lucky looked back one more time before beginning his walk down the established trail to see Takezo hauling the rope back up the sandstone face.

Five

Agent of the Authority

The man dressed in the dark red cassock with matching red skullcap and seated at the small round table was a curiosity. His garb was uncommon, but familiar. It marked him as an agent of the Authority, and most of his colleagues dressed like that. Another agent in the same outfit sat across the marble floor, next to the bar.

The remarkable thing about the agent at the table was the magnitude of the pannus under his cassock. His people were typically thin. He was an exception. His girth mandated the use of a bib at meals.

His skin was light pink and opaque. His eyes were red, a shade lighter than the color of his apparel. His eyebrows were thick and black, and he had a thin scaramouch tattooed on his face. A pair of sunglasses, with a bridge shaped to fit the anatomy of his nasal ridge, perched atop the skullcap.

His fingers turned his drink coaster around in impatient circles. He looked irritated and unhappy, and he wore it well. The prominence of those two traits in him was reflected in the demeanor of the man sitting across the table.

He wore gray, the color of slaves. He sat on the edge of his seat, his hands clasped in his lap, squeezing each other. He was thin, nearly gaunt, with golden eyes and cream-colored skin. An oversized bowler hat covered his head and half of his eyes. The fat man tipped his drink.

"Thomas! "he said, "When was that babysitter supposed to be here? I cannot be late for my meeting with the bursar from the Authority. I have spent too much time and gone into too much debt to have this project scuttled because some damn clinical developmentalist can't find their damn keys."

"Please, Augustine," said Thomas, "I've never seen you so upset. Why are you so worried about the bursar?"

"Because I know the bursar better than most. I had to get funding for a similar investigation about 3 decades ago. He was a nosy twit and a tightwad. I found out later that most of what the Authority paid him was in the form of undistributed funds that he administered into his pocket.

I need to limit his chances of doing that with this operation. I have already depleted nearly half of my voucher. I must have compensation."

"Please be patient, master, for the sake of your own health if nothing else," said Thomas. "The man said he was preparing the child for his debut. Don't worry about the bursar. You assigned me to take care of the bursar. I have recruited some assistance for that. He should have somebody on him round-the-clock."

The authority was what passed for government among the calculators. It was a loose organization, with funding derived primarily from incredibly long-term investments, some of which may have originated in the time before the dendritic radiation of events existed. Although technically, anyone who wanted to become an agent of the authority could do so if they passed an interview and a written test, the position was, in fact, hereditary.

Badges passed from the adopting relative to the child, along

with a stamped copy of the new agent's test results. Over the last four decades at least, each candidate achieved superior marks on the exam with an uncanny uniformity in the specific questions answered correctly and

incorrectly. For the most part, an Agent's job was not a serious one. The sorts of problems that sometimes blew up into disruptive violence in other cultures tended to take care of themselves among the calculators.

Though it would be hard to believe, were an outsider to eavesdrop on their conversations, the society's membership cared little for money. It interested them only as an indicator to others of their status. In addition, every last one of them carried a voucher. This was a small cylinder, with colorful markings on the outside, and clan banking records going back to eras long-lost on the inside.

One task that the Authority regularly performed as part of its respon-sibilities was an occasional audit of those bank records. It is said that many centuries ago, the Authority distributed copies of that report to all the members of the Species.

Today, a single copy decorates the bulletin board outside The Authority's central office at the Node 3 access point to the dendritic event radiation.

In living memory, a slow, steady increase in the funds available marks the only change from one audit to the next..

Augustine stopped fiddling with the coaster and picked up

A flyer balanced on the leaves of a potted plant behind his right shoulder. It was an advertisement for experts in metallurgy, weapons design, astro-physics, and theological psychodynamics—the task requiring that array of specialties was nothing less than the destruction of the deity.

Contractors would be privileged to use the facility hosting the project for their own research. The facility in question was none other than the renowned Bilateral Nephrectomy Center of Excellence.

According to the flyer, the contest provided a unique opportunity for networking among specialists in esoteric disciplines. The contractors would also have the rare opportunity to be present at God's death and the anticipated manifestation of stable "gray space" expected to follow.

The only monetary reward went to the winning design, which amounted to a small fraction of the other benefits.

Leaving the flyer on the table, Augustine pulled a companion brochure done in the same style from an envelope marked "Sensitive Material: Fraud Investigation with Alien Involvement."

"What do you think?" asked Thomas.

"It looks like a scam to me," said Augustine.

"Yes," Thomas said, "but is it a scam run from afar or a scam run nearby? Do you think they really have a means of observing an outbreak of gray space? What about the creation and programming of the nachinaks? Those are high-stakes endeavors for the most experienced operators. Whoever is in front of this scam must have at least a couple of high rollers backing them up..."

Augustine cut him off with a dismissive, drawn-out," Naaaah."

"Alien fraud? All these alien fraud cases turn out to be run remotely because

that way they can get by with no overhead, granted with a few large-scale historical exceptions. You said it yourself, though, all the things that this pamphlet

advertises are way too dangerous actually to carry out," said Augustine, "Alien
fraud investigations are not very rewarding, but take away the investigation part,
and there might be something in this one for us if, by some miracle, we happen
to catch the scammers before they clean things up. The cost-benefit analysis for a
shakedown is pretty good. Why don't you keep your ears

open on this one? Let me know if anything makes a noise, but no payments
and nothing rough."

"Thank you, master." Thomas said, "I thought it might be of interest, and
perhaps worthy of a small investment, that's all."

Augustine stared at Thomas.

"It must be bankrolled by high rollers?" said Augustine," Come on! If you
seek to entice your mark into the snare, they have to believe that it was their idea.
That means you can't tell them what to think along the way.

Now, do you want to push it until I 'm forced to respond, or are you going to
quit whining and remember why you are my slave and not the other way around?"

Thomas looked down and nodded.

I want all our resources focused on this contest. I've tried

to make it ours, and I've succeeded so far. I need those funds from the Authority to pay off the contractors, and we should be able to kick back and let it
happen, with exquisite scrutiny of course."

Augustine folded the paper up and put it in his pocket. He turned back to the
flyer enthusiastically, holding it up and pointing for Thomas to see.

"This is it," he said, "this is the way I get that bastard Laplace. This is too big
for him to orchestrate and fund on his own. The Center of Excellence isn't just
renting him a room; I'm sure of it. I'll get him and that creep he calls his
brother."

Six

Brotherhood

The man looked remarkably comfortable sitting on the locker room bench in the Node 8 access point. His tattered and patched pressure suit, and especially the "538" badge stuck to his helmet, marked him for ostracism, yet he leaned against the locker with his hands behind his head and his legs crossed as if daring anyone to comment.

He did not bear an abacus like most of the morning's sojourners in the Node, only a tarnished loop of beads. Traffic was light, so everyone except for one had the luxury of avoiding God's Helping Angel. No one walked close enough to risk a sermon. No one paused to gawk at his bone-white skin and pink eyes.

The Helper did not acknowledge Laplace, who approached from the direction of the Node's offices and took a seat on the other side of the bench.

"Good morning, Luther, "said Laplace.

"My blessings as God's," said Luther, "Have you come to return my slave?"

Laplace swiveled on the bench to sit side-by-side with Luther. "Why

would I do that?" Laplace asked, "I am here to discuss God." "Blaspheme away then. We will exact God's punishment for your sins in due time. I thought that you would have seen by now the wisdom of my offer to take Gerard back. How many times have agents of the Authority come to call since you stole him away from his home with us?

He will never be accepted, and this spiritually bereft society will never appreciate his art. Only our Society has a place for him."

"I am here about God, and that's it. You have the best early detection system around, and I would like to monitor it as well," said Laplace.

"What are you willing to pay?" asked Luther.

"A cache of damaged nachinaks that nearly doubles your current contingent by my count. "Said Laplace.

"Don't you still believe that they are conscious, or have you finally outgrown that childish notion?" Luther asked.

"They are, as we all are, episodically. Their episodes merely occur under conditions that we don't find intuitively familiar," Laplace countered. "I don't like handing them over to you, but they are all I've got."

"That is a lie. Gerard will be part of the bargain. When your project is complete, he returns to 538 with you, and he gets to choose between his quixotic relations and the Society of God's Helping Angels," Luther said.

"Give me the coordinates for your monitoring outpost," said Laplace.

"Transmitted. It is all a waste of time, you know. You will never have your utopia. This world has no place for it. Our sins have leached into its bones. It is only fit for a scourge. That's what the artists among us, including your brother, feel. They are warning us," Luther said.

"Do you want a scourge or annihilation?" Laplace asked," You say 'scourge' but you seem to want it all erased, so your God can do it over the right way. There is no coming back from annihilation, and if that is our future, then none of this makes sense, for man or God."

"Annihilation," said Luther, "that is the way of the Lord."

"I thought your God sought justice? If so, he expects the current state of affairs can be set right. That will be impossible if there is no state of affairs to remediate," Laplace said.

"Don't speak to me as if you were a servant of God who knew His will. I am the word of God. I can tell you what is in His heart, and it is ash. He has already given up. He could never produce virtue in creatures that had no innate capacity for it, in a world without purpose.

He can force repentance, but it will only last until the next temptation or threat, because the great emptiness at the end of it all provides endless room to run, endless space to hide, and no constraints. But it is no refuge for the wicked.

SIX

It is ultimate freedom, and what is Hell if not ultimate freedom? Annihilation is the only relief.

Can't you feel it, Laplace? You must. Look at them," said Luther, gesturing at the ballroom's occupants, "they are biding their time, aren't they? They await salvation through quick extinction, to spare themselves from dissipation in the void. After this cycle of rebirth and death ends, I will see you back at 538 with Gerard. Perhaps you will have come to your senses by then and will stay with us too."

Laplace stood to leave, then stopped and turned on Luther.

He leaned down and

pointed his clawed index finger at Luthe r's face. "Yes," said Laplace, ""I will be there."

Seven

We Were Never in Kansas

It was a good morning for a walk. The water reinvigorated Lucky. Despite the strangeness surrounding him, he walked with an easy gait, his shoulders relaxed. He had enough medication to go for a while. The weather looked like it was going to hold. All he had to do was throw the tent and the sleeping bag in the back of the vehicle and get back out on the road.

No one had returned to work on the trail or the trailhead parking lot. As he walked down the fire road, he thought he heard odd noises off to the right in the thick brush. He veered away from the road onto a trail running parallel to it but below the road grade. Before he arrived at the state highway, he got a look at the flat desert area where the paved road crossed the wash as it headed into town. He felt confident that he could hear several voices in conversation.

Although his luck with surprise encounters had been reasonable, he took a wide arc to the left of the road to ensure that the people could not see him. There was still no traffic anywhere. He had forgotten to ask Takezo about the state of affairs outside of the little chunk of

Sonoran Desert they could experience directly. He struck out for the subsidiary ridge where he had come down from the forest road. He hadn't marked the way as he went because the terrain was so favorable, and the best way forward seemed so obvious.

As he approached the foot of the ridge, he encountered an area with much denser brush than anything he had encountered on his way down. He searched for a game trail or other passage through, but he found nothing except catclaw Acacia. The shrub's hostility surpassed all others in a land of hostile flora. It hooked whatever touched even a single twig and wrapped it in thorny tendrils drawn to the interloper by movement. The growth of these thorn bushes was so thick that he couldn't traverse to the crest of the ridge. He did his best to work around the brush, but he couldn't seem to get past it, even with the machete's help. He spent several hours backtracking and heading off at different angles with no progress to show for it. He began to walk faster and swear intermittently.

At last, he gave up. He turned around and went back to the forest service road that led from the off-ramp of the freeway to the branch road where his car was parked. He relaxed again when he stood on the road.

It was only a short walk to the first switchback. However, when he reached the spot where the road started its climb up the ridge, an overhanging slope of sand and loose rock confronted him. The roadbed had collapsed.

He whipped the pack off his shoulders and threw it on the ground. As he dropped to his knees beside his only belongings, something caught his eye.

Behind the bushes surrounding a telephone pole at the edge of the road sat a duplicate of the white, six-legged creature in the cavern beneath the cliff dwelling. He shook his head in disbelief.

This one was in much worse shape. Black splotches peppered its surface, and charred residue filled the shattered dome housing the eye. The wreckage faintly smelled of ozone. He took a few minutes to compose himself. After a final curse for whatever had thwarted him, he put his backpack on and began the march back to the cliff dwelling.

A profound paranoia encumbered him. He stayed out of sight as much as possible by following intermittent trails crisscrossing the hillsides above the main road. He moved up almost to the ridge crest as he reached the turnoff onto the forest service road leading to the trailhead. He could not see the convenience store, and he heard no engine sounds or voices this time.

He passed the trailhead and the section of the trail leading into the canyon without incident. Nothing seemed different. He stopped where the small Creek bubbled out of the rocky wash. He filled all his water containers, although he had trouble closing the zipper on his pack and finally had to remove the machete to make everything fit.

He felt ridiculous carrying the thing in its sheath attached to his belt, but it was the only reasonable way to proceed. When he arrived at the slick rock wall, the sun had dropped below the canyon rim. His plan was sketchy beyond that point. He looked around the base of the sandstone again but found no good spots to rest for the night. At best, he would have to stick around through the next day and

then most of the day after that before he could expect to see Takezo with his rope. He looked up at the hand-and-foot-trail and the structure above. One should never second-guess the wisdom of the ancestors. He paced back and forth for a couple of minutes, and at the end of his last lap, he broke right and started climbing. He carried a heavier pack on this ascent, but some part of his central nervous system retained the first climb's lessons,

and the second time up seemed much more secure than the first.

He looked around the ruin again but couldn't find a better spot to sleep. He sat down in his old spot on the second floor but got up again in a few minutes and went down to the ledge that traversed the sandstone ramp from side to side. He looked at the buildings and then down to the hole in the cavern wall leading inside to the stairwell and passageway. He shook his arms out and rolled his neck. He stowed his hat and machete and struggled down the loose ground where the slickrock met the canyon wall.

Daylight would soon be gone, but it was still bright enough outside to illuminate the relevant items inside the cave. The small skeletons lay as he had left them. There was no sign of the six-legged mechanism.

He proceeded with much greater care on his second trip to the stairwell. He turned on his lamp and examined the floor methodically. Although skeletons lay in the middle of the room, most of the bones were clustered around the corner where the machine had been. Except for one trampled rib cage, none of the remains bore any sign of damage, and none appeared displaced.

There were footprints in the dust. Three clusters of circles, a little bit bigger

45

than the palm of his hand in diameter, roughly in two rows, marched across the room to the tunnel carved through the rock.

There, they joined a jumble of unmistakably bipedal prints. All was silent. He could not see around a distant bend in the corridor ahead. He switched to the red light on his headlamp and tiptoed forward.

The passageway extended for several hundred meters. He encountered nothing additional until he was about two-thirds of the way through. At that point, the builders had carved out a 10-foot semicircle on either side of the main passage. The space overflowed with crates and boxes, several long fluorescent lights, wire shelving, components for multiple CCTV units, and, taking up most of the right-hand storage area, the six-legged machine.

Unlike its twin, this one looked completely intact. The eye was dark. He proceeded down the passageway until he saw a hint of light in the distance.

He turned his headlamp off at that point and felt his way forward. He saw a streak of indirect daylight at the end of the tunnel. He had lost his sense of direction at about the midway point.

The afternoon was mostly gone, and the sunlight angled into the pas-sageway almost parallel to the shaft, so he must have been traveling mainly west and slightly to the north. He didn't dare to go any further. If he tried to exit that end, the sun would be in his face. There was a dormant but probably operational machine behind him, capable of who knew what, and he could see a hint of movement in the upper right corner of the doorway in the distance.

It may have been a trick of the light or the product of overwrought imagination, but he wouldn't risk it. He crept back along the corridor, using the red light on his headlamp as much as possible to conserve the batteries. He made it back to the dwelling as twilight faded. He looked around the buildings again and even returned to his spot on the second floor, where he lay down for a few minutes. No matter how he

fidgeted, he could not get comfortable this time, and he had to get back up.

In addition to all the other factors working against a more or less restful night, now his right leg itched.

He left the cliff dwelling and crossed the ledge to the forest on the canyon's rim. He looked around the area near the tree that Takezo used to anchor the rope. The juniper was right next to a naturally worn trail that negotiated a short rock step on the way down to the sturdy tree and then intersected with the ledge leading to the cliff dwelling. At the base of the step, he found a small overhang with a reasonably level floor.

After he cleared a few small rocks from it, the ground was comfortable enough, and the hollow offered a little protection from the wind. Most importantly, from that vantage point, no one could pass him unnoticed on their way to the juniper tree. He took some medication, drank, and folded the backpack with the water bottles inside to act as a pillow. He squirmed

a little until he got the bed worn in, scratched one more time, and then dropped into a deep sleep.

Eight

The Costs of Doing Business

Laplace floated in the dome of the person-sized observation window. He wore a pressure suit in place of his customary boots, hat, and slacks. His tense posture reflected limited experience functioning in free fall. He kept looking at the dome's edge, where the transparent material joined up with the metal skin of the spacecraft. He had good reason to be nervous beyond zero G discontents.

If the pair of God's Helping Angels had their math wrong no one was ever leaving. They were the only ones who operated event horizon observatories so close to the invisible point of no return. It was also most likely why their predictions of God's appearance were more accurate than anyone else's.

Four nachinaks attended him. By his side stood another device, resembling a nachinak save for its size, leg count, and single optical sensor. The unit only had three pairs of very sturdy legs to support a dense body the size of a shoebox.

The faux-nachinak was an external power source. His true nachinak needed the power source to fold Laplace and his equipment into the dendritic

radiation of events in case of emergency.

The power source did not contain enough charge to accomplish that substantial feat all by itself. It did have enough stored energy to tap the Species' network of generators with the complete power request and the proper instructions to accomplish the transmission. Laplace looked back at what was happening beyond the protection of

the dome window.

Two of his kind relaxed in their enhanced pressure suits and EVA packs some thirty meters in front of him. Thin tethers connected them to the spacecraft.

From all directions, smaller nachinak types gathered around them. The scene was pitiful.

All the little devices coming together around the two calculators were damaged. They moved slowly or fitfully. Some of them spiraled off course, and the kin of their creators didn't bother to round up the errant casualties. Out of the blue, one of them swooped into the side of the observation window, startling Laplace. He jerked away from the motion in his peripheral vision, which set off a tumble. As he was spinning, the nachinak seemed to recover from its collision and began to move off again towards the gathering, only to flip 180° unexpectedly and dart back towards the observation window, colliding with the glass dome again. After the second impact, it

moved no more.

Laplace reached out cautiously to the window's rim and arrested his spin. When he stopped, he was eye to eye with the nachinak. The golden irises were completely dilated, and the trunk had almost torn off. It was missing four legs on one side.

"It's criminal how they have mistreated you," said Laplace. "Even the lighting does you no good. It makes you look more like seafood past its prime than the inheritor of a proud pedigree with unique capabilities purchased at a dear price. They don't care. To them, you're just a bottle for the message."

Static crackled in his headset.

"Hear us, oh Lord!" The two people in spacesuits implored, lifting their hands over their heads with their palms up, "We return to you the

instruction that you gave us."

After that brief prayer, they began to work on the assembled

nachinaks, fitting them with a small plug inserted into the end of the trunk. Beyond the collection of machines and the astronauts, a black void waited. It had a shimmering, bright ring around it but no stars within.

As they finished equipping a broken device, they threw it into the void.

Laplace rolled his eyes and turned away. He activated the external power source. It began to hum, and his skin prickled. A brief spell of interference affected his headset. As the static dissipated, he touched a red marking on the nachinak above his right shoulder. A young man's voice came over the system.

"Yes, sir? What's the emergency? Do you need full deployment?"

Laplace took one more look at the ceremony that was taking place outside the ship.

"No, nothing requiring reinforcements," he said. "I don't think we need these superstitious louts after all, Danilo.

"I think I'm sold. on the new unit's capability. I have a little more to review from the material the archives provided. Tell my brother to have the membrane ready by Friday and tell him to make room in storage. I won't be selling our surplus nachinaks after all."

He reached up and activated the nachinak above his left shoulder, then the one by his left leg, and finally the lower nachinak on the right. Waves of heat rose from the external power source. He took a look around. Conditions were satisfactory.

He pressed the lock mechanism in the back of the helmet, and the whole pressure suit automatically folded itself into the headpiece. He gave the helmet an admiring once-over. Another garment just like it hung from a latch beside him, and he helped himself to it as well.

He tucked a helmet under each arm and turned to stand directly

under the nachinak on the upper right. He reached over to the left and touched a small red polka dot on the tail of the upper nachinak on that side. As he turned to align himself completely with the right nachinak, the machines on the left moved to position themselves above and below their counterparts on the right. When the left and right devices paired up, the area from the floor to the uppermost machine rolled in on itself, taking Laplace with it, while the external power source he left behind began to rumble and smoke.

Nine

God Smack

Laplace, MD, PhD, FCOE, JD, FCCLU:

Thank you for agreeing to speak at our commencement. The executive secretary will reach out to you soon to schedule.

In the meantime, please find enclosed the summary information that you requested from the Species archive:

═══

According to Species archives, God first appeared around ten million years ago. He may be an occasional visitor since historical records in affected areas do not mention his existence for centuries between eras when his activity dominates the written accounts. The case is not open and shut, however. God is a thoroughly local phenomenon.

Being a small deity in a vast universe and lacking any detectable signature (such as radiation emissions, gravitational effects, or characteristic mathematical and arithmetical associations), it is still possible that there has always been at least one God in existence over time. Most research theologians still advocate for the sporadic existence theory, invoking parsimony as their justification.

The mechanism behind his emergence is even more controversial than the history of his existence. Immediately before he begins to exist, the affected

area in the event radiation becomes difficult to navigate.

Nearby event horizon observatories shut down. In the last

moments before he arrives, gray space breaks out. The phenomenon occurs sporadically in association with a handful of other events

but God's advent is the only one that is predictably associated with large and relatively durable occurrences.

NINE

The correlations suggest a process at work in the basic structure of the dendritic radiation of events: an imbalance or excess that periodically resolves via a reaction whose product is God.

In recorded history, fewer than a dozen firsthand accounts describing the deity's appearance exist. The non-academic press preserved the accounts in remarkable detail. The popular accounts remain in circulation in much the same shape as their original copy, indicating an enduring public interest in this subject.

Although the accounts are fascinating, they are also repetitive and technically unenlightening.

They all describe a brilliant flash of light, in five cases employing the same simile, "like being inside a lightning bolt." Coincident with the flash, the deity appears on a vector with a variable directional component but a highly conserved velocity component (20% of the speed of light), all four limbs outstretched, naked, and screaming.

At first, God produces no intelligible words. A few fortunate observers had a fast vehicle at their disposal and managed to catch up with him before the end of the screaming, keeping up through the initial verbal exchange.

Following a now familiar pattern, observers learn little from God's first words.

He does not say anything unique to the situation. Instead, he embarks on a non-sequitur reiteration of one of his familiar rants. He flies in a straight line, without any change

in his conformation, until he hits something. Sometimes the something is a neutron star or the like. That's the end of the monologue in those cases. He frequently impacts some less frightful object, however.

After he recovers from the abrupt transition between nonexistence and existence, an ethical dilemma confronts him immediately. No witnesses to his appearance or subsequent activities disagree on that point. He takes pains to educate everyone he encounters about his moral crisis, which is also their moral crisis. His presentation has some variable details, but the basic outline is consistent.

He informs the audience that he has broken out of hell and is the only denizen of the infernal realm that has ever escaped or will ever escape. He has never clearly elucidated the events preceding his sojourn in the underworld. He describes hell as a place where sinners are condemned to consciousness and perpetual stasis. As a consequence of his immobilization, the world's tableau was frozen in a slice of time laid out for his perusal, and being the deity, he comprehended it all.

Subsequently, he has complete knowledge of everything that is, as well as the interdependencies undergirding all events. Usually, omniscience would put him in a good position to undercut the Calculators with a preemptive shot at utopia. To his chagrin, the gift of comprehensive knowledge comes with the curse of impotence. He knows all but can do nothing. That is clearly the case when he is trapped in hell. It is uncertain whether he escapes the curse with emancipation.

The nature of sin figures prominently in the list of early topics. Since he has never claimed to be a creator, he is not saddled with the thorny issues surrounding divine creation and sin.

Unlike the deities of other, more popular religions, God takes
a hands-on approach to sin. He substitutes an exquisite divine sensitivity for rules and requirements carved in stone.

When a person steps on an ant, God feels her carapace crack open and realizes she will never get the rice grain in her mandibles back to the Queen,

rendering her life completely meaningless. When we think of such incidents, we tend to think in terms of linear causation. The ant suffers existential failure because her exoskeleton was crushed when the shoe came down on her.

This viewpoint is incorrect, however. Before the ant reached the spot on the sidewalk where she met her demise, the farmer who grew the rice moved his grain to a more secure location when he saw ants carrying away a few of the kernels. He needed every last one of those grains to support his girlfriend in town and to maintain his drinking habit, which he developed during his courtship with the exotic dancer.

The bartender at the adults-only bar was the farmer's cousin and knew very well that there was a strong family history of alcoholism, with both of the man's parents affected. However, the cook was the farmer's brother-in-law and was happy to bully the cousin into serving alcohol in whatever quantity the rice farmer desired.

It turns out that the farmer was also an angry drunk and began beating his wife when he came home from the bar, unbeknownst to her brother, the cook.

The farmer was in a nasty mood on the ant's fateful day, for he did see the little insect making off with his grain of rice, and he intentionally altered his course to step on it, hoping that it would suffer the fate he wished upon his wife and brother-in-law.

God had a million of these stories. If you tracked down all the horizontal associations and completed an explanatory description of the sin, it all looked like the ant murder. There was no such thing as a minor sin. There was no such thing as an innocent man. Everyone got sucked into the wickedness that

was their birthright. It got just a little bit worse, too.

Over time, everyone learned of God and his teachings. The record shows it.

People wrote down all his repetitive rants and passed them around, so God could rest assured that all the creatures in the known universe capable of speech knew his dilemma. In that case, they knew fully what they were doing to him when they stepped on an ant or gave a latent alcoholic a whiskey sour. Since he was all-knowing, he suffered more from the ambient transgression than the criminal populace could even imagine.

Here is the ethical dilemma. Just as he understands the weakness and callousness of the rest of the conscious realm, he also understands his own condition. He knows everything, so he knows that justice cannot be done. The price can't just cover damage to the primary victim. It includes moral injury to a being (God) who suffers the harm as only an omniscient being could. Even if he tortures every last one of the sinners that he can get his hands on, their punishment could never be adequate.

Given their limited knowledge, the criminals could not comprehend the severity of their crime, nor could they appreciate the degree of misery that their punishment must entail.

Being omniscient, he knows that if he does not punish these people, no one will. But if he levies punishment befitting their crimes, the sinners experience existential retribution. He punishes them for being.

He recognizes such punishment–necessarily inadequate for his purposes and gratuitous from the sinner's perspective as a sin worse than the original crime.

Yet, he also knows, as only he can, the obligation omniscience entails.

The nature of the problem ensures failure, regardless of what he does.

God's solution was to preload his side of the scales with some additional suffering. He contemplated self-mutilation first, but it only led to another paradox since it again required him to commit a crime to punish crime.

After God abandoned the self-harm strategy, he began encouraging his followers to gather Universal Tissue Donors for consideration of martyrdom. Most people thought that the UTD saga was where he got his ideas about the mortification of the flesh anyway.

The Universal Tissue Donor Project marked the end of a previously fruitful collaborative practice among universities, think tanks, and venture capitalists. The initial boondoggle occurred 5,500 years ago, during a catastrophic epidemic. A prion-mediated genetic disease took hold in the Species' population. It had an incubation period of up to two years and an accelerating course of illness once symptoms started. The only effective treatment
was radical, aggressive organ and tissue transplantation. The Species quickly exhausted its healthy slave supply. The future looked grim. As their population neared the precipice, ambitious fellows stepped up to save their people.

A university consortium issued a call for papers. A libertarian think tank posted a call for volunteers and offered a prize for a curative treatment.

The university soon had a very promising phase-one trial up and running. The think tank promptly poached the postdoctoral researcher whose work formed the project's backbone.

Subsequently, the pittance given to the postdoctoral researcher caught the attention of a venture capitalists' cabal. The investors bought up every relevant right and patent. They established a company to manufacture the end product and then deployed their lawyers to make hostile contact with the research team.

NINE

In addition to a further 40% discount on the academics' services, the investors leapfrogged several cumbersome steps in the development process. They brought a successful product to market in one-third of the anticipated time.

The result was a universal tissue donor. The manufacturer used a scaffolding matrix that reproduced a generic anatomical model to fabricate these creatures. Technicians loaded pre-differentiated tissue samples into the appropriate sites.

Epigenetic modifications allowed guided development from tissue to organ. After a few weeks of incubation, a universal tissue donor walked out of the nutrient bath, sealed the communication between the two sides

of its circulation, reabsorbed the fluid in its lungs, and began to breathe.

In the interest of pragmatism, the manufacturers left the donors with enough neurologic function to get around. In the interest of compliance with the institutional review board, they left the donors with insufficient neurologic function to do anything more than get around. The treating physician had complete control of

tissue development via the enhanced epigenetic tool. However, a physician would rarely need to step in to make corrections, as the tissue communicated directly with its designated host using retroviruses. The transplant team just needed to plug it in occasionally and let it do its job. Once the donor finished assimilating the host's cell surface markers and immunologic memory, it was ready for the operating room. For those patients who required multiple transplantations over time, the donor remained viable with proper storage for six months or more.

What happened next has been the subject of many controversies. The short and truthful version is that it didn't work.

During assimilation with the host, donors sent repeated warnings about unpredicted contents of the genome. Donors also started to ask unusual questions of their own, despite their limited cortical volume.

Donors wanted to know if their lives and the host's lives were one life or two. Almost every donor wanted to know their Species classification in light of pangenomic semantic contamination.

Researchers with the Universal Tissue Donor Project discovered the contamination while programming retroviruses to assimilate cell surface markers and immunologic memory from hosts.

Across galaxies, astrobiologists recognized astonishing similarities among life forms. Convergent evolution received credit for the curious finding. Still, the geneticists on the project discovered the Species' fingerprints, among many others, on the loci for common, shared traits.

The geneticists found no evidence of grand schemes or dark purposes in the alterations. The reasons for normalizing alterations to alien genomes

boiled down to chauvinism, carelessness, and hubris.

Wherever they went, spacefaring races made themselves at home. They had already become comfortable with modifying their own genome, so it was easy for them to countenance manipulating other Species' genomes to make things a little bit homier in strange and distant lands. It was very inconvenient to limit the dissemination of changes to target genomes or to preserve the original genetic makeup of those Species, so

they didn't. The same pragmatic laziness tainted the UTD's management. Clinical trial records, obtained during discovery, contain an astonishing paucity of information regarding the donor's psychological status. Expert testimony revealed profound skepticism about the possibility of UTD

consciousness.

The cortical volume was too small, they said, to allow conscious expe-rience, though it could generate a limited EEG pattern. They attributed the donors' verbal behavior to inadvertent instructions transmitted during conversations with optimistic trial personnel. The proper sort of question evoked the proper sort of response. The proper sort of response prompted the next leading question. The process repeated as needed until it established the respondent's consciousness.

AI systems had burned consciousness optimists that way. The ex-optimists weren't about to repeat the mistake.

Enough of the trial personnel doubted the possibility of UTD conscious-ness to provide the rest with an adequate excuse for changing nothing. It was a comfortable path; speaking creatures took up solipsism long before anyone suspected a computer might be conscious.

The UTD persisted in demanding rights despite admonitions to abandon their consciousness delusion. Finally, donors objected to transplantation altogether. Several tragic instances of graft-versus-host disease ensued, leading to the program's termination.

Of course, the termination was not terminal.

Various organizations have revisited the universal tissue donors' potential from different angles, with the same results. The latest attempt was the

trial two study at the Bilateral Nephrectomy Center of Excellence, which almost resulted in hostile UTD overrunning the entire facility.

At the end of the initial UTD trial, God saw his chance and

dispatched his followers to gather up UTD and bring it to him for consid-eration of martyrdom. UTD sacrifice should have scored even better on the divine redemption scale than the martyrdom of the innocent or divine self-mutilation because it also ended the UTD's unnatural existence and the horrible suffering that must follow from it.

When shipments started rolling in and the Helpers made the first few sacrifices, God found the benefit lacking. It was still better on balance for UTD to keep its suffering to itself than it was for the donors to suffer innocently and willingly die in God's name. Even with measures of suffering, sacrifice, and punishment distributed optimally, God still got the short straw. Things didn't quite add up on his side of the books. He was doomed unless some exculpatory factor prevented him from fulfilling his duties.

The factor was power. He could avoid loads of anguish and would never need to repent again if only he had no power. When his devotees brought the idea to his attention, God rejected it without a moment's hesitation. He contended that he was actually all-powerful but had somehow been stripped of his ability when he went to hell.

The tension produced a curious spectacle. God insisted on the one thing that would keep him on the global justice hook, while his followers sought to excuse him by exposing his abject weakness. Observers noted that God never did much outside of the autobiographical rants. The experimental theologians studying God were the ones most fascinated with his aversion to action. He was surrounded day and night, and wherever he travelled, by a swarm of nachinaks, which remained in his company until they were destroyed, or he was.

These were mostly old and damaged units, and most bore a piece of add-on programming that could be traced back to some of the first

records of divine encounters contained in the archives. The nachinaks did his bidding without question.

His followers were also a significant complicating factor in the dispute over God's power to act.

Like God, a subpopulation of the Species had always labored under a weighty metaphysical burden. For this fraternity (the vast majority of its members were male) of God hobbyists, the world wasn't just amenable to categorization; it was made of categories. Time was a list.

Causes ran in a straight line. Determinism was a table full of billiard balls. Members of the Species predisposed to this attitude came together and got semi-organized. They insist that their organization has been there from the very beginning. The archive has no record confirming or refuting that claim but reports of their activities date back to the end of our Archive's record. They meant to assist the deity in any way possible, and they resolved to build a Corps of helpers for him. They became God's Helping Angels, and their extreme helpfulness quashed practical arguments in favor of effective divine action. They were the first to put forward the notion that God was epiphenomenal. That would explain his curious inaction. The idea had some problems. God was complicated. He could suffer from a dilemma, for example. A complex identity was a hard thing for an epiphenomenon to pull off. In God's case, he was God if he shot out of a gray space outbreak, crashed into a planet, gave several lectures on justice and divine punishment, etc.

The multiplicity of things that God must depend upon to be God over time posed a problem. Suppose he crashed and stepped on a pebble, which hurt his foot. Next, he saw a flower that looked pretty. He then had another pain when he put weight back on his foot and compressed the bruised area where the pebble had injured him.

His experience with the flower is no trouble because it is an isolated incident. The encounter with the pebble is another matter. It isn't so much the initial incident, but what happens when he puts his foot back on the ground and experiences another pain.

The injury from the pebble caused the second pain. He now consists of the first pain, the pebble injury, the second pain, and the condition of his foot required for the second pain to occur. Forget whether or not the pebble moved when he stepped on it; he has begun exerting causal influences on himself.

As soon as he acquires the ability to carry over dependencies from one experience to another, his epiphenomenal status is lost, and with it, his only chance for redemption.

The situation initially caused much consternation, but advocates of God's causal ineffectiveness proposed that a solution might be available in the transition from one arrangement of constituents to a subsequent arrangement of constituents. They suggested they could simply peel away that first layer of continuity over time.

They noted that God certainly looked uncannily well-preserved. He could regurgitate rants, but those were a kind of fact. They needn't be congruent or even understood to be stated, however elegant the statement may be. He had no memory whatsoever of his previous incarnations. He expressed no narrative account of his existence.

It did look suspiciously like he disregarded time. Perhaps he was like the still frames in a movie projection. The individual frames don't cause the motion picture the audience sees on the screen – that's up to the projector's actions and the representation recorded in the series of frames. If you cut out a single frame, the motion picture persists. If you shine a light through the single frame, an image appears, but it isn't the movie and won't be unless it goes back in its place and runs through the projector. If God's existence really was a constant conjunction of independent moments, with no contiguous dependencies, then there was no God movie, and the problem was solved.

The hobbyists who favored the taste of epiphenomenal theory accepted the argument and carried on assembling the helper corps. Those who felt nauseated at the slightest whiff of an epiphenomenon returned to their research and stopped talking to the others entirely. And aside from a few

small-scale massacres over the dispute, that's how they left things for many centuries. They couldn't be blamed for failing to come to a decisive answer to the question of what God was. It wasn't germane to contemporary theological issues, once the corps had assembled an adequate contingent of nachinaks, reprogrammed, and tasked with carrying out the divine will. Furthermore, God showed little interest in the issue from the very beginning, and over time, he exhibited increasing hostility towards anyone who attempted to resume the research.

Ten

Roosting

Laplace reached up and touched the gold filigree on the silver ring clipped to the lower ridge of his auditory meatus. He wanted to listen to the report on God from the archives one more time. He sat at a plain, wrought-iron frame table with a marble tabletop, nestled in a solarium at the top of a shining chrome high-rise building. He owned the building, though the large sign in front of the sky-scraper advertised, "Sonnamarg: secure living in a gritty urban environment at an affordable price." He had thought of the slogan himself and was in the habit of mentioning that fact to his staff and slaves, who were the actual tenants. He seemed to think it was clever because of the building's true purpose.

It was a roost, and a roost was a domicile, staging area, fortress, and storehouse for high-status calculators. Sonnamarg, like most roosts, stood situated boldly next to a node. Everyone who was anyone in calculator society had investigated the optimal configuration for a roost. They ran computer simulations modeling the day-to-day functions, associated costs, and vulnerability to the most common, likely, and most dangerous assaults

and infiltrations. The
simulations arrived at a consensus. They invariably concluded that access to the event radiation without external power sources was more important than the security advantage the roost gained from sitting at the bottom of some forsaken swamp on some backwater planet.

The roost owners were predisposed to favor that answer anyway. They wanted to hide and did not want to be attacked, but there was something better than se-curity to be gained from the setup. To hide without hiding too hard meant that they would still be secure from the amateurs out there who sought fame in graduating from the ham-handed criminal bourgeoisie with its bombings and frontal assaults to the more sophisticated league of operators who settled scores and achieved notoriety via intrigue, infiltration, and assassination.

The hidden message sent by the visible hiding place conveyed some valuable information to the community. It advertised the owner's respect and humility. The roost owner plugged into a node or similar publicly accessible utility, acknowledged the limited effectiveness of hiding from the upper echelons of the Species' society. Legerdemain kept the little people away; nothing could keep the heavy hitters off of you if it came to that.

There was one last, vital deterrent that went with every roost. It stemmed from a habit of mind pathognomonic of the Species' defining psychological characteristic—a habit of mind frequently cited as the source of their endurance and the most likely cause of their eventual demise.

According to one of the few human legends adopted by the Species, the king of one of the warring states hired General Sun Tzu to help the monarch with his dire strategic and tactical situation. His army was in the field battling an enemy to the south. From the North, his scouts had spotted another rival's

army marching towards the capital. He could not disengage in the South

without risking a rout and, therefore, the serious possibility of losing his army. On the other hand, he was completely undefended from the north. Gen. Sun Tzu walked the battlements, took an inventory of the city's weapons and stores, observed the troops remaining for the defense of the capital on their maneuvers, and read reports from the King's scouts detailing the logistical as well as the fighting strength of the opposing army.

Furthermore, he sought out sources who knew the enemy king well enough to comment on his nature. At the end of it all, Sun Tzu came to the king with this advice.

"I have made a thorough account of the city's strength. You cannot prevail in a siege. You might not even have the strength to force a siege. I have also assessed your other option. Victory is not assured in the South. If your army there turns its back on a well-matched foe, it will be destroyed, and no one will even be left to bury you. I have reconnoitered your enemy as they march from the north. Their king is an opportunist, and their army has set out on an adventure rather than a well-planned expedition. Here's what you must do. Withdraw all your scouts from the north so there is no sign of your military there. Tell the populace to evacuate or hide. Open the gates and set fire pots around the inner palace so it fills with smoke. Remove the populace to a location invisible from the city. Take all the guards off the walls and dismiss your personal guard. You will then dress in your ornate armor and seat yourself in the middle of the throne room on the floor with your sword laid across your lap."

The king's advisors begged him to send Sun Tzu away without pay and to ignore his deranged advice. The king was wise

enough, however, to understand that there was no other option. He was also wise enough to understand that the plan required his complete commitment if it were to have any hope of success. So, on the day the northern army showed up on his doorstep, the king was dressed in his ornate armor, sword on his lap, seated in the middle of the throne room, and the city was silent, wide open, and filled with smoke. For two days prior, the northern army had marched through an empty, silent countryside with no sign of enemy

forces or the civilian

population. The king of the northern state summoned his generals. "What is the meaning of this?" He asked.

"We do not know," the generals said, "Something is brewing. We are already overextended. We advise caution."

Rather than risk the king or the high-ranking officers, the generals sent scouts in to see what was in store.

The scouts reported back that the king was the only living person that they had encountered, and he was seated in the middle of the throne room, with no defense other than his personal equipment, surrounded by clouds of thick smoke. They said that they could not approach him due to the open ground between their last cover and the seated king, obscured as the approach was by the smoke on all sides.

Upon hearing this news, the northern king ordered his army to withdraw rather than risk an encounter with the unknown.

A roost was the upper crust calculator's smoky throne room in an open city. The final and most important message it conveyed was: "Go ahead, try me. I can bluff anybody, but isn't that what I would say if I wanted you to call my bluff?"

Laplace removed the earpiece and put it in his pocket.

He sipped a hot drink as he sat contemplating something in the distance, far beyond the walls of the high-rise. After the moment's reverie, he put the ring back on his ear.

"Danilo," he called, "would you come up here for a moment?" "On my way, master."

Laplace sat quietly, waiting for his slave's arrival. The tap, tap, tap of his index finger on the marble countertop gave the only hint to his mood. Danilo sheepishly opened the door to the solarium. He was not one of the Species.

He had hair over his entire head and face, with a tuft on top of each of his small, triangular ears, a tuft projecting downwards from the lower margin

of each ear, and a more prominent tuft projecting downwards from the angle of his jaw on both sides. His mouth projected slightly, and he had thin lips with a midpoint division in the upper lip. His eyes were large, with round pupils and black irises. His nose projected 3 to 4 inches beyond the bridge, and the nose tip had prominent, opposable flaps above and below the nostril.

His knees flexed backward, and the lower leg had a short foot with a thick nail across a pair of pads formed from the fusion of the three metatarsals on either side of the foot. He was lightly built, with six long, thin fingers on each hand.

His movements were timid and guarded. He crossed the tiled floor and knelt beside Laplace.

"Yes, master?"

Laplace spoke without looking down at him, "Danilo, what were you doing in the city yesterday?"

"I was checking on the aid stations master," Danilo replied. "You said I could do that, as long as I checked in and checked out. As long as it was on unallocated time."

"Yes, I did," Laplace said, "despite your previous difficulty following directions when you were down in the city. You haven't been pursuing females or seeking out your offspring lately, have you? You haven't been dabbling in politics again, have you?"

"Of course not, master," Danilo answered. "You gave me very strict instructions."

Laplace looked down at him sharply.

"I know you're lying to me. I also know that you're smart enough to know that you couldn't get away with it. Insubordination of this nature typically warrants severe punishment. Why would you risk that?"

"I honestly can't say," said Danilo, looking up from beneath his brows at Laplace with a steady, insolent gaze.

"I'm about to take a big risk," said Laplace, "and the odds favor the

ascendancy of my little enterprise here in case I succeed. If I fail, I'm afraid the rest of you will be wiped out in short order.

"Didn't you ever wonder why I made you my slave, Danilo? You must have.

Enslaving members of other Species is simply not done in our tradition. You must have wondered about that too. What about the history that you learned while I owned you? Have you ever wondered why the Species' history differs from all the other cultures whose histories tell the same sordid joke? "They start out free from other people, free from possessions, free from greed and jealousy. But then they trade it all in for a bowl of pottage and some certainty. Soon, they are subjugated by a society that's taken over the task of self-perpetuation from them. They don't know why they're angry, but they need to go to war, so they do. Sometimes they win, and the weight

of the

spoils drag them down.

"Sometimes, they lose, and then their chains drag them down. No matter their advantages or who advises them, they will leap back into the pointless cycle. Have you ever wondered why we never crushed them in the name of aesthetic offense, if nothing else?"

"I will gladly answer any questions you direct me to answer," said Danilo, his eyes fixed on the globes staring at him from behind lightly tinted, transparent lids, "but I fear that Master will not be pleased with my responses. Would you answer the questions for me instead?"

"Oh, please, indulge me," Laplace said. "You mustn't forget that these conversations we have from time to time are for you. I don't expect to learn anything from them, but you should.

"I already know the answers. Answers don't please or displease me. Their means of discovery and subsequent use may. But this is not news to you. Very well. Let's set aside the answers for the moment. Why do you wish to hear me speak to them?"

"I wish to hear you speak them, master, if you will, because I want to

know if you really believe them," Danilo said.

"Among all my slaves, Danilo, you remain the favorite," said Laplace. "Academics have parsed out volumes detailing nuanced variants on the single reason for our attitude towards other Species, but they don't improve on the primary answer: we simply don't find them very interesting. None of them can attempt a calculation. Most of them cannot even survive a brief visit to the dendritic radiation of events. They don't understand where they live. Not understanding where they live, they don't know what's valuable and what isn't.

"They mistake power for something that is valuable, and they mistake the approval and admiration of the masses for power.

"They mistake safety for something valuable, and then they mistake walls and bars for safety. We ignore them because they don't merit our attention," Laplace leaned down to speak into Danilo's ear, "save the occasional exceptional individual who piques our interest.

"If I fail, you will be free, for however long you are destined to enjoy it. The extraction nachinak is preprogrammed to seek you out. It will remove the subjugation nachinak from your leg when the transition is complete. I also know that you are prepared to make your move soon anyway. I look forward to it; I am sure that it will be brilliant. Whatever happens, you are still not one of the

Species. You are one of the others, so you remain vulnerable to their afflictions. Do not make mistakes about what is valuable."

"May I go now?" Danilo asked, looking down. "You are dismissed."

Eleven

Curses and Club Med

Takezo watched Lucky sleep from a safe hiding spot. He remained intent on his subject and kept his watch without moving. An hour passed. Lucky roused briefly and adjusted his makeshift pillow. Takezo sighed. He settled back and resumed waiting as Lucky relaxed again. Almost 90 minutes into the next sleep cycle, Lucky made a quiet whimpering noise. Takezo perked up and leaned forward ever so slightly.

Lucky whimpered again and twitched. Something like a swarm of gnats, but denser and much darker, gathered near Lucky's knees and began to spread across his recumbent form until he was entirely engulfed in the swarm.

Though each dot appeared to vibrate, the apparition was silent. Lucky said something incomprehensible and twitched again. In conjunction with the movement, the swarm altered its shape, adopting the appearance of a shaggy bipedal creature with a pair of long, erect ears that came to a point. Its form constantly shifted, but Takezo got a steady impression of empty eyes regarding the world around them with a ravenous glare and an upper

lip

lifting to reveal a sharp canine. Lucky had settled down, and the swarm seemed to fade when the eyes flicked towards a hint of movement on the trail above.

Takezo looked in the same direction and saw someone break cover and bolt up the trail. He was not able to pursue the spy. A change in the swarm around Lucky demanded his attention. After a few flickers lasting no more than two seconds total, the swarm vanished, along with Lucky.

Takezo leapt up, a sharp "Uso!" escaping his lips. A sleepy voice spoke, "What?"

ELEVEN

Takezo froze. He heard some scuffling noises coming from the overhang in the small cliff band, followed by a deep breath, and then silence. The next moment, Lucky was back, curled up in the same position with the swarm surrounding him. It briefly assumed its previous shape, stabilized, then flipped into a crouch with its eyes' bottomless voids locked on Takezo.

Takezo took a step back.

"No," he said, "I know you. But it was my dream, and I've seen you die a thousand times. I have tasted your blood!"

His legs wobbled. The color drained from his face. He dropped to his knees and retched. Lucky sat up, looking groggy and uncertain of where he was. He heard the retching then and scrambled to his feet. The swarm dissipated. "Takezo?" Lucky asked, "Is that you? Are you okay? What the hell is going on?"

Takezo slowly got to his feet. He spat to clear the taste of bile from his mouth. His eyes were downcast. Lucky put his headlamp on and gathered his pack. He stumbled sleepily over to Takezo.

"I'm sorry," Takezo said quietly, "I'm unable to answer your questions at present. I need to reflect on what I've seen. Will you allow me that luxury? As a sign of good faith, let me tell you everything I know about those questions." "Sure," said Lucky, "Hey, I owe you. The least I can do is return your water bags and give you some space. Besides, as you can see, I did not make

it to the station wagon, so I'll be imposing on you if your offer still stands. Although I am currently lodging in the manner to which I am more accustomed," Lucky said, sweeping his hand backward to indicate the little hollow under the rock step, "I have decided that I might benefit from a spa vacation."

Takezo smiled.

"Have I told you that you have a way of putting things that makes me feel better about them, even if I shouldn't? Yes, my invitation stands, and now I will insist, having seen your last two bungalows. I can't stand by and watch while your conditions deteriorate. At least your last spot was not directly on the dirt."

"That's more like it," Lucky said. "I prefer this over the vomiting. Lead the way, Sir."

As they climbed up the short step by the light of their headlamps, Lucky's phone buzzed in his pocket. He fished it out and took a look at the screen. The battery was getting low. He pushed a couple of buttons and gazed at the screen for a moment more.

"Do you need to respond?" Takezo asked as he studied Lucky's expression intently.

"No," Lucky said with a frown.

"Okay," Takezo said, adding, "Do you know how to work those things? I mean all those other things besides the phone and messages. I've been so busy since I got one that I never bothered to learn how to use it. "

"Yeah," said Lucky, still frowning, "I mean, more or less. I can show you in the morning if you like."

"Yes. Thank you."

The path climbed onto a plateau and widened out to a double track, which subsequently joined a proper fire road at about the 2-kilometer mark. A large rock formation loomed ahead of them, due north, but the road turned off before reaching the base.

It forked, with the main branch continuing toward the Center of Excellence

and the other branch turning downhill. The sidetrack then switched back four times down the steeper slope and took a long, gradual right hand turn down to a valley with a spring-fed creek running through it.

Lucky's headlamp had started to dim by the time they got to the little complex of buildings on the valley floor, but the sky had grown light by then, and he could turn off his lamp before it ran out of battery power. Takezo stopped just before the road cleared a small woodland at the entrance of the little valley. Lucky could make out the outlines of two structures a short distance ahead.

"Well, we have arrived at a very inopportune time of day. Would you rather stay up and see a little bit of what this place has to offer, or would you rather sleep?" Takezo asked.

"What I want to do is the first one," Lucky said, "but what I'm afraid I'm going to do is the second one. As soon as I stop, I am pretty sure that I'm going to crash. I guess it would be better to do so on a bed."

"Follow me then," Takezo said, turning onto a brick footpath that bore to the right, towards the larger of the two buildings just taking shape in the predawn light.

The path led along the north side of the villa. Looking down the longer dimension, Lucky could see that it was about twice

the length of the short side, about 35 m. A stairway with four steps led to the broad front entrance. A small arch provided access to the central patio and rooms on that side of the building. The roof was red tile, and the walls were whitewashed. All the wooden components were made of thick boards, timbers, shutters, and frames, and were crafted from dark hardwood. The central patio featured a round table with a Lazy Susan in the middle. Eight white, overstuffed chairs surrounded the table. A replica Cretan mosaic covered the entire floor.

"That's interesting," Lucky said, "This is modular."

"Yes," said Takezo, "I take that as a good sign. I think it indicates that they want this place to look nicer than it is and that they are willing to pay for an attractive perk, but not too much. That means they are genuinely committed to retaining me for the project and diligently monitor the budget.

CURSES AND CLUB MED

If I'm working for people with those attributes, I usually can get what I need to produce a high-quality result, and I don't have to do anything unethical to receive the payment that they agreed upon when the project is complete." Lucky smiled and nodded. Takezo produced a handful of keys from his pocket. He looked through the tabs until he found one labeled "Room 4." He turned the key in the lock and went through the doorway first. He stood to the side while Lucky entered. The room was spacious. There was a small table in the middle with a chair beside it. A sink with a counter and a single burner sat adjacent to the wall on the left, along with plates and cooking utensils, pots, glasses, mugs, and bowls on the shelves underneath the counter.

Beside the end of the counter closest to Lucky, there was a small refrigerator and a wall of shelves above and to the left of the refrigerator stocked with pantry items. In the corner to Lucky's right, there was a bathroom. A large window looked out onto the patio. A vertical blind stood stacked in its cubbyhole at the far end of the window frame.

Underneath the windowsill and running to the far end of the wall was a set of bookshelves, extending to the ceiling as the frame passed the end of the windowsill. The bed was queen-sized with linen sheets and a hybrid foam mattress. It had a nightstand with a lamp and electrical outlets on either side, including several USB ports. Lucky walked around the room, circling the table. He smiled and nodded his head.

"This is pretty impressive, Takezo," Lucky said, "Are you sure I'm okay to stay here? I mean, I'm happy to stay here. In fact, I think I might have trouble leaving when the time comes." Takezo shook his head and wagged his index finger.

"No. No. I am being thoroughly undercompensated for this job. It will all make more sense to you when we can sit in the sun, feeling rested, and have a cup of sake or two while I explain."

Lucky shrugged.

"Ah. There you go. Thank you for that and the room."

"I don't want you to think that this is all in the name of altruism or pity.

Something is happening to me. I don't know what it is," Takezo said, his face grim, "but I know you are involved in it, though I don't know how or why.

"I am hoping for some answers from you. That may take time, but rest assured, I will spend whatever time it takes. There is a threat in this change creeping over me. Of course, I'm saying this to see how you respond, but I also think you have a right to know. Do not concern yourself with my clients. If we need more time, they will give it to us."

Takezo bowed, never elevating his gaze from the floor,
and turned on his heel to leave.

"Takezo," Lucky said as Takezo laid his hand on the doorknob. "We'll get this sorted out …I promise you."

"I think we will," said Takezo "unfortunately, I fear that as much as I fear the alternative."

Twelve

The Harsh Realities of Heritage

The Mother trembled and gasped. In a daze, she turned to look for her child. He was barely distinguishable from an adult by now, but he stood next to her, holding her hand. He still did that from time to time, but she sensed that something else was amiss. She looked over at his face. He stood very still, staring straight ahead. Before she had time to panic, he mirrored her shocked gasp and then her bemusement.

"Damn!" he said, "like jumping into an ice bath!" The Mother knitted her brow.

"Mother?" The child asked, an expression of fear and concern on his face, "Are you okay? Was that what we were told about in the first lessons?"

"It must be!" he answered himself, a smile displacing his worried expression, "Wow," he said," Much respect. That was cleverly done."

When she didn't respond, he took her hand and led her to a café table. "Here," he said, "you should sit briefly while you get your bearings."

She walked slowly over to the seat. Behind her, a waiter not of the Species

hurried around to bus the dirty table.

"Is this a dream?" she asked. "No, I decided the last time that this was not a dream. What are you talking about?"

She looked around as they spoke, hoping for a cue to start her orientation. They sat in front of a small café under a blue and white awning dripping with moisture from the misty rain. Several bridges spanned a small river that ran past the café's storefront.

An ornate metalwork fence atop a small stone wall guarded the river on both sides, as far as she could see. A pedestrian walkway of dark red paving stones cut through the manicured green space between the shops and cafés and the fence.

Downstream, past a bakery, tall, dark green trees bordered a park, blocking the view. She swept her gaze back and forth along the banks until finally, near the third bridge upstream, she spotted a familiar sign over a tall, round, windowless building with metal skin and an industrial look to it. The sign read, "Node 3."

"Yes," she said, "that's what this is. It is the presentation, which occurs at the end of your developmental phase."

"Waiter!" she said, waving the server over to the table.

"Yes, ma'am, pardon me, ma'am," he said. "I will be with you to take your order very soon. Is there something you need more urgently in the meantime?"

"Just a simple answer to a simple question," she said, "how long would you say we, I mean this young man and I, have been here? That is, how long ago did you first see us?"

"Well, I'd say an hour, maybe even two hours," he said, cocking his head to the side, "you have been up and down the street several times, it looked like you were window-shopping,

for as much as I could see."

"Thank you very much," she said.," It doesn't look like we'll be able to stay for a drink, but we'll likely be able to come back later. Please remember

us if you see us. We would be delighted to have you wait on us again."

The Mother stood and straightened up her clothing. She tapped the boy on his shoulder and motioned for him to get back on his feet and hurry. Without a word, he did as she asked, and the two of them walked purposefully toward the bridges upriver.

Thirteen

What to Do With a Second Life?

Anisa clenched and unclenched her fist. She was as close to the end of the tunnel as she could safely get, with video surveillance and the guard watching over the passageway. The guard was dressed as a slave. There was no way, without additional identifying information, to tell whose slave he was, and therefore who she was really about to attack.

She scrolled through the current messages on the cell phone in her hand. She had broken through the encryption without any difficulty, but one could never be sure with these things that there wasn't another link or storage site lurking unseen. She went back to the main menu. The screen flashed, and she gasped slightly despite herself as she pressed the phone to her chest, hiding its glow. When the light switched off, she looked back at the screen. It had a few application short-cuts scattered in the background, and in the foreground, large block letters that read "Jim's phone," She searched through the apps,

She had lost count of the number of times that she had done this. She went to the contacts and scrolled down to the one marked with a capital "D," she then scrolled through all the messages until she found

one that looked acceptable for her purposes.

She didn't even know why it worked, but it kept the recipient tied to the area. She pushed several more buttons and then hit "send." She had distributed her attention between the phone and the guard while she finished looking for the message she wanted.

With the phone stowed, she again focused her full attention on the guard and the goings-on visible through the doorway. She could see four vehicles parked in a small asphalt lot in front of a convenience store about 60 m down the gently sloping field.

Three men were busy with boxes and crates from the vehicles, transferring the containers to the store's interior. She squinted, trying to make out the details of the cargo's contents. She recognized a couple of additional closed-circuit TV units, like the ones monitoring the tunnel exit. The rest was standard convenience store fare.

She felt a short buzz from the phone. She quickly pulled it from its zipped side pocket on her pant leg and entered the password. The screen opened to the image of a bedroom. The image flickered; someone was turning the phone in their hand.

As the view flipped, she saw a familiar human face briefly. The face drew a rapidly thickening swarm of tiny, vibrating black dots which swirled and hovered around the image, then flowed into a form suggesting an animal's face and head, though the image wavered and shifted too much to be sure. It had long ears that came to a point and bottomless eyes that pulled a steady flow of the circulating dots into their depths. She got the impression of long teeth threatening her, though no image of a tooth appeared. The screen flickered again, and all she could see after that was the image of the
bedroom.

She put the phone back in her pocket and zipped it tight. She bowed her head and rocked back and forth, hiding her face in her hands. The lapse was brief. With a desperate effort, she controlled her breath. As she regained her composure, she dropped her hands

to her sides and clenched her fists once more. Her gaze fixed on the guard at the end of the tunnel, and her face contorted with an expression of unslaked hatred as she crept down the last few meters of tunnel toward him.

Besides the guard, one other member of the Species stood by the vehicles, supervising the transfer of goods into the store. The other two were humans. The guard did not spot her until she was very close. By then, she had already turned her attention to the nachinak hovering in the upper right-hand corner of the doorway.

She carried a loop of engraved beads slung across her body. As she broke into a trot, she whipped the loop of beads over her head. The flaps of tissue lying against her abdomen and thorax snapped out from beneath their covering filaments.

As the loop of beads cleared her head and left arm, its arcing swing cast four nachinaks sequestered beneath it into the air.

The filaments were already manipulating the beads as the loop settled around the flaps in a crisscross pattern.

Meanwhile, her nachinaks darted for the device hovering in the doorway's corner. It had begun spinning up a vortex, but it was too slow. One of Anisa's devices matched its rotation and seized the enemy machine's legs, bringing the spin to an abrupt halt. The other device flitted to the front of the imprisoned unit and spread its orifice until it could slide over the opponent's trunk.

The opposing nachinak froze. Its pupils dilated. The unit clasped to its body rotated 90 degrees. The guard had noticed his predicament by that time.

He produced a large, chrome-plated, semi-automatic pistol from his belt and pointed it in her general direction, but without aiming immediately.

Instead, he looked desperately from side to side and then behind him, only to find the other nachinak that he'd been counting on crumpled and smoking on the ground, and Anisa's 3rd device hovering right above it.

In the time it took to make a brief glance over his shoulder, he lost his meager opportunity to survive.

The rotating triplet of nachinaks generated a small line in the air, stretch-ing vertically from the ceiling to the floor in the middle of the passageway.

Anisa jumped for the line, rotating midair to catch it perpendicular to the doorway's plane.

A pop and a flash of light came from farther up the tunnel as the air folded around Anisa. It seemed impossible that she would make it through the gap, but she did.

She was almost completely obscured by the time she rotated into view of the guard. Through the sliver in the air in front of him, he glimpsed Anisa with her string of beads cutting through the gap toward him.

She was still turning as she fell back into a bubble afloat in an infinite ocean of shifting shapes and colors. Then, the loop was on his arm, pulling him to his death.

He tried to brace himself, but it was impossible by then.

As it yanked him off his feet, her traction on the loop pulled Anisa forward, and she rotated past him, briefly looking straight into his terrified face as his hands scrabbled to grasp something of hers that would end up outside the contracting exclusion sphere and the event radiation with its promise of certain death for the unprotected.

As Anisa spun her body through the narrowing gap and into the sunlit meadow outside the passageway, the guard managed to get one hand through the closing fold.

Her angular momentum dropped, and she flipped the circle of beads up, arresting their flight with a sharp downward tug and an abbreviated motion in the opposite direction when the ring cleared her head.

The double loop clattered into place across her body from right shoulder to left hip, while the last remnant of the fold into the

dendritic radiation of events disappeared.

The guard's empty hand, abandoned on the rusty sand of the high desert, had already evaporated into a thin, curling pool of reddish smoke which

melted into nothing as the fold closed.

Anisa risked a quick look over her shoulder to assess the tunnel situation. She smiled. There was a rapidly brightening, yellow/orange light in the depths and roiling waves of black smoke from the doorway.

Something downhill and to her left made a loud click. Without turning her head, she dove backwards, swung her right hip and leg across her body's axis, and pushed off into a sprint as the ball of her right foot hit the ground. Simultaneously, she heard an explosion in the parking lot.

She crossed the threshold of the convenience store's back entrance at full tilt, scanning the space above the counter for an image on the video surveillance screens.

THIRTEEN

In an odd frame-by-frame, she saw her little destroyer, the nachinak that had taken out the enemy machine by the vehicles, lying on the grass, a blackened, smoking mess of ruined legs and torn skin held together now by little more than the cohesion of its tarry, homogenous innards.

Next to flash past was an image of her external power source accessory, the one responsible for the havoc in the tunnel as well as the condition of the two humans whose bodies lay in a pile behind the front counter with their clothes smoldering and the cartons of cigarettes behind

them beginning to catch fire.

The nachinak had its legs wrapped around the top knob of a joystick.

The last screen displayed a feed from the camera that covered the door and the parking lot, now two steps ahead of her.

She had successfully traversed the store without crashing. The camera kept turning, to show a shadow pass beneath it and then resolve into the image of the other calculator, striding toward the open door in front of her, as he lifted the butt of a semi-automatic shotgun to his shoulder.

Every one of the Species that has run, even the humblest calculation, is familiar with the experience of pseudo-time dilation. Though it occurs routinely in the intensive, cognitively demanding setting of a calculation, it may pop up sporadically in critical situations of all sorts, and it was what

happened to Anisa, just two quick steps from the doorway and the barrel of the shotgun.

Time slowed. As she passed the smoldering bodies, she noticed something ahead of her, on the last shelf before the doorway.

It was a collection of folk art. The bottom shelf held prefab garden gnomes and river stones. On the middle shelf were bird feeders and birdhouses, yard signs and a few planks with pithy aphorisms burned into the wood for houseguests to enjoy while they stood and urinated.

The top shelf held three

medium-sized turtles made of smooth rocks glued together to suggest the limbs, head, tail, and body, all augmented with glued and painted features for the realists among the artists' potential patrons, who the artists correctly surmised were most of them.

Anisa's attention oscillated rapidly between the turtles and the TV screen. She was reasonably sure of the gunman's position, but she was still heartbroken when the frame swept past him. The camera rattled to a stop at what she took to be the end of its arc of motion but then began zooming in on a view of the open trunks, truck beds, and crates of junk stacked on the ground.

She was now in reach of the turtles. She ripped one off the shelf and bounded to the door, pivoting on her heel to sling the turtle through the plate-glass bordering the doorway on her left.

Glass sprayed over the parking lot. The turtle landed with a thunk, having missed its target, and the shattered bits of its appendages scattered over the asphalt. As she passed the threshold into the lot, Anisa did her best to continue her sprint while transitioning into a crouch.

The shotgun blasted out another shell, pushing the barrel skyward and the gunman backward. He stumbled but didn't fall to the ground.

Anisa made for the cars and the pile of crates stacked around them. Each step she took pushed her weight farther over her toes. She heard the crunch of glass underfoot nearby, behind her, and to her left. She raised her head

and spotted a red blinking dome nestled among the junk stacked on the tailgate of a faded blue pickup truck.

The vehicle was parked in front of a shrubbery about three meters ahead and slightly to the right of her current trajectory.

The inevitable stumble began as she drew even with the rear axle of the truck. She tried to salvage her momentum by converting the stumble into a dive. Her effort was largely unsuccessful, landing her short of cover at the base of the first shrubbery in front of the

pickup truck. She was trying to crawl further into the bushes when she heard the crunching footsteps stop behind her. She curled up and waited. A loud pop, a brilliant blue flash, and a violent jolt extinguished everything.

She tried to lift her head as she woke, but she ran into an oil pan. She set the back of her head on the asphalt again and looked side to side. To her left, she could see the gunman. The shotgun lay on the ground behind him. His right hand and arm were smoldering. A charred stump was all that remained of his right foot.

She scooted out from beneath the truck as fast as she could. She stood and peered over the side of the truck bed. Someone had torched the contents. She walked past the convenience store and up the gentle hillside that opened into the meadow leading to the sandstone passageway.

Her right hand was mildly numb. She looked over the arm and hand as she walked, noting a painless burn on her palm and the back of her forearm. She had another burn on the back of her left lower leg. She looked panicked as she stopped everything to feel around her calf and knee on both sides. She found nothing unusual.

Up at the tunnel, she could still hear voices in the depths. The smoke had diminished, but it was unlikely that someone would survive an attempted crossing without a breathing apparatus. She walked back to the store and the vehicles. She reminded herself to keep an eye on the time. She was beginning to feel the residue of the fight, and it felt like it was going to slow

her down.

She looked through the items in the store, careful not to touch anything she didn't intend to take. A few of the foods looked palatable. She found a cache of sleeping bags on a shelf

in the stockroom and beside them, three large daypacks. She took one of each. The front display cases yielded a decent knife and a box of shotgun shells loaded with slugs. The two key nachinaks that had opened the fold to the event radiation were already sequestered in the loop of beads over her shoulder.

She gathered the remains of the destroyer into a resealable plastic bag. There wasn't much else of value in the cargo. While digging through the junk piled in the truck bed and on the ground around it, she found her savior and its preferred weapon.

After she escaped, Anisa made a habit of hijacking

shipments of rare items and antiquities destined for the Bilateral Nephrectomy Center of Excellence for study and exhibition. She found an instruc-tional recording for the creation and use of external power source accessory nachinaks that had paid off today.

She had traded for the power source accessory several years ago, before she knew its true value. It was a relatively large unit, about the size of a chinchilla. It was ornate in nachinak terms. Its distinguishing features were an unusually long trunk, a large mouth, and a slender pair of fins that arose from the middle of its back and tapered down to a paddle-shaped end on each side. It had the same twelve pairs of legs and yellow rimmed red buttons as the rest.

She had picked up some information from the hijacked manual regarding this type, which made it much more useful to her than to the average member of the Species.

It was not considered an impressive device because it worked almost exclus-ively with external power sources. Those machines had a bad reputation to begin with. They could malfunction and did on occasion.

Malfunctions were exceedingly rare but inordinately impressive when they did occur. That went double for the larger units.

Usually, they communicated with the Species generators to ensure smooth, safe, and reliable power transfer. Their infamy derived from misuse. Although they were robust to most insults, a power source like the Species generator sys-tem could overload the small units with an imperceptible surge. Many belliger-ent individuals of means modified their external power sources to request a surge on command. Although external power sources were familiar and unarguably useful instruments to most members of the Species, few of them had any call to be lugging one about. They were unseemly for other reasons, too.

The

only case in which the power supply was critical also happened to be the most common reason for its use: to spring or escape from an ambush.

For a Species member with the means to orchestrate a surprise attack on his peers, or famous enough to attract unwanted attention of the same sort, the ob-vious way in or out of those operations was a fold in or out of the dendritic event radiation.

THIRTEEN

An old-fashioned, unadulterated, normal spacetime hit was still on the table, and a few admirers of that swash-buckling tradition arose in every generation to perpetuate the practice. For most of the Species, though, especially the elite who had a real chance at completing a calculation, intentionally involving yourself in a shootout in someone else's roost or, even worse, someplace like a node, was just stupid.

That behavior exposed a person to crude weaponry that came down from a barbaric past, and persisted over the ages, because it was so damned effective. This was the attitude towards things like bullets, nerve agents, blister agents, and the millions of different instruments created to inflict blunt force trauma.

The attendant gaggle of overengineered and extremely dangerous nachi-

naks, certain to participate in the classic shoot 'em up, served as a big disincentive, too. Such was the company external power source accessories kept.

As she prepared to leave, she spotted an odd package in one of the crates. She knelt, turned it over and inspected the contents more carefully. It was only a box full of candy. She stood and gave the crate a solid kick, scattering the candy down the curb and into the shrubbery.

A bag with a very unusual label caught her eye as it flew across the parking lot. It was dark red, and the back of the bag bore no markings at all. On the front, two finger-breadth white lines broke the ox blood plastic into three segments. In the large, upper segment was a symbol: an oval patch of white as big as a thumbprint with a line drawing of a pointed mustache and beard. She started to curse, then stopped herself and stood up.

She looked back over her shoulder, and then she looked at the bag again. It was open at the resealable closure. She frantically hunted down all of the lollipops bearing the mark on their wrappers. When they were all sequestered in the bag, she stuffed the bag into the day pack and set off in the direction of the cliff dwelling.

Fourteen

Man's Chief End

Laplace waited in the depths of the event radiation. Over a dozen nachinaks hovered around him. One unit positioned itself directly in front of him at eye level. A thin vortex stretched from three of the units positioned at the apex of the exclusion sphere toward the dimmer and less complex territory above.

The vortex ran through the circling legs of four more nachinak as it rose, ending at the last device far out of sight in the distance. Laplace raised a small, glass rectangle to his eyes.

On the surface of the glass, a light blue Mobius strip pulsed. Its beat was irregular but averaged 50 bpm. He looked over the whole arrangement yet again. A pair of power source accessory nachinaks were minding the line of key-type machines stretched along the vortex above the sphere.

Another pair of key-type machines was spinning quietly at either end of a horizontal line stretching between them. A shimmering, undulating surface waited just beyond the line in the foreground of an indoor amphitheater. Laplace deftly flipped through a well-memorized series of calculations depicting

aspects of the connecting 'vortex's terminus. His nachinaks sped up their beating legs and shifted in conjunction with the change in descriptions that accompanied each aspectual alteration.

Very few of the Species had cultivated a talent for the sort of calculation he was attempting. It wasn't something that directly applied to a complete calculation. However, the ability to shift descriptions from one aspect of events to another often affected the life expectancy of those who aspired to that larger goal. Laplace cultivated his talent for such calculations and other areas of expertise considered impractical, as he was seeking something besides a complete calculation.

Paradoxically, like every member of the Species who rose to his echelon, he was secretly convinced that the real reason that a complete calculation had not occurred was the simple fact that he had not attempted one. Yet even the towering self-confidence that came with superior talent could not quell a growing doubt about the consensus methods used in this quest, and perhaps even about the nature of the project itself.

It was difficult to say how much those larger concerns weighed on his mind at the moment.

He faced a more immediate and possibly more confounding question: How do you catch something that cannot cause anything?

According to one of the more helpful of the reliable sources, a series of causal dependencies led right up to God and stopped. He was an isolated endpoint. The literature contained an

inordinate amount of conjecture regarding why that should be. A variety of ontological arguments prevailed. In order to be the supreme being, God must be incapable of sin. That much made perfect sense. Sin was a transgression against God, inclusive of his extensions. It would not do for God to be capable of self-transgression.

Yet, as God himself liked to remind whoever would listen to him, if sin and the principle of causal closure of the physical world were taken seriously at

once, to act in the world was, sooner or later, to be guilty.

Therefore, God cannot act. Even for the academics and the theologians, divine causation was a theoretical concern. For Laplace at that moment, divine causation's details were a matter of success and possibly survival. His plan required an ironclad understanding of the qualifications for causal dependency and for exemption from causal efficacy.

Causation was notoriously tricky to pin down. Counterfactuals were so enticing. Take the example, "The bullet killed John." You can simply define the cause of John's death by saying that if the bullet had not struck John as it did, John would not be dead.

Yet there are myriad possibilities left open by the formulation, from overdeterminations (John is shot, but before he dies from the direct effects of the gunshot wound, he hits the ground after a 20 story fall), to contrib-utory causes (let's not forget the gunpowder or the man who pulled the trigger), to the trivial proximal causes (John died of cardiopulmonary arrest, because everyone who dies, dies of cardiopulmonary arrest). To be exempt, an entity's participation in events should not support a counterfactual or qualify it for contributory causal status.

Laplace's background did not predispose him to this kind of thinking. Nevertheless, he concluded through his research that God never struck a planet or directly instructed a nachinak to alter its behavior.

On the other hand, God incurred little risk of causation should he rave endlessly to his followers about eternal torture or put on a light show for them. Similarly, if the nachinak that followed him everywhere took it upon themselves to attack sinners based on instructions programmed by their mortal creators, it wasn't exactly God's fault.

A distinct instability in the event radiation correlated with the deity's appearance. Laplace built the nachinak with the rows of rust-colored spots now floating before his eyes to detect that instability. As long as the anomaly wasn't directly due to divine action, everything else would fall in line. If anything else were the case, then divine causation was real, and he was in deep trouble.

The nachinak hung motionless, but the blue Mobius strip's pulsation

became more regular and its rate accelerated.

Laplace responded with a series of quick adjustments on the abacus. The strip tilted and rotated slightly on its axis. Laplace adjusted again.

In the layers above him came a flash of light, then rapid dimming. Two more nachinaks became active, providing a view of the far end of the vortex. Laplace noted at least two, and possibly three, familiar figures. They were other ambitious members of the Species who came to see what they could extract from the imminent disruption. A series of gray discs snapped into existence. One of the prospectors had positioned themselves too close to the outbreak of gray space and got engulfed. Laplace didn't have time to note anything more. The image was getting fuzzy. He made one more small adjustment and then looked back at the Mobius strip. The shape blinked out, and the display switched to a flashing red exclamation point. The ropelike vortex extended up from the fold with its shimmering surface just beyond, through the legs of three more nachinaks and ended just below the underbelly of the fourth nachinak. The fourth machine revved the motion of its legs in an instant, causing the vortex to expand and its eye along with it.

The opening propagated in a series of segments, one after the next, at precisely equal intervals, faster than the eye could follow, giving a steady rate of propagation at 20% of the speed of light. In a flash of blue and gold brilliance, the expanding segments of the vortex reached the fold and went through.

The four nachinaks that held the fold open seized to a stop, which left two of them smoking, inert, and missing legs. The fold closed instantly.

Laplace opened another with his abacus and stepped through, with his nachinaks surrounding him. Two external power sources waited on either side of the large table in the front and center of the amphitheater. A pair of large nachinaks hovered over the table, generating between them a disk of coiled vortices made of dark grit and crackling with electricity.

Three of his slaves stood at the ready as well, two with shotguns and

the third with a dart gun containing a syringe full of neurotoxin. Laplace had one hand behind his back, holding a rotating silvery torus with a fluid surface that swirled continuously into its center.

The table held a scale model of an academic campus, which also served as the housing for a 3D projector. Across the model doorways at the entrance to the diorama, a banner read, "Welcome to the Bilateral Nephrectomy Center of Excellence."

Above him, behind the projector, a large box sat securely anchored to the model and attended by a pair of nachinaks. The entire container measured three meters by three meters. The box did not have a lid. Inside, a shimmering tube flipped itself inside out at regular intervals too short to see. A roaring noise came from the tubing, and the sound undulated with the tube's frequency. Everyone stood motionless and silent, stunned by their unmitigated success. Laplace was the first to speak.

"Why," he asked the room, "did you shrink him?"

They all looked at each other without responding. Finally, another of the Species who stood across the table from Laplace and who bore a striking resemblance to him replied.

"We didn't do that," he said, "he came that way."

Laplace dropped his hands and stepped forward to examine the container's contents more closely. He looked at each of the slaves in turn with clear intent. They maintained their weapons at the ready.

Focusing on the tubing, he saw a small object vibrating right in the center of the tube. The object pulsated too fast for him to get a good look at it. He turned to his doppelganger, who was also approaching the container.

"Well, I can't make out what's in there, but it certainly isn't moving at 20% the speed of light anymore," he said. "Brother, would you please?"

"Certainly," said his brother.

He reached into the model of the campus and turned on the 3D projector

attached to it. A steady image coalesced about the table. It was a human with ringlets of dark hair and dark skin, his eyes squinted shut, his mouth wide open, producing the scream audible in the background. He was completely naked with all four limbs outstretched.

Silence fell across the assembly once again, except for the unwavering scream. The slaves let their weapons slowly drift down.

"Well then," Laplace said, "congratulations are in order for all of us. Wonderful job, everyone."

"When," asked his brother, "Do you think he will stop screaming?" "Should be any time now," Laplace said, "if you believe what the old records say, which I'm beginning to believe more than I had ever imagined

I would."

89

FOURTEEN

"Carry on with the plan," said Laplace, "no changes at this point. Continuous monitoring and leave the nachinaks active on standby. We've got enough juice to keep them on alert for as long as we want. This building must remain secure. Nothing overt, though; the COE must maintain business as usual. Make sure that the signs for the renovation closure get posted at intervals on the outer walls and at every entrance. We don't want people passing the outer corridors and starting to wonder about the quiet." His brother crossed over to stand beside Laplace. He gestured for the two of them to proceed to the backstage doors, where faculty typically entered

and exited. Laplace

hoisted his abacus up and began walking slowly to doors.

"How stable is this setup?" his brother asked. "Perhaps we should take advantage of the situation as it stands and just try to kill him right away by means of our own ingenuity. It seems that one of your close competitors was lost in the outbreak of gray space today as well, which puts us at an additional advantage. It might be less risky."

"No. In light of all that has happened, I believe the situation is very secure. We will gain much more from letting him live for a bit, trust me."

"You will be staying with us for a while, then?" asked his brother. "In anticipation, I prepared your regular quarters, with room enough for your slaves, and I have moved some of our basic research staff to another wing of the building to give you access to additional laboratory facilities should you need them."

"Yes. Thank you," said Laplace, "I will be back."

"Really?" his brother asked, "You would think that the successful apprehension and incarceration of the Almighty would be enough for the day."

"Yes," Laplace said, "but I'm told now that I am summoned for some kind of Node 3 business. The news is informal, of course, at this point. I just want to get rid of that loose end before we are neck deep in our research and can afford it less."

"I understand," said his brother. "One day, we should do something about those parasites."

"You see," said Laplace, "that's exactly how it happens that I barely had the

90

opportunity to admire our catch when I have to deal with something else. Don't overbook us. Besides, this appears to be something different than the questing noses of the shit hounds, and I'm curious to see what it's about."

15

Fifteen

Kanpai Then Confessions

The sun was almost overhead by the time Lucky woke up again. He'd been able to remove his outer layer of clothing before going to sleep but was still dirty from the last few days of hiking and camping, not to mention any of the other stuff. He took a shower, dusted his clothes off as best he could, and headed out to the patio. Takezo was there, seated at the table, reading a newspaper.

He stood and folded the paper when Lucky approached.

"Oh good, you're awake," he said, "I thought you might be even later. As you see, the food is still fresh. You would have caught me unprepared if you had awakened 30 minutes earlier. We have rice, natto, tamari, tea, coffee, and bagels in case you have never had natto."

"Many thanks," Lucky said, waving his hand dismissively. "I have not had natto before, but I'll try most anything, and I like most everything in the end."

"Okay," Takezo said, "I will be fair to the natto and show you how it is prepared and best enjoyed. The natto goes in a small bowl or sauce dish.

The rice is by itself, and another sauce
dish contains the tamari. Put the natto on top of the rice, dip lightly in the tamari, just enough so that the rice grains do not separate, and enjoy."

He assembled the ingredients in their proper vessels as he narrated the description to Lucky. When he was done, he placed everything in front of Lucky and sat back to watch, with his arms folded across his chest.

"Not to set the wrong tone," Lucky asked, "but what is this again?" "Fermented soybeans," Takezo said.

Lucky opted for a spoon instead of chopsticks, scooped up examples of all three elements comprising the meal in the proportions instructed, and tried a bite. He paused as the aroma struck him. He tried again and got it past his nose.

"Not too bad," he said.

Takezo smiled and nodded before sitting down to his own bowl.

In the managed to eat most of the rice and about one-third of the fermented soybeans. Takezo insisted on taking the dishes back to his room to wash and insisted Lucky should have the blueberry bagel as well. After the dishes were set in the drying rack, Takezo returned with three bottles of sake and cups.

"I don't usually consume alcohol during the day but today is a rest day and a day for somewhat serious talk," he said.

He poured them each a cup. "To the joy of solitude, "said Takezo as he raised his cup.

"Really? Yeah, okay, I guess," Lucky said, raising his cup and downing the contents in a single gulp.

Takezo poured each of them another cup.

"Oh yes," Takezo added, "I wanted to tell you about one thing before I forget. I do have another guest staying on the other side of the house. You probably won't even see them, due to their

schedule, but I must ask you not to go into that side of the house or attempt

to contact the other guest."

"No problem," said Lucky, "let's get to the main event now. It seems we both have questions, and they may be the same questions. Who goes first?"

"You should go first," said Takezo.

"Okay. I am getting texts. They're once or twice a day. They don't have any identifying information. They're not about anything very important; they feel kind of generic. They are from my wife. But that's the only time of day I think about her. I can't seem to bring her to mind unprompted. I don't remember what she looks like. I don't remember the sound of her voice. But I remember how her texts read. The last time I thought about her spontaneously was when I pulled off the freeway to find a camping spot.

And that's the other thing, why can't I get back to the car? I know I can get lost; I'm not so foolish as to believe I can't lose my way, especially when I'm in the thick brush. But I don't get lost easily, especially not in a landscape I'm very familiar with and during daylight hours, with landmarks all around me. What do you know about that?" he asked.

as for the difficulties with navigation., I have the same problems. I can offer some information that may help.

Where we are is not in the real world. Please listen to me before you react. I mean to say that the real world is bigger and more complicated than we expect. The connections between elements of the real world and elements of this world do exist, and people who know how to do so can alter

those connections. I think that is why you have so much trouble getting back to your shelter and transportation.

Someone is thwarting you for some reason. I think I may be restricted also for another reason. But that requires a little bit more thought and a little bit more information. I experienced the same problems with navigation when I tried to venture into the area where you left your vehicle. I cannot even follow the highway to the bridge over the wash. I can get to the old country store at the foot of the Mesa.

Obviously, I can get to the dwelling. Also, if I continue walking down the slope behind the old country store, I can walk for a little over a mile, and at that point, I will come upon a small encampment of security personnel guarding a doorway. The world where we live stands beyond that door. It is where I was ushered into this world.

A man named Augustine hired me. He provided me with a workshop and tools as well as access to information regarding my craft, some of which I thought irretrievably lost. He, in turn, is bidding for a share of the reward that will come from the construction and proof of a weapon. It must be a hand-held weapon, and once we have a winning prototype, we will turn it against God and destroy him."

"What?" Lucky laughed and shook his head.

"Umm, if you believe in such things, that's not supposed to be possible, "he said," And he's telling you this has to be some kind of spear or axe or something like that? That seems weird. Are you sure that this guy is not up to something else and isn't just trying to distract you for some hidden and malign purpose?

By the way, did he tell you just how he was going to find God and pull the greatest trick the world has ever seen by conning the all-knowing, all-

powerful, and omnipresent deity into a compromising position where he can use this weapon?"

"Yes," Takezo said, "it seems like he might be mentally ill. I rejected his request out of hand when I first heard it, but things have happened since, and I

am at the point where I'm willing to believe almost anything is possible. To address the metaphysical concerns that you raise.

Whatever this entity is that has aroused predatory instincts in my patron, it is not what Christians or Muslims, or any of the other popular religions, would call God. It claims to be all-knowing, but I'm not sure whether it claims to be all-powerful. It is certainly not omnipresent because it regularly appears

at odd locales in the universe, and it is regularly killed by something, only to reappear at a later time and different place."

Lucky rolled his eyes in exasperation.

"Please listen," Takezo said, "You must understand what I'm telling you, and you must believe it. If you do not understand or understand and do not believe, we will be unable to help each other."

"Are you sure, Takezo?" Lucky said,

"As you're speaking, I'm feeling that we have less and less in common. And to be honest, I'm not sure how you could use my help. Nobody is hiring me to build some outlandish weapon. No one set up a house for me to live in while I work for them. If you can't get yourself out of your current trouble, I don't think it makes a damn bit of difference whether I'm helping or not."

"You are mistaken," Takezo said.

"I have seen what I needed to see about you to confirm your necessity. I cannot succeed if you are not able to help me. I saw what happened to you in your sleep."

"Hold on!" Lucky said, "What the hell do you mean by that? You are watching me sleep? This is really getting out of hand!"

"Forgive me," said Takezo "I promise you I can explain. Look around you and tell me that the possibilities you were able to consider yesterday are the same as the possibilities you can consider today. Let me finish. If we come to the end of this tale and you still think it is nonsense, then you can leave this house, and I will not try to convince you otherwise."

Lucky nodded and sat back in his chair with his arms folded across his chest.

"Permit me to try another approach," Takezo said, "I will tell you what my work is like.

I am a metallurgist specializing in the fabrication of implements of all sorts. It is something that requires utmost care and concentration. If my

frame of mind is correct, I can make use of my senses in a way that translates into specialized knowledge. The limited old depiction that the division between a phenomenon and its explanatory reduction has enforced on our experience crumbles in the light of this new manner of representation. I will be bold enough to claim the mantle of knowledge for this new understanding, even if it means ripping that symbol from the defunct body of our direct senses."

Lucky sat up a little taller in his seat.

"What are you implying? That we don't know anything from what we see, feel, or hear? As far as I can tell, that's all we know."

"How do we speak of these things?" Takezo asked as he paced back and forth in front of Lucky, "I say that I know something by its feel or by its scent. There are properties on display in the world that our senses mediate entirely.

These are

things like solidity, bitterness, density, brittleness, heat transfer, and so on. You can see by this small list that there are very complex properties and very simple properties, Properties

that are easily quantified, and properties that are difficult to quantify, with this one thing in common: they are phenomena woven by our senses. They do not require, nor do they refer to, ideal shapes, or numerical or mathematical entities. They represent at least a class of properties, if not all properties that function together as a coherent whole."

He cast about wildly in search of an adequate example.

"Aha!" he said, patting the tabletop with his right hand, "Take solidity. If I put my hand on the table, it feels solid. I push, and it pushes back. However, if I see it drop from the back of a truck onto the concrete, or if I strike it with a hammer, I will also be able to tell that it is solid, and how solid it is by its appearance as it strikes the ground and in the aftermath, and the sound it makes when it hits."

How it feels, not to my hand, but to my hand as my hand feels a hammer's

impact upon a tabletop. Any of us who speak of solidity also have this nascent extension in mind. The condensed memory of how it felt to hit a tabletop with a hammer, including all the instances of recollected hammer blows, comes to mind as a single thought with my experience of the current instance.

The conditions that inform our sensory experience, in addition to the immediate sensory impressions, constitute our field of consciousness.

Our senses could represent a bizarre underlying reality, just well enough for us to survive. Conversely, it could be that our phenomenology is what is real, that we see directly what is really happening when the hammer. strikes the table.

All of our mathematics and scientific inquiry is merely leverage. It adds detail to our phenomenology as it subtracts completeness.

"In either case, the senses still represent properties for us with the help of our field of consciousness. We can't make our eyes sharper or our fingertips more sensitive, but we can educate our minds to bring more of our field of consciousness to bear."

Takezo picked up a spoon from the table and held it in front of Lucky, " "When I pick this up, I feel a coolness to the surface which goes away at a precise rate, a resistance to movement in my hand, a resistance to bending when I push on it with my fingers, a surface which is smooth and has a certain shape, a smell, were my nose so sensitive."

"My education," Takezo said as he leaned in closer, maintaining the focus of his attention on the spoon, "consisted of learning all the correlates of these properties provided by the theories of physics, chemistry, and mathematics."

Lucky felt a wary, specific nervous feeling growing in him. He recognized obsession when he saw it. It made people unpredictable, and he had made it a habit to avoid active cases; however, in this case, he was trapped in the chair.

"That must be very satisfying," Lucky said.

"No!" Takezo said, his focus shifting to Lucky's face, "That's the thing.

It has never been satisfying. There has always been something missing, but no longer! Now, I can use what I know in the way it was meant to be used. When I pick up a piece of metal, I can feel, smell, see, and hear all of those properties that make it suited for one use and not another. But I can also tell what I can do with a tool, from a tuning fork to a spectrometer, to get a precise understanding of a metal's properties,

What I can do now is an entirely new craft. From alloys to finished surfaces, the quality and speed of my work are beyond anything I was capable of before. I would guess it is beyond anything that anyone was capable of before."

Lucky nodded hesitantly, encouraging Takezo to continue. "I know this sounds terribly improbable," said Takezo.

"I am not about to help you with that. I'm afraid you must either accept it or not. I have had a thorough medical examination. The medical scientists cannot tell me how or why I can do these things.

I have only been this way recently. For almost my entire life, I have been a good metalworker, but a normal one capable of the normal sort of thing a metalworker can do.

I began to realize the difference after I had a dream. That is the only positive information I have regarding the onset. "

"Now, this is the part you can help me with," Takezo said, narrowing his eyes and sharpening his scrutiny of Lucky's unease.

Lucky pushed back in his chair. The late-morning sun was hot, and it intensified the effects of the sake. He felt woozy. He began to think about how he could extricate himself from the situation.

"This is what I need from you.," said Takezo," You may have guessed that we have come here for a purpose. In fact, we have not come here for any purpose of our own. Someone brought us here, for some purpose of theirs, and now I know it has to do with this dream we may share."

"I cannot tell you everything that happened in my version of the dream. I can feel that there was much more, almost all the dream, in fact, that I forgot immediately upon waking. I can tell you that it was not a normal dream. It lasted an entire night and into the next day. I walked in my sleep,

something that I have never done before or since. They found me sitting in the field where I kept my horse, staring at the ground and unresponsive. And I can tell you that I still have the residual effects of that dream, which can recur for me day or night, out of the blue.

The main thing I remember was a sensation of tremendous pressure. I knew that something had ahold of me. Somehow, it was responsible for the pressure over my entire body as if an incredibly dense fluid poured over me until I was suspended in it. At that point, it contracted like a muscle, and I was unable to breathe or move, and I was helpless while I felt it crush me to death.

But I did not die. I could not accept it, so I pushed back. I felt it give, so I pushed back more and more and more until I began to feel a horrible rage and deep hunger for the destruction of whatever was trying to destroy me!" Takezo was shouting. He paused for a frightened glance over each shoulder and went on in a whisper, "I could feel that it was weaker than me. I yearned to destroy it all the more because of the audacity of its attempt to destroy me. Then it gave way. It broke. And with that, my sight returned, and I could tell all the parts of my body again, feel hot and cold, taste, and

smell.

I saw that I held something in my hands. It was the body of a creature my size, my build, but without any features on its face, just fur, but not even fur, just a swarm of small creatures which brought to mind insects, but they were not insects. They swarmed together to form the image of the creature, its fur, its ears that stick up on top of its head and come to a point, its eyes that pull in everything they see and would consume it, and I felt my eyes return that gaze and its desire to take even though it could not possess anything. I came back with the impression that I had seen teeth that were sharp, long, and white, though I could never summon any image of teeth from the memory. Blood poured out of the shrinking body!"

His voice had risen to a scream, and Takezo was standing now beside the

table. He was looking in Lucky's direction, but he was not seeing anything of the present. His fists rested on the tabletop, and he was panting. His eyes were wide, and a strange bubbling erupted in the centers of the pupils. Lucky stared aghast and leaned back even further in his seat until he pitched over backwards.

With that, the spell was broken, and he dashed to his room, closed the door, and locked it. He crouched down by the far side of the bed and tried to remain as still as

possible.

A fist hammered against his door. He looked up, shaking. He could see Takezo's silhouette against the blind over the window in the door. It was smudged and indistinct at the margins. Takezo pounded on the door again. Lucky saw a flurry of small fuzzy dots explode outward from the blow and then circulate back in toward the center of the impact.

After a moment, Lucky came to himself. He stood back up, took five long strides to the door, flipped the lock, and flung it open. Takezo stood there in the midst of the swarm. Eyes that yearned to consume the world stared at Lucky. They blinked.

"I cannot see you," Takezo said, "Lucky?"

The eyes crumpled and dissipated, along with all the swarming dots. "I'm right here," said Lucky, and he grasped Takezo's wrist.

Takezo yanked his arm away.

"Have I lost my mind?" Takezo asked.

"I would have said so five minutes ago," said Lucky, "but now I can't deny what I saw. It sure puts all that stuff about knowledge and experience in a little different light."

Lucky straightened up and put one hand on Takezo's shoulder. "Buddy, you are not crazy," Lucky said," but both of

us may be."

They stood with their eyes downcast for several minutes. It was Lucky

who spoke first.

"You're right, I had almost that same dream," Lucky said, "it turned out different for me, though. It happened as I rode through the desert. I was trying to get away from something, I can't even remember what it was. I just knew that if I kept riding, I could outrun it. It was cold, and I was so tired that I was falling asleep lying out on the tank. I woke up when the bike started to drift or when my hand would drop off the throttle

as I dozed. I knew that any minute I was going to fall asleep for real and crash, and that would be it, and I just gave up.

But instead of crashing, I felt that thing on my back. And then I felt the crushing start just like you said, and it got worse and worse and worse. Finally, it crushed me out of existence. At least, that's what I've always thought.

Listening to you and considering the implications, I now believe that I am still here, at least in some kind of way. Maybe it didn't crush me out of existence; maybe it crushed me into something else.

The trouble is: how might I figure out what that something is? Because I'm remembering a little bit of what I forgot when I pulled off the freeway. The first thing that I remember after the dream was the road rash on my forearms and the realization, as I stood there looking at the scrapes, that I had wrecked. Blood was coming out of a cut on my scalp and my right ear. I could hear the sound of traffic on the highway, so I walked in its direction until I came to the road, and somebody packed me up and took me to the emergency room.

They said that the head injury must have set something off in my mind, so it didn't work like it should anymore. I had headaches all the time. It was hard to concentrate or get anything done. I found that I could read, though; that was something that I never really had a talent for in the past. I read everything I could get my hands on. All the reading didn't change how I felt, though.

101

FIFTEEN

I would describe how I felt to the psychiatrists and neurologists. I

remember the looks on their faces. They told me I needed an antipsychotic. I took one, and then a different one, and then another different one. They all had intolerable side effects. That medicine I take now? That's a medicine to help me move after the antipsychotics made my muscles stiff and threw my balance off.

I never told anybody about that dream. It was bad enough. I

did not want to relive it. And people already thought I was crazy. Eventually, I wandered out into the desert with my pack, some supplies, a tarp, and my sleeping bag. I think I was on the same mission that I had been on with the motorcycle.

I would call and check in with my family. They were very upset at first, but when I showed up dirty, but not in such bad shape otherwise, they accepted how it was, and they did their best to help me. I would come into town now and then to see if I could pick up a disability check or mechanic work for some bikers I knew, or both. I never liked to sleep there, though. I knew where I stood with the coyotes and snakes, and if I came to harm in a conflict with them, it would be in the context of a relationship based on mutual respect. Who knew with humans?

I pulled off the freeway two days ago to get my bearings and let the medicine start working on my nerves and muscles. I was on my way back from buying that car. My wife's name is Diane."

Lucky shook his head.

"I still can't remember my own name, though."

"We can look for your name," Takezo said, "I'm certain we will find it, given the success we have experienced so far."

Lucky poured himself a cup of sake, threw it back, and then poured another.

"All kidding aside," Lucky asked, "where do we go from here? I'm honestly not sure what to make of this. I think maybe I should be angry about something, but I'm not. It's nice to have the riddle solved, but the practicalities remain the same. Plus, I am involved in your predicament now as well as my own."

"When you look around and all is confusion and turmoil, the best thing to do is to sit and wait with your eyes open..." Takezo said, "as for your involvement with me, you should learn to curtail your obligations to others. You are responsible for yourself and no one else. I do not presume to hold any claim

on you. You have no claim on me and my problems either. We can certainly help each other, but not on the basis of a ledger of accounts or the rules of human relationships endorsed by society. All the work that comes from that forge is a variety of chains or manacles."

"I don't know Takezo, that sounds kind of stingy," Lucky said.

"Most people," said Takezo shaking his head, "underestimate the re-sources required to ally themselves with others and overestimate resources that they and others possess."

"Wait. What are you saying to me? That if we form an allegiance, it is setting us up to fail, or that it is setting me up to fail? Or do you mean that we are beyond help-you, me, both of us together?" Lucky said, "Permit me to straighten your thinking out on this one, because I am an expert in failure, so you ought to listen to me when I'm offering you free advice on the subject."

Lucky stood and finished off, by his count, the morning's fourth sake.. He swayed a little as he tilted his head back. Takezo watched him with bemusement but kept quiet as Lucky gazed into the middle distance and held forth.

"You must know already that failure isn't necessarily the end of the line," he said," I mean, when you fail at something you ought to take a hard look at how you failed, what you are trying to do, and the resources that you can give, and that you want to give to succeed. Stopping to take an inventory like that can keep you from banging your head against the wall.

That's what the psychologists said. How would they know? They're always banging their heads on someone else's wall, never their own. But I'll give this one to them, reluctantly.

Sometimes, it can change your mind about what you really set out to do. When I looked hard at my ambitious goals, I discovered that I was more interested in pursuing the smaller pieces of the big ambitions for their own sake, and that I had been on the trail of that other goal because all the footprints converged on its track."

Lucky paused to see if Takezo was paying attention. Takezo sat with his elbows propped on his legs and his head sagging. Lucky took the opportunity to pour himself one more sake. When the pause became noticeable, Takezo raised his head and gestured for Lucky to continue.

"I know you'll be able to dismiss this stuff as just another apology for failure by those who have gotten good at it," said Lucky.

He nodded as Takezo looked up at him abruptly

"Yeah, I know about that too. Everything we do gets better with practice, even if we don't want it to.

However, to dismiss what I have to say on that basis would be a mistake even more serious than pushing your failures aside and leaving them in the past unreconciled, because I don't intend to apologize. I'm not trying to dumb things down. Failure is nothing less than failure, and nothing more. Taking a hard look gets you two things: number one, it immunizes you against the dangers you face when you succeed. If you understand and accept the causes of failure, then when you succeed, you won't think it was because you were just that good or the powers that be owed you or loved you, or an opponent believed something that made them weaker than you all of those lures that trap people into trying to win because all victories are moral victories, end of story.

Once people step over the rim of that pit, they hardly ever escape in one

piece. It's their fate to learn someday that all else being equal, the person who fights to survive will defeat the person who fights to win every time."

"Second: Previous experience with failure lets you know when

it's all over and that means, you will never despair.

If you figure that you still got a chance, then take it, even if it's a bad chance. Suppose you really have used up everything you got and there are no flags on the horizon heralding friends come to rescue you.

In that case, you can at least go down knowing where you're headed, showing no incoherent doubts or regrets, and representing what you have intended to represent."

Takezo stood and came around to Lucky's side of the table. He poked Lucky's chest with his index finger.

"Even if things don't look good, and you expect that you will lose, retaliate. Neither wisdom nor skill has any place in this. The man of good character does not think of victory or defeat but instead rushes headlong to an irrational death. Do this and you will awaken from your dreams."

"The words of Yamamoto Tsunetomo," said Takezo," A man who never got the chance to lose a fight."

Then, Takezo began to laugh, hard enough to require the table's help to remain upright.

Lucky flopped back down in his chair. "I wasn't joking, you know," he said.

"No, no," Takezo said, "I am laughing at myself for harboring those false expectations that I had just been cautioning you about. I need some time to put everything in its proper order. How would you like to spend the rest of the day? I can show you my workshop here, or we can pay a visit to the Bilateral Nephrectomy Center of Excellence. I also have a rose garden down by the pond past the far side of the house. It is a small rose garden, though, and probably would not be interesting to you if you were not a gardener."

"I'll admit, I'm not much for growing plants., "said Lucky, "I want to understand what happens in that workshop, so I think the tour

should wait for another day.."

.

I had an idea while we've been sitting here. How much battery have you got left in that cell phone?"

"85%," Takezo said.

"Okay. Get the phone open, now slide it over to the main screen and pick out this picture of the jungle under games," Luck said, as he scooted his chair around to look over Takezo's shoulder, "all right, the objective is to get through the obstacle course as quick as possible. This is how you jump; this is how you run..."

FIFTEEN

Lucky continued his instruction without any change in his voice or demeanor, despite the rising column of black smoke he saw in the distance. It originated from some point fairly close to the end of the Mesa, marking the Northwest boundary of the territory that he now understood to be his prison.

Sixteen

Belongings

Francis squirmed uncomfortably in the chair that the executive assistant had directed him to take when they entered the office 45 minutes earlier, having been told that they should hurry up so that they wouldn't miss their turn. He was a little less than a head shorter than adult members of his Species, and that was the only way that people would otherwise typically identify him as an adolescent. His eyes were relatively large and round with yellow irises. The lids dipped down on the outside corners, giving him a slightly sad look. His eyebrows were thin and dark. He had a reddish complexion and a broad nasal bridge.

He did not have any cosmetic alterations, nor did he wear jewelry or other adornments. No child of the Species was allowed such things before their presentation to a volunteer adopting relatives or authority-chosen family members. Only the Mothers knew what younger children of the Species looked like. They were never seen outside the confines of a developmental center.

When a pregnancy occurred, it resulted in a blastocyst surrounded by male genetic material encased in a series of

durable membranes, which filtered nutrients from the mother's blood-stream or preserved the blastocyst to begin gestation at a time

of plenty in the future. The full, purely biological process of fetal development likely had not occurred for at least the last several million years. After the embryo formed, the mother reported to an office of the Foundation for Clinical Developmentalism and Neuropsychological Development, where, in the privacy of a tasteful, clean, and climate-controlled booth, she pushed out the tiny products of conception, placed them in a reinforced jar which contained a circulating nutrient broth, and delivered them to the front desk, where an intake worker took down a family pedigree, collected a genetic sample, and labeled the bottle for transport to a Developmental Center for nurturing.

Though the records certainly may be incomplete, no adult other than one of the Mothers was known to have set foot inside or even seen a Developmental Center.

The developmental specialists intentionally drew candidates for the Mothers from a pool of marginalized individuals. They were people who had never been enslaved, but who also had no extensive wealth beyond what was available to them via the vouchers, no active interactions with family members, and no meaningful capacity for calculation. They were almost inevitably volunteers, though the Foundation did run a program for those facing enslavement, i.e., those who had an implanted subjugation nachinak but had not yet completed the process.

The Mothers were given an amnestic after they volunteered and before they could leave the building or take any other meaningful action. Once they were unconscious, they were lifted from the gurneys where they received the medication, placed on a conveyor belt with an identification badge and transceiver, and transferred to a pod for the journey to their assigned developmental center. The transport proceeded at fast, sub-light speeds as distance allowed.

Legend has it that the Mothers were kept in stasis, but that is widely doubted given the durability of historical fast sub light vehicles and the benefits of relativity in the Mother's situation. A handful of long-distance transports reported sighting vessels with foundation markings near legacy ER bridges, but few took those anecdotes seriously, considering the source. The Mothers then apprenticed for several years while they learned their art. They trained in basic academic subjects, reading and mathematics, both formal and intuitive, early childhood development, nutrition, exercise and sports physiology, ethics, and pediatrics. When they tested out of all of their disciplines, a newly activated blastocyst awaited them.

They were with the blastocyst, now turned embryo, day, and night from then on. They maintained its nutritional support devices and monitored its development until it wore through the final membrane and emerged in its infantile state. The Mother continued nurturing her charge throughout its childhood development and early education until it became an adolescent. The hormonal transition from child to adult among the Species was gradual and subtle.

The child graduated from the developmental center based on age rather than on any physiological benchmark. Again, amnestics were involved, but another form of travel delivered the Mother-child dyad to the beginning of its next phase in life. No one knew what that mode

of transportation was.

Wormholes were a popular candidate, but they would create a lot of disturbance and require an impractically large amount of energy, even for the Species' generators. Other suggestions are things like macroscopic tunneling, interfering gravitons, and, lastly, passage through a very short corridor in the dendritic event radiation. The last option would make the most sense economically but would prove dangerously subject to intrigue. Somehow, they arrived and found their way to a Foundation office associated with an authority outpost. What followed was something known as a presentation or

debut. The Foundation, with the help of the Authority as necessary, gathered related members of the Species as they wished to participate and introduced the child to them. These ceremonies were not solemn but were not typically possessed of a celebratory atmosphere either. Most of what went on was introduction, paperwork including waivers and permissions, gifts of equipment, and bargaining for favors, work, and position.

When all involved completed the steps that concerned them during the presentation, the mother said goodbye to the child, and the child set off on their new life. The outcome of the entire performance was either a new member added to a fairly well-organized, protective clan or the equivalent of a minnow tossed over the side of a boat in full view of hovering seagulls. Francis visibly sighed with relief when one of the Foundation agents who had been part of his intake opened the door to the office and signaled for the Mother to accompany him. Francis started to rise as well, but the agent

gestured for him to sit back down. He did so, hesitantly.

When the door closed, Francis stood up and began to inspect the office. He checked the pictures on the walls. Those seemed legitimate. He looked at the chair, the desk lamp, the desk, the blotter, and the little projector that gave access to the electronic portion of the foundation's records. Nothing sinister turned up. He swallowed hard and looked towards the door. He walked over and put his auditory meatus against the center panel. All was silent. He tiptoed back to the desk. A file folder lay on the corner of the desktop, carefully aligned with the edge of the blotter and the upper corner of the projector lens. He put his finger on the corner of the folder. It had a small picture of him paperclipped.

to the top of the file. It felt like there were more than ten pages within, much more than he had expected. He closed his eyes and took his finger off the corner of the folder. He shook his head and started to reach back down, then paused and shook his head again

.

Instead of picking up the file, he quickly went through all the open drawers on the desk. He found nothing helpful. The drawer under the desktop was locked, and the lock had a very complex mechanism. If he had some tools and some time, he thought he might be able to get it open. During the search, he began to relax and move with purpose. By the time he had assessed the lock, he was no longer ambivalent about the file. He picked it up and opened it.

The face sheet was incomprehensible. He guessed that it detailed all the salient results of his genetic profile. He recognized the code pattern typically associated with that type of information. He flipped through the next few pages cautiously. He couldn't afford to tear any of the papers. The foundation's staff compiled these files manually and typed them out on a manual typewriter. Anything the subject of the file did not want to keep for themselves got incinerated immediately. The file's security was unparalleled.

On the last four pages, he found what he was looking for. On the upper right corner of those pages, the technicians attached a picture of the page's subject, in the same format as his picture on the front of the file. The page contained the subject's matched genetic profile, contact information, favorability score regarding the child presented to them, and any instructions regarding the relatives' wishes surrounding the presentation.

The first sheet showed a picture of an older-looking man. He was well-dressed and held an abacus. A stamp across the bottom of his picture declared him deceased. The next sheet showed a woman in her middle years. Her clothes were plain. She had some engravings on her

bio-prosthetic limbs, but no other cosmetic interventions or decoration. He memorized her contact information and turned to the third page. The picture showed a boy, not much older than him. The subject had not relaxed for his portrait. He wore an expensive shawl across his shoulders and

embroidered slacks. With the boys' contact information memorized, Francis turned to the last page.

The picture in the corner made his jaw drop. It was a man of indeterminate age. He was of an indeterminate age because he had undergone extensive cosmetic interventions. His treatments induced local/regional tissue transparency. He confronted the world with dark red, glaring orbs rather than lidded eyes.

The central nervous and circulatory system structures sat suspended in the red-tinted background of altered tissue. Like the man on page one of the profiles, he held an abacus, though his was clearly the superior instrument. On top of it all perched a ridiculous hat that clashed with anything a person might choose to wear with it. He closed the folder and slinked back over to the door.

All remained silent. Carefully, he turned the knob. It opened. What happened next was no surprise. A loud, undulating buzz began. He felt a sharp pain in his left hand, where it rested on the doorknob. He thought that it was a static shock at first. Then he saw the drops of blood rolling off the hollow core needle protruding from the center of the orb. He stared in horror and braced himself for a gruesome death by poisoning.

Nothing happened. He shivered and turned back to the hallway. He beheld eerie inactivity. He had come through the door now opposite him at the end of the hall, on his way from the waiting area and intake tasks to the office. The space beyond the door's frosted glass window was now dark, as were the offices

111

facing each other across the hallway ahead.

He walked on tiptoe for two steps and then stopped. He shook his head. Anyone wishing him harm would already have a weapon pointed at the door. He tucked his chin and set off running. He struck the glass panel with the back of his shoulder, across the shoulder blade. The impact knocked the breath out of him. The window stood unharmed as he bounced off it to the right. As he lay there, stunned and gasping, a flash of light penetrated his tightly shut eyelids an instant before the slap of a pressure wave from the

exploding door struck him. He was unable to get up for a few more seconds afterward. As Francis lay immobilized, the sound of coughing and an angry voice echoed in the smoking waiting room.

"Idiot! Why didn't I follow my first instinct and ignore the advisor from building security?" The voice screamed, punctuated by a loud thump and a squeal of pain, "I never should've armed any of you."

Silence began to creep back into the offices. Francis got his shaking legs back under him and stumbled to the nearest wall, seeking cover.

"Will one of you go retrieve the unarmed adolescent that you just blew up?" the voice prompted; its tone filled with disgust.

Shuffling sounds came from the waiting room, and then the sound of a door opening.

"Hello?" Came the voice of a newcomer, "I'm with building maintenance. I got a work order here."

"You've got to be kidding me!" The first voice chimed in, "Now you hold your fire? Do you really think he's from building maintenance? Shoot him! Shoot him! Shoot him!"

Before the end of the shouted order, came the sound of several hisses and a light "pop."

Right then, Francis allowed himself a peek around the corner. The explosion had completely demolished the waiting area and service windows. Chairs were scattered all around. The man

who was the subject of the final dossier in Francis's packet stood just inside the doorway. He had several of the small helper robots from Francis's textbooks attending him nearby.

Two pairs of them hovered slightly to each side and behind him. Between them, they held a convex, billowing, translucent spider web. The man held a box containing a number of canisters the size of the distal third of his small finger. Each canister came equipped with a thin needle protruding from the nose of the black and orange striped vial. Two of them hung in the air above the web, their outlines smudged by high frequency vibration

One additional, slightly different robot hovered about a foot behind the man's head and faced back toward the reception area. It had the shape of the others, with the square black box comprising the back of the head, the two eyes just in front of the box, the short trunk, and the numerous legs. But this device curled over the top of a reflective torus, which rotated slowly around its center, while the surface circulated through the same central point.

Opposite the coalition of exotic armaments, three men crouched behind a pair of tables flipped on their sides. All wore the red garments that served as the unofficial uniform of the Authority. Two of them were armed with shotguns, while the third held an assault rifle with an attached grenade launcher. Behind the gunman stood a man dressed in a gray robe, and a round hat too big for his head. He was pointing a pistol at Francis's relative but did not take a shot. Four bodies, also dressed as Authority agents, lay in front of the tables.

"Danilo!" Francis's relative commanded.

Simultaneously with the command, a line like a razor cut in the air appeared at the feet of the man in gray. It rapidly propagated

upwards, and the surroundings seemed to fold around the man as the line extended. Francis jumped out from his hiding place and waved his hands, "Hey, hey, over here! I'm your legacy!" he yelled to his rescuer. Francis never got to hear the response.

He felt hands on his shoulders and a hard pull that tipped him backward into a frightful, disorienting abyss of shapes and colors. The hands on his shoulders spun him around to face a pair of the little helper robots he had seen his relative commanding. They hovered at the endpoints of a vertical line in the air.

SIXTEEN

He felt a push from the hands, a tingling sensation, and then a feeling of pressure over his body's front and back surfaces. He blinked and found himself back in the normal world, but no longer anywhere near the Node 3

offices. He was not entirely sure that his fortunes had improved.

He stood in a dimly lit room with piping and conduit running along the walls and ceiling. The room contained several crates packed with vacuum bags like the ones used for military field rations. There were two tables stacked with paper folders and small 3D projectors for computer access. At least a dozen people crammed into the room, and they all stopped to stare at Francis.

They were not members of the Species. They had prominent, triangular ears with projecting tufts of fur at the tips, with similar Tufts at the angles of their jaw. They had small snouts that could move independently. They came in various colors, but mostly dark brown or gray, and stood about 1 ½ meters tall. Francis gawked at them, dumbfounded.

He felt the grip on his shoulders loosen, and a hand was now on his right elbow. It belonged to one of the little creatures, who swung around to stand in front of Francis. It looked into his eyes for a moment and then pulled him down so that they were

face-to-face. It smiled. Francis felt a stab behind his right knee. "Ouch!" Francis cried out.

To which the small creature in gray robes replied, "Gotcha!"

Seventeen

Touristus Maximus

The next morning, an uncomfortable silence prevailed at the Villa. Despite their elective mutism, neither Lucky nor Takezo seemed inclined to avoid the other, and there were no problems with breakfast. It was natto all around this time. They went over Takezo's progress with his video game. He had already exceeded the score of an average intermediate player. Lucky cautioned him on the poor battery life of most phones. Nobody talked about dreams or prisons. They briefly discussed plans for the day. Lucky wasn't too specific, but he passed again on the invitation to tour the workshop. He said that he did not feel like he could give it due attention, which was true. Takezo had to get to work, and so that was that.

Lucky wandered around the grounds for a little while. On the south side, beyond the south end of the building, a Koi pond sparkled next to the rose garden. A small gravel walkway ran from the set of benches overlooking the pond in front of the rose garden to a small gazebo. A tool shed graced the southwest corner of the rose garden. The grass was fairly long, and Lucky got the impression that it was treated with intentional neglect.

On the level field in front of the two buildings and the small shed on the southeast side of the K oi Pond, the grass was short and neat, with no burned areas or gravel inclusions. A small bulletin board next to the four steps linking the edge of the field with the marble walkway to the house displayed a flyer advertising Takezo's competition, hung from a pair of thumbtacks.

Several more copies occupied the wooden boxes below the cork board. The board held only one other item. It was a small, single-page ad, front and back and in color, for fencing lessons taught directly by the master. Pictures bordered the top, sides, and bottom of the flyer. All were photos of Takezo in action, receiving prizes, or standing for portraits with a variety of fencing apparatus, from an épée to a shinai. The classes ran three times a week in the evening.

The ad displayed a contact number above the line of photos at the bottom. Lucky took his phone out of his breast pocket and turned it on. To his surprise, there was an alert pending. He entered the phone number into his contacts and went back to the text menu. He opened the unread message.

"Hi, no new news. We miss you. I know you're good at taking care of yourself, but please be extra careful. See you soon."

He turned the phone off and put it back in his pocket. He walked through the little forest of junipers to join the gravel path where it exited the forest. He continued up the switchbacks to the east/southeast extension of the main trail.

It was still fairly early, though the entire ball of the sun shone above the horizon. He was surprised to see several people walking in either direction already. He noted several human workers along with members of the Species. Judging by their clothing and equipment, they all seemed to be involved in construction work. He noted several members of the Species marked as students by their identical shoulder bags emblazoned with the renovascular anatomy in gold on a red background.

Lucky decided to follow the students. As they walked, more and more people joined the parade. Now, the travelers were exclusively members of the Species. He noted a couple of odd creatures occupied with various tasks among the occasional side buildings set back from the Promenade. However, he saw no more humans from that point onward. He got a few stares and even one or two startled gasps. It was enough to dissuade him from trying to blend in with the crowd. Instead, he walked on in the middle of the path with his shoulders straight and his head up, displaying no anxiety or hostility.

The walk was quite a bit longer than anticipated. He estimated it at about 7 km. Fortunately, it was relatively level walking, with just a few small rises and no steep gradients. For the first several kilometers, the path was wider than a double track and paved with gravel only. For the last 2 km, the construction on the sides of the road got denser, though it was still all isolated buildings surrounded by parkways and small undeveloped lots, which may have been meant as parks.

The way passed a few shops set back from the roadside. These wore signs in an unfamiliar ideographic script, judging by their appearance. Soon, buildings proliferated alongside the path, and the road expanded to a proper size, with three lanes: one lane for walking and two lanes for vehicles coming and going. Small, self-driving electric vehicles made up most of the traffic, with a few electric scooters or motorcycles here and there. At its end, the road veered to the right and split into a tangled

Delta of smaller roadways connecting discontinuous blocks of houses and service industry businesses. The building style, components, and general layout of the individual buildings, as well as the residential areas themselves, looked quite familiar to Lucky. The wealth on display, however, put to shame all the other cities that Lucky had visited. Nothing was ostentatious, but everything was nice, new, and tastefully assembled. If anything, the architecture displayed a nostalgia for the metropolises of postmodern Europe, though the similarity was almost certainly coincidental. Where the road curved right, a hill stood at the beginning of a line of foothills, low and rounded, in the foreground of distant mountains unfamiliar to Lucky. Running a kilometer at least from the beginning of the curve in the road along the hillside, there were massive flights of stairs carved out of a volcanic mineral that yielded a smooth, shiny finish on the cut surface of the black and red

stone. Lucky's eyes widened, and he looked down at the side of the road.

Without his noticing it, the soil had transformed from the red, sandy loam of the Southwest high desert to a black volcanic soil. The black soil held no more moisture than the desert's red stuff. The same general class of flora grew in the vacant lots, on the sides of the hills, and along the green spaces in the neighborhoods. On closer inspection, however, the specific plants were completely different from the Species growing in the desert back home. Most of it looked hostile, of course.

There were varieties of cacti, spiked, small, leafed plants like the familiar crown of thorns and Palo Verde. To his great delight, Lucky did not see anything

117

equivalent to cat claw Acacia. Low spreading trees with dark green and dark red leaves sprouting from limbs on chocolate-colored trunks and boughs sprouted from planters at intervals along the stairways. A pair of lamps illuminated each planter's area in addition to lighting

set into the front surface of the steps. No railings disrupted the upward flow of the stairway. Lucky was slightly winded by the time he got to the top. In front of him lay an extensive plaza, with a few booths on the periphery. It was as wide as the stairway, and that distance at least across.

Facing the stairs across the square's expanse stood a circular wall with many portals. Interwoven trunks, limbs, and tendrils of vining plants formed the barrier. The wall was three meters high and capped with a shingled wood roof. Lamps projected out from wrought-iron fencing forming the wall's core to a point just beyond the eaves.

The result was a circle of lights along the inner and outer

faces of the wall. The trees' planter was continuous and acted as a small moat at the base. Numerous, narrow, arched doorways penetrated the wall. Ornate iron gates secured the outer opening of the tunnels while transparent swinging doors protected the inner gateway.

Several of the plant Species comprising the wall grew colorful fruits, while others bore plain flowers colored white or yellow, which produced a subtle, calming fragrance. A few security officers stood next to the doorways but did not constitute a threatening presence. Lucky took a look at the roof and the depths of the wall of trees as he ambled towards the central plaza beyond the wall. He could not be certain due to his lack of familiarity with the technology, but from what he could see, the planners had not skimped on security in their effort to make the facility inviting for guests. He saw a line of slots following the curve of the fence and harboring a mechanism with periodic regularities in the shadowed depths, which he took to be drones.

He leaned into the shadow cast by the lights inside and outside the short corridors between the outer and inner doorways. He

found only a small portion of the wall that permitted a glimpse of the shaded area, but when he poked his head inside, he saw that the middle of the wall adjacent to the central fencing was crawling with nachinaks.

A small, three-tiered fountain occupied the center of the smaller plaza inside the wall. The pool surrounding it was below the surface, with a simulated beach in textured and rounded stone, a few flowering aquatic plants, and a small population of colorful fish. Students bearing golden kidneys and aorta stamps on backpacks and shoulder bags made up

most of the inner Plaza's traffic. He didn't notice any other identification associated with the passersby.

He kept looking, and just as he attracted the scrutiny of a security guard, he spotted what he sought. Several buildings opened out onto the far side of the plaza where the wall intersected the entryway of the outermost structures. A pair of security personnel stood at the bank of tinted, transparent doors of the most southerly building. The middle building was well-lit, with clear sliding doors and large plate windows. It was reminiscent of some familiar hospitals, and Lucky avoided it. However, the next most northerly entryway had a person outside of the two pairs of double doors who greeted visitors and appeared to be answering questions. In the foyer, four members of the Species staffed a long table, and behind them, a long display contained rows of symbols over smaller blocks of subtext.

A small crowd stood around an individual whose dress closely resembled the clothing worn by the desk attendants. Lucky waved off the greeter while pointing his finger to- wards the foyer and the group of people gathered at its northeast corner. He barely made it inside when the security guard caught up with him. Lucky felt a hand on his shoulder and jumped, which made the security guard jump. The touch of the hand was not what

he had expected. It did not feel cold or hard, like metal, but it did not quite feel like the touch of a human hand. They stood facing each other for almost half a minute, each sizing the other up. Lucky made the first move.

"Oh hey," Lucky said, shrugging and holding his hands palm up.

Lucky felt another hand on his other shoulder. He slowly

turned to see who had arrived to back up the guard. He was face- to-face with the group leader. The group itself stood close by, looking him over and chatting

119

among themselves. The group leader held up a small gold ring with silver inlays. In a slow, exaggerated motion meant to forestall any defensive response from Lucky, the group leader grasped the upper and lower halves of the ring and gently twisted them. The ring opened along an invisible line. The person slipped the gap in the golden hoop over Lucky's left earlobe and gingerly closed the ring until it was secured in position on the lower part of Lucky's ear. With the tap of a finger, the gibberish buzzing around Lucky resolved into intelligible speech.

"Better?" Asked the woman as she took a last look at the positioning of the ring.

"Now, please explain to us why you are here. Indeed, how you are here? I have some specialized education related to my position that allows me to classify you as human, but your Species is exceedingly rare, and I can't imagine that you are standing here because you came for the Center of Excellence tour."

"Thanks very much," Lucky replied, "no, I'm not doing any- thing on purpose right now. I guess that's the problem. I'm the house-guest of a contractor for the Center of Excellence, and I really don't have much to do. So, I decided to have a look around. I feel like I ought to take advantage of this opportunity since I'm

not likely to be back this way ever again."

"Yes, that makes a lot of sense," she said, "but the center hosts many research teams investigating a very broad variety of topics. Some of those topics are highly sensitive and

potentially hazardous.

We cannot have guests wandering about the campus un- escorted. You will need to speak with security for clearance, and they will determine whether the tour is suitable for you or not. We may meet again based on their assessment."

"Okay," said Lucky.

He shrugged and turned to the security guard, "I guess I'm coming with you?" Without a word, the guard took him by the elbow and led him from the building foyer into a side corridor and then through an open doorway into a claustrophobic maze of cubicles and partitions. They wove through the narrow aisles until they came to a small office.

The room looked like it had been stuffed into the corner of the maze as an af- terthought. The door opened outward because it could not have opened inward.

A small desk occupied the distal half of the room. The guard indicated that Lucky should take a seat on the closer of the two chairs facing opposite each other across the desk.

The guard pressed his index finger against the desk drawer. It popped open to reveal a bag of equipment sealed across the top. The guard applied each instrument to Lucky in an orderly and matter-of-fact process.

From Lucky's standpoint, it didn't look much different than the booking procedure for jail, and he became more uncomfortable with each sample and measurement. When the guard finished, he packed everything back up in the bag and summoned a clerk to pick it up.

Afterward, they sat for a few more minutes waiting. The guard neither moved nor spoke. Lucky resisted the urge to do both. At last, a man opened the door and leaned through

the doorway. He motioned for them to come with him.

Lucky's companion rose briskly and ushered Lucky out with a hand on his elbow. Two men in gray robes flanked the man in charge as he led them all through the other side of the cubicle maze, into a large meeting room. The leader sat down at the end of the table and gestured for Lucky to come stand in front of him. No one else sat down.

The man was a few inches taller than the rest of the Species in the room, so about the same height as Lucky. He was slender with a narrow face. His irises were yellow, and his skin color was a light reddish-brown. He wore a lab coat and a surgeon's cap over scrub pants.

"I am Gerard," the leader began, "you understand that we must know how and why you came here, given the unusual nature of your presence. Without that knowledge, our options are to detain you indefinitely or to cast you out. With that knowledge, we have the additional option to release you into the care of a responsible person. All of our exams up until this point don't indicate anything that would preclude that last option. So, now it is up to you."

Lucky shifted from foot to foot,

"It's like I told the lady from the tour; 'said Lucky," I'm the houseguest of a

121

contractor for the center. I got bored. I'm tired of sitting around looking at the same four walls, so I went for a walk, and I followed the road to this place."

"Here is my problem," Gerard said, pointing a finger at Lucky, "no one will claim you. We don't have a lot of contractors working for us in the first place. The few contractors we do house on site know the rules about visitors, which are quite simple: no visitors!"

Lucky stared at him in shock.

"Just a minute, "Lucky protested, "I can show you where the house is."

"No, that will not be necessary," said Gerard with a dismissive wave of his hand, "send him out through the Node 8 access point."

"Shall I send him with a minder to be sure that he gets through?" Asked the guard at Lucky's elbow.

"No," said Gerard as he rose to leave, "I think that will not be necessary either."

Lucky panicked. He jerked his elbow away from the guard's grasp. The guard had already tightened his grip, however. The extra resistance threw Lucky off-balance. He fell to the floor and rolled partway under the table. One of his feet swung around and struck a chair on the other side, slamming it into the wall. He froze in expectation of an impending beating.

Several heartbeats later, nothing bad had happened, so he stuck with his winning strategy. He was facing the wall on the populated side of the table. He heard footsteps running away from the room, and someone stooped down to look under the table. It was one of the gray-robed attendants.

He was almost face-to-face with Lucky, but it seemed not to register, and he jumped back up to search elsewhere. A few more seconds passed until the room was empty save for Lucky.

He moved as quickly as he could while remaining silent. He heard some commotion in the direction of the cubicles, so he turned to go the other way. He nearly ran into the guard who had brought him to the meeting room.

Lucky stumbled around the man without making contact. Still, the man was in a position to notice another person with him in the narrow hallway.

Lucky went undetected.

The hallway turned left abruptly after the next two meeting rooms down the line. A thick, steel-clad door blocked the short passage in that direction. Lucky pushed it open. He was blinded by the glare on the other side for a moment. As the heavy door swung

shut, lights on the walls outside flashed in company with an undulating shriek. An automated voice repeated, "An emergency condition exists in the first-floor offices of the COE at the access point to the hospital entryway." Lucky looked left and right. The voice had given a pretty good description of where he was standing.

He moved as quickly as he could through the hospital's glass doors. Clerks seated behind the admissions desk ahead of him worked hard to lower and lock the barriers in front of their workstations. None of them looked up as he strode past them. Behind their desks, he noted a sturdy door, not as heavy as the one he had exited, but still something that would not easily succumb if it were locked. He made right for that door.

In a welcome departure from the preceding events of the day, the door swung open, and he went through it without suffering any injury, insult, or threat. Up to his right, stairs climbed into the dim reaches of the hospital's wards.

To his left, a short section of wall blocked a direct turn, but a doorway with its door propped open admitted him to the ground-floor hospital facilities, including the physical plant. He jumped down two flights of stairs to the boiler room, an imaginary space bounded by a red painted railing alone.

He hid behind the boiler, where it was close to the wall and right beside a small office on an adjacent platform. He could not see or hear anyone active in the ground-floor work areas. Looking a bit more relaxed, Lucky moved with a determined step in the direction of the wooded area behind the hospital. Soon, he could see the far wall of the ground floor.

Two-thirds of it was devoted to loading docks. Roll-down security doors barred the way in front, but a short stair at the northwest corner of the loading docks led down to a concrete pad behind the hospital.

Lucky took a look from side to side before he broke out into the open. A crowd gathered at a muster point across the concrete pad and the wide gravel parking area.

He estimated about thirty individuals in the crowd, all of whom chatted happily among themselves with apparent gratitude for the break in the workday. He slipped into the woods. The forest was similar to the high desert Juniper woodlands where he lived. The black soil and the low, spreading trees differed, but not by much. Most of the trees had spruce-like needles in variegated dark reds and black. There were a few shrubs with smooth, burnt orange bark and red leaves shaped like Laurel. The leaves from those shrubs covered most of the soil on the hillside.

In contrast to the aberrant sterility he'd found in the land West of this forest, he saw a few birds flitting through the canopy and bioluminescent insects pulsing fluorescent green on the tree trunks.

For all appearances, he had escaped. He relaxed and sat down against a large tree trunk. The hour was late.

Momentarily, the shrieking alarm went silent. The gathering behind the hospital broke up, and the celebrants filtered back to their desks and cubicles. He looked over the campus from his new vantage point. The hospital building in front of him stood twelve stories high. Its architects had not tried for anything too adventurous. It was square.

The rooms were spaced evenly across the outside walls. Floors two and three lacked regular windows. The intake area and emergency services occupied the first floor, whose roof covered an area from the northeast corner of the hospital over to the matching corner of the administrative offices, and up to the edge of the round Plaza, where the hospital doors and entryway formed the north side of the open space.

The hospital was not the largest building in the complex. That honor went to a metal vase of a structure tapering upwards from the base for about 10 stories and then flaring back out for another four stories to the roof, where a large, covered pool served as the centerpiece for an extensive garden with arbors, and a walking path around the edge of the roof. Just two windows broke the metal walls' smooth upward sweep. Spanning the waist of the building, a round sign with white lettering on a black background and a narrow green border stripe proclaimed, "Node 8".

Beyond the main hospital stood another four-story building, broader than it was high. White stone, which might have been marble, constituted its walls. The building remained dark as the sun set, and lights came on across the campus. To the south and separated from the immediate surroundings of the main hospital were several long, three-story buildings with walkways and green spaces running between them, and beyond those, a cluster of shops and restaurants.

Finally, on the southeast side of the Plaza, a three- story building of dark stone sprawled over several acres. On the south side of the building, the windows were dark, and several scaffolds hung from the walls.

It had a small, rectangular Plaza at the front entrance. A wall surrounded the Plaza and extended over to a covered entryway near the southeast terminus of the main plaza's wall, suggesting contiguity.

Lucky climbed to the ridge's peak in the interest of a better understanding of the lay of the land. He saw another set of ridges leading up and running parallel to the ridge that he crested. The parking area behind the hospital tapered to a two- lane road as it switched back and forth down the steep slope northeast of the hospital. He could not see clearly beyond the bend in the road marking the end of the switchbacks, but the geographic trend suggested a major river valley. He walked down off the crest. The prevailing wind blew out of the Northeast.

About halfway down the Southwest slope, he came upon a fairly level patch of bushes surrounding a large tree. A scant covering of dry leaves offered potential bedding material. He stood for a long time looking at the nest. Finally,

he turned away and walked back down the hill towards the back of the hospital. As he neared the bottom of the slope, a single light appeared in a fourth-floor corner window of the otherwise darkened marble building beyond the hospital.

Eighteen

Dancing With Mother

Laplace stared at the Mother, studying her as if some irregularity of dress or fleeting expression would tell him what he needed to do with her, if only he looked hard enough to flush it out. The Mother waited, unconcerned as usual.

Hostile forces had already gathered, both in the node above and in the back offices of the reception area where he now stood, assessing the damage. He leaned over and casually pawed through a stack of paper files containing the identifying genetic information, strengths and weaknesses, physical health, and personality profiles of the adolescents scheduled for review of their heredity for that date. Most would go on to a presentation with the nearest blood relative who was willing to take them in.

When he came to Francis' file, he dusted it off and opened the cover. He looked at the genetic signature and screening. He skipped past most of the information regarding academics and personality assessment. Finally, he opened the page that held his picture neatly affixed to the paper in the upper right-hand corner. The report lacked any descriptive power. It contained

almost no record of his actual accomplishments (though it hinted at some of them), instead

focusing on his less useful, safe, and unambiguous successes. He could have done without all those achievements. It mentioned a thesis paper on reprogramming nachinaks to carry out search and rescue tasks. That project got top billing as the primary example of a foundational propensity to pursue humanitarian ends, despite an uncomfortable correlation between his humanitarian successes and his investment portfolios' growth spurts. The Authority, with the Foundations' permission and assistance, devoted the last third of the report to his involvement in criminal activities, including violent crimes. He closed the file and tossed it scornfully back on the stack.

He looked at the Mother again.

"Why are people so fascinated with these genetic foibles?" he mused. "It is a brute fact," the Mother explained.

Laplace chuckled.

"Well, the fascination at least, is itself a behavior," he scoffed, "and it's hard to see how the rest of it, you know, the sniffing around with RNA probes and restriction endonucleases, the family trees, the unhealthy focus on glory transmitted through gametes all that nonsense is nothing but a set of behaviors as well. In that case, behaviors are not brute facts. They bear explanation, actually, they demand explanation lest they persist past their usefulness or begin to deceive their practitioners regarding the in. principal sanctity of any behavior."

"Behaviors don't need justification in all cases," the Mother corrected. "Do you need permission to understand what I'm saying to you right now? What justifies a word's meaning if not simply its use? Furthermore, behaviors aren't justified by mere association with other behaviors. A Boy can join a gang to protect himself and his associates from other

gangs, but it only makes sense if the boy and his associates actually care for each other. Otherwise, they're just brawling their way from one pragmatic excuse to the next. It's nothing but a rhetorical tautology, a circular

justification. In other words, nothing at all," she looked at him sharply before continuing,

"You must orient yourself on something in this life," she said," You can't understand how you relate to all the things around you otherwise. A brute fact is just fine for that purpose. And we're all born with one handy in the form of kinship, just imagine."

With that, she looked away again.

He continued to eye her suspiciously for a few moments. He looked back at the files, and after a brief reconsideration, he snatched the file belonging to

Francis from the top of the stack and swung around to grab the mother by the upper part of her arm.

His grip was not rough, but it was firm enough to encourage her to move and to keep up. Melodic clinking rose from the tufts covering the front of his body. The flaps of connective tissue and muscle between the rows of Tufts flipped outwards to reveal a wire circle threaded through a large collection of intricately engraved beads wound around the appendages and nearly ringing with the speed of their rotation and impact as the filaments worked on them.

Laplace and the Mother moved briskly through the area of rubble and an enclosed hallway to the top of two flights of fire stairs.

They passed through a doorway onto an outside deck with another automatic door on the other side. A projected image of a directory designated the building they left as the address of the Authority, and the Foundation for Clinical Developmentalism and Neuropsychological Development. A sister image projected above the door across the deck read "Node 3 Access to Dendritic Event Radiation. Please review your equipment checklist before joining the queue."

Laplace shifted his gaze to the rooftops across the street. That very specific maneuver constituted the sole practical use for his extravagant, bizarre, and disturbing cosmetic interventions. Because he could see through the tissues of his lateral orbit and cheek, not to mention the adjacent areas of

his eyelids, he didn't need to turn his head, and the rotation of his eyeballs was only discernible at a very close range.

"Must they persist in this charade?" He lamented under his breath.

Two of his anterior flaps disengaged from the loop of beads and flipped a pair of nachinaks into position above each shoulder. A pair of darts appeared on each of the re-extended flaps. He swung the Mother back under the small metal awning over the door.

"I sincerely apologize for this," he told her, "But I'm afraid we're going to have to absorb some fire at this point. You may also have to witness several," he cleared his throat," unpleasant deaths. I can't do anything about either of those things. However, I can assure you that we will survive, barring any very recent, major revision to their rules of engagement. Once again, I can assure you that I follow all changes in those rules with extreme rigor."

Before she could ask any questions, he swept her out onto the deck, still holding her by the upper arm, and walked briskly across the decking, while taking care not to allow the mother to drift out of position by his side.

Something exploded in the vicinity of his left ear. He kept walking, although he suffered one of the many disadvantages related to his tissue transparency treatments. He could not blink in response to glare or flashes of light. He had to slow down a little bit to keep from running into the railing on the far side of the deck.

A transparent web now enveloped

Laplace, the Mother, and the four nachinaks, generating the defense. The floor of the deck was a metal grate, the only flooring that made any sense in the rainy climate of that land. Muffled clanks on the underside of the decking tracked their steps as they crossed it. Puffs of bright white mist swirled up around their feet. Tendrils of gray vapor answered from a series of vials that dropped from loops on Laplace's belt to burst 5 cm above the deck grating.

"Ha!" Laplace allowed himself a derisive laugh as three of his darts flew through the railing toward unseen targets below.

They continued their brisk walk through the automatic door and into the Node 3 access point hallway. The hallway bifurcated to form a large

loop around a central, low-ceilinged ballroom. One hundred round cages, accommodating up to four people normally equipped, occupied all of the floor space. The hallways had low, arched ceilings, benches on the outside curve, and a subjugation nachinak locker space.

Laplace kept moving quickly. They walked almost to the middle of the left branch before they came to his stored equipment. His abacus lay halfway out of the locker. The sound of claws scratching on plastic emanated from behind and below the instrument. They caught two agents of the Authority by surprise as they were attempting to drag the body of a third agent out of range of the abacus. They dropped the body and fled.

Laplace freed the abacus with an effort, allowing four additional nachinaks to

129

escape from the locker. He looped his string of beads around the outside of the frame, near the supports fitted to his anterior flaps. As he lifted the abacus, it locked into place, giving him some assistance with the weight. He took hold of the Mother's arm again and guided her over to a nearby cage on the ballroom floor. He stepped down, made sure that her feet were completely inside the

bars, and closed the cage. A seam opened in the air, and he guided her through before stepping through himself. The last thing he saw before the fold closed completely was an empty ballroom.

Nineteen

The Dirty Bomb

Francis woke to find himself in the same room where he had passed out. No one had further assaulted him, but no one had moved him either. The small gray creatures continued with their business. It looked like they were preparing for war. The creature who had kidnapped him noticed as Francis stirred and rushed over to him.

"Wait! Sit for a minute before you try to stand. With everything else that follows a typical encounter with a subjugation nachinak, the victim often has trouble remembering that a subjugation nachinak causes vasodilation," advised the little fellow as he gently urged Francis to sit against the wall. "My name is Danilo; I am your new master."

A brief, tittering laugh escaped him. Francis regarded Danilo with a mix of anger and revulsion.

"How is that possible?" Francis demanded. "It's hard enough to get the subjugation nachinak properly programmed to work on other Species when the master is one of ours."

"It is possible," Danilo replied in a hurt tone. "It was hard

to imagine at first, especially because of the way the first three died so quickly. But I found the right books, and I had it down after a couple more tries. Don't worry, you won't die until I say you can."

Activity over Danilo's shoulder drew Francis's attention. Several of his captors, who wore helmets and protective vests, had begun lining up others of their kind, who bore no military trappings.

"Oh yes!" Danilo exclaimed, "Time for the concubines. Follow me and stick by my side. I will tell you your role in this while I take care of things." Francis struggled to his feet. He did feel somewhat lightheaded. He looked down at his leg and noticed that a subjugation nachinak was attached to the upper part of his right calf. Danilo bounced down the short stairs into the corridor, which ran several hundred meters beyond the room in either direction. A line of Danilo's small furry kindred lined up naked, with their hands and heads against the wall. Danilo approached the first in line. Francis

had a moment to notice that all of the assembled creatures were female.

Then, to his horror, Danilo undid the flap on the front of his garments and produced a long, thin appendage. Francis thought it might be a tentacle at first, but its mobility was limited, and given the situation,

he quickly surmised the thing's actual purpose. Danilo squared up behind the first in line and inserted the appendage in an orifice between the thin legs. He gave two quick pushes followed by a muffled squeak, and then he was on to the next. He spoke to Francis as he went from concubine to concubine.

"I do this at least once every week, whether I feel like it or not," he explained. "I will be remembered. You, on the other hand, will be forgotten. I promise you that. But not until after some good times. Some really, really good times. I can't wait to see

the look on the master's face.

I know his praise is empty. What he seeks is an advantage. He has the information, the results of all my study and toil. I discovered a way to immunize other Species against the most severe effects of the dendritic event radiation and a way to move through it without using a loop of beads or an abacus.

I found a way to modify the nachinaks, making them more independent and powerful and allowing one nachinak to control an opposing device. I left all those things sitting in plain sight. That way, he knows. Besides knowing I have you, he knows I know what you are. There," he declared, having finished with the last concubine in line, "you are to stay next to me until I tell you otherwise."

Danilo clapped his hands and smiled,

"Oh, I see now why they do this. It feels good."

They made their way down the rest of the hall, then took a narrowing passageway to the left. The structure changed as they turned down another passageway to the right. They entered a maze of tunnels, some lined with bricks, others lined with tiles or concrete. The smell confirmed to Francis that they were in the sewer. He guessed that a city lay above them based on the extent of the drainage system.

He estimated that they had traveled about 3 km from their starting point when he began to hear deep booming sounds from the network of passageways ahead. The sounds became louder as they walked. They had not seen many other people in the network of tunnels previously, but after passing the 3 km mark, they came across more and more soldiers, who bowed their heads and placed one hand over their chests when Danilo walked by.

The volume of noise was alarming now. Francis could feel it through the ground now as well as hear it. The passages filled with smoke and an acrid odor. Ahead of them, dim sunlight illuminated a pile of rubble.

Danilo looped a small transceiver from his breast pocket over his ear. As he

activated the device, he turned to Francis.

"This is my army," Danilo proclaimed. "Wait till you see it up close; it's beautiful. Right now, I have to defeat those of my own people who would resist me. My victory will be quick and complete. Then, I can turn my attention to bigger objectives.

You people haven't bothered with other Species for a long time. And other Species have ignored you back.

You are like our crazy uncles, tinkering around in your simulated reality, no longer interested in the real world. Well, that's about to change. Wait until you see the collection of subjugation nachinaks that I've amassed. Wait until you see what a neat trick I have taught them."

By now, a squad of soldiers surrounded them. One of them brought forward a pair of polished hardwood boxes. Danilo opened them up to reveal, on the left, a large weapon, about the size of a squad machine gun, with a coil of thick insulation spiraling down the weapon's body to the muzzle. It had a large ammunition canister slung below, a shoulder strap to help support it, and a curved butt with a substantial layer of gel padding. The other box contained a large nachinak, about the size of a small cat.

With the assistance of his bodyguards, Danilo set the weapon against his shoulder and positioned it properly to allow somewhat accurate fire. He touched three red contact spots on the nachinak. It rose from the box, and its legs began to circulate.

Francis recognized it as an external power source accessory. But it was larger than the average specimen of its type. Danilo laughed and made his way up the pile of rubble to the surface, with Francis trailing close behind him. They emerged in the middle of a firefight. They were close to several friendly firing positions, which provided cover. Francis could

see that the protection would not last for long. Enemy forces occupied several positions in the median of the wide street in front of them, as well as in the buildings and on the rooftops. At the end of the Boulevard, an armored vehicle traversed its turret in their direction.

"Oh, look at it!" Danilo shouted with delight over the din of gunfire, "This

is me! I did this! It's glorious!"

Bullets skipped off the blocks of shattered concrete just in front of them. Francis saw something flash by the right side of his head. Almost immediately afterward, the ground lit up and shrugged forcefully, nearly sending them back down the rubble pile to the bottom of the tunnel. Smoke obscured their view down the Boulevard.

Two pairs of nachinaks hovered in front of them. Francis looked around in a full circle. Two more pairs of nachinak guarded their flanks. Strung between them, a diaphanous web of transparent spider silk floated on the breeze. A wad of similar material lay on the ground in front of the protective devices. Charred and smoking, it bubbled with flashes of contained detonation.

Danilo laughed again and then devoted all his attention and effort to raising and aiming the weapon he carried on his left side. Danilo finally managed to stabilize it and then directed its muzzle toward the armored vehicle at the end of the Boulevard.

He pulled the trigger, and the weapon jumped in his arms with a loud "thunk." The round it fired left a scintillating track behind the projectile. The exhaust trail curved slightly to intersect with the vehicle.

In the instant before contact, the round flared into a spinning pair of incredibly bright jets that careened wildly through the armored vehicle. The vehicle's surface threw back a couple of gouts of flame, indicating the presence of an

Electromagnetic shield, but

the tumbling plasma disc hardly slowed. It slashed an 8-foot gouge through the vehicle and the stairs behind it, disappearing into the depths of the basement beyond.

Danilo pumped his fist in the air. The defensive web absorbed a hail of rifle bullets as well as another cannon shell from a cross street to their left and an incendiary grenade from somewhere above them.

The deluge of projectiles sobered Danilo up. He produced a single bead

from his hip pocket and touched a series of features on its surface. Nachinaks swarmed toward them from all directions. Francis gawked.

No one should be able to manage so many devices simultaneously. They did not assemble once they reached the launch point. Instead, they proceeded directly to their targets.

Several torus generators dodged in and out among the fighters contesting the building to their right. They were as effective as textbooks described, but two of them began to behave abnormally and then became unstable. Great globs of compressed space flipped off their mirror surfaces. They wobbled erratically for a few moments and then exploded. The building was destroyed, and the dust from its collapse washed over them.

Danilo tried to coordinate with some of his troops outside of the dust cloud. He couldn't sort out their positions well enough to allow a second shot with the plasma disc.

Francis and Danilo remained in position, their view completely obscured by the dust cloud, while the sound of fighting quickly receded. As the world around them gradually faded back into focus, a squad of Danilo's soldiers found them and escorted them to a nearby forward command post. Danilo handed off the heavy weapon to an aide and stood by the

communication hub, watching the

battle proceed around them and listening to reports from his officers. It was quickly apparent that Danilo had been correct. His army routed the opposition within 90 minutes. Within three hours, his special operations teams delivered him the heads of the military leadership on the other side, followed by the heads of the political leadership on the other side.

Francis remained quiet for the entirety of the war. He said nothing the following day, the day after that, or the next day after.

Danilo was so busy that he seemed to have forgotten his new slave. However, each night, he directed an aide to provide Francis with an air mattress and blanket. Neither of them had much to eat due to the workload.

Francis did not feel hungry anyway. Danilo arrived early at Francis's bivouac on the fifth day after the war. He tossed a file folder down beside Francis on the air mattress. Francis looked at the folder and then back at Danilo.

"Open it," Danilo ordered, "and read it. All of it."

Francis did as he was commanded. It looked like the same folder that he had lifted from the desk at the Foundation for Clinical Developmentalism and Neuropsychological Development. He rapidly flipped through the familiar material.

The only thing different was the last page. Instead of Laplace, a picture of a man named "Augustine" occupied the folder's upper, outer corner. The biographical information focused on Augustine's long-term and hereditary association with the Authority. He specialized in organized crime, especially financial crime within that category.

He was famous for coming as close as anyone had in the last two centuries to completing a calculation. He had a long-standing feud with Laplace. It had recently been quiescent, but it had a history of escalating to violence from time to time. The hostility

stemmed from Laplace's interference in Augustine's attempt at a completion.

Francis looked through the remainder of the report, but it was no easier to understand the genetic reporting in this dossier than it had been with the first one.

"So?" Francis said.

"No. What?" Danilo asked incredulously, "You can't read the genetics report?"

"No, I can't, "Francis admitted without shame. "I never really found that topic very interesting."

"Oh, this is too sweet!" Danilo laughed "Well listen up you stupid piece of shit. What that shows is that you are a chimera. That means your cells are a mixture of two genetically distinct lines.

Chimeras do occur sporadically. But this one was no accident. Your real kin is that fat turd in the picture. The mother's side of the family is no longer with us. You see, this Augustine person found out that one of his girlfriends had become pregnant. He generously offered to deliver the blastocyst to a Foundation office for her.

After all, the Authority was paired with their organization traditionally. She refused, and she was quite irrational about it. That rubbed Augustine the wrong way, so he killed her and extracted the blastocyst postmortem.

Like all of these upper-echelon twits, he is always looking for an angle. He didn't really want some clumsy child weighing him down when it emerged from a developmental center in a few years. He'd been waiting for this opportunity; he planned for it.

So, he altered the cells in the dormant blastocyst. He had a genetic sample from Laplace. Laplace is a notorious criminal and sociopath, so he has had a number of nonfatal interactions with the Authority, unfortunately. Augustine had access to the evidence room, and it was quite a simple matter for him to obtain

a sample without anyone noticing.

And so here you are, really the long-lost son of that pig, loaded up to look like the progeny of Laplace and slipped under the door to destroy him, and to do it in the most thoroughgoing, prolonged, and painful way. Wait till he finds out you're counterfeit and then finds out that you might not be a counterfeit.

What is he going to do, I wonder? You are screwed. Laplace is going to toss

137

you on your ass as soon as he finds out. Then it's just a matter of who snatches you up. It'll be too late by then, though. Way too late. You'll be dead in a few months, no matter what. You might've guessed that it was no accident that Laplace showed up at the Foundation office just when he did. It wasn't an accident that the needle in that doorknob stuck your hand.

You had a virus packed away in your chromosomes when Augustine had

hold of you. It resides in your cellular immune system.

It needs two things to activate it. One is a catalytic enzyme to activate the dormant code, and the other is a provocation to the cellular immunity to promote replication. The needlestick kills two birds with one stone.

Once it's loose, the virus destroys your immune system and eats away at your marrow. The virus is more than 95% infectious as well. All I have to do is give you a touch of IV anesthesia and drop you off at the roost.

You'll notice that Augustine appears unconcerned with the prospect of unleashing a catastrophic plague. He is unconcerned because there will be no plague. Augustine was cautious. He waited until he had the opportunity to create a chimera. A cluster of proteins whose structure is encoded by genetic loci unique to Laplace and you provides the only binding site for the viral capsid. We shot you with a silver bullet."

"What is your further role in Augustine's murder plan?" Francis asked, "There's something else you want, or you wouldn't be telling me this."

"Oh yes," Danilo said, "I don't feel the punishment is adequate. Maybe for you, but you're not the one who's been the worst in all this. As I have thought it over these last many weeks, I have concluded that I'm not really angry at you at all. I mean, I don't think I would save you at this point, even if I could, but I wouldn't go out of my way to harm you either. That's why I'm going to offer you a fair deal."

Danilo reached inside his jacket and pulled out a linen cloth and a second one. He unfolded both bundles to reveal a pair of nachinaks.

"These are my offer," Danilo said, "one for him and one for you. You take the extraction nachinak, use it, and you die a free man. In the meanwhile, Laplace becomes my slave, and I make sure that he drinks his cup of humiliation to the dregs."

Twenty

Good Times at the Five and Dime

Takezo paced in front of his workshop. Lucky had been gone for almost 2 days. No one had paid a visit with questions or news, so Takezo could safely assume that Lucky was not dead or detained. The process of elimination could take him no further.

He put a couple of items into a day pack, including Lucky's machete, and set off through the patch of Juniper Forest and up the switchbacks to the main trail. The trail had more than the usual amount of traffic that morning. Takezo passed by the usual stream of people with business at the Center of Excellence. He noted an excess of technicians and members of Species other than the Species, especially a variety of short, gray, furry people, most of them bearing heavy backpacks. He noted recent signs of passage on the side trail leading down to the cliff dwelling.

Someone had put substantial work into the main trail. It was now a level two track with a gravel surface. An additional side trail ran up to the base of the large Mesa overlooking the system of canyons and valleys, including

the cliff dwelling, and stretching southwards. The trail ended at a shed built into the rock wall. The improved trail led past a meadow and through

a growth of trees and brush, right to the doorstep of the old country store. Its proprietors had improved the store as well since Takezo's last visit. It sported a new façade in log cabin style. The proprietors replaced the old, scratched plate glass windows with old-fashioned framed windows. The glass sliding door was gone. A solid wooden door with a doorknob replaced it. Several coolers lined the outside wall in the front. They had built a porch

in the back as well, with open-air seating.

The parking area had moved to the gravel pad behind the building. Takezo opened the door and stepped into the dimly lit interior. Only two other people, both members of the Species, were shopping. The goods on offer had not changed, except for two aisles devoted to folk art on consignment. Those aisles were gone, and two racks of magazines and postcards stood in their stead. A single male human tended to the counter. He didn't look up when Takezo entered.

He had a cigarette and a coffee mug in one hand and a tabloid magazine in the other. Takezo strolled over to the counter and slapped his hand on the surface. The man jumped but didn't drop the mug or the cigarette. As he looked up at Takezo, he took the opportunity to have a sip of his drink and a long pull on the smoke.

"Yeah?" He asked as he leaned forward and set the cup down, "What is – aw shit, I mean, good afternoon sir how may I assist you?"

Takezo took an involuntary step back. The liquid in the cup was bargain bourbon, and the cigarette was not a menthol.

"Good afternoon," Takezo responded, "Is the boss in?"

"I haven't seen him for a while," said the cashier, "but the last time I checked, he was out back somewhere."

Takezo nodded his thanks and went around to the porch.

Two steps led up to the platform. The structure was large and ramshackle enough to require a line of supports down the middle. The roof was low and made of plywood panels covered in white plastic sheeting. The proprietors had devoted most of the space to eight two-to three-person tables with the requisite number of chairs. Luncheon guests occupied only one table at that time.

Two construction workers sat at the table farthest from a grill and steam table set up on a platform separate from the porch itself, and just in front of a cinderblock building connected to the store. The cinderblock building was completely new since Takezo's last visit. The unpainted walls held three windows.

The third window out supported an air conditioning unit, while the other two were closed. One of the Species and one human manned the grill. The woman was showing her companion, who was familiar to Takezo, how to tell when a steak was ready.

"Excuse me," Takezo interrupted, "I need to speak with Augustine if he is here."

141

"What?" Said the woman, "I don't know no Augustines…"

"But you know that I do," said Thomas.

"Yes," Takezo said, "Thank you, Thomas. I have a very short list of additional materials and several simple questions for him."

"Let me check in with him," Thomas said, "he has been very busy over the last few days, and he may not have time today."

"Thank you. I thought that might be the case, I've arrived with time to wait."

Thomas bowed and slipped past the steam table. He walked briskly around the back of the building. Takezo heard a screen door open and shut. He took a seat and watched the woman poke at the steak on the grill.

"You know," he said, "it's all mystery meat to them, if they eat meat at all."

"Well, we are all in luck then, "she said, "because I ain't making it for them."

"Yes," said Takezo, "we are all in luck."

Fifteen minutes went by before Thomas returned.

"Okay," Thomas said, "he'll see you. But he told me to warn you that he may need to interrupt the conversation for calls and messages."

"Thank you," said Takezo, "I will be brief, I assure you."

Augustine's office was just behind the junction between the store and the cinderblock addition. Takezo entered through a door across from the store's rear entrance. Augustine's desk was a couple of steps to the right. It took up most of that half of the room. A single chair sat facing Augustine, across the desk. A bank of video monitors for the security cameras inside and outside the store lined the top of the far wall. Another door, currently propped open, gave access to the area behind the store's counter, where the clerk still sat, cup and cigarette in hand, reading his tabloid.

Augustine was talking to someone remotely as Takezo entered.

"That is not my problem," Augustine told the party on the other end of the line, "whatever you choose to do besides the delivery is your own concern. Just make the drop. After that, we are done."

Augustine tapped the silver loop hanging from the rim of his auditory meatus.

"What is it?" Augustine asked.

142

"I have a short list of materials that need to be filled. You will find that it is nothing too exotic," Takezo said, as he set the paper list on Augustine's desk, "I also had a couple of questions.

that I thought you might be able to help me with."

"Go ahead," said Augustine.

"Why have you put up the flyer for my fencing school on the bulletin board?" Takezo asked," And why did I receive an invitation to attend the demonstration of a weapon prototype the day after tomorrow in my own workshop?"

"I thought you would be pleased," Augustine said, "the answer to both questions is to throw people off. And it is not your workshop; it is my workshop. I'm lending it to you until you're done with your weapon

prototype. That's how it is

because it can't be any other way. You are not the only person I've contracted with, and I need someplace to review their submissions.

My workshop is equipped to conduct the trials, and that's where the trials will be conducted. Anything else?"

"Just one thing," Takezo said in an even tone, "I have seen someone poking around the place over the last two days. Nothing has been disturbed, but I did not recognize the person either. Have you heard any news of an interloper from your people here, at the fold, or from the security department at the

Center of Excellence?"

"No," said Augustine.

"Back to work then," Takezo said, "I like what you've done with the place, by the way."

Augustine was scowling at the cashier. "Yeah," he mumbled, "see you."

Takezo let himself out. His walk back to the compound was uneventful. When he arrived, he dropped his pack off at the workshop and made a beeline for the house. He stopped in front of the door to the south apartment and knocked loudly. There was no response. He took the key from his hip pocket and opened the door. He walked across the room to lean against the nightstand as the door swung shut, ignoring the person hiding in the corner to his left holding a knife, with a nachinak floating overhead.

"Don't kid yourself," he said without looking up. Anisa lowered the knife.

"I thought we agreed not to leave or enter this way unless the need was dire," she said.

"You must tell him. Everything," Takezo said.

"I will not. I don't know what his part is in all this. We both have our questions for him, he has answered your questions, and now we all have to wait. For his answers to mine."

"Do you know where he is?" Takezo asked as he slowly looked up to glare at her.," It has been two days since I saw him."

She threw up her hands,

"And you waited until now to tell me this? You know what you've really been waiting for? Our destruction. It is probably on its way right now."

"I think it is not," Takezo said, "the signs are not there. I am untroubled by anything right now except for your duplicity. And I mean all of your duplicity, not just the dishonest treatment you have given him. I don't know what else you are up to, but you are up to something.

As I told you, I will not demand anything. I will advise you, though. You should begin to unravel this now. Otherwise, you will get caught in the tangle."

He did not wait for her to reply. He walked out and slammed the door behind him.

Twenty-one

Sonnamarg Smokescreen

Laplace sat on the bar's middle stool, swaying slightly with the music. The artist was an indulgence of his. Though the roost was not the musician's only gig, he spent most of his time there and enjoyed very generous compensation for it. He gave every indication that he didn't mind the effect that private concerts had on his renown; he didn't even seem to mind the occasional performances for an audience of one, like this one. The musician played a large string instrument exclusively, which looked and sounded much like a sitar.

The napkin under Laplace's drink was nothing but gray mush. He swirled the remnants of his drink in the glass to mix the melted ice with liquor. Hardened windows were extravagantly expensive, so Laplace's roost, like most, only had a few. The bar had the biggest window of them all.

It took up most of a wall and looked across a large square to an airfield and launch site, with a huge lake stretching beyond to the horizon.

Wide boulevards converged on a roundabout at the far end of the square,

and an abstract statue occupied the center pedestal.

A manicured lawn and flower beds covered the rest of the space, cut by an "X" of stone-paved walkways. The giant sun was sinking into the lake. Atmospheric moisture and particulates attenuated the looming star's red light, turning it to alpenglow. He didn't move when he heard the door open behind him. He took a deep breath and turned to address the musician, signaling for the tune to stop.

"Splendid, as usual," Laplace acknowledged. "Are you able to come back later? I have to speak with this person, and I don't want to neglect the music. You'll get paid for a second session. "

TWENTY-ONE

The musician took a shallow bow.

"Don't worry about it, I'm happy to come back. Just give me a call when things are ready.

We'll call this intermission."

The musician turned and left, nodding to the Mother on his way out. She stood quietly, staring straight ahead.

"Come in," said Laplace, "take a seat. I prefer to give you more time to recover after all that's happened. Danilo has chosen a complicated path, however, and I'm afraid we are all dancing to his tune for the time being."

The Mother sat down on his right side. She asked the bartender for the same thing Laplace was having.

"I owe you an apology once again. If you feel angry with me, I certainly understand. I know that I've played a role in ending your life," Laplace said. "I'm still here," the Mother said. "I am not angry with you. You saved me during the attack at Node 3, from whatever it was that they would have done with me. It was my decision anyway to threaten him."

"Oh yes," Laplace laughed, "had I been there, I would've advised you not to do that, though I would've enjoyed seeing the reaction."

"I didn't think I had anything to lose at that point," she said, "he had committed a one-in-a-million violation, which could

have been catastrophic. When I arrived with Francis, I'd already chosen my exile, and I understood that it was a half-measure, and if there was even a hint that it was to be unsuccessful, then the complete measure meant my death."

"And mine as well," said Laplace, "if your information and its logical conclusion are correct."

"Do you have reason to doubt them?" She asked with alarm.

"I do not. The little man may look timid, but he is not a liar or a coward," Laplace reassured her. "In his master's place, I would've done the same thing, if not more."

"More?" She asked, "What do you mean by that? Is there more to come? On your part, that is."

"I wouldn't tell you one way or the other," Laplace replied.

146

He sat up straight abruptly. The filaments overlying his abdomen stirred, and two nachinaks drifted free. Both were oversized. One had black stripes running the length of its body and a head at each end; the other had an elongated pair of fins on its back. He nodded to the bartender, who returned the gesture. He swiveled his chair and spoke to the Mother over his left shoulder.

"Please go behind the bar and do not come out until I tell you to," he ordered.

She complied while he stood and took two steps to the middle of the room. Two more nachinaks emerged from the filaments covering his chest. One stacked itself on top of the other as they floated into position above his left shoulder. A split in the air formed in front of him and slightly to the right. He quickly adjusted his position to face it. The split grew slightly, and an unconscious Francis tumbled out of it. He did not hit the ground. A floor tile opened and spat out an exceptionally large nachinak with a cylindrical body and a stubby trunk. It began spinning rapidly as it cleared the retracted edges of the tile and the mouth at the end of the trunk opened wider than the diameter of its body, sending a thin,

frosted sheet of material spiraling out as it sucked air from the room. The fabric enveloped Francis and snapped shut at both ends. Even before the wrapping was complete, another seam in the air appeared, running from the two devices above Laplace's left shoulder, down to the floor.

Laplace stepped through quickly. A similar split was starting to close across from him in the wall of the exclusion sphere. He reached through with both arms and pulled his Abacus into the excluded space. The sphere, which had been shrinking, stabilized. A host of nachinaks poured into the space around Laplace as he fought to stabilize the fold as well.

He began to work the beads and cylinders. The kaleidoscopic scene outside the sphere gradually darkened and became less crowded with transforming shapes. A filament touched four symbols engraved on the surface of a single bead. Four nachinaks swooped out of their formation on the periphery of the sphere and took up station next to Laplace. They were large, blocky machines. Each had a unique pattern of red spots, black stripes, and gold frog eyes scattered across its body.

147

TWENTY-ONE

The first assault did not catch Laplace by surprise. The attacker failed to adequately close the distance before sending out a disruption wave, accidentally triangulating herself.

Laplace's defensive team deflected the disruption without difficulty, and as they did so, Laplace dispatched two standard-type machines to lay a vortex tunneling into the opposing exclusion sphere. They darted out to intercept the other sphere.

The enemy coordinating the attack managed to deflect one of the nachinak, though she did not destroy it. It circled until its checklist came back zero and then resumed the attack. It broke off before it reached the target, though, as its twin had already completed the mission. She had hesitated slightly before activating her personal defense – a common occurrence among the more aggressive disputants frequenting the radiation, since its field scuttled the user's own offensive devices in the process of saving their life.

When a neurotoxic dart sensed a countermeasure coming online, it would explode in an attempt to give its target a fatal spritzing of nerve agent,

which added up to a droplet the size of half a poppy seed. The dart's full shot delivered a hit equal to an entire bagel's worth of poppy seeds. Laplace's first opponent took a full shot in the upper chest.

She crumpled. The abacus slid off her body, and the nachinaks it contained emerged to mill about in confusion until all of it dissolved into red mist and diffused in the event radiation.

The second attack came right on the heels of the first one and did catch Laplace by surprise. His experience saw him through this time.

He felt something behind him. He did not turn, flinch, or freeze like many of his fellow calculators did when they encountered this tactic. Instead, he detonated one of the darts he kept hovering right above him for that very purpose

The "pop" from the exploding dart overlapped perfectly with the "pop" from an anti-toxin vial's detonation a few milliseconds later.

The timing had to be just right. The nerve agent matured on the target membrane channel on contact, practically as fast as the antitoxin decomposed the nerve agent. Too much delay in the system, and he would die from his own nerve agent. Early detonation gave the enemy a share of the antitoxin. Hours of practice backed by a string of successes gave Laplace the ice-cold confidence in the tactic needed to make it work.

As he collapsed, the victim bumped Laplace, who shoved the body to the bottom of the sphere.

Laplace could now see the rest of the force arrayed against him. Two calculators, one a late arrival, navigated separate spheres dangerously close together. Just in front of them, in the middle, was Danilo. He was managing two loops of beads and a pair of nachinaks that Laplace had never seen before. Their bodies were round and long, with a distinctly snakelike appearance that set them apart from the average device. They had a black base color with narrow red stripes running from the trunk down to the end of the body.

There was an aperture at the end of the body as well as in the trunk. The pair of strung bead loops whipped through the bodies back and forth while the bodies themselves adjusted relative position on the loop.

All this led to a wriggling motion in the loops, which became more and more difficult to control and avoid as the speed of the process increased. Danilo's body language suggested that he was very close to losing control. Laplace stared daggers at him.

Danilo was doing the smart thing. He was trying to describe an aspect that would allow him to easily bail out of his current situation, likely at the bargain price of a single lost nachinak. Two more enemies arrived. They took up positions on either side of Laplace and waited.

Everyone knew what was going to happen next. Any one of the Species would have known. From eyewitness reports in the archives to mythology recorded by secondhand sources, the prelude and the subsequent events had repeated themselves through history. They formed the core of the Species' cultural identity.

Laplace tucked his chin and leaned forward slightly. The boxy device on the lower left beside him started to vibrate. Moving with dexterity earned from thousands of repetitions, his left hand yanked a wire out of one of the cylinder caps and fed it

to the nachinak buzzing next to his left knee. The response was alarming and nauseating. The surroundings pulsed and swirled in a flux of changing color and brightness. After 30 seconds, the boxy nachinak began to wobble and smoke. Without further warning, it dropped from its place by its creator's side. Laplace snatched the wire from its mouth and connected it to the next unit above. He looked at his fellow travelers.

All of them were still with him, but they looked unsteady. He burned through the next two units and plugged into the last. Danilo was almost invisible as he took his off-ramp in hopes of escaping. Laplace screamed defiance as the last of the devices failed.

They had driven him forward with the compiled descriptions from countless trips through the events comprising the universe as known to the

Species, everything within its light cone. He took over the calculation seamlessly. A single point of yellow light glimmered above him, and one below him. Otherwise, darkness surrounded him. In the faint illumination from the distant lights, vague, misty shapes stretched out around him on all sides, but he was almost clear of them. He was almost completely separated from the vast projection of events. He began to shiver, and the bare globes of his eyes skipped over the scene before him.

There was an asymmetry. He was at the point of conclusion. If he proceeded one movement further, he would find out whether his answer was correct or not, and consequences would follow. He stopped and plucked a nachinak with two heads and black-and- white stripes running the length of its body from the formation of devices above him. The two opponents who had accompanied Danilo passed by Laplace without slowing down.

The first one did not seem to notice anything amiss, but the second turned to look at Laplace with an expression that quickly evolved from puzzlement to panic. Neither of them avoided the featureless expanse of gray

that flashed into existence before them. Only one of his enemies remained. Instead of proceeding down the probability gradient in the hope of supervening on a base dense enough to resist the outbreak of gray space, he wrote a description of the final member of the Species to show up for the party. As he finished the calculation, he raised his hand as if he were going to throw the striped nachinak.

He stopped being in his exclusion sphere and started being behind the person described inside their exclusion sphere. His arm whipped forward. The Nachinak's mouth smacked into the back of the man's neck, and then Laplace was back in his own, rapidly shrinking exclusion sphere. He knelt beside his abacus and did his best to work quickly despite the awkward position. Thick, bright, colorful shapes flowed past in the following second, and then the man with the black striped machine stuck to his neck reappeared, along with Danilo with the other end of the nachinak stuck to his neck. He still had his loops of beads and began trying to sketch his way

back to an easy aspect.

Laplace took over and diverted the pair towards a dimmer zone along his path to the edge of the complete calculation. A gray disc bulged through the circulating shapes, and then another, and another. They grew and coalesced, then split back apart into smaller circles, and repeated the cycle. There was no way for Danilo to escape. Just before he contacted the surface of the disc in front of him, he turned, pulled a fleshy tube out of his pants, and began waving it in Laplace's direction. He started laughing, but the gray space cut him off.

Twenty-two

The Empty

Lucky crept as quietly as he could towards the entrance of the white building. He skirted the one guard encountered between the gate in back of the Center of Excellence and his objective. He nervously eyed the cameras over the door and on the corner of the building. He continued moving, despite his misgivings. He got to the door without incident and checked it. It was locked. He kept moving around the corner to his left. He came across an emergency exit about one-third of the way down the side of the building.

It, too, was locked. However, as he turned to move on, he noticed a dim light shining through a grate at the base of the wall ahead. He aligned himself with the grate and faced away from the building with his back against the wall. Slightly off a direct line from the grate and beyond a paved walkway about 10 m from the building, a pair of metal plates covered a portal.

On closer inspection, the plates formed doors to a freight elevator. The doors had a latch to secure them, but it was hanging open. He pulled on the plates, and they swung open easily. The elevator did not activate, but it had no roof, and even though the platform was about six meters down,

a series of rungs set in the wall of the shaft allowed access to the platform. He climbed down and transferred onto the rungs.

He could not see any way to close the access doors from the inside. He quickly descended the rungs and squeezed through the opening between the elevator and the outer door frames. He pushed the up button, and the car rose to the open access doors. He pressed the down button, and the car returned to the bottom of the shaft. In addition, the access doors at the top of the shaft automatically closed. He moved down the hallway before him, passing several storage rooms on the side. A short ramp at the end of the hall led to a maintenance room. Its door was unlocked. He opened the door a few centimeters and looked out. There was no one in the hallway.

He walked slowly down the hall until he reached the corner of the building where he'd seen the light. He heard a bump in the hall ahead of him. He froze. The stairwell door on the opposite wall swung out, and a nervous-looking member of the Species in gray robes and an oversized bowler hat walked into the hallway right toward Lucky. The light in the hallway was bad, but it should have been adequate to give Lucky away.

Instead, the man walked past him within one meter without seeming to notice. Under his right arm, he held a miniature version of the strange, six-legged machine that Lucky had encountered in the lower room of the cliff dwelling.

The door was swinging shut, and Lucky nearly missed it. He ducked through and waited for it to close completely before proceeding up the stairs. To his relief, the door at the top was open. It led into a short section of hallway that terminated in another doorway. The door had a label in the Species' script. To Lucky's surprise, the characters twisted around themselves and then reformed in English to read "Vault One." He turned the handle, and the door swung open. The room beyond was small, scarcely

large enough for the desk chair.

it contained. The table was polished hardwood, and the frame of the chair

matched. The tabletop was empty except for a 3D viewer permanently attached to the wood and facing the chair. Two whole walls of the room held windows looking out onto the back of the Center of Excellence campus. There were several panes of glass in each frame. Lucky sat down on the chair. He looked at the viewer with some trepidation. It had a retractable, adjustable arm with several rows of crystals attached by thin wires to the projection head. The vital piece was a clear crystal orb. It had a single button at the base of the arm. Lucky shrugged and pushed it. A heavily pixelated image popped up.

The only legible contents resided in a label at the upper right. It read "Report to the Institutional Review Board on complaints against surgeon 'Gerard.'"

The next page was blank. On the page after that, the initial part of a recorded interview played. The camera view was over the interviewer's right shoulder. Seated across from him, on an additional chair in the very room where Lucky sat, was the man who had sent Lucky to his doom that afternoon.

"Would you please state your name for the record?" asked the interviewer. "You know my name. I can see it on the readout," Gerard replied.

"A formality, you're correct," the interviewer said. "I prefer plain speaking anyway. You know that you have been accused of murder."

"Have you called for someone from the Authority to bring me in, in that..." The image went blank again and then resumed two pages later.

"How do you suppose my actions were unethical?" asked Gerard.

"Besides violating an oath you took to adhere to the ethical standards and guidelines of this institution, as well as the signed oath to operate within the rules governing this facility, which include the requirement to log in any requests for OR time and resources. You brought somebody to the operating table, and that person died on the table."

"That is true," said Gerard. "Let me tell you about that person. Michael

came to me requesting a bilateral nephrectomy right after we had ended the trial for a universal tissue donor transplant program.

The procedure was a death sentence at worst, and the patient would face a lifetime of dialysis at best. An evil act if ever there was one, wouldn't you agree?"

The recording captured the sound of the interviewer clearing his throat before speaking,

"It would appear so, "he said," That is, in large part, why we are here today,"

"Indeed, it is," said Gerard." Hear me out; there is more to it." "Michael suffered from severe congestive heart failure, "said Gerard." He had stage IV disease, which meant he was experiencing difficulty breathing

at rest. His life was miserable.

I understood that Michael would not be receiving dialysis, per his request, after the surgery, and that he would be allowed to die under anesthesia as soon as I procured the organs. Do you think I did wrong?"

"Perhaps not," the interviewer admitted hesitantly."

"Many would disagree with you and tag the procedure as evil, no matter the mitigating circumstances," Gerard continued," How do they explain themselves? The variation in the non-moral properties involves changes in the estimated degree of evil. Still, the state of affairs does not transition into evil as most people use the term. Moral facts are moral or not, regardless of the relative seriousness of the fact's moral standing.

The moral facts vary with non-moral facts when we consider their relative magnitude as a moral property. They do not covary reliably with any non-moral fact when it comes to assigning their status as a moral fact in the first place.

We can measure pain with morphine, but we can define it that way as well. Two mg of morphine makes the pain 50 % better. 8 mg makes the pain go away.

By contrast, there is nothing to keep not observing the Sabbath from appearing on the same list of moral ills as murder.

The interviewer shifted uncomfortably in his seat.

"Do you mean to say that these things–ethical things-do - do not exist?" asked the interviewer

"So, what do you think?" asked Gerard, "Do you really believe that there are facts to go by in such a case.

"There is some absolute quality to evil, according to those who think it is a property of various things in the world, just like greenness is a property of various things in the world, but that quality alone gives us a categorical and unique reason to shun it, they say.

"The situation across moral terms is even more absurd. Not all that is just is good, and not all that is good is just. Yet so often they are. So, in case they are not, which prevails?

"If an act is generous, then it is a transfer of resources, and it is good. If an act is kind, it is a response to another individual's needs, and it is good. To say that kindness is good, therefore, if I want to be good, I ought to be kind, doesn't tell us much about good. It doesn't tell us anything at all.

"We need to know what good is that we should want it, but we can't have

155

that information up front. We can label many states of affairs as good or evil, but no state of affairs encompasses good or evil.

"You have put some thought into this,' and I commend your efforts, "said the interviewer," but don't you think this schema works out a little bit too well for you?"

"The words of a man who cannot even offer a response to my position, much less a refutation," said Gerard.

"I am the one conducting this interview. If we are living a moral fairy tale, then where are the Fairies? Who is telling us this insidious story, and why does such a transparent fiction persist?" Asked the interviewer.

"Ask who it empowers," said Gerard," Look for the little men trying to go big who need a stick to beat everyone else down, since they aren't getting any taller. I'd recommend the mirror as a good place to start."

"Philosophical niceties are beside the point. If you had just come to us with the case, we might have approved the procedure," said the interviewer in a sympathetic tone, "and all this would have been unnecessary," he

continued in a decidedly less sympathetic tone,"

Yet, you chose to ignore your duty to this institution deliberately, as far as I can tell. What could possibly motivate you to do that?"

Gerard rose and began to pace back and forth across the far side of the room.

"Ah, you got it right away: motive," he said, "it is the key to... well, to everything or at least everything we consider valuable enough to act upon. The trouble is that our motive has no bounds, but other people do. Shriveled, decrepit borders that persist without justification and constrict year after year.

There are those of us whose motives are transcendent. We possess a philosopher's stone which we apply to the weaknesses, the fears, and even the pain and revulsion which have been our oppressors since we learned to speak! We transform weaknesses into virtues. From pointless suffering and emptiness, we make art!"

With that, Gerard sprang across the table onto the interviewer, carrying them both out of frame.

"Of course, I didn't ask your leave to do the procedure. What permission does art require?" Gerard asked, "If I had, the beauty of Michael's insight would have been lost doubly. Both his description of the experience he had with my knife and the paralytic without the veil of anesthesia and my interpretation for him and posterity, of the beauty, all the sensuous joy in the experience, unobscured by the filters of an erroneous morality supported by a culture whose only need is false reassurance that it is not dying."

For three more seconds, the image of the empty chair floated above the table and then disappeared.

Lucky stared at the projector for a long time. His legs were stiff by the time he got up. He took a couple of his pills from
the emergency stash in his front pocket. He slipped over to the door and turned the handle. It did not move. He stepped back in disbelief.

A dead-end like this should not be locked from the outside. He sat on the floor for a few minutes, contemplating the situation. In the end, he lay the back of the chair down on the floor to substitute for a pillow and went to sleep.

It must have been early in the morning, judging by the way he felt when a sound from the tabletop awakened him. It was the sound of somebody opening the door to the room. He looked toward the door as he was scrambling to rise, but it was not moving.

He turned around quickly and saw the image of a man of the Species wearing a red robe opening the door into the room. The man was very fat, and he moved awkwardly as he squeezed through the doorway. He went over to the corner of the room formed by the two large windows. The point of view was now above and behind the man, so Lucky had difficulty making out exactly what he was doing. After a moment, a doorway hidden on the far wall slid open. The man walked over to the door and poked his head inside. "Ugh," he spat, "that is disgusting! Get back in there you piece of shit!"

With that, he kicked at something in the doorframe. There was a damp smack, and then the door shut.

The recording went back to a blank screen. Lucky went to the window and felt around the corner at the top. His finger pad rubbed over a slight metal edge. He got his fingernail underneath and opened a small tab. It snapped into place, and as it did, he heard a click from each door.

The hidden door in the wall retracted and slid to the side. Lucky ran over to the door at the entrance and pulled on the handle. It opened. Behind him, he heard swirling water and a series of slaps on the floor.

He looked behind him and saw one small figure standing in front of the chair and table, dripping a fishy-smelling liquid on the floor as it struggled to breathe. A light from below illuminated the opening in the far wall. Two more figures like the one standing before him struggled to exit the doorway from a pool of liquid filling the shaft below.

Lucky dashed through the door and tried to block the small creature's exit, but it was too close behind him. If he struggled, the others would be on

him before he could shut the door. He chose to slam the door shut. To his relief, it locked. He turned towards the single escapee from the vault.

It looked like a child-sized member of the Species. However, it lacked the Species' distinctive features, the filaments and tissue flaps covering the chest and abdomen. Its skin was bare and frightfully thin, like a premature baby's. It stood still in front of him, looking at him but not seeing him.

Lucky puzzled over the hostile impression he got from the creature. Within a few minutes, he had an epiphany. it came from the creature's eye movements. It didn't try to read the emotions in his shifting facial expression. It saw no meaning there. The stragglers pounded on the door. Lucky waved his hand in front of its face, and it turned its head in response to the movement.

The clamor on the other side of the door faded over the next ten minutes. Lucky sat watching the creature all the while.

"What the hell am I supposed to do with you?" Lucky asked. It turned to face him and said, "No."

"Yeah, that's what I thought.," "said Lucky.

Lucky opened the next door and held it for his new responsibility. It did not move until he stepped back inside and took its hand.

"Takezo is going to have a field day with this," Lucky complained.

On his way through the ground-floor physical plant, Lucky stopped by the office adjacent to the boiler. He took a clean coverall from the coat hook on the back wall and a respirator mask from the desk drawer for his companion. The coveralls fit better than Lucky expected once he managed to get all four cuffs rolled up. Lucky moved cautiously along the loading dock. When they got to the door leading to the outside stairs, Lucky paused. He looked over the makeshift disguise.

"Well, my friend, let's hope nobody gets too close. OK, Casper, time to make

like a ghost, and maybe we can get you back to my room unseen."

Twenty-three

Afflicted

Laplace, Francis, and the Mother sat at the bar.

"Get Francis a drink," Laplace said to the bartender, "but make it something mild. He's earned it, but none of us have earned it completely, and he will need to remain as sharp as possible."

The bartender looked confused as he examined Francis's pressure suit helmet.

"Look," said Laplace, "you have the reservoirs over here on the left." He pointed out a couple of canisters that fit into the neck of the helmet. "Francis," Laplace asked, "how loyal was the officer corps to Danilo? Did he rule them by fear, incentives, promises, or virtue? Were you able to pick up much during your time with them?"

"I'm sorry," Francis replied. It's not that I was inattentive; I just didn't know that I needed to be spying at the time."

"Understood," said Laplace, "you will have to wear the pressure suit until I get better arrangements set up. Those arrangements will be elsewhere, as we are not safe here now. The situation is contained, but that is all."

"You have no idea," Laplace asked the Mother," how Augustine got into the center? Everyone is still at risk as long as that knowledge remains at large. It must be traced to root and branch and expunged. Otherwise, anyone else with a personal grievance can resort to the same method."

"We assume that he came by it through the Authority," the "Mother said, "his clan is burrowed deep in that organization. They also have the necessary connections within the Foundation. If they have identified a betrayer there, I don't see how the status quo can be restored.

We will never know whether that critical information could be leaked again or whether someone has it locked in their vault as insurance. I fear that the developmental centers will all need to be destroyed and then restored by slave labor or volunteers. When construction is complete, everyone involved must be eliminated. I'm not sure that the Species is up to that anymore."

"My main concern," she said, turning to look directly at Laplace, "is for Francis' well-being. What is to become of him? Have you called for a medical assessment?"

"Of course," Laplace said, "they took samples and assessed his current status before they packed him into that souvenir spacesuit."

"The virus is more sophisticated than I first suspected," said Laplace. "The designers took advantage of differences between the two genomes to induce limited guided evolution. Although you favor the hypothesis that Augustine concocted the whole scheme, I'd say there must have been someone else involved. Certainly, Danilo is - sorry -

was smart enough to come up with this supplemental deviation, but I did not think he had the resources to make it work. If we leave this thing to replicate, it will eventually lose the mutations

restricting its pathogenesis to people with my family's genetic markers. Combined with the problem you identified regarding the developmental centers, that will end the Species."

"So that means," Francis said slowly, "you're going to kill me."

"If I were smart," Laplace said, "and cautious, that's exactly what I would do. If I were going to do that, I would have already. I'm smart, but I'm not cautious. I don't want to just get out of this with my skin intact; I want to win. So, I'm not going to kill you.

"Besides, I don't owe a damn thing to the Species. End up hating about half of them. Anyway, we're off to join my brother at the Center of Excellence. It's a defensible space, and besides, he has access to the services of a virologist and some equipment that will speed up the process of emancipation."

Twenty-four

Danilo, and Danilo, and Danilo

"Who is in charge here?" Danilo said to Danilo.

They stood face to face in a rear command post. The two Danilos were indistinguishable except for a missing ear on the part of the Danilo at the door. He gave Danilo a light headbutt.

"It is no longer the Danilo who navigated the dendritic event radiation; Laplace destroyed him, and in the process, his unique nachinak. We could have funded Armageddon if you defectives had just listened to me!" Danilo said.

"You generic mother fucker! Come back to speak with me when you've done something," said Danilo one ear "Meanwhile, shut up because I'm coming to you now, before you have the chance to do something incredibly stupid! Do you know what's happening with the females?"

Danilo paused momentarily, then answered, "Of course, I know what is happening with them. And I am getting ready to do something about it. But as a good tactician, unlike certain other people in this room whose names I shall not mention, I am trying to stabilize existing encounters before adding a new one to our list of problems. The females can wait."

"Look," Danilo One Ear said, "I have information that…"

"No!" The unblemished Danilo said, "Laplace and the rest of them, they are killing our future! Soon, it won't matter how many of these skirmishes we win. Our dominance will be questionable. We cannot have that. Do you think that any of us, in the end, could tolerate such an injustice? Or do you really believe Laplace? That's it, isn't it!

"You think he picked us out of that basement, that filthy, stinking, verminous, cozy, happy basement, because we were special. He picked us because we were the easiest to catch. We were the easiest to subdue. He took one look at us and knew that nobody gave a shit about us so nobody would give him any trouble if he took us and did as he pleased."

"But..." One Ear began again.

"But," the unblemished Danilo cut him off, "that is the same injustice, if not worse, than the one that drove us to this extreme. We thought we were the lowest kind of person when he took us. We had no idea what it meant to be nothing. We didn't understand the immense gap between low and nothing. But he taught us, didn't he?

"He always insisted that one could only truly learn through experience and example. When he "lost" us in the nameless city, he knew those monsters were waiting for us. He knew which abomination merited banishment to that place. Everyone knows what happened when they caught us. None of us would tell, not in a million years, because they knew what all the rest of us would do if they squealed.

"We won't let this go. We can't let this go. He taught us that we were worthless by making us worthless, and the only way to know if it is true or not, to know for sure that we did not somehow deserve this, not even one speck of it, is to do what we planned.

"If we cannot do this, there is no hope of becoming something other than what we are. We must expurgate as much of the universe as we can reach. We will burn Laplace, the old races, new civilizations, all of it, and after the bodies are turned to ashes, we will wipe every last memory of them from existence."

"Yes," One Ear said, "that is the plan, but you don't understand, you idiot!"

"Yes, I do!" The unblemished Danilo said, "They are killing their infants. It's too damn late. There are already too many of us. We can always make more, too, as long as conditions are better controlled."

"Holy shit!" said Danilo One Ear as he smashed unblemished Danilo to the ground with a single punch. "They are killing themselves! First, they kill the baby, and then they kill themselves. It is blowing up like a forest fire. If you stand here and bitch about justice for 10 more minutes, they should just about be done."

Danilo stared at Danilo and blinked.

163

TWENTY-FOUR

"I have ordered all the off-planet harems into lockdown with strict communications quarantine," said Danilo One Ear. "That won't last, but it may be enough."

Twenty-five

Eau de War

Augustine laid a cold stare on Dion until the cashier put down his cup and stared back over the top of his magazine.

"Well," Augustine said, "show me what you got on him."

"Hold on, hold on," the human replied, "I figured I would just give him enough time to get down the road a ways so if he changed his mind about buying a pack of gum or some such thing we wouldn't have to suffer the embarrassment of being caught analyzing his bodily fluids."

"Right. Now cough it up," said Augustine.

Dion reached down and pushed a button hidden under the counter's lip. The 3D projector in front of Augustine flickered, and he smiled.

"Excellent," Augustine said, "The levels are perfect. He should be ready for the implant any day now. What about the other one? Any progress?"

"I am perplexed by that situation," Dion said. "It doesn't seem that we missed anything, but the implant didn't take. We compensated for differences in metabolism between humans and the Species. We picked

the right subtype of subjugation nachinak for his personality. His identity as the subjugation nachinak sees it has a lot fewer subvening elements than a normal person's, but that should make the nachinak's job easier. It's possible that we got bumped.."

"By what person?" Augustine asked in exasperation, "he's almost impossible to spot, much less follow."

"I don't know," Dion said, "but I think our other ghost would be a prime suspect."

"No, I got her under a microscope," said Augustine. "It must be one of the others associated with the Center of Excellence. I will go over there and see what I can shake loose. Put someone on him dedicated. Find out what's going on. If we have been bumped, I want that subjugation unit back."

"Sure thing, Mr. Authority," said Dion.

"If you see Thomas before I do, tell him where I've gone," said Augustine.

It was late afternoon when Lucky got back to the house. He had stayed off the roads and trails between the center of excellence and the small hanging valley where Takezo's workshop stood. He stood just before the trail junction for a long time. The workshop was silent, but an occasional

wisp of conversation brushed his ear from the far side of the little villa.

Hugging the tree line, he walked quickly and silently along the path to the house. The conversation became more intelligible with each step as he entered the little courtyard. One voice belonged to Takezo, but the other was likely a woman's voice, judging by its register, and one that he did not recognize. He would have to get closer if he wanted to make out the words clearly. The brushy slope behind the domicile was out. The front of the building was too exposed. The roof was all that remained.

He tried to jump or belly flop onto the eaves but couldn't manage to swing his leg over the edge. He had better luck with the corner. By applying maximal counter pressure with his hands, he could flex his hip and catch his knee on the edge of a tile. He was up. He weighted the roofing tiles cautiously.

Fortunately, they were primarily decorative, so they bore his weight and remained in place as he climbed. He peeked over the ridge of the roof. Takezo sat on a bench by the rose garden, speaking with none other than Lucky's acquaintance from the brush pile.

Takezo enjoyed a lollipop during the conversation. When it was his turn to speak, he removed it from his mouth and used it as a swagger stick, gesticulating with it to make his points.

"You have chosen the path of solitude, yet you still harbor ill will. You do not prepare yourself to endure your memories or cast aside your desire for justice. I give you six months until something snaps. Then you are back in this game despite yourself. Then you are dead," Takezo said

"I will not leave the game until it is won. Isolation is the price of victory, "the woman said.

"You cannot win," Takezo said. "If you kill this Laplace, do you think the others will leave you alone? Especially if they guess what you have wielded against him."

"No. They know well enough to avoid my weapon. It has a name in legend," she said.

"You think so?" Takezo said. 'Carnivorous animals don't give up on marked prey. They appear to abandon the hunt but circle back as soon as the brush obscures them, and stalking resumes."

She turned her head away abruptly.

"I see that you are committed to this foolishness. So be it.

I will still help you where I can," Takezo said." I will renege on my promise, though, if you do not tell him the truth before you embark on this hopeless war."

Lucky scrambled back down the roof and let himself drop to the ground as quietly as possible. He turned the corner to the left, out of the courtyard, and directly to the forbidden apartment's door. He tried the knob, and to his surprise, it opened. The room inside was a carbon copy of his own. He ignored the contents, grabbed a chair, and set it squarely in the middle of the floor, facing the door.

He crossed his arms over his chest, straightened his back, and mustered up the best scowl he could manage. He waited. His back began to ache slightly from maintaining good posture. His facial muscles started to ache as well. He was just about to stand up to stretch his legs when the door opened.

His dead acquaintance from the Kiva stood stiffly in the doorway. She was quiet for a moment before speaking.

"Come to the table in the courtyard," she said, "I will explain everything. Takezo has made food and that horrible rice wine."

Twenty-six

A Simple Procedure

"Are you telling me," Augustine asked incredulously, "that I am a prisoner?" The slave shook her head.

"Perish the thought," she said, "because of recent safety concerns, including several serious breaches of the facility, we are encouraging visitors, including our partners in scientific research, to limit their activities, and to travel within the facility or without, in the company of armed security provided by the Center of Excellence."

Augustine stood in the doorway leading from the Node 8 access point, with its lockers lining the curved wall of the building and its ballroom filled with spherical wire cages, where ancient machinery created the folds and their associated exclusion spheres. The slave stood firm.

"Those are the directives. I have no authority to modify them or make exceptions. If you wish," she said, "I can summon our director to discuss your concerns. Please be advised that if you arrange such a meeting, it is still quite likely that nothing will change.

"Great," said Augustine, "that director is still the murdering scumbag who calls himself Gerard?"

"Though I would never refer to the director in those terms," the slave said, "given the context and source of the question, I believe that we reference the same individual."

"Well, now that we are clear on the subject of this conversation," said Augustine, "I should very much like to see that scumbag, Gerard. I am here on business from the Authority. Be sure that you communicate that to him. You may also tell him that some of that business involves him directly."

"I will do so," said the slave, and with a curt bow, she left. Augustine stepped into the hallway and shouted at her back,

"Tell him to hurry up. I have other things to do. I will be in the lounge. And bring me those records I requested."

He spat on the floor. When her footsteps were no longer audible in the echoing metal chamber, he turned around and headed in the opposite direction. As he walked the gentle curve of the hallway, he heard snippets of calming music. The tunes grew louder, and soon, he came upon their source.

The lounge had an oval-shaped entryway almost as long as the bar and dining area combined. On the opposite side of the room from the bar stood a small bandstand, occupied by four musicians: strings, percussion, woodwind, and brass. There were two other people in the room.

Augustine recognized one of them as a well-known up-and-comer. He already had an extensive file with the Authority. He had not done anything indicative of sociopathy, however, so the Authority simply monitored him. Augustine did not recognize the other person. Nothing about the unidentified individual suggested that he was anything but a middle-class worker, likely involved with some ancillary aspect of the node's activity.

It was not unusual to see that class of person in the lounge at any of the nodes.

The facilities were generally self-sustaining by design. They never required a technician or maintenance person on a continuing basis, so the workers were involved in scheduling, promotion, and logistics. They fit the profile of typical lounge-goers across the universe. Their jobs were complicated but superfluous. Most of the workers identified with their jobs, even though, deep down, they knew those jobs were meaningless.

They felt an irresistible attraction to the lounge, where they could purchase liquid affirmation while watching others drown their petty sorrows.

The room was dim; the lights favored the lower frequencies of the spectrum. Augustine took a table in the corner next to the bar. He motioned to the bartender that he needed service immediately. Once he had his cocktail and a snack, his wellspring of patience quickly ran dry. He made it through about one-third of the drink before he summoned the bartender again. "Hey, do you know that slave who dumped me here?" Augustine asked, "You must, come to think of it. Anyone working in this kind of shithole is going to need a couple of drinks after work if they weren't able to load up at lunch. And judging by the quality of the service and the liquor, it would seem that there are precious few alternatives to your establishment," Augustine leaned closer to the bartender and added in a conspiratorial tone, "I'd bet you could help me a lot, given all the tales of woe and discontent that you must hear from the pathetic drunks who wash up at your bar.

"Tell you what, why don't you round up that slave for me, and her director, and my files? You look like you could manage that, and without leaving the bar. That way, we can use the time I'm left waiting here to discuss the future of our new relationship."

The bartender nodded to Augustine, turned around, and made. himself busy behind the bar. Within ten minutes, he set off to the bandstand with a loaded tray of drinks.

The band cut its set short when the refreshments arrived. The drummer

and the string player excused themselves, presumably to go to the restroom, though they walked away from the bandstand in opposite directions. On his way back to Augustine's table, the bartender stopped to check on his other patrons.

The semi-famous calculator ordered another drink. The worker stood while his payment was processed, then strode past the bar and down the right-hand hallway. Within a minute, Gerard appeared from the same direction, leaving the bartender without enough time to finish bussing the dirty table. Gerard did not acknowledge Augustine's presence. Instead, he went behind the bar and helped himself to a glass of top-shelf liqueur.

"Efficiency, "Augustine said, "is an underrated virtue."

"Yes, indeed," Gerard said as he threw the other half

of his drink in the garbage, "So, you cannot tour the facility unchaperoned. No exceptions, per the recent reaffirmation of the Guidance Counsel. I have looked over your list of documents. All of them are mine and of little interest to someone like yourself. Besides, illustrative demonstration is an underappreciated mode of communication. I hope I have made myself understood today."

"Oh, I think I get the message," Augustine said, "I'm just ignoring it because the Council has some interim guidance. They have banned all surgical procedures involving patients who are incapable of consenting for themselves. They issued the revised statement in response to reports of pediatric patients undergoing surgical procedures at facilities that are not licensed for pediatric care. These reports involve several of the newly debuted Species from a developmental center and infants of

other Species. Two of those reports specifically named the Bilateral Nephrectomy Center of Excellence."

"The care we provide here is for adults only," said Gerard. "This is also a research facility, so the care we provide is experimental and subject to an institutional review board in every case."

"Well then, give me the records to prove it," Augustine said. I want to know what's going on here. It appears you have something cooking with a couple of other centers of excellence. I see numerous voucher transfers without valid receipts or authorized recipients.

Unless you have something else to show me that contradicts my natural assumption that this whole thing is a scam aimed at defrauding the Authority and its associated banking and investing institutions, I'm going to have to ask you to halt operations here or begin paying a 30% penalty on disbursements to the named centers of excellence."

"Thank you for your devotion to efficiency. I thought we were going to have to wait quite a bit longer for the truth," said Gerard, "you won't be getting any money from us. At least, the way things stand currently. The state of affairs could change in your favor, however.

I don't like you. I have never liked you, not from the moment I saw your disgusting form squeezed from a fold. Since that day when you dropped by to tell me that you were taking over jurisdiction for your predecessor after his tragic, sudden cardiac arrest, every interaction I've had with you has just confirmed my first impression that you were a vicious simpleton with a savant talent for corruption."

Our mission here, however, is of such critical importance that I cannot indulge my own prejudices or aesthetic principles at the mission's expense."

With that, Gerard turned to the bartender. "Lock it down," said Gerard.

The bartender flipped open a panel underneath the bar and tapped several buttons on a keypad. The lights dimmed further. A slot hidden in the joint between metal plates forming the corridor wall slid open on either end of the lounge. Eight nachinak issued from each slot, unfurling a wispy sheet of defensive spiderweb behind them.

Augustine jumped to his feet, knocking the chair over behind him. Six nachinaks dropped from the hem of his cassock. They took positions, forming a truncated circle from the floor over the top of Augustine's head. One more device appeared from the collar of Augustine's robe.

It was a large type with clear nodules sprouting from its back and sides. As it rose to its position immediately in front of Augustine, its legs flexed, shattering the nodules into thousands of slender shards, which began to swirl around the device.

"My what memories that arouses," said Gerard, "I had one of those once upon a time. I loved it. It will be unnecessary this evening. If you would come around the bar and follow me, preferably without breaking anything during your passage."

Augustine slipped his right hand into his left sleeve. The devices surrounding him gradually descended to resume their previous hiding places on his person. As the offensive unit pulled back, the crystal shards returned to their nodular conformation.

Augustine kicked the chair out of his way and waddled around the end of the bar. Gerard, meanwhile, opened the stockroom door and proceeded through it without waiting for Augustine. Augustine strolled across the bar mats, brushing several bottles of wine from the shelf as he went, knocking them to the floor where they miraculously landed just to the side of the mats and shattered. The large stockroom offered no plausible opportunities for accidental contact with breakables. Gerard

173

opened the door at the far end and could be heard directing a slave to bring up presentation videos and documents. By the time Augustine reached the doorway at the end of the short hallway beyond the stockroom, Gerard was the only one left in the meeting room. The hallway continued to Augustine's left and turned another corner.

Augustine could hear a door close behind him as he entered the meeting room. Gerard sat against the wall across a steel table with places for twelve. A projector poked through a hole in the middle of the table.

"Take a seat where you please," said Gerard.

"It would please me," said Augustine, "to sit where you are sitting." Gerard stood and walked to the far end of the table. He remained standing

191

and gestured for Augustine to occupy the vacant chair. Augustine lowered himself onto the seat, watching Gerard suspiciously. Gerard burrowed a finger under the tuft of filaments on his left upper chest. A heavy door slid down from a pocket in the ceiling of the short hallway outside the room. Augustine did not blink.

"This is the test, isn't it?" Gerard said, "What happens when it's just the two of us?"

"Enough charades," said Augustine," let's keep this efficient, shall we? Pitch me what you got, or let's see what else you got."

With a movement from the filaments in the same area of Gerard's left chest, the projector came online with an image of a presentation cover page.

The page read: A Modest Proposal, Dreaming of the Last Great Challenge in Medicine.

"At the end of the trial, two universal tissue donor debacle," Gerard said, "we were drifting. We had no

purpose or direction, but we still possessed substantial resources and a gathering of talent and expertise rarely matched in the modern history of medical science.

Although I believe that the circumstances provided a suitable environment for the events that followed to take root, it was not money, wisdom, or the ponderous force of the scientific method that produced the first sprout. It was Revelation. Revelation gave us the wherewithal to reassess our goals completely.

"Revelation allowed us to change our direction.

"I had a dream, you see. It was a dream of nothing. At the beginning of the dream, I was aware of myself. Then, in the dream, I slept. I lost my self-awareness, but in the last moment before my consciousness collapsed into nonexistence, I held onto the reassuring certainty that this was sleep. I had experienced this moment and what followed thousands and thousands of times. It was the most certain thing in my life.

I did not merely wake from the dream sleep into normal wakefulness. I woke to the continuation of my dream. Instead of feeling refreshed and awake, I suffered a profound weariness. I knew that I felt the weariness preceding death.

Again, I began to lose consciousness. But in the moment before I ceased to exist, I knew that this time was not like any of the times before. I knew that this time, I would not return to dreams or anything else. I would not be. All would be made naught with the next inevitable tick of the clock.

I would have traded anything to hold onto that moment before the tick. But there was nothing that could accept my payment and nothing to trade for that one more moment. I woke. Ever since I woke, I have lived in fear of that moment before nothing. I've come to understand what my dream meant. It was the last and most vicious malady: the burden of consciousness.

"Every conscious creature lives
at all times under the threat of that moment. They don't fear annihilation; they fear confrontation with the moment before nothingness. It holds their heads in its grasp, pries open their eyes and forces them to see how foolish all their hopes have been, as they watch the contents of their lives crushed out of existence in the singularity just before it consumes them as well."

"That's heartwarming," said Augustine, "but you are not giving me much to work with. I like how Revelation sounds as much as the next person does. I'm not devoting any time, money, or other resources to somebody else's 'Revelation.'"

"Never fear," said Gerard, wagging his finger," You will not be asked to do so. You need to understand the magnitude of the discovery as thoroughly as you can."

"Got it," said Augustine, "get on with the rest of it."

"When I truly woke the next morning, I had a mission. I gathered all pertinent literature available to me. I began to comb through it for any evidence that my predecessors had recognized this problem and, if so, what they might have done about it. Of course, it turned out that some had considered it. A handful of those who had considered it had

also investigated the pathophysiology of the affliction. They immediately recognized the same thing I had:, it isn't the fact of the matter that causes the disease; it is how people feel about it that causes the disease. The enlightened few worked feverishly to discover the nature of those feelings and their correlations. They devised Neurosurgical approaches to map out the pathways involved.

"They found that the prodrome was lifelong. The afflicted organisms experienced changes in identity, including loss of function, inescapable pain, helplessness, and psychological

instability. The suffering born of uncertainty that accompanied

their instability imprinted itself on the brain, as well as on parts of the peripheral nervous system and even the metabolism."

The resulting pathological structure altered psychology. An ideal, healthy individual's world contains key concepts such as distributed individual identity and restricted autonomy. The psyche needs those concepts lest it suffer runaway anticipatory planning. "

"Yeah," said Augustine as he rose to leave, "this is very amusing, but I don't think I'll play along anymore."

"Please, please!" Gerard said, "Give me 15 more seconds and then decide." Augustine reluctantly sat back down.

"We fixed it," said Gerard. "You see, once a creature is locked onto a fixed identity because it anticipates a catastrophe as the endpoint of change, it cannot deliver itself from the affliction. That has been the problem with every approach to a cure so far. Psychologists reason with their patients. Theologians offer an alternative narrative. Psychiatrists cool the overloaded circuitry with chemicals. All the therapies treat the outcome of the neuropsychological dysfunction but leave the derangement itself intact. Our method excises and replaces the diseased organ with a functional one."

"So what?" Augustine said, "What is this supposed to sway me to do? It sounds like you have figured out a way to fix something in people's heads that they may not want fixed and may not even think is a problem in the first place – "

"Wait," Gerard interjected, "they will give you the answer themselves."

Gerard scrolled through the presentation, almost to the very end. As the recording played again, the camera panned across

the

large plaza in front of the hospital at the Bilateral Nephrectomy Center of Excellence. Three members of the Species, two of whom bore the stigmata of the upper echelon, and one who looked middle class stood in front of a restless crowd. Gerard addressed the three in front from somewhere off-camera.

"We will get to that directly," said Gerard. "First, you must explain yourselves so that others may understand why we are asking for support for this endeavor. Who wants to go first?"

"I will," said the middle-class man, stepping forward. "I am Henry, and I was one of the first participants in the study. I was pretty hesitant when I signed up. I did not like the idea that I would be consenting to something without any prior explanation of the procedures involved. The orientation booklet didn't even lay out the purpose of the experiment. All I knew was that it promised to make me feel better in the end."

Once it was all over, I understood why the methods had remained secret and the endpoint had been vague. I understood that, without the gift I received from the treatment, I would not have been capable of informed consent. Like the rest of the participants, I wouldn't have believed I had the problem stated in the study's abstract. Now I understand, though."

Everything that weighed me down throughout my life originated from that single defect. I no longer harbor bitterness about my social standing. I no longer think about my old insecurities."

I don't covet goods or experiences, so I no longer suffer from jealousy. I also don't feel anxious about what may happen or about what I may have

done differently in the past.

"My friends and clan members have witnessed my transformation. That is why they're here with me today, asking that you move this procedure out of the experimental phase and make it

available to all."

"I share Henry's sentiments," said the younger of the two aristocrats. "I am Venita. Before the treatment, I was troubled by the same worries as Henry's. I spent much of my time feeling anxious, angry, fearful, and depressed. Like all of us, I aspired to complete a calculation. I was consumed by the desire to succeed. I was terrified of failure. I was terrified of the gray space and my rivals."

All those entanglements had their roots in the diseased circuitry of my brain. Once that was repaired, I was free. I no longer felt those awful things that had troubled my past. I also feel that this procedure is so monumentally beneficial that it should not be kept from the world a moment longer. Please, consider opening the protocol to the public as soon as possible."

The last of the spokespersons stepped forward.

"My name is Dennis," said the man, "and I would agree with what my two friends have said already. I will add that the effects of the procedure go beyond the good it does to the patients themselves. It affects all the people in the patient's life as well."

Before I underwent treatment, I was frequently in conflict with those around me. I spent much of my day tallying up my grievances. At night, I would dwell on the injustices I had suffered."

I had two groups of people in my life. The first was the group whose thoughts and opinions of me were an ongoing source of anxiety, feelings of inadequacy, and disappointment. Those were my friends."

The other group consisted of people I was suspicious of, envious of, and disdainful towards. Those were my adversaries. Now, I see all the nuances that I had missed before. I do not suffer from the imagined slights and judgments of others. I am free in a way I had not imagined possible before

the procedure. Please make this treatment available to the public as soon as possible."

The crowd roared its approval. Gerard switched off the presentation. "Now do you see what I mean?" asked Gerard. "You understand the

significance of this discovery? In effect, I have completed the calculation. Utopia is at hand."

It was always foolish of us to think we could establish a perfectly harmonious society through direct intervention in the causal chain of events. If we truly accept determinism, it simply can't be so. Utopia does not reside in its political, economic, philosophical, or aesthetic components. Utopia resides in its people. There is the fulcrum we may use to shift the fraternity of conscious beings into the ideal state of affairs."

Augustine rubbed his forehead. He sat silent for several minutes while Gerard waited.

"Why me? I keep coming back to that question. Why are you talking to me about this? Do you expect to convince me to bankroll this? Even if I had the inclination, I don't see how I could convince anyone to give you money. Everybody knows that I hate you, you poisonous degenerate."

"Precisely," Gerard said, slapping his fist against his open palm, "if I can convince you, despite our mutual antipathy, how can potential patrons discount the significance of this work?"

"Uh-huh. You've got partnerships listed on your cover page: the Center of Excellence for Neurosurgical Reconstruction of the Septal Vellum, Center of Excellence in Pursuit of Surgical Innovation in the Use of Biomechanical Adjuncts to the Functional

Capacity of Intelligent and Semi-Intelligent Persons and the Quantitative Happiness Project," Augustine said, narrowing his eyes, "just what is it, exactly, that you are doing here?"

"I don't think I understand what you're getting at," Gerard said. "Are you ask-

179

ing for details of the procedures? As you've implied, our techniques were years in development and span multiple medical specialties. The protocols are extensive and likely beyond even a well-informed layman's comprehension."

"Try me," Augustine insisted.

"Very well. You were forewarned," Gerard said

"The treatment has two phases, one psychological and one neurosurgical. We repair the pain/pleasure perceptual imbalance first. The Center of Excellence for Neurosurgical Reconstruction of the Septal Vellum, Supplied us with an electrode and diagnostic equipment to deliver pleasant stimuli directly to the pleasure mediating neurons in the vellum. We provided noxious stimuli through direct use of electrodes in the thalamus and surgical stimuli. With balance restored, we employed microsurgical techniques to maintain system stability while conditioning the patient's response to the malady of consciousness."

"Back up a minute," asked Augustine, "what do you mean by surgically induced stimuli?"

"Stimuli delivered by surgical means, calculated to match the opposing stimuli administered through the probe in the pleasure centers of the brain as closely as possible," Gerard said.

"Like what?" Augustine asked.

"A simple procedure derived from antiquated skin graft harvesting techniques, "said Gerard.

Augustine sat back in his chair and pointed a finger at Gerard. "You mean that you skinned them alive, you tortured people" Augustine said.

"That is completely off base," said Gerard, in a calm tone with a hint of smugness. "You heard the testimony of the subject named Henry. What he said is absolutely the truth. We went through the motions of obtaining consent before carrying out procedures on all subjects in the program, but none of them could give consent

due to a qualitative gap in their understanding, which could only be corrected by successfully completing the treatment.

Augustine spluttered.

"You needn't worry about the ethics of all this," Gerard said. "The brain

180

learns without the assistance of consciousness and conscious memory. They were not under anesthesia for any of the procedures. However, they were sedated with a medication that erases the conscious memory of experiences that occur while under its influence.

We corrected the circuitry during the procedures, and then, from their perspective, the subjects simply woke up from a refreshing nap. It was as if nothing at all had happened."

"Very tidy," said Augustine, "and perfectly innocent."

"Quite, "Gerard said.

"Until one adds a little context, "Augustine said, as he withdrew a small projector from a pocket in his cassock and laid it on the table.

Augustine activated the viewer and watched Gerard's face with satisfaction. An image flickered into existence above the conference table. It depicted a small room with a central desk and a single chair lying on its side. A voice spoke from behind the camera's field of view.

"Of course, I didn't ask your leave to do the procedure. What permission does art require?" asked Gerard's voice, "If I had, the beauty of Michael's insight would have been lost. Both his description of the experience he had with my knife and the paralytic without the veil of anesthesia and my interpretation for him and posterity, of the beauty, all the sensuous joy in the experience, unobscured by the filters of an erroneous morality supported by a culture whose only need is false reassurance that it is not dying."

Augustine left the recording playing on a loop.

"Do you think I am stupid, or is it possible that you have come to believe your own lie?" Augustine said, "You are no humanitarian. You are a sick individual. You are a psychopath, a sadist, and a murderer. "

"Back to the same old meaningless recriminations," Gerard said, "If I did enjoy the procedures, then I was the only person who was affected. I challenge you to bring this up before the council or whatever ad hoc gathering of peers you may choose to carry out the day's petty, bullying persecution.

You may bring this record of your voyeuristic perversion, and I will bring my

181

neurosurgeons, my anesthesiologists, and my patients' testimonials. Take your time. I eagerly await your response. "

"Oh no! Oh, hell no!" Augustine said," With all I've got on you, you are even worse off than I imagined, to think that I would leave here today without you chained to my abacus, whether on foot, in a cage, or in a bucket!"

"What do you think you have on me – reports of an ethicist AWOL? You should strive to balance efficiency with rigor in your research, agent of the Authority. It turns out that even ethicists sometimes suffer from ethical deficiencies." said Gerard.

"We will find the body," Augustine said, "we
always do."

A crease formed in the air beside Augustine, and he deftly slipped into it as he swiped the projector from the table in a single movement.

Twenty-seven

What Do You Know, Danilo?

Coincident with Augustine's departure, more fissures split the conference room, too many for the space to contain.

Where the folds crossed, parts of bodies spilled forth with the bits rapidly dissolving into red mist. Neither the living nor the dead were members of the Species; they were Danilo's troops. Those who survived deployment came under crossfire from the string player, positioned in the stockroom, and the bar fly, who stood at the hallway junction.

Both utilized a weapon commonly encountered during misguided attempts on nodes, roosts, and other high-value, urban, indoor objectives. It resembled a backpack vacuum, and on the inside, it carried an array of coils, sensors, and charge mapping processors, all of which tapped into the Species' power system. They turned every surface in range into a potential origin for a fatal arc. Despite their superior numbers, Danilo's followers were doomed.

Great, writhing sparks jumped at them from the floor, walls, and ceiling.

Thick smoke, smelling of burnt hair and ozone, quickly filled the rooms and corridors adjacent to the conference room. The

small furry soldiers rapidly suffered a total disciplinary collapse. On two occasions, Gerard's personal defense system caught otherwise fatal volleys of bullets from a particularly determined squad of Danilo's soldiers that managed to push the musician out of the stockroom. However, just as they seemed to be gaining momentum, one of the squad members covering the rear inexplicably turned on the squad leader and shot him in the back.

The rest of the squad escaped into the event radiation moments later. Suddenly, the conference room was silent. Gerard shut down his defense system, brushed off the chair at the head of the table, and took a seat. The building's climate control caught up with the rancid vapors left over from the skirmish. Gerard looked up at the sound of the stockroom door opening and closing. The musician began his report as he entered the conference room.

"Drusilla gave the all-clear, boss," he said, propping his weapon against the wall by the doorway. They were poorly disciplined. As soon as they realized they would not overrun us, it was every man for himself.

"I am afraid that it was more than just inadequate training that contributed to the chaos you observed. Do we have prisoners?" Gerard asked.

"Only four, "the barfly admitted. "It was a real struggle to keep a couple of accidental weapon discharges from wiping out the lot of them."

"Not to worry," Gerard said," four is plenty."

Laplace observed the technician tinkering with the subjugation nachinak in Francis' leg. He worked as smoothly within the confines of the sterile field as he did with both hands outside it. Francis showed no discomfort, either from the scraping and probing about the mechanism embedded in his upper calf or from the hostile attention of the four Danilos

under armed guard

just across the room. Laplace came a step closer and looked over the technician's shoulder as he worked.

"What do you think?" Laplace asked, "Is there anything referring to genetics in the programming of the subjugation unit?"

"I can't see anything," the technician said, "as you know better than any of us, the hardwired stuff in these units is very difficult to interrogate completely. I can't guarantee that there is nothing in there waiting to bite. However, the same things that make them difficult to interrogate also make them difficult to modify. The good thing, from Francis's perspective, is that most of the failed modifications result in a failure of the entire unit as well. I know every reported incident of a successful modification and the details of each one as well. This subjugation unit is free of all known modifications."

Laplace turned to observe the Danilos. He could not distinguish one from the other; even their mannerisms were identical.

"Which one of you is Danilo?" Laplace asked. "I am Danilo," said the Danilo on the left end. "I am Danilo," said the Danilo on the right end. "I am Danilo," said the left–middle Danilo. "I am Danilo," said the right–middle Danilo.

Laplace lifted his hat from his head to wipe away the sweat from his brow. He paced back and forth before the assembled Danilos for a few passes.

"What has become of all the females of your Species?" Laplace asked. "You must know that your traditional treatment of the other gender was a central factor in your enslavement. I felt that your cultural background had prepared you adequately to accept our tradition.

Though it seems I have failed in my role as your master for the most part, I still feel quite certain that the training you received was at least technically sound. I know you must have at least two more fallback plans. Will you tell me what they are, or must I elicit them?"

The four Danilos met his request with sullen stares.

"I will ask a different way," said Laplace. "There is a familiar story about a boat that sailed across many seas. I told this several times in the course of

Danilo's education. It was a utilitarian vessel, designed for trade, and had no name to begin with, or at least no name anyone remembered. The routes it plied were difficult, and not many ships survived the passage for a single round, but this ship managed the entire course thrice.

The accomplishment attracted the attention of wealthy merchants, expert sailors, and adventurers, who became the crew and sponsors of the vessel. It soon set forth again and made another successful round, and another, and another. Each passage was a feat in and of itself, and the ship never came through completely unscathed.

Carpenters and outfitters in ports along the way repaired a plank here and a mast there until no original piece of the ship remained. However, at each point, the repairmen took exquisite care to craft replacement parts true to the originals, down to the most minute detail.

By now, people had given the ship a name: the Ship of Renown. It had become so famous, in fact, that its admirers began to commission exact replicas of the ship of renown to sail the trade routes beside the original. Some philosophers puzzled over the identity of the Ship of Renown.

It had been thoroughly replaced in all of its parts over time. Was it still the same ship? At first, there seemed to be an answer to that question. It would have been more straightforward if you had just asked the question of the

irreducible constituents. Is this carbon atom identical to that carbon atom?

Superficially, they are the same, but each carries a distinctive history and context that gives it an identity. So, the story of the ship was not over.

In every detail, down to the number of atoms per plank, Replicas of the Ship set sail from shipyards in every port of call for the original. Soon enough, no other type of seafaring vessel existed except the Ship, for short. Before many more years had passed, people even forgot why it was called the Ship. Now came the important and truly difficult question: Did the Ship of Renown still exist? Is it more right to say that it evolved beyond its name's utility or that use erased its identity and the name along with it over time? Those were the questions that the philosophers should have asked, but none of them remembered to ask them. How could they?"

The Danilos shifted uncomfortably but remained silent. "Oh, I may have struck a nerve," Laplace said.

"Well,

then, I'll show you what I know unless one of you has something you'd like to share about what you know."

He looked at them each in turn for a long second. Their prehensile noses twitched and curled as if the appendages could hide themselves within the nasal cavities. Two of them began to whimper.

"No one has anything to say?" Laplace asked one more time.

There was a sharp click, and one of the Danilos jumped and screeched. He began searching frantically through the fur on his abdomen. The area started to smolder. He pulled a golden, metal sliver, no larger than a mosquito, from the now-sparking patch of skin. He threw it to the side as the fingers that grasped it themselves began to spark and burn.

The screaming was unbearable. The other Danilos cowered at the feet of the guards and tried to cover their ears.

Though the burning victim tried to run to his comrades, the fire was consuming him too rapidly.

He only took a few steps before he was reduced to useless flopping as he turned to char.. Everyone in the room coughed and retched on the smoke.

Laplace produced a handkerchief from a pocket in his trousers and held it to his mouth and nasal passages. The remains were smoldering but cool enough to preclude damage to the polish on his footwear as he poked through them with the toe of his boot.

"Here we are!" he exclaimed as his probing pushed something non-Danilo from the ashes. Before the object lost contact with his boot, it shot up from the ground at him. It was not quick enough, however. One of the tufts on his left lower abdomen stirred and flicked out an external power supply

accessory, which latched onto the projectile, immobilizing it immediately. The attacker was another nachinak. It looked exactly like a subjugation nachinak, despite its behavior.

"What a beauty," Laplace said, "Shall I confirm its identity? It will avail you nothing for me to demonstrate the source and extent of my knowledge on this account."

None of the Danilos replied. Their eyes remained downcast, avoiding both Laplace and the pile of ashes.

"This is ridiculous," he chided.

The filaments surrounding a chest tuft on the right stirred and unrolled to reveal a nachinak of a different sort. It was the same size as a standard unit, but its occipital cube flared around the posterior edge like a frill. It had a double row of legs between the terminal pairs. The legs oriented towards the ventral surface of its body were similar to those found on more common varieties. However, the legs oriented caudad ended in a small bundle of

filaments. They had no joints, resembling tentacles more than articulated appendages, although they maintained a bend in the middle that preserved their orientation. It was covered with red and black splotches, no greater than a millimeter in diameter, and irregular in shape, so it was difficult to tell whether it was a black nachinak splattered with red or a red nachinak splattered with black. It stretched and shook itself. The golden irises of its protruding eyes dilated and contracted.

"Don't get me wrong," said Laplace. "I am impressed and quite proud of Danilo's expertise surrounding our little companions. His knowledge nearly rivaled my own, but not quite."

The red and black nachinak cast off from the filament platform on Laplace's chest and landed squarely on top of the subjugation nachinak. Its tiny trunk dilated and snaked down to cover the prisoner's trunk. Laplace touched the silver and gold filigree ring clamped to the rim of his external auditory meatus. He stood for several minutes listening intently. His concentration broke with a small sound of disgust.

He looked at the remaining Danilos and shook his head. "You really didn't understand what this would do to you

, "Laplace said," It appears to have been a case of motivated ignorance as well. That makes it even worse. You can't hide long enough in the event radiation, you know. You have lost. You have lost on your own merits. You no longer have my sympathy."

"I don't need anything of yours," said one of the Danilos., "You don't know what you're talking about. I am the victor here. You should prepare yourself for a severe disappointment."

Laplace laughed and waved his arm dismissively in the direction of the prisoners.

"Perhaps if you had known a little more about skins...Dispose of them, please," he instructed the guards.

Laplace turned to address the technician still working on the device burrowed into Francis's leg.

"How much longer?" He asked.

"It shouldn't be too long," the technician estimated, "several hours, to be safe."

"Take the time you need to be safe," said Laplace. "We are running out the clock on our immediate problems anyway. After that, I will need Francis's assistance for what's to come. He will need to be at his best if we are to finish matters properly."

Twenty-eight

Sound, Noise, Trees, and Tarski

Lucky gave Anisa a considerable head start before rising from his chair to walk out to the table in the courtyard. She stood at one end of the table. The filaments covering her chest and abdomen rippled impatiently. Takezo sat on the opposite side of the table, looking unhappy.

"Okay," Lucky said, "I'm here for my explanation. I have questions of my own, too." There was silence all around. Takezo slapped his hand on the table and stood to speak.

"This is Anisa," he said. She will tell you everything you need to know and answer your questions as best she can. I will be here to guarantee accuracy."

Lucky nodded and turned his chair to face Anisa. He crossed his arms over his chest.

"I brought you here," she said, "because you have something of mine, and I need it back. I had to act with great care because the item is valuable. Besides, I am a runaway slave. Any of the Species that recognize my status is likely to try to detain me or report me to the Authority. My master has actively pursued me as well. He is prone to kill escapees that allow

themselves to be recaptured.

All of the unusual events that interfered with your trip back home pertain to my enslavement. Our society claims a broad swath of benefits derive from the institution of slavery. I can see only one: it engenders in the slave a single-minded, unwavering desire to escape.

I have had that desire since the day that my master stabbed my calf with that evil little device."

Anisa walked over to Lucky. He watched her suspiciously but without any sign of intimidation. She planted a palm firmly on each arm of the chair and leaned uncomfortably close.

"You are mine," she said, "more precisely, you are me. You see, once a slave has escaped, their one preoccupation is how to hide effectively. They already know what it means to be stuffed in a hole. They want to walk free but not be seen. A fine dream, but not a realistic one – at least, that's what I thought until I began researching it.

After my enslavement, I uncovered a set of skills that I would never have imagined belonging to me. I am a good researcher. I am a good thief. I am good at navigating the dendritic event radiation. I don't mind killing people when I have to. That set of skills enabled me to succeed and realize every slave's dream.

Long ago, a group of slaves under one master conspired to modify subjugation nachinaks. Many of those slaves died in the process but blessed as they were with the unflinching determination to escape, they had an inexhaustible supply of volunteers, and soon, they had nachinaks modified to do exactly what they wanted."

"You mean they invented a machine that would make them invisible?" asked Lucky.

Anisa leaned in even closer, inspecting his left eye and then his right. "Not exactly, a normal subjugation nachinak works by modifying the slave's identity to look like it shares elements of its supervenience base with the base elements of the Master's identity. As you might imagine, the

modifications aim to be as essential as possible.

I

For instance, a slave born in the highlands of my home world will have

fond memories of the mountains, will know how to ski, and will be slightly shorter than the average lowlander. Perhaps the master went to the mountains on a ski vacation twice in the past. The subjugation nachinak marks those intersections between master and slave with a metaphorical fluorescent stain. It seeks elements of belonging tied to a specific place, culture, or family. It chains the slave with elements of their identity that they will not readily abandon.

The circumstances create a reflexive aversion in the slave to any threat to the status quo. That is in addition to the more pedestrian forms of leverage sub-

191

sequently available to the master. The slave's hesitancy aligns with the shared base elements of identity, rendering the slave easier to recapture should they escape.

The slave can no longer truly hide. The links can be traced with an abacus in normal space-time and even more efficiently in the dendritic event radiation.."

"Why does that process trouble the slave, except by marking them?" Lucky asked. Anisa smiled and leaned back until she could rest on her locked elbows. "Causal closure of the physical world, or strong supervenience, if you want to use the event radiation's model, is why. Laplace used to regale us slaves with the story of the Ship of Renown to explain it. The point is:

imprecise identities fail to exist.

You may begin to see where I'm going with this. There is a way to modify the subjugation nachinak so that it provides a safe disconnection from the master while obscuring the slave. That modified nachinak was the grand achievement of the cooperative.

Going forward, the nachinak identified the slave's base elements with local conditions without continuity over time.. The slave sacrificed a few minor elements of their identity to give substance to the lie, but in return, the device described an imprecise identity to everyone in range.

It doesn't just convince the observers that they can't see you, it convinces

them that you do not exist." You are a rhetorical tautology.

"So, what you're telling me is that you think I have this cloak of yours, and you want me to give it back to you?" asked Lucky. "But I have never heard of, seen, nor heard of any such thing until this very moment."

"No," Anisa said, "it isn't a cloak; it's a skin. That's what they called it, the ones who first successfully modified the nachinak. That's what we still call it. It isn't just a piece of clothing that is separate from you. It is a skin of yours. In this case, it's my skin, and you are it. Go ahead and feel just below your knee on the right side."

Lucky reached down and felt the area. There was a firm mass in the deeper tissues.

"What the hell have you done?" Lucky asked," Where are you going with this?

Do you mean to kill me and wrap yourself in my hide, so you can take this thing back? Don't I get a little bit of credit for rescuing you from the cliff dwelling?"

Anisa took a step back from Lucky with a puzzled look on her face. Takezo also backed away from the table and pulled a long-bladed knife from a sheath stuffed through the back of his belt.

"I don't plan to kill you," said Anisa. "I can't kill you because you're not alive. You never have been. Takezo, can you see it? Can you hear it?"

"Yes," Takezo answered, "Lucky, I do not believe her. The basic facts are correct, but her representation is wrong. Please bear with us. You do not control the skin right now. We can only continue to communicate with you if you become calm enough for us to see you as you are once more. She cannot see you at all, and I see what we both dreamed of in the past. I will teach you how to control this thing – "

"What?" Anisa objected, "That isn't what we talked about! Just restrain him. I will remove the disassociation nachinak from his leg, and then I will have the skin back. That will greatly simplify this discussion.."

"Urusai! Baka ona!" Takezo shouted, "Lucky —" "Let her finish, Takezo," Lucky said.

"A wise decision," said Anisa, "because of what we are, we cannot avoid each other. Circumstances will always conspire to bring us nearer to each other. That will always be a dangerous situation. You can still be tracked, albeit with great difficulty. But should you be found, you would have no real defense, and neither would I. They can get to me through you. That's why I separated myself from you many months ago. I wouldn't have done it if I had known then what I know now. Without stable references, the histories tell us that the skin displaced from its owner will rapidly disintegrate. However, if it detects a complete identity within its nachinak's perceptual field, it will latch on; that is the corollary to the Nachinak's dissociative program. That means a

reckoning for both the skin and its new proprietor.

One identity will be predominant, and the other one will be subsumed. That is what happened to you. That is what happened to Takezo. For him, it happened long, long ago, and he prevailed. For you, it happened two years ago, and you lost the struggle for predominance."

"So that's what happened that night in the desert on the motorcycle," Lucky said, "but it wasn't exactly what happened, was it?. The story got changed by the winner. That's why I have the gap in my memory between the wreck and the folks picking me up on the highway. That's why things have been fuzzy since then."

"That's right," said Anisa, "your name was Jim. Your wife's name was Diane. She died about 8 months ago. I knew that you would find your way to me, so it was easy to bring you into the corridors I established around the freeway in the canyons.

Localizing you within that area was going to prove more difficult. I was able to procure her phone. I have been recycling texts. The contact seems to keep you in the vicinity. I regret doing so. I'm sorry."

"But you don't regret killing me," Lucky said.

"I don't regret reclaiming the elements of my identity that have borrowed components of your defunct identity to sustain them," said Anisa.

"Lucky, you are not who you think you are. You are the universe's stale memory of the person who got crushed out of existence in the desert that night, and ever since, you have served strictly as a reference, a waypoint on the map, acting to stabilize the predominant identity."

"He has learned. He has established an alliance with me," Takezo said. "These are not the actions of a ghost made of unchanging memory."

Anisa looked down and shook her head.

"He already had a connection with you. He has merely played out that pre-existing bond. He has learned things," she said, "but his acquired knowledge is superficial. Observe him more closely, Takezo. He reacts to new information, but he cannot interpret what he learns. He cannot find initiative in what he learns. His spontaneous behaviors are rote.

He will tell you that he is conscious because that was the established belief of the person from whom he derives. Don't you see how he reacted when I informed him of his wife's demise and the source of the text messages he has received since he's been here? He had no qualitative experience of any of that news. None of it altered him in the least. Why don't you ask him what he makes of all this?"

"Lucky?" Takezo asked, "How do you feel about what Anisa has told you? What will you do now?"

"I think she is lying about Diane," Lucky said. "I don't know how she got hold of that phone.

When I get out of here, I'm going to go home. In the meantime, I will do what I can to help you complete your project. I can't see any possibility of release before your work is finished."

"Case closed," Anisa said.

"Only if the judge relies on her prejudiced ear alone," Takezo said.

Rippling swarms of black specks wove about the space in front of Lucky's chair. They resolved over a few seconds, first into the figure of the starving wolf and then into Lucky.

"I learned that quickly enough," Lucky told Anisa, "and without much

help from anyone. No offense, Takezo." Takezo laughed.

"Is that supposed to prove my hypothesis or yours?" Anisa asked. "He performed as prompted as far as I could see."

Takezo just laughed harder.

""Don't we all? I have no interest in your interpretation of this ink blot," Takezo answered," Come back to us when you have something to redeem your speculations.

Time for sake."

"Keep laughing. Don't call me, though, when the unblinking eyes are upon you," Anisa said.

"I will call you," Takezo promised. "This person has come to represent fear itself to you. You must be there when the duel occurs, or you will never be rid of him."

Anisa said nothing.

Takezo and Jim turned to the food and sake. She spent the rest of the evening watching them talk, and she was the last to retire as the sun touched the rose garden with color for the new day.

Twenty-nine

The Demonstration

In the confines of the store's tiny office, Augustine paced, swore, and sweated. Dion and Thomas occupied the other side of the desk. Thomas was wedged in the corner of the room while Dion had pulled his chair up to the desk, to rest his drink on it.

"Those rotten little freaks were next to useless," Augustine said. "Thomas, I thought you said they were good fighters and reliable. What happened in there?"

Thomas squirmed uncomfortably in his chair.

"I, I don't know," he said, "when I observed them at Danilo's invitation, they were highly effective troops. It's as if there has been some collective deterioration.

Augustine bumped against the corner of the table as he turned to address Thomas. The impact made a curious, hollow sound. Dion did a double-take. "What the hell was that?" asked Dion. "Did that sound come out of you, boss?"

After a moment's contemplation, Augustine said, "I can't

afford to kill you right now. It would be difficult to hide the body. You're a little more useful than most of these twerps anyway. I can let you in on a secret, but you should know that this is a real secret, one that could be fatal if divulged."

"I can keep my mouth shut," Dion said.

"What do you think, Thomas?" Augustine asked.

"You heard him," Thomas said.

Augustine raised the hem of his cassock. It revealed the easily replaceable limbs seen on every other calculator. Nothing stood out, at least until the edge of the cassock lifted over his lower abdomen.

He was a portly fellow, without a doubt, but not nearly so portly as he appeared at first glance. What looked like a substantial pannus of abdominal fat was actually a large Abacus. Relative to others of its kind, it was more of everything that an abacus aspired to be. A chocolate-colored wood with an intricate grain constituted its frame and body. It housed two more rows of cylinders than the typical Abacus, featured extensive carvings over the entire body of the machine, and boasted a plethora of covered drawers and pockets in the wood.

Dion let out a low whistle.

"I see," he said. "Don't worry, Boss man. I won't tell anybody that you're walking around with a gold-plated Stradivarius strapped to your gut."

Augustine dropped the ball of fabric gathered in his right hand.

"All right," Augustine said, "that's enough show and tell. We have a lot less to work with now. However, it should still be enough. We have to focus on the smith. He's going to get us back into the Center of Excellence, and he's going to keep them from coming after us overtly. I am going down there this afternoon for a little inspection. You two just have to keep this

place running smoothly, all right? If anything appears out of sorts, please call me right away. Do not act on your own initiative, regardless of the circumstances. Do you understand me?"

Thomas and Dion nodded.

Augustine opened the door behind the sales counter but stopped short of going through. He looked sharply at Thomas, who was still sitting in the corner and showing no sign of impending movement.

"What the hell is that?" Augustine asked, "Spit that out, and put any more that you are holding on the table in front of you."

Thomas reluctantly removed the lollipop that he had just begun to enjoy from his mouth and laid it on the desktop. He searched his pockets and produced three more of the same.

Augustine narrowed his eyes in suspicion.

"Did anyone give those to you, or did you just find them?" he asked, "and how long have you been sucking on them?"

"I'm sorry if I did something wrong, master," Thomas apologized., "I found them myself, in one of the boxes that had been torn open during the raid on the store. I think this was going to be my third one."

"You are not to have one more of those," Augustine said," they're one of the things I use in the preparatory phase of enslavement nowadays. They make the subject suggestible. No more!"

Augustine squeezed through the space behind the counter and exited the vacant store by its new doorway. He took a sharp left as soon as he stepped outside to further improve his chances of escaping before anyone in the outdoor dining area spotted him.

He made his way across the small, forested slope and through the dry, brown meadow without encountering anyone.

A workman waved

at him as he passed by on the widening trail. The man was installing equipment in the pair of sheds that now occupied the space in front of the tunnel that ran back to the cliff dwelling.

By the time he reached the side trail leading to the hanging valley where the workshop and villa lay, Augustine was sweating profusely. He sat down on a log bench at the trail junction but soon began to catch a chill. The switchbacks were easy walking, and he arrived at the workshop's door, if

not refreshed, then at least not irritated.

He could hear the smith conversing with someone. He paused for a moment, but the sliding door, which took up most of the front of the building, was wide open, making effective eavesdropping impossible. So, he kept walking right up to the forge in the center of the room.

The smith was dressed for work, wearing a heavy, insulated apron, a welder's mask, a helmet, and thick gauntlets. The other person looked utterly out of place. He was a human, with short hair and a crooked nose. He wore an orange plaid shirt and blue jeans, with flat-soled running shoes. Even though nothing about him suggested short-term travel plans, he wore a tattered day pack on his back.

"We are fortunate indeed this morning," said Takezo as he turned to bow "This is Mr. Augustine, our sponsor. Mr. Augustine, this is Jim. He is a relative of mine by marriage and is considering an apprenticeship with me. I hope you don't mind if he observes my work."

"No, I'd be thrilled," said Augustine, "since that means that there will be work to observe."

"You see, Jim. I told you he had a wonderful sense of humor," said Takezo. "he is always ready to share a joke or a good story. Perhaps he would be the one to field your questions about the practice of slavery among members of his Species."

"Yeah, well, I've got to have a sense of humor. This whole

damn thing is a joke. It was a joke to name this anomaly God. It's a joke to insist on forging a utensil to destroy it. The only thing that isn't funny is the fortune we stand to make by conjuring up a private patch of gray space when and where we want it," said Augustine., "I came all the way down here to see what you've done so far. I think you have to find somebody else to play amateur anthropologist. All I'm interested in is seeing the weapon."

"Mr. Augustine, you are the only one of your Species we could turn to for such explanations," said Takezo., "There are serious issues pertaining to this matter for Jim, and so for myself, and so for you."

"How does slavery concern someone like this," asked Augustine, "who is not a member of the Species, and would not appear to have any means or purpose for dealing with any members of the Species?"

"Do not judge this man too hastily," Takezo said, "he's a good negotiator and skilled at finding rare and hidden objects. I have asked him to track down some materials vital to our project. He has succeeded but must convince the fugitive slave who has access to allow us to purchase those materials."

"You could just give me the name and location of the runaway slave, and I can pick them up for you. That is part of my job description," Augustine said.

Takezo bowed.

"Thank you for the offer, but this matter demands a type of persuasion unavailable to persons in positions of authority, especially persons of the Authority."

199

"Fine," Augustine sighed, "don't interrupt. You need to know a couple of things about the Species for context. First, we live a long time compared to most of the intelligent races – about four hundred solar orbits as you people would reckon. We have been

around for a long time, too— millions of years. Many millions. We no longer remember our origins or much of our history.

We have seen it all, and most of it is nonsense. Of the few important things we have learned, two stand out. First, it is impossible to govern intelligent people. Give me a rabble of idiots, and I will turn out a real juggernaut of a state, ready to conquer a galaxy. Give me a bunch of eggheads with a dozen years of education each and it's another story. Knowledge paralyzes people. Analysis bogs everything down. It makes people weak and indecisive.

Second, a society and its culture need a purpose. It can be a religion, scientific inquiry, exploration, or genocide, whatever. The project doesn't matter, as long as it provides society with a validating goal and the culture with guidance. Otherwise, when the people finally realize that no one is going to reward them for existing, and they have tried the last color and

pattern for their scarves without satisfaction, everything falls apart.

That said, people still need protection, demand justice, and merit correction. In lieu of a government institution to cover those needs, we have a cultural institution: slavery.

Let's face it, in every community, you will find people who are unprepared to live responsibly on their own when society expects them to. Those are the people who end up getting enslaved. They are then protected. Their status insulates them from distracting responsibilities. They can learn from their master, who is their tried and proven superior. Being a slave allows them to learn what it is to serve. It teaches humility, endurance, vigilance, and ingenuity. It provides a reliable feedback mechanism as they assess their skills and preparedness for an independent life, especially if that life will be devoted to reaching a complete calculation.

The institution has its

problems, just like any methodology. Methods are all necessarily incomplete and impersonal. Sometimes, a slave will just fail to become independent. Slaves live by many rules that are of no use in the free world. Some of the enforcement mechanisms associated with the institution may seem harsh. Still, they must be considered in light of the severity of the risks that an independent calculator must navigate. "

"Thank you for your thorough treatment of a delicate and complex subject, "said Takezo.

Augustine replied with a flat stare, then added, "I don't know what led you to get involved with a fugitive slave. I don't want to know, and I will not go back through my archived Authority bulletins to find out. Don't be fooled; this is a family business, and you are not even a second cousin twice removed. If you step in, even to criticize, there won't be a question-and-answer period."

"I appreciate your candor," said Takezo. "Now, shall we examine the prototype?"

He stepped behind the forge and lifted a 2-meter-long metal shaft from a

hidden rack. The whole weapon tapered evenly and symmetrically from the indentation that formed the grip to the point. It had a small counterbalance at the base of the grip.

The design was plain, which accentuated the remarkable appearance of the material. It resembled frost feathers wrapped in a slice of the night sky. Judging by the handling, the instrument was heavy.

As Takezo approached, a slight hum became apparent.

"An amorphous solid. Osmium and osmium-iridium alloy. The point and edges are reactive, and the whole thing holds a charge. The nature of that charge remains a mystery," Takezo said," It does not behave like an electroweak type of force. " Augustine extended a hand to touch it.

"These gloves would be the minimum level of precaution advisable," Takezo said, as he withdrew the weapon beyond Augustine's reach," Though I would recommend not touching it at all for the time being."

"Of course, we have a weapon that must be hand-held, and the first line of the owner's manual is a warning against holding it in your hands," said Augustine "At, least you remain consistent."

Takezo paused for a moment and let the point of the weapon dip. He took a deep breath, blew it out, and shook his head. He put the weapon back in its cradle. Without further discussion, he pulled an insulating cover off a large piece of equipment occupying one side of the workshop, in the area behind the forge. The item stood chest high. It had a rectangular base with a disc on top.

The base had a sliding door in front, which allowed access to the instrumentation within. The disc was made of dull gray metal. It measured forty centimeters thick and one meter in diameter.

Takezo opened the sliding door in the base and turned on the instruments inside. He made a few adjustments, then clipped the weapon into its cradle. On the right side of the workshop, a small cart bore a harness to hold the cradle in a pendulum frame. Behind the frame, an actuator lined up with

the base of the weapon, allowing the operator to remotely swing the blade point -first.

Takezo unscrewed the bolts anchoring the actuator to the cart and set the machine aside. He pushed the cart across the workshop floor, then maneuvered the wheels into a set of slots in the cement pad. As the wheels settled into their places, a locking

mechanism at the bottom of each slot automatically secured them. Takezo put his hand on the weapon's grip and lowered the face shield on his helmet. He pointed at the forge, indicating that Jim and Augustine should take shelter behind it. Takezo then secured the weapon cradle to the frame and pulled the weapon back with both hands.

"Hey, I'm just joking," Augustine said, "here's no need…"

Takezo swung the weapon forward forcefully. It contacted the disc on top of the experimental instrument with a crack, and the loud screech of metal scraping across metal.

Jim and Augustine both ducked but didn't take their eyes off the action. A dark flash accompanied the initial progress of the point through the metal disc, like the world had blinked in response to the impact. The point carried through the disc.

It would have stood almost half its length beyond the back of the target if the disc had kept its form.

The Instead, the metal target shattered into shards, ranging from nearly microscopic vapor drops to marble-sized flaming steel blobs. The observers ducked the rest of the way behind the forge and avoided serious burns.

When they emerged to reexamine the weapon, it had changed. The cradle and frame were smashed, and Takezo held the blade in a guard position. His arms trembled slightly as he supported it.

Throughout the prototype's material, the frost feathers withered and ceased to reflect light as they had prior to the test. A dim violet glow surrounded the distal sixteen centimeters of the blade down to the point. That portion of the blade now looked dark red, almost black, with a few

silvery flecks scattered on the surface. The changes near the
point resolved quickly, but the alterations in the frost feathers persisted.

Takezo hoisted the blade to chest height, walked over to the forge, and dropped it on the anvil surface. A hint of smoke came off the palms of his gloves, but the gloves themselves appeared intact. He suffered damage from the molten metal shrapnel, which ruined his helmet, visor, and apron.

"It does that just once," Takezo said," it can re-accumulate charge, but it takes several days, and I have not identified a means of accelerating that process."

"Yeah, now I take it all back. Don't worry about the recharging problem. I think I have an easy solution," said Augustine, "however, the solution will require my presence and active participation at least until we have a stable system that we can set and forget."

"I will not refuse any assistance. Can you return to work on this solution shortly? Takezo asked.

"Two days," said Augustine as he left the workshop.

Takezo and Jim stood listening to the fading huff and shuffle that accompanied Augustine whenever he traveled on foot. When Augustine was well on his way, by silent mutual assent, they retired to the Koi pond.

"Now you must speak with Anisa," Takezo said when he was sure that Augustine was out of earshot, even with a hidden microphone's assistance. They sat in silence for a while. The day was warm, with a scattering of clouds and a light breeze. Takezo stretched his legs out in front of him and leaned back, letting the wind blow through his hair. Jim sat passively

watching minnows in the pond.

"Do you think she will speak with me?" Jim asked.

"I think she will. She has passed from uncertainty into uncertainty. She needs to get her feet back under her and find the edge of the path again.

Nobody can do that for her, but nothing clarifies one's thoughts more

than listening to oneself speak them aloud, especially if the listening occurs in the course of explaining those thoughts to another person.. I hope you will help her. I hope she will revise her opinion of you. I hope that she will reconsider her destination," said Takezo.

"I'm surprised to hear all this coming from the champion of solitude and self-sufficiency," said Jim.

"There is a place for everything. Solitude and self-sufficiency are the destinations themselves, not the road."

Thirty

Disingenuous Lessons

Francis squirmed in his pressure suit. He stood in a light rain on the rooftop deck of Sonnamarg, Laplace's roost. The Mother stood next to him. An umbrella kept some of the rain off her. Still, the present shower came with gusty winds, and she was gradually getting soaked by drops blown under the rim. She began to shiver intermittently.

The glass-enclosed warmth of the nearby solarium beckoned, but Laplace had cautioned them to remain in the open while they waited on the rooftop. The moment they disembarked from the drone, Laplace rushed down-stairs to a storeroom without leaving them an itinerary. Francis put his arm around the mother in a symbolic gesture of solidarity. No actual warmth was transferred through the pressure suit.

Fortunately, Laplace returned before hypothermia set in. He crossed the roof quickly, without looking around. Four nachinaks hovered by his head and shoulders. Several more of the devices were nestled in the filaments covering his chest. Two larger devices clung to his left arm. He held a

pressure suit on the right, half-draped over his shoulder.

"Follow me," he said, "I apologize for the wait – security protocols. No sign of trouble?"

"None so far," Francis said.

They made for the door on the opposite side of the roof from the solarium. Francis increased his pace to reach the exit first and assist Laplace. He did not have the chance to look back until he was holding the door open. Laplace sprinted past him.

The Mother struggled forward at less than half his pace. She was shivering again and looking like she might collapse at any moment.. Francis caught a hint of movement against the clouds. He let go of the door and did his best to run to her. She looked up at the sky, then back at him. She frantically waved him off.

He tripped over his own boot. As he struggled to his hands and knees, he heard a sound like hail in a thunderstorm.

The face plate on his helmet cracked. Blows fell heavily on his back and legs. He felt something tearing at the suit, then at the skin beneath it. He flailed to dislodge whatever was digging into him.

A heartbeat later, it all stopped. He could still feel something in the suit with him, poking into his lower back. He popped the quick-release on the helmet. The seams on the suit zipped open, and four nachinaks fell out onto the deck. He threw the helmet off and looked around in desperation.

The Mother lay on the deck a few meters from him. Her face was unrecognizable, and her clothes were in tatters. Blood seeped from both ears and pooled on the tiles.

He looked away.

Nachinaks hung in the air all around him, their legs gently circulating in standby mode. Something heavy clanked on the deck behind him. He turned to see Laplace accompanied by an external power supply. About a meter over Laplace's head, four of his own nachinak writhed against each

other in interlocking circles as Laplace silently regarded the disaster surrounding him.

"Neither of you deserved this," he told Francis. "I am the only one who deserves this. This is what Danilo meant. This is how he won."

Laplace held up a bead and tapped a small indentation in the engraving. The ball of nachinaks above his head stopped turning and convulsed. Every hostile device within view followed suit. The formation overhead resumed its weave and rotation. The rest dropped to the ground.

Laplace quickly examined the inert devices. Francis picked up one that had impacted his face plate. It was missing legs and had a gash across the midsection. It looked like a subjugation nachinak, but it had a modification to the trunk.

There was an added structure inside, just behind the ring of teeth. Laplace noticed Francis puzzling over the damaged machine and went over to have a look.

"Would you please give me that?" Laplace asked.

Francis handed over the specimen. Laplace examined it closely. He carefully extracted the anomalous part from its trunk.

"Oh no," he whispered," Oh no."

"What?" Francis asked apprehensively.

"We have to go. Get your new pressure suit on. I left it in the stairwell landing, outside the hatch. One of my security personnel is waiting to decontaminate everything as soon as you are dressed," Laplace instructed. "They will take care of her as soon as it is safe to do so."

"What about you?" Francis asked, "You are infected now, aren't you?"

"No," said Laplace, "the virologists at the COE are among the

best. I have been immunized with positive confirmatory titers and a brisk lymphocytic response. You are the only one left to worry about

Thirty-one

Immodest Proposals

Jim sat with his back against the warm sandstone. The sun was low on the horizon. Shadows already occupied the space between trees on the slope below, but he was still basking in golden rays. He observed the occasional passersby for any sign that they noticed him.

All of them strolled down the trail without batting an eyelash. He had learned to control the skin. Now, he just had to hope that he properly understood the rules of the enchanted forest. Confirmation soon crept up the hillside from the hanging valley.

When she turned in the direction of the COE, he jumped up and ran after her.

"Anisa!" he shouted," I need to talk with you."

In response, she ducked into the brush. He followed at a trot. She would have surprised him if he had lost his concentration. He almost bumped into her as it was.

"Anisa! Why are you running from me?" Jim asked as he relaxed his guard and became noticeable again.

She plopped down in the red dirt. He stood a respectful distance behind her and waited for her to speak. Presently, she drew herself up, but instead of addressing his question, she

started back down the slope to the villa. She didn't break stride until she came to a stop at the edge of the pond. She refused to look at him.

"Get it over with," she said.

"I have a lot of questions and a few requests," he said.

"Get it over with," she said."

"I didn't get most of your conversation with Takezo –" said Jim.

"–That's because you are not conscious," she said.

"Okay, so there's another one right there. Why do you keep saying that?"

"Because you are not conscious," she said.

"I disagree. How come I can carry on conversations, get scared, and brush my own teeth instead of someone else's if I am not conscious?" Jim asked.

"You are an amalgam of two complex systems," she said," You retained many capabilities – enough to pass unless challenged. What is your name?"

"Jim"

"Before I told you that your name was Jim, did you know it?"

"No"

"Did you experience any associations when you learned your name?" she asked.

"I don't know," he said, "What are you getting at?"

"When a computer receives a new piece of data, it checks a

set of rules to classify the information and then associates it with a category. Once the association is established, the machine can refer to that information in future operations, but always in a single aspect – the one determined by its programmers' rules.

For instance, if the machine receives data about a rose, it will associate that new information with things that are flowers, things that smell good, red things, etc.,

as the rules dictate. The computer refers to the item by its category to utilize

its knowledge. Are you with me so far?" Anisa asked. Jim nodded.

"When a conscious entity receives new data, the entity can use rules to classify the information so that it is available for reference," Anisa continued,," but she also experiences the data acquisition.

The scent of the rose comes to her in the garden that her adopter kept, and now it is part of how the garden feels to her and how her adopter feels to her. The scent forever bears the mark of her feelings about the garden and her adopter.

In addition to a location within categories, she also has a narrative of her collective experiences, where rose scents feel like gardens, gardens feel like spring, and spring feels like cold dew on her socks. She has an explanation that can adjust, expand, and yield access to other aspects of rose scents – chemical, cultural, psychological – that would need to be added by a programmer otherwise."

"Okay, it did not feel like anything when you told me my name, but I wanted to know it," Jim said," Doesn't that count for anything?"

Anisa wagged her finger.

"No, "she said," The skin Nachinak's program maintains local consis-tencies. Jim, before the amalgam, would have wanted to recall his name, so those are the directions that you got."

"Alright, I also want to know why you were enslaved," he said." What about that?"

"Takezo told you to ask that question," she said. "He thinks he is my therapist for some reason."

"No, the question is mine, "he said.

"Then he suggested it to you."

"Well?" he asked.

She turned on her heel and marched off to the villa. He did his best to keep up. She fumbled with her keys at the door to her room, and when it finally

opened, she pushed the door so hard that it bounced back and hit her on the shoulder. Jim caught up in the few moments it took her to swear at the door and regain her composure. She went directly to the bookshelves and rummaged through them until she came upon a thin tablet. She turned it on and tossed it at Jim.

"This is in libraries, schools, and rental units. The copy in your hands came with the room. Read it. Then I will tell you."

A paper entitled: "The Current State of Cultural Institutions: the Happy Case of Slavery, A Review of the Literature.

The Proceedings of the Center of Excellence in Sociology Abstract:

The health of cultural institutions is key to the Species' long-term survival. Given the special status and age of the Species, it is challenging to draw conclusions regarding

the currency, effectiveness, and evolution of our cultural institutions. Yet, given the minimalist approach to governance adopted long ago and still favored with near unanimity in every survey on the subject, the solidity of those institutions is vital if we are to continue in good stead over the next millennia. One of the most debated institutions, especially by races that lack experience with it, is slavery. As a result of the increased scrutiny by outside sociologists, slavery has a strong database to go by. In the following paper, we review the database, its implications, and the surrounding literature, finding that the institution of slavery continues to serve the Species well and is a robust tradition heading into the next millennium.

As cultural institutions go, slavery, in one form or another, is one of the most commonly encountered traditions across Species and ecologies.

Despite its popularity, the judgments ultimately rendered by

societies that adopt the institution vary to the extreme. One culture may sing its praises while another may condemn it, and yet another may tolerate it on the fringe of society. Slavery among the Species has proven to be one of the institution's most successful and enduring iterations.

Due to the initial conditions surrounding maturation, the Species has been one of the easiest to study. While bias is always a potential confounding factor, the aforementioned variability in cultural experiences with the insti-tution, along with the persistent differences in the intercultural practices of slavery, suggest differences in the structures of key elements (e.g., the master/slave relation-ship) of the institution as the most likely causes of the observed discrepancies. Because of the likelihood that the social contract governing the master/slave relationship determines the success or failure of slavery as a cultural institution, we have focused our efforts on that relationship.

Our data accumulation on this subject is exhaustive. It includes double-blinded functional neuroimaging, observational and interrogative soci-ological and psychological investigations, and large-scale, longitudinal, double-blinded, controlled experimentation, which has followed various interventions on sub-jects recruited upon emergence and followed across their entire lifespan. We have obtained several reproducible results related to the analysis in question: the suit-ability of the enslaved for enslavement.

"Oh shit," Jim remarked as the tablet hit the floor.

"Yeah," she said, "exactly."

"I don't feel well," said Jim as he stumbled out of the room and headed back to the pond's edge. Anisa went on speaking as they walked.

"It goes on. Their statistical analysis is valid. But you see the truth left in the dust with the final preceding statement – 'the suitability of the enslaved for enslavement.'

They came upon the rose garden again as the flowers displayed their subtle and most beautiful shades, visible only in the light filtered through the thick of evening.

Anisa's lips curled into an expression of rage and resentment. She kicked the nearest flower. The petals exploded and the thorns dug into her foot.

"Why was I enslaved? Because I wasn't good enough. Because

I was gullible. Because I convinced myself that I was managing my relationship with Laplace, when the truth was that he had run the whole game the whole time.

"Love will set anybody off their guard," Jim said.

"Oh my!" she laughed, "love had nothing to do with it. Ambition was the foundation of my association with that ghoul. I thought he wanted a protégé to carry his research and exploration forward.

As soon as I woke that night with the subjugation nachinak burying itself in my leg, I found out that what he really wanted was a sucker to prospect gray space for him.

It took a long time to straighten out my head after enslavement. I heard all those lies in that paper a thousand times between my years in the developmental center and my subjugation day. I still believed them on some level. It took almost 6 months for me to reject slavery altogether, and I'm afraid that I still live with residual dissonance.

I was a slow learner, but I have learned well. Sociologists say that slavery is educational. Slaves learn responsibility in service to their masters, they say. It is impossible to teach responsibility without allowing people to be responsible. Responsibility is incompatible with coercion. To give you a

233

familiar analogy, anyone who thinks that a prisoner learns something from making license plates at gunpoint is kidding themselves. The process of control and coercion is toxic to the existing virtues of the individual upon whom it is perpetrated.

Subjugation sends a powerful message. It tells the slaves that their lives have instrumental value only.

They must eventually reject their own intrinsic value altogether. What does it do for them except provide a point of leverage? Instrumental purpose is their only birthright.

The slaves begin to despise themselves because they learn to see their condition as a travesty. Every time they encounter something outside of their confinement, they feel its ridicule. The only thing that they have left for themselves is a misplaced desire to survive. We all want to survive, but not merely for the sake of taking another breath. When a person gets to that point, they are lost without any means of finding

their way back.

They can only defend themselves from within the prison walls. They hold the fort by discounting the free world in principle.

Then the locks and guards can go away; nobody will escape. The slaves have learned to fear the masters' punishment not as a mere injustice but as an existential rejection. Rather than have the master punish them, they will punish themselves and each other.

I told him about Shelly and Carmella, two of his slaves who escaped with me. I thought he knew I was planning to run, and about the Skin. He was going to let me run anyway, just to see how I would do it."

"Are you sure he's still chasing you?" Jim asked. "Maybe he saw what he wanted to see when you escaped, and he has moved on."

"I believe he did see what he wanted, and that was the skin," she said, "I don't think he has just let me run off with it again."

"Technically, you don't have the skin," said Jim.

"I have the skin extraction nachinak,' she said.

"Yes. That's the one I gave you in the cliff dwelling, isn't it?"

"Don't beat yourself up," she said," I was going to take it anyway."

"Which brings me to my request. I had a couple, but just one significant one," he said.

"What is it?" she asked.

"Don't kill me," he asked.

"I can't –

"Yeah, yeah," he said, "I'm not alive in the first place. I'm not even conscious. I told Takezo that I would help him with his project and find out why his thinking and memory are messed up. I want to keep my promises."

"Find out what is wrong with his mind? I am not sure I want to sign up for such an open-ended program," she said.

"You could lend a hand," Jim said, "That would speed things up."

"I will consider it, "she said as she turned away from the pond.

She patted Jim on the shoulder without looking at him retraced her steps back to the villa and her room.

Jim stood looking at the black, flat water as the last of the day's light left with the sunset's colors.

Takezo came down from the workshop and stood by him. Still, Jim did not speak. Finally, Takezo asked the question on everyone's mind.

"Well?"

"Do you think you can teach me to fence? I'm looking for a crash course.

"

Takezo laughed.

"Five AM," he said, and set off for the villa as well.

"Why can't it ever be easy with you people?" Jim remarked under his breath.

Thirty-two

War Crimes for the Refugees

Laplace and Francis stood in total darkness, listening. Metal creaked as it shrank or expanded, making echoes. Further off, the wind whistled through gaps in the structure. They heard no voices, footsteps, or any other sounds to suggest that anyone had noticed their arrival. Laplace turned on the light in the domed optical array on the external power source beside him. Moments later, Francis did the same. The beams followed their head movements as they surveyed the ruined event radiation access point.

Whatever destroyed the ballroom and its cages did so in the distant past. All of the bars forming the cages had corroded, and undisturbed dust lay thick on the floor.

"Not what I was hoping for," Laplace said" Let's see what this cost us."

He hit a button on the two power sources, and a number popped up above the optical array on each unit.

"We won't get out of here with the charge we have left," he said.

He opened a compartment on his abacus. Two nachinak bearing paired fins on their backs emerged and took up their stations above and behind him on either side.

"They could detect this, but only if they are looking for it specifically," he

told Francis," You don't want these people to capture you. This button," he said, indicating a large, circular polka dot just behind the base of the skull, in the power source's midline," will overload the unit within 30 seconds.

The same

person must push it again within 30 seconds to prevent overload. Francis gazed into the distance without responding. "Did you – "

"I push this button if I want to die in an explosion. Yes, I heard. When do I get better?" Francis asked.

"From what?" asked Laplace.

"What do you think? Mother is dead. I couldn't get to her in time," Francis said, as silent tears welled up again.

"That never gets better," Laplace said. "You just run out of grief eventually,"

"If it doesn't get better, how do you stand a lifetime's worth of these tragedies?" Francis asked.

"You avoid them. You dole the misery out to other people, capable or not, deserving or not. You drink. You blow yourself up. You pursue justice or revenge because you can imagine the payback being sufficient. Trick yourself into getting back on your feet, however you can, because if you stand, you will remember how to walk.

"Then you walk away.

"You start walking and keep walking until the horrors fall behind.." "Laplace said.

He reached up to activate the two external power source accessory nachinaks hovering over him.

"I had hoped to lead them away from the center of excellence, but I must say that I'm not disappointed to have missed them. I have other reasons for being here, and as I think about it more, I'm not sure that picking a fight was the best idea in the first place," Laplace mused, "said.

" Well, we're here now. I might as well complete my errand. If they have genuinely lost us, the hunt will keep them off the center of excellence for a

while, perhaps long enough. We may yet encounter them here, anyway."

Francis looked at Laplace and frowned.

"Are you all right?" He asked, "You sound uncertain."

"I'm well enough, thank you. This place brings back old memories, the bad kind," Laplace said.

"Remember, do not let them get their hands on you," he. said, "The Helpers' theology, in particular, its emphasis on justice and divine punishment, attracts a particularly nasty class of sadistic psychopath. That is why they are relegated to places like Unsalvageable Remnant 538"

Laplace led them unerringly through the buried ruin. The architecture was an odd mix of huge and delicate alongside squat and rugged. The clashing styles did not stem from a schizophrenic aesthetic. Laplace and Francis discovered two sets of airy glass monuments. One was very old, according to the inscriptions on the cornerstones.

The ancient structures favored a minimalist style. Their remains hinted at soaring curves of thin, polished frames supporting sparkling clear glass. The newer set had been more colorful and complex, with tiered balconies, domes, tinted glass spheres, and arches

The most recent construction paid no heed to art. Its products aimed to endure. The buildings' flesh and bones were reinforced concrete laid down in oppressive thicknesses. The concrete structures stood, but they had not saved the people who lived and worked inside the hard shells.

Something had destroyed the new and old at once. Fire had gutted almost every building. Piles of wreckage occupied corners and sidewalks next to the old and new buildings alike. Inside, empty cans and military ration packaging lay strewn across the floors.

Every public facility had a notice stenciled on the wall beside the main entrance. The marks were fragmentary, and Francis had almost stopped

detouring to read them when he spotted a legible specimen.

"Get back here! We have nearly made it to the outskirts," said Laplace.

He looked up at the patch of night sky framed by the limestone rim of the natural cavern enlarged to accommodate the city. A tiny light traversed the starfield.

When Francis ignored him Laplace hurried over to the doorway. Francis read the notification aloud:

"Unsalvageable Remnant number 538

the Authority has declared this world unsalvageable due to malignant cultural deterioration.

an evacuation order is in effect. As of the time of this notice, the Authority will provide no further assistance

including evacuation transport

"Malignant Cultural Deterioration? What is that? "asked Francis.

"This," said Laplace, pointing at the ground, "it's what happens when people mistake hard times for a zero-sum game. As you might imagine feedback of this sort from the Authority doesn't help the situation. Now hurry, we may be at more risk of detection than I had thought"

As Laplace predicted, the urban maze of ruined buildings and debris thinned abruptly. What had been vacant land beneath the cavern roof's shadow now held a patchwork of bunkers dug into the ground after the MCD by the survivors in the vain hope of continued survival, in anticipation of the collapse. Laplace detoured around the bunkers ' fortifications but showed no interest in them otherwise, except for a single subterranean vault on the city's most desolate outskirts

"Wait here, Francis," Laplace said, There may be something helpful in this one. I'll take a look. You keep watch out here."

"Isn't that an unnecessary risk?" asked Francis.

"I don't think so," Laplace answered. "It is just as abandoned as the rest. I won't be long. The external power sources will stay with you until I get back."

Francis gave an exasperated shrug and sat down on one of the power sources.

Laplace practically strolled up to the hatch that provided the only access to the underground fortification. The roof had a few mines scattered across it, but they formed no systematic defense. The person who placed them didn't bother to overlap their proximity fields.

The hatch was open, and the rungs descending into the dark interior were polished to a shine.

Laplace climbed down the shaft to the floor, about twenty feet below, and stood debating whether to turn on his flashlight.

"You might as well come in," said the vault's occupant as he shone a light in Laplace's eyes." "Nobody is home."

He turned off the flashlight, and emergency floor lighting illuminated the room. The speaker was Metizian, one of Danilo's people and familiar to Laplace.

219

"I thought you had escaped," said Laplace." "I couldn't believe it when I got the notice from your subjugation nachinak."

"Notice?" the Metizian asked. "Then you did build a seer unit after all!"

"I'd rather that weren't common knowledge," said Laplace.

"Who that would care might I tell, Luther?" The Metizian asked.

"Perhaps," Laplace replied cautiously, "where is Luther, by the way?"

"Out fomenting a schism, where else?" sighed the Metizian.

"Then you could leave right now. You know your way to the developmental center. You know who to talk to once you get there. There's a good chance that they would take you in. Why are you still here?" Laplace asked.

"Won't you please come in? That will make all of this easier," said the Metizian.

With that, he turned and opened the door behind him. He walked into the bunker's single large room and motioned for Laplace to follow. Laplace was stuck in the doorway.

The room resembled nothing more than a natural history Museum in its

layout. It was a carpeted maze of pedestals, display tables, glass cases, and holographic figures. The contents, however, had nothing to do with extinct plants or woolly mammoths; the displays were all about Gerard.

Papers of his on topics, such as pain perception, near-death experiences, and ritual mutilation, filled the glass cases. The holographic projections depicted surgical procedures performed without anesthesia, accompanied by subtitled commentary. The tables and pedestals supported both surgical instruments and instruments whose sole purpose was to inflict pain.

"What is the meaning of all this?" Laplace asked as he wandered from item to item.

"You're in the reliquary of a new religion," the Metizian said. "Luther, among others, had a falling out with God. In that situation, a person of faith has only two choices: confession or heresy. Luther has chosen heresy, and I, along with him."

"What is Gerard's role in this new religion?" Laplace asked.

"He is our teacher," said the Metizian, "both he and God are preoccupied with pain. In God's opinion, pain and death possess moral qualities, and He seeks to balance the distribution of these qualities across the population of conscious entities. He refers to virtue and immorality in passing because virtue and immorality provide the measures for his task. He is not concerned with virtue or immorality beyond their usefulness to him in administering justice. Pain's virtue is Gerard's only concern."

"His fascination with those subjects, and pain in particular, is due to his neurologic condition," Laplace said.

"That is not true. Even if it were true, it would not matter. Pain and death confront us no matter what. When the Society of God's Helping Angels caught me, they subjected me to the worst kinds of torture, sexual abuse, and degradation. At first, I tried to hide from it. Then I tried to wish it away. Finally, I sought solace in planning my revenge. None of those strategies stopped the torments. Nothing restored what the Angels took, "the Metizian said. "The torture was inevitable. After all else failed, I accepted it. I took on the lesson. I had nothing. I was nothing. When I made those confessions,

suddenly I was free.

There was nothing to experience the torture. The pain became a disinterested visitor and an object of curiosity for me. I learned on my own what Gerard has to teach the rest of us.

Our only freedom is the freedom to dismantle ourselves before pain and death come to do it for us."

"The lesson you describe is supposed to supplant the faith in God? I guess it doesn't promise anything that it can't deliver." Laplace said, "Freedom's false promise notwithstanding, this is your last chance to leave with me. You are already emancipated, based on the interrogation of your subjugation nachinak.

"I will stay. May I see it, though, before you leave?" asked the Metizian. The filaments covering the middle of Laplace's chest quivered and parted to reveal a rare Species of nachinak. It had a long and delicate trunk, and a pair of delicate ridges bordered in red lace that adorned its dorsal and ventral surfaces. Its body was thin and elegant. Tiny black and red speckles covered its white skin.

The unit drifted over to the Metizian and alighted on his outstretched palm.

221

THIRTY-TWO

"I never imagined I would actually see one. The descriptions don't do it justice," he said as he dropped his hand and allowed the nachinak to return to its hiding place.

"Farewell."

Thirty-three

Don't Bring a Gun to a Sword Fight, A Friendly Ghost Will Do

"When the weapon comes toward you, move," Takezo said.

Jim dropped his sword and threw up his hands. The morning was getting on, and they had made little progress.

"Maybe if we tried a different weapon?" Jim asked.

"No, we start with the épée. It is harder to pick up bad habits with this weapon, and it is easier for me to demonstrate guards and blocks," Takezo said.

"I feel a little weird in the costume, and you know, the sword is more like a knitting needle than an instrument of destruction. I can't help but feel a little silly," Jim said, "I think it is kind of holding me back. Just a suggestion, though."

"Even more reason to stick with the épée," said Takezo., "Pick it up, and we will go back to the number four block and riposte. Try to maintain tempo."

They stood in the courtyard of the villa. Jim was beginning to sweat in his

mask, vest, and fencing gauntlets. Takezo had already spent three hours working with Jim on stance and distance, footwork, and basic defenses. Jim tried to do as Takezo instructed.

As Takezo stabbed at him in the midline, he performed the block and stabbed back along the same line. The sequence repeated successfully once, twice, three times, and then Takezo called a halt.

"Mind the angle always," he said. "You block just using your arm and hand. That means you are not in a position to attack when your time comes, so you are also not in a position to defend when your opponent's time comes."

"I'm sorry," Jim said.

THIRTY-THREE

"Don't be sorry," Takezo said, "Perform the technique correctly. Okay, I see that look on your face. I think we are done with learning for the day. Take the equipment off and have some orange juice."

"I'm – "Jim began.

"Stop! There are no apologies in sword fighting. Apologies mean that you wish things were some other way. You must accept your current situation without a second thought and go from there. Anything less cedes the initiative to your opponent. Starting today, we will strive to eliminate all sorts of wishful thinking from your mind," said Takezo.

Jim had already poured himself a glass of orange juice. He raised the glass and then downed the entire contents. Takezo smiled and nodded with approval as he poured a glass, too. He drank slowly and had not yet emptied his tumbler of juice when loud and angry voices from the vicinity of his workshop interrupted the refreshments.

He and Jim set their glasses down and ran off towards the commotion. As they reached the steps down from the villa, they saw Augustine shouting and gesturing angrily at a pair of unfamiliar persons who stood outside the

workshop's open sliding door. Both of the strangers were
calculators.

The one who directly confronted Augustine wore an articulated metal frame covered with adherent silver laurel leaves. In his left hand, he held several loops of chain, and in his right hand, he held a hammerhead attached to the far end of the chain. The chain and the hammerhead emitted a light orange glow.

"This is no beauty pageant. You can't appeal to the rulebook. There is no rulebook!" Augustine said to the fellow with the chain weapon., "A lot of people have died pursuing a weapon of this nature, and a lot more people are going to die in the pursuit. If you are not happy with the compensation, you may leave."

As Augustine was speaking, the two newcomers noticed Jim and Takezo approaching.

"Aha! Here they come," said the chain-wielding man, "now we shall have some answers. Hey, you!" The man said to Takezo, "I propose a contest."

"Look at this," the man said," he has involved two extra-Species individuals whom he has supported and paid extravagantly to design a God killer. What positive difference could this progeny of a younger and weaker race make in the effort to realize this weapon? I think that the sponsors never intended to succeed. I think this has all been an underhanded trick to steal everyone else's ideas."

"Shut up," Takezo muttered as he strode past, walking right between the newcomers and Augustine.

Without another word, the man began swinging the hammerhead on the chain. It sparked and crackled as a wavefront built on the leading edge of the hammer.

"Proposal accepted," Takezo said quietly as he slipped on his welding gauntlets and grasped his creation by its indented handgrips.

Augustine ran to take cover around the far corner of the building. The second

challenger pulled an automatic pistol from a holster on his left leg and began trying to get a bead on Takezo.

Jim looked from Augustine over to the nascent fight and back again. He dashed toward Augustine's hiding place.

"Yeah!" Augustine said, "You don't want to get slaughtered. Over here." Jim cut left abruptly before he rounded the corner and dove behind the forge. Meanwhile, Takezo picked up his hammer from the integrated Anvil and worked to advance while keeping a stack of crates and a block and chain

hoist between himself and the pistol.

Jim broke cover and made for the opposite wall. The gunman shifted his aim towards the movement and fired. The shot went wide, and by the time the gunman regrouped, his target had disappeared. He stood and gaped until Takezo's hammer erased the incredulous look from his face. The chain-wielding opponent then took his chance.

The hammer arced towards Takezo's head, but the weapon was slow on offense. Takezo ducked and shifted right, arriving at the gunman's body before the primary opponent recovered his hammer. Takezo snatched the pistol from the floor and emptied its clip at his opponent.

With the first shot, the collection of silver leaves stirred on the frame. They flowed to each bullet's point of impact with a loud snap. When they arrived, they clung to the frame and each other like ants, forming a bridge of their bodies across a chasm. The shots bounced off.

Takezo had not waited for results from the pistol. As soon as the last round was away, he took two running steps and then jumped across an intervening crate to close the distance. He raised the blade above his head and then dipped the point straight

down to the middle of his opponent's chest, while his hands continued over the top of the arc and back down to match the point's vector as it made contact. His opponent tried to block the anticipated head cut with a length of chain stretched between his two hands. The point had already slipped by and struck his chest before the chain came into contact with Takezo's blade.

The entire collection of leaves stacked itself against the blow. The world blinked, and the leaves exploded, creating a wall of shrapnel.

The shards missed Takezo, who continued to move to his right as soon as his feet struck the ground. Although he had learned to weather the shock through repeated exposure, it was still enough to knock the weapon from his hands. He scrambled back to the left to retrieve the blade.

By the time it was back in his possession, his opponent had regained his feet. The enemy kicked off the remainder of the metal frame that had supported his reactive armor. The hammer arced towards Takezo. In mid-swing, the opponent yanked the chain downwards, and as the hammer whipped on its new trajectory, the distal meter of chain stiffened and flew like a spear at Takezo's legs. He leaped back but still had to take some of the impact on his blade. The contact made a deafening screech of metal on metal as sparks showered both combatants. Takezo was injured. He held his weapon in one hand as he shook the other hand, trying to restore feeling.

At that moment, he glimpsed a flicker of movement above him. He struck by reflex and felt the blade contact something very light. A second later, half of an external power source accessory nachinak landed to his left and the other half to his right.

"You stupid, clumsy brawler," said Augustine, "do you have any idea what it took to make that thing? I can't believe that I'm trying to help you!"

The chain was coming at him by then. He raised the grip of his weapon in a covering guard. Again, he glimpsed movement overhead.

He had no time to attend to it. He was still tracking the path of the hammer towards him when a second nachinak lit on the pommel of his weapon. He heard a snap followed by buzzing from the far corner of the building.

In response to the sound, his blade came alive again. The frost feather markings blossomed to their full extent and brilliance. The dull discoloration disappeared from the point.

The chain hammer and the blade clashed one more time. The hammer exploded into molten droplets, taking almost a meter of chain along with it.

Liquid metal peppered Takezo's skin and clothing, forcing him to disengage. In the pause, the enemy stood and began to gather what remained of his weapon for a renewed attack. When the man had the remnant of his weapon in order, he stood to face Takezo again.

Instead, a small pale creature confronted him. It walked slowly and steadily in his direction. It stopped as the man raised the chain over his head.

"No," it said.

Before the man could respond, Takezo's long knife struck him in the throat. Jim became noticeable again.

"Great," said Jim, "I guess I should give you credit for doing what you could. Come over here before something happens to you."

Casper turned without a second glance at the man dying on the ground in front of him and walked over to Jim with Takezo following in his wake. Casper stopped two feet in front of Jim.

"No," he said.

"Thank you," said Takezo to Casper. Casper stood impassively.

Augustine waddled into the conversation.

"Where did you get that thing?" Augustine asked.

THIRTY-THREE

"I bought it from an exotic pet store in the town below the Center of Excellence," said Takezo.

"I suppose there is no law against having one of these, and I guess it's good that someone's finding a use for them at last. Beware, they can turn on you," said Augustine, turning from Casper to Takezo, "As I was coming to warn you, word has gotten out that you are building some kind of weapon for us. The sponsorship aspect is now common knowledge. In other words, everything that our late friend over there with the hormone problem was beefing about is widely known. That means there's going to be more of this," he said, sweeping his hand across the ruin before them.

"On a more hopeful note," he said, "I have found out how to charge that weapon quickly using an external power source and power accessory

nachinaks. Currently, you get about one recharge from a full external power source. The cost is likely to improve as demand and resource costs stabilize and adjust. I'm confident that we will be able to increase the number of charges per power source as we gain experience with the pairing. Right now, though, it is still one and done. The external power source overheats easily, and we already have several damaged units in for repair."

With that, Augustine turned around and began the long trek back to the Old Country Store.

Takezo and Jim turned to cleaning up the wreckage in silence, with sober expressions to match the
grim prospects of their new circumstances.

When they were finished, both took a seat on the floor in front of Casper. "How long have I had a new tenant?"? " Takezo asked. "

"Takezo, this is Casper. Casper, Takezo," said Jim, "Casper has only been with me for a couple of days. All he does is
stand around and sometimes say 'no.' I don't know what to do with him. I think he was part of some kind of medical experiment, so I feel sorry for him, but I'm not sure whether that makes any sense. He doesn't seem to be suffering. He

doesn't seem to be anything at all. If I feed him, he will eat, but I suspect he would starve to death if I left him to his own devices."

"He is here now, so he belongs to us," said Takezo, "he is clearly a creature without a spirit. The world does not make creatures without spirits, nor does it tolerate them if they come to be when a creature somehow loses its

spirit. Come, I have an idea."

Takezo rose and walked to the back of the shop, to a door in the northeast corner. He pulled out his keys and unlocked the deadbolt. Behind the door, a long room contained a woodstove with firewood stacked alongside and a steel box stacked full of volcanic rocks on top. A bucket and ladle took up the other side of the floor beside the stove. Two tiers of benches surrounded the stove, and behind them, a large wooden tub with deep ladles and a selection

of soaps on the floor beside it.

Takezo took Casper's hand and led the creature into the sauna.

There, Takezo sat Casper down on the lower tier of benches and explained the purpose of everything in the room. Upon completing the orientation, Takezo assigned Casper the bathhouse keeper's title and duties.

"What do you expect will come of this?" Lucky asked.

"A place for it. If it lost its spirit, how can it find a new one with no directions or landmarks? I have given Casper those things, now time will tell. "

Thirty-four

Araceli's Gamble

Five Danilos and greater than three times that number of nachinaks lay inert on the gangway. Laplace and Francis stood at the hatch, waiting for someone to let them in. The two external power sources continued to clank along beside them. The noise caused anxiety at first, but as they had picked their way through the ancient, decrepit buildings, it became apparent that no one remained to hear them. Yet, the ruin was not wholly abandoned. When they exited the city limits, they came upon a massive launch and recovery facility dug into the bedrock like the rest of the city.

The machinery showed signs of recent salvage activity, and the old scrap yards contained wrecks of current vintage. They proceeded more cautiously, but their luck held, and before encountering any hostiles, they discovered a large gathering of females from Danilo's race.

The males had packed them into a fast, sub- light vehicle and set off for UR 538. However, the females rebelled and took control of the ship's vital systems. The Danilos hung on and fought their way out of the ship when it landed and besieged the airlock until Laplace and Francis arrived. Even after Laplace

and Francis showed live footage of their captors' dead bodies, the women were still wary. They sent another delegation to the airlock. They were considering the additional guarantees and reassurances Laplace gave to them. The conference was into its second hour.

Francis picked at a rubber seal on the gangplank with a screwdriver that he found along the way as they journeyed from the offline node to the launch and recovery center. The center was enormous. At its peak, it handled numerous launch and recovery operations daily. Like so many similar facilities, it also benefited from the legacy self- repair mechanisms installed when the structure was new, many forgotten millions of years ago. With those caveats, it still looked a little bit too well-kept for comfort.

"Stop that!" Laplace snapped at Francis.

Francis sighed and tossed the screwdriver over his shoulder.

"Stay alert. I'm sure that somebody still lives here," Laplace said. "It's only a matter of time before we meet them. We must

have the first move. If we don't, then we are done."

"What's wrong with them?" Francis inquired, indicating the fallen Danilos. "They are making bad decisions, more and more as time goes on. And their behavior is erratic, sometimes even bizarre, even for Danilo." "Good observation," said Laplace, "for lack of a better term, they are

devolving. You see that every one of them has a subjugation nachinak?"

"I was wondering about that," said Francis. "Who could they possibly

refer to? One person couldn't hold that many slaves. So, what does that nachinak bind them to?"

"You guessed close to the mark. Given the background, I'm assuming that you took the Danilos for clones, as it would make

the most sense. Most are clones, but a substantial minority are converted from a previous individual.

Danilo started the conversions when he discovered, by accident, that the modified subjugation nachinak he had created was capable of the feat. That modification not only subjugated the host but also made continuous,

recurrent corrections in the host system to align it with the original Danilo's supervenience base Laplace said, "These are not Danilo clones, who would share a genetic identity, but with different lives. These are copies, each possessing the exact memories, experiences, knowledge, and perceptions of the original Danilo.

The problem is that no system is perfect. The copies are subject to error compounding. That's what you see before you. That's why they want the females. They technically no longer need them. What they're doing right now is as close to male parthenogenesis as possible. They were hoping that the females would mitigate the deterioration, as the genetic material in a natural pregnancy undergoes recombination."

Laplace took a peek through the portal. The conferees had requested that he cease checking as they began their deliberations. They told him that they found his cosmetic modifications disconcerting and could not tolerate interruptions every 15 minutes, no matter who was peeking through the glass and tapping on the door. This time, he was in luck. They had wrapped up their discussions. One of them approached the door and spoke to him over the intercom.

"Although most of us still don't trust you, we also don't see a way forward without your assistance. You may enter." The small creature released the hatch and stepped aside. Ten of her sisters rose from the floor and offered a lukewarm greeting. Laplace acknowledged them and then turned back to the woman

who was now locking the closed hatch.

"You are in charge here?" he asked.

"In this room, yes," she answered.

"I'm sorry, but the spokesperson never mentioned your name."

"I am Araceli," she said

"Araceli, I need to see the engine room, the navigational computer, and the records," Laplace said as he walked to the airlock exit door and down

the corridor that she indicated, "I am not too fond of space travel, but I can usually sort out where I am, and what I need to do to get where I am going, whether or not I am travelling by spaceship."

"Whew," she replied without looking up, "You can't imagine how relieved I feel to hear you say that."

"Really?" Laplace asked as he stopped in the middle of the hallway.

"No. That was a joke," she said as she walked ahead of him, "but I'm not too worried. How could it be worse?"

Laplace seemed ready to say something but then thought better of it and resumed the walk. They made their way through the maze of passages, Laplace, and Araceli in front, followed by Francis and the two external power sources. The delegation of Metizians took up the rear.

The trip to the engine room was short. Laplace made a show of bringing up all the displays that he knew how to activate. He reviewed the data, nodding occasionally to express his approval of the readings he saw.

There was a workstation to access the navigation computer in the engineering section. It took him several minutes to find his way into the system. The ship's current proprietors made multiple attempts on the navigation computer for several days after the rebellion, and their efforts triggered additional layers of security.

Laplace waded through several outdated launch and recovery plans before arriving at what he was after. At the very end of the search, he found a library of forbidden files. Laplace was unable to open the library, no matter what he tried. Before the forbidden files, the most recent flight plans indicated that the ship was launching from the planet of origin for Danilo's race. It was listed as a military transport and was destined for UR 538 from the beginning.

During the trip from Metiz to UR 538, someone revised the flight plan and sent the vessel around a binary consisting of a medium-sized black hole and a young, massive star. The close pass got them to a better E.R. bridge and

accelerated the ship to a very early arrival at the UR 538 launch and recovery area. The ship landed in a commercial zone instead of the military resupply transfer area designated in the original flight plan. After he had thoroughly reviewed the information, he called Araceli over.

"Do you know who changed the flight plan on your way here?" he asked.

"I did. I took it from one of Danilo's officers. He was a navigator, and we imposed upon him to show us how things worked around the ship," Araceli replied.

"Where is he now?" Laplace asked.

"Freeze-drying in the vacuum somewhere between the binary system and UR 538," she said.

"Was it his idea to change the course?" Laplace asked.

"No, he did not encourage us to take this route. It was my choice, but it didn't seem like much of a choice in light of the alert," said Araceli.

"What alert? There's no alert showing on my screen, "Laplace said.

"It's right over here," she said, "when you zoom in on the launch and recovery zone. "

She came closer so that she could see the map better. She recentered everything several times, zoomed in and out, and scanned the zones on either side of the no-go zone in question. No alerts popped up, and there was no unusual activity.

"Well, it was there. It marked that entire zone as no- go. The details said that the helpers controlled that part of the zone and that one of their ships was scheduled to land there in the next 7 to 10 days. "

Laplace stood and strode back into the hallway. "Where can we access records?" He asked.

"In the wheelhouse. It's the closest, and it's the other way," she said, pointing down the opposite hall.

He pivoted and increased his pace. As he passed the group, Araceli had to break into a trot to keep up with him.

"Hey! Now you have passed it!" Araceli shouted down to the next hallway junction. Laplace stopped short and walked back to her without saying another word.

"Please do not disturb me. Stay here for the next few minutes. I need to concentrate," said Laplace.

The others were catching up as they spoke. Francis overheard the entire conversation and spoke before Laplace could duck into the room.

"He was here, Danilo, that is," Francis stated.

"More than once," LaPlace said, "given the current state of affairs, I'm no longer too worried about him. The ongoing problem is Augustine. Danilo couldn't get here by himself. He needed someone from the Authority to help him. We need to determine the extent of Augustine's knowledge. We need to know how many times he has been here and where he went during his visits. Complicating our lives even further, he's likely to have left several deterrents along our way. I don't

think he suspected that we would find out about all this, but such measures are standard operating procedure, and I don't see him deviating from standard operating procedure in this circumstance."

"What about us?" Francis asked, "We are contaminated with knowledge too, and we are on a trajectory to become even more contaminated. Are we just hoping to keep this all quiet, or should I resign myself to imminent death? Hang on... You've been here before, haven't you? You have been here before, but you didn't go far enough to bring judgment down on you."

"Stop thinking until I tell you to start again," Laplace said, "All of you need to leave me for a few minutes so that I can concentrate on extracting what we need from the records." Without waiting for a response, he stepped through the door and closed it behind him. The room was narrow and lined on either side with a row of utilitarian desks with benches, all bolted securely to the wall. Laplace chose a desk in the middle of the nearest wall to reduce visibility in case anyone decided to peek in. He tapped a button on his desk's projector, and the index of records popped up. Most of it was inventory and

log entries. Laplace scrolled past to a specific date. It was a date that should not have existed, but the calendar had opened to it. The file for that date contained one highly secure entry. Laplace pulled up the entry and tried to break into it, armed only with his own guile and average hacking skills. When he was clearly stymied, he grimaced and reached into a compartment on his abacus to retrieve a set of instructions handwritten on a sheet of paper. He unfolded the note and entered a series of commands as the text instructed. Presently, the image of his brother Gerard came up associated with a dossier.

THIRTY-FOUR

Joint task force report: Conclusions.

First: Diversion of resources from the Developmental Center, practice of medicine beyond the scope of training, perpetuation of untreatable neurodevelopmental disease in violation of Developmental Center policy and procedure.

Second: enticement to violate the security of Developmental Centers, willful violation of Developmental Center security, religious contamination of Developmental Center personnel, physical and psychological abuse of designated Mother, 48 counts

This report is the final summary of the investigation into incident number 277 at the developmental center accessed via the fold maintained on UR538. The original Mother, the one responsible for the sequestration of the ovum, acted on her own initially. She was the driving force behind the whole incident. The only mitigating factor was religious contamination. She expressed admiration for the Gods Helping Angels Sect. The source of contamination was a relative of hers who was a member of the sect. Specifically, she was motivated by the sect's taboo regarding the destruction of an ovum. She drew an unsalvageable ovum, and instead of turning it in

after her intake evaluation detected the problem, she hid it in her quarters, intending to maintain the developing child until it reached presentation age. Much of the apparent deficiency in the investigation, manifesting as a long delay between the commission of the original crime and its detection, is due to problems she encountered with the disposition of the individual who matured from the blastocyst. She maintained stasis for a number of years. During that time, she was tracking potential adopters among the child's relatives. When one appeared ready to emerge, she

reinitiated development and pursued an accelerated program. The child's disorder was progressive derangement of the cortical levels. A treatment does exist for the condition. However, the treatment is not curative and produces an improvement in the course of the disease that is below the established benchmarks for treatment. Nevertheless, the Mother in question managed to obtain the treatment, which she herself administered to the child without the proper credentials or professional guidance. When the child reached presentation age, she apparently just released him through the fold. A gap in our evidence remains between the purported release and the subsequent reappearance of the individual in question. A laboratory test obtained in the course of admissions to medical school flagged his genetics. The authority chose to defer action at that time in favor of longitudinal observation.

Redacted

Laplace did his best to restore the redacted pages, without success. He searched the records twice over but could find no entries referring to Augustine or Danilo. He saved a copy of the report and sent a copy to Francis with the attached message: Read this. He leaned forward, put his head in his hands, and swore quietly to himself for two minutes. When he emerged from the viewing room, his anger and frustration were apparent.

"Augustine covered his tracks well, didn't he?" Francis said, "I don't

think we'll learn anything more here."

"I thought I told you to stop thinking," Laplace reminded him. "Here is the rest of it. I had visited UR 538 as well. I was trying to find the fold that permitted entry to the developmental center. My brother's illness was worsening rapidly. He needed more of the medication that the Mothers had hidden there. When we were close, he started to remember what happened to

him the last time around. He panicked. He hid in a patch of thorn bushes, and I could not persuade him to move. I had to sneak into the center by myself and hope that he hid well enough. I avoided summary execution at the hands of the section AI, thanks to the original Mother.

Besides being a devout woman, she was a brutal bully. She trounced anyone who came into her section without permission and a chaperone. Being an artificial person brought no credit with her either. She abused the AI as if it were a fully conscious entity, just in case. Fortunately, she died a couple of years before I set foot in the center, so I never had to deal with her. I suppose I should be grateful to her. She took the risk of altering my profile and diverting my incubator to a different center. I can't forgive her panic at the end, though. She dumped him on the street, after all of that.

She had passed down her secrets and the therapy pack for her charge to a colleague. That was your mother, Francis. When I returned from the center, my brother had disappeared.

It was too dangerous to stay, so I went back to Sonnamarg to regroup. I had enslaved Danilo and three of his brethren. I thought that they were adequately prepared when I took them back to UR 538. I was wrong, of course. They had my brother by then. He was persuaded by the helpers, or by his own ruminations, that he was one of them. They had done things to him by then – the sort of things that leave marks and impairments. He ran me off the first time I attempted an extrication. That was when the helpers caught Danilo. Danilo never recovered from what they did to him,

though I convinced myself otherwise. I knew that the helpers would take the Metizians to the center for interrogation. They are contemptible fanatics, but they are sworn to protect the centers and remain as faithful to their oath as any Agent of the Authority. I set up at the fold and waited. That was one of my best days. They did not stand a chance. I wiped them out to the last man. Danilo and one other Metizian survived. Danilo helped me subdue my brother and transfer him out through the radiation. The

other Metizian escaped while I was occupied with the transfer calculations. Were you listening, Francis?"

"I was," he replied.

"Give me a summary and tactical analysis based on what I have described from previous encounters and your observations," said Laplace.

"Our assets are superior resources in the form of the devices we have with us, as well as those we can bring in on short notice. We have an advantage when operating in the radiation. We have a fast sub light transport that is probably faster than anything the opposition can field. Currently, we have better intelligence; they are unaware of our presence yet. To our disadvantage, we are on their home territory. There are more of them than there are of us. Their vessels are better armed and have more naval combat experience. Unknowns are the enemy's desire to engage and the capability of our Metizian personnel. So, we should avoid launching this ship. We should hide as long as possible. We should find out whether Metizians can fight or not. We should utilize the event radiation to move and, if necessary, relocate the fight to the event radiation. And might I add, "Francis continued before Laplace could butt in, "we should clarify our objectives before we do anything else. What are we supposed to do with the Metizians? What about the center? Do we contact them about the security breach? Do you even know who to contact?"

"Yes, what do you plan to do with the Metizians?" Araceli asked.

"We have to contact the center. I will do that myself. They are long past the days when they would shoot on sight anyone trying to enter. Even before

the events surrounding Gerard and Francis, there had been intermittent reports of people walking around with knowledge of a center's location. It is

common enough that the Mothers developed a protocol for it. We now accept this reality, and nobody jumps to evacuate the place and then blow it up as soon as someone knocks on the door. Nor do they immediately put a bounty on anyone who learns one of their secrets. What Augustine did is different, granted. He also tampered with equipment and children and enlisted a center staff member to assist him. Nevertheless, he has not disclosed anything vital. He has no discernible motive to harm the centers. I will pass on what we have learned to the staff. The final decision is theirs. That goes for the fate of the Metizians too. The Foundation for Clinical Developmentalism and Neuropsychological Development is their only hope. It is the only organization equipped to take them in and the only organization capable of the large-scale genetic engineering that the Metizians will require to survive.

"What makes you so sure that they will take us in?" Araceli asked, "I'm not going to ask the group to act on your suppositions or the requirements of a deal yet to be done."

Laplace indicated that they should begin walking. The leader started back to the junction of the hallways at a leisurely pace. Everyone fell in behind her, with Francis taking up a position next to Laplace on the left.

"I would not suggest a gamble," he assured the leader. "Remember, the center's staff, from the slaves to the Mothers, are members of the Species who sacrificed any opportunity to participate in the quest that has shaped not only our culture but our physiology over countless generations. Their work at the centers takes the place of the quest for Utopia. They will not be able to resist the opportunity that your people represent."

As Laplace concluded, the leader turned a corner, and they stood in the doorway of a large room containing rows and rows

of reclining chairs. Each chair had a support arm with an IV fluid bag attached to it. None of the chairs was occupied. Scattered groups of Metizians sat on the floor, talking or playing games. They were all adult females. The leader continued to the other side of the room, returning shouted greetings and gestures of solidarity along the way.

She opened a pressure door in the far wall and continued into another cross-section of the ship, this one partitioned off into numerous small compartments. Each compartment held four groups of four beds outfitted for passenger stasis during extended flights. Araceli passed through several rows of stasis rooms to a command area in the center of the section. She stopped and indicated for the rest of the group to take a seat on the floor. Laplace sat down on the back of the nearest external power source instead. Francis waffled for a moment and then followed suit.

"I will take report from my officers now and present your wager to them. It should take 15 to 20 minutes," Araceli informed them.

"By all means," said Laplace.

While Araceli gathered her officers in a far corner of the command center, Laplace took stock of the technology. Superficially, it all looked antiquated. Every fast sub light vessel had that look to it. The ships were all utilitarian and built to withstand severe physical stress. The instrument panels featured both analog and projected readouts. Thick bolts through welded plates secured anything that couldn't be integrated with a wall, floor, or ceiling panel. It all looked clunky, whether the ship was new or old. Laplace did not note any chipped paint, mismatched instrument components, or loose nuts on bolted attachments. As he was looking over the wall displays, something caught his eye. He recognized the picture on one of the video feeds as the view from a camera above the air lock door where they had entered the ship. It looked like a leaf blew past in the background, but there were no trees or bushes nearby. His gaze lingered on the scene. After a few seconds, nothing more unusual had happened, and Laplace was about to move on to the next monitor when the

scene abruptly went black and flashed a symbol resembling a black sun on a silvery background. The scene outside the airlock then reappeared. Laplace sat up straight.

"Get the leader and tell her to bring all the fighters that she can gather in the next five minutes to the airlock door," Laplace told Francis.

Francis started to object, but Laplace was already gone. The two external power sources clanked after him, and a gathering flock of nachinaks swirled overhead.

Thirty-five

Try Our Intentional Inexistence

Despite some initial hiccups, Jim had taken to invisibility quite well. He maintained the effect without difficulty now. It no longer flickered or distorted. He could walk down the middle of the road, approaching the center of excellence without a care. He needn't skulk around in the hostile vegetation anymore. The trip was over before he realized it had begun.

He occupied himself along the way with a debate about which forbidden locale he would visit first. He made it all the way to the first Plaza at the top of the stairways without a final decision. He stopped for a moment to review his choices. Night had fallen by then. The relatively poor lighting on the

eastern side of the campus made it look foreboding. Besides, he had already been there. He turned right and took the sidewalk that skirted the hedge and continued southwest to the stairs in front of the medical school lecture halls and amphitheater.

He found the front doors unlocked but encountered more serious roadblocks just inside. The building was getting a makeover. The contractors had torn out the walls. Black and yellow tape forbade entry. For those who missed the initial notice, the contractors had also posted 'no trespassing' signs on the exposed members of the frame. Jim cautiously ducked and sidestepped his way through the demolished hall. The construction ended ten feet from a set of fire doors that led down to the stage in front of the amphitheater. Jim brushed himself off at the end of the demolished section. He pushed the release bar and opened the left-hand fire door about half a handbreadth. His jaw dropped. The divine hamster habitat slowly gyrated above a large diorama of the campus. A slave armed with a semi-automatic rifle stood at attention on either side. Two external power sources waited by each guard. A pair of large nachinak floated above the diorama, their legs beating lazily. They supported interwoven tubes of black sand circulating between them. Jim slipped through the fire doors, easing the left-hand door closed after him. He tiptoed down the stairs to the stage. A voice came from the tube sculpture above the diorama.

"They don't notice you. You don't need to sneak around."

"Yeah, I know. It makes me feel better, though," said Jim.

As he drew nearer, Jim could see the voice's owner, floating in the sculpture of transparent ductwork. It was a small,

naked man with cold blue eyes, dark skin, and dark ringlet curls.

"Hello, I'm Jim. Who are you, and what brings you here? Are you in trouble?" asked Jim.

"I am. The Lord thy God," said the little man.

"Whoa! Not so fast. How do you know that you are my God?"

"Because I am omniscient. Therefore, I know who I am, and I know that your God is who I am One way or another, you will follow me. All who are caught in the present will follow the omniscient," God stated flatly.

"How is that? Maybe I'll walk the other way," Jim said. God sighed.

"I know where to walk so you will follow."

"I hate to quibble," said Jim, "but does that mean I'm following you, you're staying ahead of me, or we're just sharing the trail?"

"Do you want to ask it that way?" God asked. "What do you mean?" Asked Jim.

"It's another way of asking where you end up, and of course, you all end up dead, so it is another way of asking the second question that everyone asks me." Said God." The first is 'Who are you?' The second is,' How will I die?'

I will tell you what I tell everyone. That information will destroy the person that you are now, because every detour around that end belongs to a different you."

"Isn't that just a technicality?" Jim asked, "You know, the butterfly effect _."

"Stop it!" God said, "Those words are forbidden. All such excuses are forbidden. You will not escape your deaths, your lives, or your responsibility. You have

243

sinned. You continue to sin. Every day, you afflict me with your sins. You sprayed poison around the shop building in the little town ten miles up the road from you," God said.

"I did," Jim said. "That was my last job."

God drew up to his full eighteen centimeters and began to excoriate, his voice growing louder with each word.

"I knew what would happen when you offered to do the job. I saw your lack of interest in discovering what you would really be doing. You did not care to understand the consequences for the 'vermin' or me. I knew. I understood. I knew exactly what the mouse went through as it bled out into its gut and

lungs. Most observers wouldn't have been able to tell for sure whether her pups died of starvation or hypothermia. It was hypothermia. So now, you are on my list. I can't bear to let your callous, casual atrocities stand. There must be justice!"

God slammed his fist against his palm, generating an unnaturally loud slap.

"You are impervious to true justice, though. You could not even be made to understand what you did to the mice," God said," much less what you did to an omniscient bystander, who had to watch what you did and who cannot ever forget it. I know the price of your transgressions, but I can never have payment from you. If I torture you appropriately, it won't refine your understanding of the sins you have committed. It will be a matter of revenge and gratuitous suffering. And then I have sinned, just as if I had shirked my duty and failed to punish you adequately or at all."

"It's quite a dilemma you've gotten yourself into," Jim said.

"You needn't pretend to care," said the deity.

"It's never wrong to be polite," said Jim.

God did his best to flop down on the edge of his habitat. The shimmering containment membrane spread out at the potential point of impact, and the tiny figure flickered into a sitting position just out of contact with the membrane and the floor of the box. He sat there glowering at the empty amphitheater. Jim sidled over a little farther on his seat.

"You might as well go ahead and ask me," God said.

The words tumbled out.

"Am I conscious or not? Am I alive or am I an automaton?" Jim asked.

"I can't tell you," God said with satisfaction, "these are things that occur within the subject, and are not facts in the world. Consciousness has signs and symptoms, but no tests or detectors can find it. I can tell you things about it, but as a report of my own, not as a sample of my all-encompassing knowledge. Before you try to sort that out, you should ask yourself why.

You are alone with the answer either way."

"You have given me a lot to think about, "said Jim. "Would you mind if I return in the next couple of days to discuss my progress?"

"You may, but you must understand that none of this absolves you of your guilt. You will be punished for your sins sooner or later, maybe even tomorrow, ".

Thirty-six

The Children's Crusade

Laplace fiddled with the screws on the airlock's ventilation panel for several minutes before giving up.

"Are these the only tools that we have available?" he asked, throwing the screwdriver on the floor for emphasis.

"We can go back and look for some more," the Metizian leader suggested. "No time," Laplace said, "we can risk forcing the doors just enough to let

my little helper get through here. We just have to be quiet about it."

He went to the pile of tools on the floor and selected a substantial crowbar. He had opened the access panel for the door controls at the beginning of the present chore. He knelt beside the panel and disconnected the power to the inner and outer airlock doors. A single nachinak hovered over him. It was an unusual creature, sporting a pair of thin ridges on its back and belly, with an intricate lacey fringe atop each ridge. The body was white with black and red speckles, and the fringe was a deep red. From the tail end, a white tube projected to about half again the length of its body, and it had an unusually

long trunk.

Laplace worked the edge of the crowbar into the gap between the doors and pulled. He broke off when he reached the end of his strength. He looked at the gap between the doors. He smiled. It had not been wishful thinking. He had felt a little give in the doors, and he could see an increase in the space between them.

"Remember that the airlock still has to work after you're done with it," the Metizians leader reminded him.

He did not reply. Instead, he worked the thin edge of the crowbar deeper into the gap between the doors and cranked it again. This time, he saw daylight on the other side. He could now get most of the crowbar into the gap, and he was able to force the door open enough to allow passage on the next attempt. He lay down on the floor and turned on his side. He wriggled until he could get his shoulders through the gap and then pushed on the edge of the door to squeeze the rest of his body through. He stayed on the floor.

The single nachinak kept its position over him. He reached back through the doors and retrieved the crowbar. He moved in a crouch to the outside doors. Gingerly, he worked the edge of the crowbar between the two doors. He added pressure very gradually. The outer doors were not as difficult to force, and he managed to get through them without slips, clanks, or bumps. Adding to his good fortune, he only had to open the outer doors wide enough to let the nachinak through. It landed on the edge of the door as soon as there was daylight from the outside and squirmed its way through. Laplace tiptoed back to the inner door as quickly as possible once the unit was out of sight.

"Check the feed from the camera," he whispered.

The Metizians' leader snatched a projector from a side pocket of her vest and turned it on. It showed the same scene as it had since his arrival. He smiled with relief. He had set his abacus

aside so he could squeeze through the doorways. He reached around the side of the door and pulled the abacus into the airlock. He secured it to his chest and disconnected one of the end plate wires on a middle cylinder. He moved as quietly as he could back to the outside doors and carefully threaded the wire between the gap in the doors up towards his best-estimated location of the camera. Momentarily, the wire moved on its own.

He completely relaxed. He walked back to the inner doors to ask for the projector. He plugged the other end of the wire into the device and turned it on. Once again, the monotonous view of the launch and recovery center appeared. He manipulated some of the beads on his abacus, and the scene changed to a claustrophobic view of the camera wholly engulfed in the trunk of an unfamiliar nachinak. The image could only have come from Laplace's own device.

"Okay, you can turn the power back on but wait until I have tossed the rest of the wire through the gap," Laplace called back to his team, "I don't want this cut because I don't have much of it and it's the only wire configuration I can use to communicate with our little friend out there."

The team complied very efficiently, and soon, they all stood outside the re-sealed outer air lock doors, admiring Laplace's assistant's capabilities.

Laplace attached the free end of the wire to the projector once more and then gave additional instructions to his nachinak.

"Please make one sweep through all the signals associated with this network," he ordered. The scene shifted every 10 seconds subsequently. Sometimes, it was obviously a view through the eyes of another nachinak. Sometimes, it was an image from a surveillance camera. Laplace made adjustments and brought up a launch and recovery center map. The map

was populated with green dots, and a new one appeared every time the view on the screen changed. Mostly, the place looked abandoned, but as the scattering of dots marched into the northeast quadrant, decrepit men began to appear in the scenes.

Most of them wore some kind of pressure suit. The suits varied dra-

matically in appearance, but they were all tattered, stained, and covered with field maintenance patches intended for use during the brief interval when a suit in use was damaged but couldn't be repaired immediately. The patches were de-signed to last approximately two weeks. The patches on God's Helping Angels must have been at least two years old. For the most part, the activity in the far northeast quadrant appeared subdued. On a single landing pad, activity was brisk. The helpers undertook the necessary tasks to prepare the pad for a new landing. Nachinaks, many looking just as battered as the men who deployed them, swarmed around the workers attending to their own jobs.

It wasn't until the dots had marched all the way across the map to the northwest quadrant that Laplace saw what he was looking for. A giant statue of a nachinak, made of gold and green metal plates, stood in a cubbyhole chiseled into the side of a limestone cliff. The opening of the statue's trunk was large enough to accommodate even the tallest member of the Species standing at full height. A little further down to the statue's left, a heavy door presumably opened into passageways carved into the limestone.

Laplace caught glimpses of precisely cut paving stones exposed here and there, but most of the original paving had long since been covered by sand. About two and a half kilometers east of the door, a collection of tents lay hidden behind a ruined administrative high-rise. Well-camouflaged bunkers dotted the field of sand and rubble between the wrecked building and the door, and an additional formation of Helping Angels had taken

up position due West, where the limestone escarpment curved back north briefly before resuming its westward extension.

It was an ambush, which was the only move that made any sense, given the helpers' situation. The door was familiar to Laplace from his previous visits to UR 538. It was the only door in or out of the developmental center, and so it was the one place where Laplace and the Metizians would have to show up sooner or later. Prospects looked grim overall, but the circumstances did allow a small ray of sunshine or two. God's Helping Angels had started their

preparations late in relation to Laplace's arrival. Besides that, Laplace had his own little red and white helping Angel with two fully charged external power sources, his best portable offensive weapon, and the four neutralizers, the latter for use if all else failed. Laplace sank into contemplation as the seer nachinak continued its survey of the enemy forces. Suddenly, he sat upright. He turned to Francis.

"You were wrong. You missed something," Laplace said.

"What do you mean?" said Francis defensively. "What did I fail to evaluate?"

"Our assets. We have one more asset that may be key, "Laplace replied. "I'm talking about you, Francis."

"What do you mean?" Francis asked. "I mean, I'm trained to use various weapons and the abacus. I think I understand how the armor in this EVA works. I can run it without any trouble, but that doesn't mean I'll be a decent fighter. Nobody knows and won't until I try to fight."

"I have faith in your ability to seize the moment," said Laplace, "but I'm not talking about any kinetic ability. I'm talking about what's going on in your blood right now."

"Oh no," Francis groaned, "I knew it was too good to be true. Will I need a transfusion after this?

Laplace chuckled.

"Don't worry, we just need a small sample. Don't be so dramatic, Francis. A bioweapon ought to be confident."

Thirty-seven

Answers in Prophecy

Takezo had to wake Jim for his fencing lessons the next day. Jim was distracted and made almost no progress. Things were bad enough that Takezo became angry.

"Stop!" he said after Jim lost control of the bind that Takezo had been trying to teach him for the last 90 minutes.

"Now, you will come over here," Takezo directed as he walked briskly from the training field to the villa's courtyard, "and stand in the horse stance while you tell me what is going on."

Jim complied.

"I can't pay attention today because I'm preoccupied with two things," Jim said. First, I'm wondering if I'm truly conscious, and I wonder why it matters to me whether I am or not. Second, I am worried that Anisa's going to kill you."

Takezo, who had been walking back and forth in front of Jim, stopped abruptly and pushed Jim hard in the middle of his chest. The shove lifted

Jim off the ground and sent him stumbling back.

"Do you think so little of me?" Takezo asked, "I have killed many men, all of them expert fencers. She would last no more than a heartbeat. Don't worry about me."

"Are you going to beat up the poison if she decides to do it that way, for example?" Jim asked.

"Get back into horse stance, and I will explain the other concern to you," Takezo said.

Jim reluctantly assumed a squatting stance with his toes pointed 45° out from parallel, his back straight, his hips fully flexed and abducted, and his knees bent at a 90° angle.

"There is one reason why we value consciousness: aesthetics," Takezo said. "Our consciousness allows us to see the whole cloth before us, immediately and with access to all of its aspectual shapes."

There is another approach to take if the goal is robust survival. The Species' grand cultural project exemplifies it in principle. Flatten out the world. Number its connections, then add them all up. You will get an answer that way, but it is an answer cursed with myopia. Even the calculators aspire to more than that brand of process and its answers. At the end of their descriptive calculation, they want to understand what it means and to appreciate its beauty.

Jim was sweating. His legs shook.

Seeing his discomfort, Takezo leaned down to Jim's face and asked quietly, "Why do you think I invited you to do this stance work? Do you think I worry that your legs are not strong enough?

What you feel now, the burning and the desire to give up that comes with it, are the reasons. If you are a perfect student, you will learn to endure the burning without hope or expectation. If you can achieve the state of mind that does not try to squirm away into such false refuge, then you will be ready to destroy another human being with a cut through the body's elegant mechanism. When the moment to cut arrives, you must act without reflection. I can teach anyone to parry, strike,

and evade in a few months. When it comes to preparing the mind
to commit the act of destruction, a lifetime is sometimes not enough.

The mind resists making the cut because it is conscious of the ugliness inherent in the act. That is why you are concerned about whether or not you are conscious, because if you are not, then what I am doing here is creating a murderer."

Jim's knees sagged, and rather than fall over, he broke his stance and stood. "I am not creating a murderer," Takezo said, "I have seen enough warriors
and enough murderers to know the difference."

Jim looked at his feet and mumbled, "I'm not sure I want to do this, Takezo."

Takezo slapped Jim on the shoulder and told him, "We'll put the lessons on hold. Think about our conversation today, then come back when you have decided, whichever way you decide."

Jim shuffled off to his room, but he did not stay there. As soon as he was confident that no one would notice his absence for a while, he slipped off to the Center of Excellence. He almost forgot his medication and had to go back to the nightstand when he was halfway out the door to retrieve the pill bottle. He was hardly symptomatic by then. He noticed that since he had achieved control of the skin, his condition had improved dramatically.

Carefree, he strolled onto campus, through the entrance to the University's amphitheater, and down to the labyrinth where God lived, still under continuous armed guard.

The deity floated in the middle of the structure in a Lotus position. "Welcome, my son," he spoke to Jim in greeting, "be seated."

"Don't mind if I do," said Jim as he sat down on the edge of the diorama. I will confess upfront that I am no closer to an answer to my question, but I think I may have found an answer

to yours along the way. I am resolved not to concern myself with my consciousness anymore. You're right about me being alone with my experience, no matter what. If that's how it is, then I must endure it either way.

For what it's worth, thanks. From now on, please call me Lucky. The name I was given means something to me, while the name I discovered doesn't. Now, this is the thing about your dilemma.

As I thought about consciousness, and specifically about how I could determine whether I have it, I could not escape the need for a measure to define it. Could it fit on a pinhead? Could it fit in a brain? Did it have a telltale voltage or color? I quickly realized that it would be impossible to find a system of measurement that could help me describe consciousness. It wasn't that I hadn't found the right system yet or that I just wasn't used to measuring things of that kind. Consciousness, as opposed to alertness, is not something that can be measured. From that understanding, I arrived at my stated conclusion, but something was

253

still nagging at me. I thought back through it, and then I saw the answer to your puzzle. You are not used to measuring things in terms of anything other than their relative severity. I think you have been handicapped by your inability to resolve the justice dilemma by appeals to sequence and time. What you need to do is go by space. Justice is local, so start with what is closest to you."

God was silent. His brow furrowed. He sat like a statue for five long minutes.

"You may be onto something," God said. "I don't see any way that preference based on proximity comes back to me."

He uncrossed his legs and stretched. The stretch went on and on, and as he stretched, he gained height and substance. He tore through the tiny maze that had housed him, and he set his feet on the diorama, crushing it into the floor. One of

the guards backed off, his weapon trained on the Lord, while the other broke and ran for the exit.

The pair of nachinaks, circulating a vortex of black sand between them, accelerated their spins. God reached through the vortex to grasp the two devices. A spark jumped from the vortex to his arm and chest. As his hand and forearm pushed into the stream of black sand, it ate away at the tissue, denuding the intruding flesh almost down to bone.

He grimaced and then laughed as his hand made contact with the closer device and crushed it. With its partner disrupted, the other nachinak veered off and crashed into the amphitheater's stage. Lucky put the time God spent dealing with his captors to good use. He focused on maintaining the mindset and concentration that fortified his obscurity. At the same time, he backed slowly toward the exit door where he had entered. Both of the guards made it to the exits.

God stamped on the external power supply units, destroying them. God had stopped growing when he reached around eight meters in height. Finding himself without nearby enemies for the moment, he stopped and looked around the room.

"Lucky! Where are you, Lucky? You have liberated me, Lucky. You freed me from the dilemma," God said as he strained to see through the effects of the skin, "though you remain a sinner and must face judgment, I also name you my Prophet."

The promotion shattered Lucky's concentration. He had almost made it out the door, but God noticed him at once. The divine gaze transfixed him. "Honored," Lucky said, his voice trembling, "but don't you think this is a little hasty?" I have to be honest with you; I don't think I'm qualified

because I don't know what a prophet does."

"That's easy," God said, "A prophet does what God says.

A prophet is an emissary sent to bring comfort to the faithful and to instill fear of divine judgment in the wicked. I will send you these messages: for the Species, you must reconsider your course. It has become an excuse for your sins. You will never escape your viewpoint. For my helping angels, I have told you to cease your ceremonial abuse of my smallest children. You

should take care what you toss into the abyss besides helpless little ones, especially wishes and questions. You never asked for my permission to act in my name, so I hereby disown you with no possibility of redemption.

For all to hear – no one will avoid judgment because you have judged. You hold sacred anything stamped with a personal brand. Don't you dare come to me with complaints about your isolation and suffering. You brought isolation and suffering on yourselves. Bear that in mind as you contemplate the judgment yet to come; it will be far worse than your incidental disappointments."

"Those are some pretty big promises," Lucky said. "Are you sure you want me to say all those things to all those people? How will you maintain control of the purgatory you are sending me to create? Am I wrong, or is that what I'm supposed to bring about: a waiting room for the damned?"

A furious expression spread across God's visage, and his fists were wreathed in lightning. He opened his mouth to speak, but at that moment, the door behind Lucky slammed open, a hand and arm shot out from behind the doorway, snatched a handful of shirt and collar, and yanked Lucky into the hall.

"Shut up," said Anisa, "and run!"

THIRTY-SEVEN

A massive impact on the door behind him emphasized the urgency of her instructions. Lucky sprinted after her.

"You are my prophet!" God yelled after them as he pounded on the walls of the amphitheater, "Don't you fail me, Lucky."

Thirty-eight

A Pale Horse

Laplace paced from one side of the airlock to the other. It had been less than an hour since he had turned over the work with the bioreactor to one of the medical personnel among the Metizians. He had some familiarity with the technical aspects of genetic engineering, mainly acquired when he was researching cosmetic interventions and during the course of treating his brother many years ago. The current task, however, exceeded his capability. He regretted the first hour it took him to admit that he was in over his head and that someone with more advanced training needed to take over. They were committed now.

Presently, another bruised and torn nachinak wriggled through the gap in the outer airlock doors and reported to the device hovering beside four groups of similarly damaged nachinaks, all lined up and waiting for instructions.

"Hello, love," Laplace greeted the new recruit. "Let me see what's happened there. I don't want you to look too good, but I won't send you out

with damage like that."

The nachinak had a split in its trunk that ran almost the entire length to the rectangle at the base of the skull. Two legs on each

side had also broken off. Laplace gathered up the distal edges of the split trunk with forceps and applied traction while gluing the laceration shut. He released his patient to join its fellows in the appropriate line. "Hello," Francis's voice came over the audio-only channel, "I'm sending the whole package down. The doctor wanted me to give you a report on my status as well. She did a check after we finished loading the aerosols. She wanted to tell you that the passive immunity treatments were working, but that the active immunization had not yet provoked a response, and I still have a high viral load."

"Good. That's good, Francis. We will just have to wait a little bit longer until we can get you out of that pressure suit," said Laplace," Ah! Here they are."

A Metizian trotted through the rear airlock entrance and laid a Styrofoam cooler labeled 'biohazard' at his feet. 'Get down here; this has taken far too long, and we may yet need you to help defend.'

"See you in a minute," Francis said.

Laplace spoke to his nachinak, "Bring them up one at a time from all of the groups sequentially." As soon as they are loaded, they can return to their areas and perform a routine sweep."

One by one, the damaged nachinaks rose from their group's ranks and presented themselves to Laplace. He removed the lid from the cooler and retrieved a rack of small vials. He loaded a vial into each unit's trunk and sent them on their mission. Each one returned to its original assignment. Once it arrived, it opened the pressurized vial and began its usual patrol pattern, while viral particles spilled onto hapless helpers below.

Adjustments to the original virus were much more straightforward than expected. Although they required a few more

sophisticated genetic alterations to enhance infectivity, the primary fix involved increasing the rate of viral replication. The template easily accommodated the change. It worked so well that they did not need to add any extra functions to prevent the illness from spreading beyond the infected helpers. Infected individuals began to feel sick within 45 minutes of exposure, became debilitated almost as quickly, and died within 4 to 6 hours of exposure.

The deployment only took a few minutes. Francis, the doctor, and Araceli stood with Laplace in silence, watching their best shot at survival struggle through the crack between the halves of the outer door.

"That's it, then," said Laplace as he sent the last of the damaged nachinaks on its way. "We are now spectators, watching our own fate unfold. If my guesses are correct, then they will be too weak to harm us by the time they realize what's going on. If I've guessed wrong, they will send out reconnaissance in strength; they will find us quickly, and we will only manage to die before they do."

"The pessimism would be tiresome if I weren't used to it by now," Francis remarked.

"Always," said Laplace with a smile, "begin with the worst-case scenario. It rarely makes a difference, but it avoids a great deal of disappointment." Francis smiled as well and took a seat on the floor with his back propped against the wall of the airlock. He activated his projector and brought up an image from the camera mounted above the outside door. The last of the nachinaks disappeared into the distance, and all was quiet. Laplace turned and left without another word. He made his way back to the viewing room, where he retrieved the ship's records, set up his projector

at the same table he had used before and closed both doors to the room. Gerard's image appeared as Laplace activated his projector.

"Brother?" Gerard asked, "Have you heard then? How can that be so? I barely got the news myself."

"What news are you talking about?" asked Laplace. "I had my reason for

this call."

"You've caught me on my way to confirm the reports, but it appears that our previously tiny, adorable God in a box has become large, frightening, and free."

"So, he wasn't epiphenomenal after all; he was just deeply conflicted. Of course," Laplace laughed, "let's have it all at once. Still, we knew this was likely to happen sooner or later. I'm assuming that the barrier around the amphitheater is still holding?"

"Yes, from the racket I'm beginning to hear ahead, I think that's a very safe assumption," Gerard said.

"You have to be extremely careful, brother," Laplace said," I think this is all still a show. He could not breach the barrier without risk to himself, but he could break through if he chose to. We mustn't give him any information that would prompt him to take the chance until we are ready. Most of all, we need to make believe that we are keeping him in the dark about who is on site. I bet that

259

he will wait until his enemies have gathered around him to strike. In the meantime, are you in a secure space?"

"One moment. Now I am," said Gerard as the sound of the door closing in the background marked the end of the thunderous hammering which had begun to make conversation difficult.

"I need you to set up a scan," said Laplace.

"What kind of scan?" I will send an order to the medical
imaging department," Gerard said.

"You don't understand. I need you to set up the scan. I am having difficulty concentrating, and I've been experiencing exaggerated, ego-dystonic emotional episodes," said Laplace.

"Oh, I see. You must be mistaken, though. That's in the past," Gerard said.

"We are never rid of the past, brother. It sticks with us, and we carry on without noticing for the most part. It's only when it snags on something near to us that we take note," Laplace replied.

"Yes, I take your meaning. But if what you fear is true, how will you return?" Gerard asked.

"It hasn't gotten that bad yet. If it does get that bad, then I'm just cashing in the same way that I always expected I would. But I'm almost at the way out, and so far, there's no one guarding the door," Laplace said.

"Very well, I will await your arrival. In the meantime, our all-knowing specimen will learn nothing new," Gerard said.

"Indeed. Although if he is paying attention, maybe he will recall how little omniscience helps a person in most circumstances." Laplace said, "Please notify me of any changes in our circumstances in the meantime."

Thirty-nine

The Node 8 Situation

Anisa collided with the man as he exited the faculty office. He was looking the other way at the moment of impact, so he had neither reflexes nor momentum to protect himself. She flopped to the floor, and he tumbled two body lengths down the hall. She gasped for breath for a few seconds.

"Ouch," Lucky commented as he came upon the crash. "Are you injured?" She tried to answer, but the words would not come out. Instead, she motioned for him to go over to the other victim, who had yet to show any signs of life after the wreck. He was lying face down. Lucky shrugged and turned him over. The man groaned and opened his eyes. In the interval between the victim's eye-opening and the resumption of normal, pre-impact neurologic function, Lucky started to look nervous.

He was still having trouble distinguishing one member of the Species from another. Even so, with its hundreds of generations of evolutionary education, his limbic system had marked this face for recognition.

"No, no, no, no," Lucky whispered as he backpedaled," it's

the guy from hospital administration!" Gerard sat up.

"What have we here? It's our curious houseguest staying with – nobody that I would know, right? You are responsible for this, aren't you?" he said, rising to his feet unsteadily.

The irregular impacts behind Lucky grew louder, and the ground shook in accompaniment. He reached Anisa and helped her to her feet. She used her first normal breath to state the obvious.

"We need to get out of here," she said.

THIRTY-NINE

Two more of the Species rounded the corner of the next hallway junction down and headed for Gerard at a run.

"Prophet!" Came the voice of God from uncomfortably nearby, "Do not rest until my way is prepared. You must bring my prophecies to those facing the first judgment. Don't shirk your duties, or you will be replaced and face first judgment yourself." Lucky shot an exasperated look at Gerard and gestured in the direction of God's voice as if presenting evidence in a courtroom.

Gerard had completely recovered his composure. He raised an eyebrow. "He chose you as his prophet?" Gerard asked, "I suppose this is proof

that wisdom does not always accompany knowledge."

"I know what you mean," said Lucky, "I think I was deputized more as a matter of convenience until he could find somebody better qualified, which is why I vote that we continue running as fast as we can back the way you came."

Without waiting for anyone to second the motion, Lucky took off towards the two guards approaching the scene of the accident. Gerard quickly sidestepped to avoid being hit again and maintained a position close to the outer wall as Anisa passed by close on Lucky's heels.

Gerard hesitated until the next blow from

the divine fist shook the hallway, at which point he followed the others as

fast as he could. The guards had drawn weapons but came to a stop without pointing their shotguns at anyone. They looked at each other and then at Gerard, hoping for some guidance. Gerard looked annoyed but said nothing and waved them back the way they came. Soon, all of the runners arrived at the construction site in the building's foyer.

A dozen more security personnel awaited them. Anisa and Lucky slowed their pace and then stopped as soon as they saw the assembly of guards. Gerard was right behind them.

"Wait! These are witnesses with valuable information. They are not to be harmed. You are to protect them at all costs. Am I understood?" Gerard asked.

The woman in charge stepped forward. She was solidly built with dark gray skin and blue eyes. She wore the gray robes of a former slave. Around her head, she had tied a folded strip of green cloth with an image of an eight-ball printed in front. She looked Anisa up and down contemptuously and then turned to Lucky. "I thought I had seen something odd this morning on my way to inspect the security measures in the amphitheater. I guess it was you. You shouldn't be skulking around, but I see that you have become involved with the criminal element. Perhaps you can be rehabilitated if we eliminate the negative influences in your life," she said, and then, turning to Gerard, added, "I understand, Director. With your permission, I'm taking these two into protective custody. Do you have additional instructions?"

"Yes," Gerard said, while assiduously avoiding eye contact with Anisa, "check them over to make sure there are no injuries that require treatment. Deploy your personnel at regular intervals around the perimeter of the secondary barrier.

They are not to speak or otherwise respond to anything that they hear from the other side. I will send some of my nachinaks to reinforce them. However, if the barrier fails, they are to fall back to the designated rendezvous points without engaging. When you are confident that our two guests are in good

health, please escort them to the Node 8 lounge. I will meet you there."

Forty

Memory Lane

The afternoon proceeded into the evening, and still, nothing stirred on the land-scape. Laplace sat reading papers from the archives until he could no longer block out the suspense. He got up and paced until his legs got tired. He sat back down to resume reading, but he only lasted a few minutes before falling asleep, slumped against the back wall of the airlock. He jolted awake at the advent of first light.

He called up the view from the camera over the doorway. The same dull vista appeared. He flipped through the live feeds from the other nachinaks conscrip-ted by his modified external power supply accessory. He saw bodies scattered here and there, with no visible activity across the entire length and breadth of the launch site. In one of the field barracks, he saw bodies piled on the ground and in the tents. Only a comprehensive surveillance with a body count would have satisfied him that the way was clear, but the available circumstantial evidence convinced him that it was safe enough to take the next step.

Araceli appeared in the doorway. Her eyes were puffy, and patches of her

fur stuck out at odd angles

"What news?" She asked. "Time to go," Laplace said.

She left to gather the small cadre of Metizians who had any kind of military training. Francis showed up shortly before she returned.

"As we discussed," Laplace reminded the 30-strong expeditionary force as-sembled in the airlock, "no yelling. Use your audio-only channels to speak with each other. Single file. Maintain your distance. I will be in front. Both of the ex-ternal power sources will come with me. Francis takes the middle. Araceli brings up the rear. Break into your fire teams and cover at first contact. Francis, what the hell is that?"

Francis held up a bulky device resembling a grenade launcher, with a cable wrapped around the short barrel. A matching bandolier holding five large shells hung across his chest.

"I couldn't sleep last night, so I wandered around the ship. I recognized this thing and thought that it might be helpful," Francis said.

"As you must know already," Laplace said, "that is a highly indiscriminate weapon. Bring it if you must, but use it as a last resort, and only on an isolated target."

With that, Laplace opened the outer doors to the airlock and began the long walk to the developmental center's entrance. The silence was nerve-racking. The occasional nachinak swooped down toward them. In every case, the modified external power source accessory took control and interrogated the unfamiliar unit. All of them were following default protocols.

Initially, Laplace expressed concern regarding his troops' morbid interest in the bodies lying here and there at the roadside. The problem cured itself, though, as every person who broke formation to view the bulging eyes, purple subcutaneous

hemorrhages, and pink froth crusted in and around the corpse's mouth and nasal passages avoided second looks and warned off their uninitiated

comrades. They stopped to rest several times, but nobody proposed a meal. When they arrived at the sand-covered square beneath the limestone escarpment, they paused. It was a bad place to get ambushed. They decided to send four of their number, including Francis, to confirm neutralization.

They checked the firing positions, abandoned administrative buildings, and temporary barracks. They found only dead Helping Angels.

While Francis's team scouted the Eastern camp, Araceli herself reconnoitered the West. No one had survived on that side either. They relaxed a little bit as they made their way across the expanse of loose sand to the door and the massive nachinak statue.

The whole group flopped down to rest at the base of the statue. The hike was long by any measure, and most of the participants had not walked that far in recent memory, if at all. Yet, even after they recovered, nobody gave the word to proceed. The Metizians looked around in an effort to discern some clue as to the next move. Some of them even went to Araceli directly. She told them that she was waiting for the plan as well and counseled patience. They kept watching Laplace, but he displayed no interest at all in moving.

Two hours later, Francis got up and began to pace. Laplace sat atop one of the external power sources with his hat tilted over his eyes. Francis made a show of warming up for some unknown upcoming activity. When Laplace failed to respond, Francis sat back down to pout for a few minutes. He was hardly near the end of his session when the wind began to roar in the East. Laplace perked up. He stood as the roaring got louder, louder than any

wind. A dust cloud billowed over the distant rim of the launch and recovery area. Flames lit the cloud from within.

"Francis, have you fired one of those before, or did you just observe its use?" Laplace asked.

"I watched someone fire a more recent model. It seems straightforward enough," Francis said

"That is true," said Laplace, "but you should still send a round downrange before your marksmanship becomes critical. Take a long shot but try to hit what you're aiming at anyway. I'm going to show you something that the manufacturer omitted from the later models. See this?" Laplace asked as he borrowed the weapon from Francis and flipped up a 6 x 6 cm screen near the stock.

"I do now," Francis said, "I never knew it had one of these." "It is a seldom-used feature," Laplace said. "Under most conditions, it functions as part of an illegal subsystem. Firing it in that mode buys you a visit from the Authority, and maybe even a trip to see the Council. A few egregious uses in the past resulted in death warrants. You shouldn't worry about that

today, though."

Laplace plucked two shells from the bandolier and held them up in front of Francis for a side-by-side comparison. They were fairly similar, but one was decidedly heavier than the other and had the symbol "Li 6" stamped on the base of the shell. Laplace brandished the stamped shell.

"This is only for use with the long-range targeting system, "Laplace said, "The unmarked shell can be used for either, though its effectiveness at long-range is limited. Nevertheless, take your practice shot with the unmarked shell, then load up the stamped shell. Once the shot is away, don't wait to

see it hit. Go through this door," he said, indicating the door close beside the statue, "and keep moving. You're going to feel lost, but I will meet up with you and bring you the rest of the way."

He turned to the Metizians.

"You're not going to like this," he confessed, "but there's something you must know about those we left back at the ship…"

"…They are on their way as we speak," Araceli finished for him. She pointed to the northwest, where the remainder of the Metizians had detoured into the shadow of the escarpment to come up behind the lead element unnoticed by Laplace and unacknowledged by others.

"What are you thinking?" Laplace said, "There are too many. They will

never approve a crowd like that. I thought we were clear on the plan. The terrain offers them some protection, and we would come back later for the survivors."

"We were clear on the plan. Recall that, though we watched what you did for us, we also remembered what Danilo told us about you. I told them to follow our track as soon as we were out of sight and to take a small detour that would keep them out of range of your co-opted nachinaks. They should be here any minute." Indeed, the leading edge of the group had arrived already and was clustering around the door. Laplace was speechless. He kicked the sand and threw the unstamped shell towards the distant recovery zone where the Gods Helping Angels' fast sub light transport had just landed. He ripped the bandolier off of Francis and frantically sorted through the remaining rounds.

Three of them bore stamps, including the first example that he had shown Francis.

"New plan," Laplace said as he grabbed Francis by both

shoulders and spoke directly into his faceplate, "no practice shots. The rangefinder says 15 km; leave it set there. It will flash green when you are at the proper elevation. Fire one, reload immediately, and send the second one without a pause."

Laplace returned the ammunition to Francis and left him tilting the weapon's barrel up and down to trigger the tone and alarm system that facilitated long-range use. The door opened easily for Laplace when he placed his hand on the edge. He swung it wide, and when he let go, the door froze in place. He stepped well to the side and motioned urgently for the Metizians to enter.

"Never mind what they told you during fire drills, run! You, up front, run! Keep going until you hit a dead-end," he yelled at them.

As he had intended, a mild panic ensued, and the crowd scrambled through the doorway as quickly as they could.

"One of us," Laplace informed Araceli, indicating himself and Francis, "has to be last. That's the only way we know the door is secure. Get all of your people inside as far as possible, as quickly as possible. This is a place where strange things happen. In particular, it is very easy to lose one's way. All your people should stay together. They should maintain physical contact with one other person at a minimum at all times. If they are lost, we will have to negotiate their return, which is difficult and costly."

He took one look back. Francis had his shot ready. He gave Laplace the thumbs up as a rocket-assisted artillery shell burst ten meters over his head, sending a deluge of shrapnel against the reactive armor covering his pressure suit.

"Oops," Laplace remarked.

The artillery round came from a long-range weapon, so it

was likely guided at least in part by a nachinak hovering above them. Laplace flicked open the lid of a drawer on his abacus and released his modified external power source accessory. Laplace held up his screen.

Immediately below the enemy Nachinak's point of view, Laplace could see Francis crouched in a crater. Laplace then spoke through the screen, ordering the enemy nachinak to return to its designated unit. It turned, and the view shifted to a long-distance shot of the sandy expanse between the crater and the platoon of Gods Helping Angels, who were mounted in a pair of wheeled armored vehicles and headed toward the camera. Each vehicle carried a cannon, a heavy machine gun, a launcher for a defensive net, and a pair of flame throwers.

Laplace turned his attention to the crater once more. "Francis!" he said," Can you hear me? What is your status?"

"I'm here. I seem to be okay," Francis said. "I think that the launcher survived as well, but I would like you to take a look at it before I use it."

"In case you forgot,' here' is where the enemy targeted you and just scored

a direct hit," Laplace said. "Get away from 'here.'"

Francis scrambled over the rim of the crater and ran towards Laplace. Before he was halfway to the door, Laplace yelled, "Drop and cover!" Francis obeyed immediately, covering the launcher and ammunition bandolier with his body.

The next round hit just beyond the first crater. Laplace had pulled the door shut, and Francis was completely horizontal as the round exploded, and neither of them suffered injury from the shrapnel. Laplace continued to monitor the on-coming vehicles through the magnified image on his glass rectangle.

He saw them pull a red and black painted box from a compartment hidden under one of the seats. They opened the box and took out the oversized shell that it contained. They fiddled with the arming mechanism situated just distal to the stabilizer fins. Laplace scrambled to open the door again.

"They are queuing up an area denial round! "He warned Francis, "You have to be quicker!"

Francis wasn't listening. He had flipped the long-range sight down and loaded one of the unstamped rounds into the breach. With some effort, he raised the weapon until he could look down the short-range sight, drew a bead on the lead vehicle, and fired. He traced the sparkling trail of burning propellant as it tracked toward the enemy vehicles.

"Next, next, next!" Laplace said.

Contrary to instructions, Francis spared a glance at Laplace. While Francis was thinking about his next move, Laplace had set up his four nachinaks in the neutralizer formation. They currently hovered about ten feet above him. His defensive web hung from its four nachinak minders.

One of his utility nachinaks raced to Francis, trailing a chain of four vials containing a clear fluid. It landed on his right shoulder and plugged the vials into the chemical weapon countermeasure slots in his helmet.

"The little one knows what to do," Laplace shouted to Francis, "you do

your job!"

Francis dashed over to the shell that Laplace had thrown into the sand. Francis' first round arrived. The leading vehicle turned hard to the driver's right in an effort to avoid the spinning plasma jets that sprouted from the projectile. The effort succeeded, but he leaned on the controls a little too hard, and the vehicle flipped.

The force of the roll ejected two of the occupants, who landed in the sand a dozen meters from the wreck. The rest of the occupants were underneath the vehicle as

it landed upside down. The plasma jets steered clumsily toward the remaining vehicle. They didn't get anywhere near the target, but during the change of direction, the blazing disc dug into the sand and showered the machine and its occupants with molten glass. It rolled to a stop as the crew did fire suppression.

Laplace looked over at Francis. The young man had stowed his remaining plasma shell in the bandolier and readied the launcher for a war crime. The first long-range projectile was on its way with a loud report and a recoil that strained the impact- dampening pads in Francis's pressure suit.

He popped the breach open and loaded his next round as fast as possible. He sent it right after the first shot and turned to run towards the door where Laplace was waiting.

Laplace gestured frantically for Francis to hurry. Though he could hear something approaching quickly behind him, Francis resisted the urge to look back over his shoulder. He cleared the door right before a massive impact drove it shut, throwing Francis and Laplace into the passageway beyond.

Laplace activated a pair of lights sequestered in the filaments near each shoulder and rapidly took inventory. His nachinaks had retreated to their holding areas as soon as he went inside, and all seemed to have come through the impact unscathed. He picked up his hat and dusted it off. It would need

professional cleaning, but it, too, was in good condition. The headlamps on Francis's helmet came on.

"What's that?" Francis asked. The sound of muffled voices came through the door . Laplace motioned for Francis to follow down the passage, away from the entrance.

"We should get farther in before the flash hits," Laplace said as he trotted up the corridor. A few seconds later, they felt heat on their backs, and then in a few more seconds, the earth

shook. The crack and rumble of breaking rock accompanied the tremor, and twilight streamed into the passageway along with a cloud of dust.

Francis saw shadows moving in the dust storm. Someone coughed, and a constellation of flashlights lit up between them and the door. Francis hesitated for an instant, and a flash blinded him, followed by an impact against his chest. The reactive armor held, but the blow knocked the wind out of him. As he lay trying to recover, he heard multiple objects pass over him in a series of shrill whines.

The next thing he saw was Laplace standing over him, offering a hand to help him to his feet. He pulled himself up and looked down. Eight bodies, all dressed in pressure suits and all with horrendous burns across their backs and the backs of their legs, lay strewn on the floor inside the ruined doorway. Francis bent to examine the nearest corpse.

"Keep your distance," Laplace said, "we ought not test our immunizations unnecessarily."

"Who are they?" Francis asked.

"The crew of the second vehicle from the transport ship," Laplace answered.

"What is this patch on the helmet— Ad Majorem Dei Gloriam.

What does that mean?" Francis asked.

"A lot," Laplace responded, with a hint of a smile, "and nothing. Not anymore. We need to move on to catch up with the others."

As they proceeded up the passageway, the light leaking through the pile

of rubble that had been the door and entry quickly faded. There were no marks on the walls, ceiling, or floor. They began to pass other corridors leading off to either side. At the first of these alternatives, Laplace sent his modified accessory nachinak up to hover above them. They

walked for fifteen minutes before they came to the end of the main corridor and faced a perpendicular hall on either side. Laplace did some quick calculations with the abacus and led them down the left-hand passageway. He repeated the process at several subsequent crossroads.

They continued walking until they finally heard the murmur of conversation ahead of them in the dark. Around the next corner, a dim light shone from a large chamber at the end of the tunnel.

"Hello? Laplace? Francis?" Came a voice from the room ahead. "Yes, it's us, Araceli," Laplace called out.

The chamber was large enough to hold several hundred people. It was not natural and appeared to be an unfinished archaeological excavation. The floor was smooth and level, but the ceiling was rough-hewn, and there were large gouges in the walls that ran from floor to ceiling. The Metizians had gathered in the middle of the room to wait for them. Araceli emerged from the group to meet them.

"This is a dead-end," she informed them. "I expect you have the answer to this?"

"Yes, follow me," Laplace reassured her.

Laplace went to the nearest wall and began walking down its length, pausing at each gouge to look inside the associated alcove. Two-thirds of the way around, he stepped into a gash in the wall and stopped abruptly. He narrowed his eyes and scrutinized the stone walls. He made some adjustments on his abacus, and the accessory nachinak made a slow turn towards the right side of the cubbyhole. He made one more delicate adjustment on a single abacus bead, and a thin line appeared on the rock face.

He addressed the hovering nachinak. "Bring them out, please," he instructed. About seven feet above the floor, a pair of nachinaks slipped out of the faint crease in the wall. As they emerged, the crease became more prominent. Laplace sighed. He instructed his nachinak to stand by and turned to Araceli, who had been watching his investigations closely.

"Now we are in for some tedium," he announced. "We have a number of these folds to pass and a few dead-ends to avoid along the way. This doesn't get dangerous for quite some time, but it is possible to get off course. Unlike temporary folds, stable folds have a precise description, and to get to the intended destination, one must follow the geometry of the fold precisely. For people who have experienced many transitions through temporary folds, it isn't too hard to get things right the first time. It feels a certain way to be on track when passing through a fold. There is a sensation of uniform, increasing pressure on the anterior and posterior surfaces of the body. The analogy used during instruction on the use of the event radiation is that the sensation one ought to feel when passing through a fold is the same feeling that a melon seed experiences as one spits it out between one's lips. I'm sorry, but that's the best I can do. Tell this to your people. It may help, but they should also note that it's almost certain that some of them will get lost. If that happens, they should remain calm. I can find them all; it just takes time. The only crucial transition is the last one, and I will take the lead there, while I will follow before that. Francis will go ahead of everyone. If some unforeseen problem arises, it will be up to him to plead our case."

Francis had fallen behind during the search. He perked up when Laplace came to a halt, and was already on his way when Laplace stepped out of the alcove and waved him over.

"I'm entrusting you with my little treasure here," Laplace said as soon as Francis was in earshot, "You have a series of folds to negotiate. They're going to be difficult to find sometimes, but a diligent search will reveal them in the end. The nachinak will help you with course corrections. Eventually, you will arrive at a duplicate of the monument to the little ones and the

adjacent doors. Our destination lies beyond the twin of the door that we entered from the launch and recovery area, but you must not enter by yourself unless a day passes, and I have not arrived. Questions?"

273

"None," Francis said.

Araceli shifted uncomfortably and took a deep breath. Laplace cut her off with an angry look before she could speak.

"Off you go," said Laplace. Francis affirmed that the modified accessory nachinak was in the proper position and then slipped into the gap in the stone. The gap folded in on itself behind him, obscuring the two attendant nachinaks in the process.

"Really," Araceli said, "no instructions? Not even a warning?"

"Absolutely not," Laplace said. "There is no place for theater in our appeal. Our case will stand or fall on its own merits. The only way we could hurt ourselves, should things go so wrong that Francis becomes our spokesman, is for his presentation to come across as coached. The situation is particularly dangerous because the audience's professional background

renders them particularly adept at recognizing a disingenuous appeal.

Laplace activated a generic version of the accessory nachinak and tweaked the abacus again. The thin mark on the wall reappeared, along with the two nachinak maintaining the fold.

"Shall we get started?" Laplace said.

Araceli gave him a sour look before turning to gather her people. Laplace smiled in response and waved to those in the front of the group who were watching the preparations. As he turned back, he noticed that the two nachinak maintaining the fold had shifted slightly. He pulled them back in line with a tap on an abacus bead. A minute ripple propagated along the crease in response. The first of the Metizians stepped up to begin their trip through the labyrinth.

"Are you okay?" She asked Laplace.

"I must be if I am doing this," he answered.

Forty-one

Reunions Are Complicated

"Are you going to drink that?" Lucky asked.

"No, you take it," Anisa answered, dismissing the gin and tonic with a wave of her hand. During the breaks between sets, if they listened very carefully, they could hear a faint echo of divine pounding still reverberating in the amphitheater.

"Boy," Lucky laughed nervously, "talk about some pent-up rage." Anisa and their minder, Drusilla, pretended not to hear him.

"So," Drusilla said, "it looks like you didn't get away after all. What do you think he's going to do when he shows up here and finds out that you let his little pet loose, exposed Gerard, and plotted with Augustine to ambush him?"

"One out of three isn't bad," said Anisa, "You won't get any information from me this way. I also won't be caught by the likes of you, and I mean the

lot of you. Tell me this, Drusilla, since there is nothing at stake anymore when I ask you these

questions. Why did you come back? How could you come back?" Drusilla pulled the garnish out of her drink and nibbled at the fruit. "Time is one answer. I couldn't stay angry forever. I worked for several

other prominent figures, but it was too risky and unsatisfying. I decided that I only wanted to work for the best, and I didn't want to die early."

"Oh my God!" Anisa lamented, covering her face with her hands.

"Oh, come on, Anisa. You have to admit that he is the best. I also have more autonomy here than I did at any other job I've held as an emancipated person," said Drusilla. "I work directly with Gerard, and he is only interested in the research side of things. I practically run the node, the University, and the medical center."

"I don't see working with that kabuki as a fringe benefit," Anisa said with disgust.

"Wait, what? What was that word?" Lucky asked. "Why?" Anisa asked, "What did you hear?"

"You just called somebody a kabuki," Lucky said. "What does that mean? That is, I know what it means to me, but what does it mean to you?"

"Okay, now I'm hearing something about a dancer," said Anisa. "Is that what you heard?"

"Kind of, the term I heard was specific to a Japanese dance style. The performers wear masks and elaborate costumes that hide their identities. It is sometimes used as a metaphor for obscure representations. Is that what the translator was shooting for?" Lucky asked.

"Maybe. I think it can't tell the difference between you and Takezo, which is legitimately funny. It may also be the closest

equivalent that the translator can use in your language. The word I used was slang and specifically refers to a person who is enslaved, subsequently

emancipated, and then refuses to wear the gray robes. The word does double duty when referring to Gerard because he's a disgusting pervert, no matter what he's wearing," said Anisa.

Drusilla crushed the remainder of the garnish in her hand and threw it back in her drink.

"There is another explanation," Drusilla said, "the word that she spoke is something that most of us no longer use in polite conversation. Polite or not, however, it does not describe Gerard. He was a captive for a while and bore a subjugation nachinak, but his captivity bore no resemblance beyond the implant to what we would call slavery. Even before that, his developmental course was complex and difficult. He's been through a lot. I can't help but feel for him."

"Ugh! I think I'm going to puke," said Anisa. "You're petting a rabid dog; you know that don't you? You're going to wake up one morning missing a major organ or two."

Drusilla clamped her mouth shut and looked away. Lucky slouched down in his seat and did his best to hide behind his glass.

They waited 10 more silent, uncomfortable minutes for Gerard. He came in through the stockroom behind the bar and took a seat at the table next to Lucky.

"I feel sorry for anyone venturing beyond the atmosphere for the next six months," Gerard said. "It appears that my brother purchased every reactive armor pad in the local cluster. Anyway, the situation seems to be under control for the moment. We will still have to bring this project to

its conclusion on a significantly accelerated schedule. I contacted the Authority and the Foundation. Representatives of both organizations expressed keen interest in seeing the results of my work. However, I was not able to give them an update on the results of your work," he said to Lucky.

Lucky sat up straight and put his glass back on the table. "Officially, I'm not working on anything right now. "

"What about this… Whatever it is that obscures you when you creep about

our campus?" Gerard asked.

"I view that more like a medical condition than anything that I'm working on. It appears that my friend has made significant progress on his design. That's what you're referring to, right? The weapons design competition?" Said Lucky.

"In any case," Gerard said, "representatives from the governing boards of each institution will be arriving four days from now. Would you do me the favor of extending an invitation to attend the program on that day to your friend? Please advise him that he should be prepared to present his work during the evening symposium, regardless of its current state of completion.

"Sure, I guess. Does that mean we are free to go?" Lucky asked.

"Of course," said Gerard,' I will keep you updated on any changes to the situation here at the Center of Excellence. I also wanted to be clear about the presentation. You are all invited, as guests."

"No monitors, no minders, no check-in?" Anisa asked. "No, I think not," said Gerard, "Do you think those things

will be necessary? Never fear; if my brother wishes to contact you, he will be able to find you without assistance. Now, if you'll excuse me, I must attend a re-assessment of the barrier's

integrity with my staff."

Gerard rose from his seat and walked away at a brisk pace. The remnants of the cabal sat for a moment, staring across the table at each other.

"He may not feel the need to monitor you," Drusilla said, "but rest assured, you will be monitored. You should not take his word as license to snoop around the campus at will."

"You shouldn't have to worry about that," Lucky said. "It's all out in the open now, don't you think? I can no longer see any need to stay in the shadows."

"We'll see, won't we?" Drusilla said as she stood and followed after Gerard. She had not left the bar before Lucky stood as well.

"If you don't mind," he told Anisa, "I'd like to take a break too. The Lord's

prophet prefers to keep as much distance as possible between the Lord and himself."

"Very well," Anisa agreed, pushing back from the table.

As they exited the Node Eight building, Lucky and Anisa encountered a maze of barriers marked with warning signs and detour instructions. Impacts emanating from the academic center came less frequently but remained audible across the campus. The detour route took them through the lobby of the Medical Center and across the inner Plaza.

Foot traffic across the Center of Excellence was well below normal, but the ruckus in the academic center drew a crowd. The curious gathered in clumps at the barricades marking a safe perimeter, craning their necks in hopes of glimpsing the source of danger. Lucky and Anisa hurried past the spectators, slowing their pace only after they passed the stairways beyond the outer Plaza. It was business as usual in the village and on the roads leading East. People stared at Lucky as he walked, fully exposed. He pretended not to notice, as did

Anisa. Soon, the traffic thinned as the road narrowed from a two-lane to a single lane. Lucky looked over at Anisa.

"What are you going to do?" he asked, "If you don't run, will you help us or not?"

"None of your business," she said.

"I beg to differ. You never did promise not to kill me. I don't see how you're going to get away clean this time without using the skin," said Lucky.

"You will have to keep guessing."

They turned the last of the switchbacks and entered the small forest. Lucky stopped abruptly, stuck his nose in the air, and inhaled.

"You smell something burning?" He asked.

"Yes," Anisa confirmed, and then took off running down the path.

Lucky kept up with her, and they soon saw the source of the odor. Smoke was rising from Takezo's workshop. There was no visible enemy around the building, which had sustained damage from shotgun slugs and rifle bullets.

They heard a loud crack, followed by the snap of a bullet hitting live wood. Lucky stopped, knelt, and looked toward the sound's origin. He immediately spotted two humans pointing rifles in his direction. He recognized both of them from the old country store. One was the cashier named Dion. The other was Marge; the fry cook and bartender.

Dion recognized Lucky in return, quickly set down his rifle, and raised his hands to indicate that he was no longer targeting the newcomers. Marge did not immediately follow suit, but after some desperate signaling and whispers from Dion, she set her rifle aside as well and held up her hands. With the danger defused, the snipers slung their weapons over their shoulders and hurried down to meet Lucky and Anisa.

"Is there anybody still in there?" Lucky asked. "No, I think we ran them off," Dion said.

Lucky had a look at Marge. He had never mistaken her for athletic, but she wasn't looking well at all now. She was sweating and breathing hard. Her skin was a little pale."

"Tell you what," Lucky said, "why don't you stand watch here, Marge, while we make sure that the workshop is clear."

Marge nodded yes and sat down on a large rock beside a juniper tree. She mopped her brow and swayed in her seat, but her eyes scanned the surrounding woods continuously while she panted. The other three cautiously advanced on the workshop. When they were about 10 m from the back of the building, Anisa signaled that she would go around the other side. They didn't hear anything out of the ordinary, so they moved quickly around the corner of the large sliding door, which stood completely open. A moderate amount of smoke obscured the interior. The prototype weapon

was gone. The forge was unscathed. They saw no blood and no bodies.

Lucky pulled the fire extinguisher out of its case and began snuffing anything that smoldered or burned with a flame. Despite the smoke, Lucky found few flames to douse.

It was becoming obvious that the attack had occurred quite some time ago, and the fire never really caught. Lucky reemerged from the building, fire extinguisher in hand. He looked around. The little kiosk was intact. So was the shed down by the pond and the rose garden in the portion of it that he could see.

The villa seemed to have escaped any damage. Dion and Anisa were almost to the front steps. Lucky ran to catch up with them. They stopped in the doorway. Seated on the table in front of them was Takezo, covered in blood splatters.

Two scabbards, one

for a short sword and one for a long sword, were tucked into his belt. He had his cell phone in his hands. He focused exclusively on the game flashing across its screen. He appeared so distracted that Lucky jumped when his friend spoke.

"I didn't get all of them," he said as the game chimed a new level of achievement. "However, I don't think any of them will be returning. Some other would-be thief will take their place, though. I will not come back here. Lucky, will you help me pack up?"

On Takezo's side of the table, two corpses lay face down on the mosaic, surrounded by a large pool of blood. The closer body's intestines lay beside it. The more distant body had a puncture wound to the chest.

Underneath the table, the final casualty lay with its torso on one side of the table and its head on the other.

Without looking up from his game, Takezo asked, "Dion, would you please take care of the bodies? Choose who you want to work with you. I have pulled sheets out of the toolshed," he said, indicating a pile of canvas tarps stacked by the entryway. Nothing fancy. Just put them in the bin by the toolshed when you are finished. Please inform Augustine of this incident. I would like to thank you for your hospitality and assistance during my stay here. Please convey those same sentiments to Augustine, along with my regrets that I shall have to leave these

beautiful accommodations he provided just for me."

"I think we had some body bags in storage," said Dion, "and I will pass

your message on to Augustine." "What about me?" asked Anisa.

"What about you?" Takezo asked, "You do as you please, as always." Anisa's face lit with a flare of anger, fading quickly to sadness.

"I will stick with Lucky," she said.

Takezo sighed deeply, set the phone down, and laid his swords beside it. Without looking at any of them, he walked off to his room. Lucky followed and found that the door was already locked. He waited patiently outside. Soon enough, Takezo emerged, a towel draped over his shoulders, wearing a bathrobe and sandals.

"Get a towel," he shouted, "anyone who needs a bath. If you need a change of clothes, take coveralls from the tool shed."

He walked slowly up to the shop and picked his way to the bath through the aftermath of the raid.

Casper awaited them. By now, everyone knew of him, at least by reputation. He sat where Lucky had left him the day before when they were done with feeding. Lucky was shocked to see him quickly rise and begin preparations for the sauna. Takezo educated Casper on the sauna's workings daily, without any immediate acknowledgment to show for it.

Now he smiled as he watched Casper act out his instructions to a T. Takezo's robe had once been white but was now stained pink and maroon. By unspoken consensus, Takezo used the rinse tub first. He went through several rounds of soap and rinse, including his hair. When he returned to sit by the stove, Lucky stared at him in horror.

281

Takezo ignored him. The door opened, and Dion entered. He had blood on his hands and

clothing. He removed his clothes and stuffed them into a plastic bag that he carried in his front pocket. He then took his turn at the tub. When he came back in, he stopped short and stared at Takezo.

"Holy shit man!" Dion blurted out, "What in the hell happened to you? No way you're still alive! How are you still alive?"

Takezo was covered with scars. The sheer number was impressive, but the incredible part was the depth and location of some. The wounds that would cause such scars were typically fatal.

"Sound diet. Meditation. Nothing more," Takezo shrugged.

"Guess I'm going to start meditating again," said Lucky, "I hope I remember what the therapist told me. Not so sure about

the diet, though."

"Natto will keep you alive, Lucky," Takezo asserted.

"Or at least make it so you don't care whether you live or die. Either way, you got a mouthful of natto, which spoils the plan," Anisa added.

The rest laughed. Shortly thereafter, they gathered their clothing and got dressed. Lucky waited while Takezo changed in the space behind the tub. He emerged wearing a utilitarian kimono, with his hair held down by a hatchimaki. He walked back to the villa to add a few items to his backpack. He picked up his swords on the way. He had the blades clean, inspected, oiled, and secure in their scabbards before the blood congealed after the massacre. The bodies lay stacked in the tool bin next to the shed. Dion drafted Marge to help him with the mopping. Takezo thanked them profusely again. He waited until they were 10 minutes gone on their way back to the store, and then he walked away from the villa for the last time. As he passed in front of the workshop, he grabbed the stepstool resting against the workshop's doorframe. He unfolded the stool

and stood on the top step. He slid his hand along to feel the top of the doorframe. When he couldn't reach it anymore, he stepped down, moved the stepstool, and felt around the next section. This time, he found something and lifted it with both hands as he stepped down to the ground.

He held the prototype weapon before him. He swung it up to ride on his shoulder and resumed his walk. Lucky fell in beside him. To their surprise, Anisa joined them right before the pavement began. Lucky gave her a sidelong glance.

"I make no apologies, "said Anisa. "I am as tempted as the next person to bear witness to history."

"What about the charging problem, Takezo?" Asked Lucky.

"That is fixed. Augustine did help me after all," Takezo said, "but not like he intended. He sent an external power source along with one of the nachinaks that could control the thing. I did not have much use for the power source itself, but the nachinak was the key. Within its programming, I found code transferable to the weapon. It can build charge in the same ways it could before, but now it can also draw energy by contacting an opponent's charged devices."

"And all this without the middleman?" Lucky asked. Takezo nodded in response.

"Have you tested the max charge?" Asked Anisa.

Takezo smiled and shook his head. "I'm afraid that would be too risky."

"When will the fight take place?" Lucky asked.

"Whenever we are both ready," he said, "this is the test. In a duel, the contest is decided already when the blades cross. Now is the time when the contest is won or lost by successfully completing the preparation ritual. First, one must bring oneself to believe that one owns nothing. As I meditate before the match,

I let go of my connections to my country and my culture. Then I let go of my comrades, then my teachers, then my family, then my memories, then the things around me, and finally myself. When I am finally empty, I can turn to look at my origin.

I see the thread of intentional conscious experience that stretches across the events of my life, binding the chaotic happenstance into a coherent personal existence. At last, I cut the thread. I am completely isolated, and I never know, however many times I make that journey, what I will find in the aftermath of the cut. But every time before, I have found the will to renew the thread. I am determined to pick it up again and carry it onward wherever time and fortune allow.

That is how I am when I come to the fight. My life is gone. I have nothing to lose. I have nothing to fear because I am already dead. My only recourse is to fight to win my life back."

"The preparation sounds difficult, "said Lucky, "which brings me back to my original question: how long does it take to achieve that state of mind?" "As long as it takes to draw a sword," Takezo said. "Once one stands in

that place, he never truly leaves it."

They completed the journey in silence. Foot traffic was light, and the atmosphere in the community built on the flanks of the center of excellence was subdued. The cafés and restaurants were empty. There was no music. The center's security force had set up checkpoints with bunkers on the upper flights of the stairway. A message warning nonessential personnel to stay clear of the area played in a loop over a temporary public address system.

Despite discouragement from security personnel, as well as loudspeakers and written warnings on the perimeter barriers, a crowd gathered on the broad Plaza outside the University and Medical Center. The inner Plaza, with its

surrounding hedgerow, was off-limits. The doors at either end of every leafy corridor were closed and locked. An armed guard stood at the entrance of each outer door. Drones and nachinak circled overhead.

From the academic building, a booming voice addressed all with ears to hear.

"You have concluded your lives," the voice proclaimed. "Judgment is at hand. Nothing you can say or do now will absolve you of your sin or spare you the full measure of divine justice. Prepare for your punishment. You know who you are... Martin, the pharmacist, do you recall the expired medication that you mixed with fresh pills and sold to Sherry, who worked at the admissions desk in the Medical Center? It was more than her liver could handle, and she became jaundiced. She faces a transplant now that she will not survive..."

The monologue continued in the same vein. God repeated his general threat and admonishment, and then he called out some individual on a specific transgression described in all its lurid detail, punctuated by the sound of the deity's fists striking the barrier around him.

Takezo strode past the checkpoint barring admission to the academic center. The guard raised his weapon to stop Lucky and Anisa from following Takezo's example and then ran after the trespasser, shouting angrily for him to stop.

Someone in command must have been watching because the guard pulled up short and covered his auditory meatus with his hand on one side. He nodded twice and then turned back to Anisa and Lucky.

"Okay, you two are cleared," the guard said, waving them through. "Give us some warning next time, will you? Good communication keeps you from getting shot."

Takezo had turned to wait for them at the entrance to the academic center's foyer. They caught up with him quickly and entered the construction zone. They turned left in a narrow passageway leading to the small antechamber behind the doors to the main stage. Another guard stood at the doors. Takezo dismissed him. Several chairs, presumably for speakers on deck, lined the back wall of the antechamber. Takezo picked out two of them, one to sit on and the other to support his feet. He indicated that Anisa and Lucky should take seats of their own.

He settled in and pulled the cell phone out of his kimono. He left the volume on half while he played the game that Lucky had taught him how to access.

God had grown silent.

Lucky looked over at Anisa and then back at Takezo. "What are we doing?" Lucky asked.

Without looking up from his game, Takezo said, "Preparation."

"I thought that happened as quickly as you could draw your sword," Lucky said.

"Special preparation," Takezo said. "It is rumored that only the hand of a believer can kill God. That is because God owes his existence to his

believers' doubts and fears as well as their faith and fidelity. Man has found many ways to set aside faith and fidelity. Doubts and fears, however, are intransigent. If doubt and fear remain, then God may remain as well. I do not fear

285

the creature behind that wall, but I have doubts about what he really is. I will wait here until he has convinced me; then I will defeat him."

Forty-two

The Last Liaison

While Araceli accounted for the Metizians, Laplace faced up to his plan's weaknesses. He had no choice because the center's Director stood directly in front of him and read down the list.

It had taken him several hours of backtracking to assemble all of the Metizians in the inadequate space outside the developmental centers' admissions clinic. The clinic's daily functions went on around them as leadership debated the fate of the Metizians and the members of the Species who had facilitated their trespass.

The labyrinth leading through the dendritic radiation to the center ended at a short tunnel lined with electrical contact plates. In a cavern at the tunnel's origin, a duplicate of the giant nachinak greeted visitors from the outside. Facing the labyrinth's exit across the tunnel, a heavy door led to a processing room, where blastocysts and the few embryos arriving at the center got sorted and processed prior to examination in the clinic.

The tunnel opened into the marshaling area for the clinic through an arch

of vines, where archetypical birds perched and idealized arboreal mammals eternally chased each other through the branches, all sculpted in iron.

The high, transparent ceiling admitted enough light to support several large trees, one in the middle of the room with a ring of benches around its base, and two others on either side of the room. The floor was paved with green tiles. Rows of shelves lined the wall across from the tunnel's entrance, containing the newest members of the Species in their incubator pods.

Two wide doorways led into the clinic itself. Between the doorways, a wrought-iron table in the same style as the tunnel archway supported an espresso machine, along with plates, cups, and condiments. Small, round, iron tables and chairs were scattered across the rest of the space. From time to time, personnel from the administrative staff elbowed their way through the milling, nervous Metizians to place additional incubators in line on the shelves.

"How did you imagine this would go?" asked the Director," At the very least, there are too many of them for us to absorb on our initiative. We would need to cover that expense in our budget request. If we do that, then the Foundation will have questions, and if the Foundation has questions, the Authority will have questions.

You understand how this works, Laplace. One does not ask forgiveness from the Authority, only permission. They will automatically say no.

This is stupid enough if you undertook it based on misguided guilt, sympathy, or ethical obligation. It is even worse if you have some ulterior motive, especially if that motive is personal.

A dark cloud hangs over this center already due to your activities and their sequelae. I'm tempted to turn the tunnel back on and send you through it this minute without further discussion."

"But here we stand, already discussing it," Laplace said with a hint of a smile, "You know me Madame Director. Whatever I am to other people, I have always been an unshakable supporter

of you and this center. Additionally, you are aware of the truth about our traditions surrounding the centers. You've read the lost records from the archives that I dug up. It has never been the case that the developmental centers were completely secret.

As far as we know, there was only a brief, recent era where the practices of summarily executing anyone who encountered a center for any reason and destroying and re-constituting any center whose location became known were actively pursued as policy on the ground.

Before you point out the weakness of such justification, I would refer to your own experience. What misfortune has befallen this center since Gerard and I have been at large? None, unless you count Augustine's mischief. He alone is responsible for that, however. I've told you what he did and how he did it.

You must admit that he did not accomplish his scheme by taking advantage of any weakness in the centers' policies and procedures or by leveraging any external weakness under the centers' control, in fact or in principle."

"You make a good point," the mother said, "but it still doesn't address the practicalities. Tell it to the representatives from the Authority when they arrive to investigate these matters."

She turned on her heel and began walking back towards the clinic doorways.

"Okay," Laplace said, "what about this: the Metizians face a unique genetic crisis."

He ran to step in front of her and continued before she could object to the imposition, "Wait now. Please listen, I'm writing your grant for you."

"The centers do not submit grant requests, nor do they accept grants if offered..." said the Director.

"And that is a crying shame," Laplace said, "Attitudes about purity in funding have changed somewhat over the years. These things are now

administered by third parties on a regular basis. I can guarantee you that numerous entities would jump at the opportunity to sponsor a one-of-a-kind endeavor like this. It would more than compensate for the center's costs in sustaining the Metizians.

It would give you the means to save an entire Species otherwise destined for extinction, and who knows what breakthroughs in our understanding of genetics may result?

On top of all that, I can wrap up the Authority's investigation into Augustine's trespass in ten minutes. No need to invite the shit hounds."

The Director crossed her arms and put her weight on her back foot. She eyed him as if he were selling her a pig in a burlap sack that neither grunted nor squealed.

With a tired sigh, she turned away from her initial path to the safe back offices and sat down at a table next to the espresso machine. She sat for a long time, picking at the lace tablecloth with her fingernail. She brewed herself a coffee and took a couple of sips before addressing Laplace.

"Ten minutes?" She asked. "If that," Laplace said.

"You know," she said, "I never wanted to turn them away."

"Your responsibilities often force you to confront an array of unacceptable alternatives. I would not want them, nor would I prove capable of fulfilling them nearly as well as you do," said Laplace.

"Don't push it," the Director said.

Laplace turned and walked into the clinic. He made his way through the hallways and treatment rooms without taking a wrong turn or hesitating. At the very back of the clinic, a spiral stairway led to a small office off of a microscopy suite.

A short man with green eyes and a pale complexion sat at the desk in the office, scrolling through histology images. Only two of the five microscope benches in the room beyond were occupied, and neither of the technicians seemed to notice Laplace's arrival.

The man in the office, however, jumped when he looked up to
see who had come to visit.

"Time's up," said Laplace. "Come with me, Morris. I made an appoint-

ment on your behalf with the director. You mustn't be late."

Morris stood, and Laplace grabbed him by the elbow. The claws on his fingertips dug in. Morris winced but did not make a sound.

"He didn't want to kill you," Morris said as they walked down the stairs. "He knew he couldn't kill you."

"Yes, but he didn't need to," Laplace replied.

Morris looked down and came along without resistance. The Director was waiting for them at the end of the hallway. She gestured for them to follow her, and she made her way to the office at the back of the clinic. She shut the door. Morris spoke without prompting.

"Nothing will happen to Thomas, will it? It isn't his fault. I was the one who encouraged him. I was the one who joined in on the planning," he said. "When did you first grant access to uncredentialed persons?" the Director asked.

"Twenty years ago," Morris replied.

The Director swallowed hard and swayed before she dropped into the closest chair. "Who?" Laplace asked.

"That was when I met Thomas. Augustine sent him to retrieve the blastocyst

290

that his concubine sent us. Retrieve or destroy was the complete order. He wandered in from the fold chamber while I was working after hours with one intake officer.

Thomas walked into the tunnel, clearly ignorant of the danger. I should have pressed the button, but I couldn't. He looked so nervous, so endearing. I redirected my co-worker, deactivated the cameras,

and went down to meet him myself. He thought I was going to

kill him. I brought him to my office, and he ended up hiding there for two days. That was as long as he could stay before Augustine got suspicious. I can't believe we did something so dangerous, but we did."

"Wait a minute," Laplace said, "According to Danilo, Augustine was personally involved in this scheme from its inception. What was his involvement?"

"Oh, I never met him," said Morris. "All of our communications were by

courier. Thomas was the courier." "Go on," said Laplace.

"Well, he came to me with this cockamamie plan and a vial full of squamous epithelium or something. I never took a real close look. From the standpoint of a genetic engineer, it was plainly worthless.

I was desperate to see Thomas again, so I volunteered our samples instead, the ones from Gerard that had long since been archived. Thanks to Gerard's Mother, I also had a blueprint for the subsequent stages of the plan. She had taken advantage of the 'one across the board' methodology. One child, one Mother, one point of contact for everyone else. Socialization without bullying, ostracism, or submission to group identity.

She used the requisite anonymity and the security structure, intense scrutiny at the perimeter, without active scrutiny within the perimeter, to keep the child hidden. All the responsibility resides with the Mother, so a single person stood between us and success.

I came to her with the report on Francis's chimerism. It is technically a criterion for exclusion, though that would be subject to appeal. I suggested that it would be safer and more straightforward to quash the report rather than risk an appeal. I was pretty confident that she would agree.

291

I was responsible for the document. All I had to do was discard one of the genetic profiles. She had already

crossed a line with her involvement in Gerard's case. That involvement not only put her in the same boat as we were, but it also meant that she was familiar with the strategies and methods we would use.

I think she felt compassion for both me and Thomas. She took the substantial risk of hiding him on his subsequent visits. Francis's development was completely normal. Thomas continued to communicate with us. He had told Augustine that we expected to be paid for our efforts.

Thomas kept the money while he continued to visit me regularly on the pretense of physically transferring the payments. We had perfected the formula for getting him in and out without being noticed. Once Francis reached the age of presentation, the project became difficult again.

I reassured the Mother that I would be able to manage any pending genetic sampling. I was quite confident that we would not get any requests for testing before he was ready to leave the center. Once the original reports are entered, it is extremely rare for anyone to request repeated sampling; everyone knows that genes don't change.

When the time came, everyone met at the quarters previously occupied by Gerard's Mother. Francis' Mother had kept the rooms in anticipation of their assignment to a new Mother.

The Authority had designated the quarters and their contents as a crime scene. However, they could not see how discovering a crime in the case would bring them any profit. Their enthusiasm for wrapping up the investigation was tepid at best.

We still had a stasis pod that Gerard's Mother had used to hold him until she could identify a guaranteed adopter. When the time finally arrived, we administered an amnestic and packed Francis into the pod. I worked on him while he was in stasis. I insinuated the virus into his genome. I didn't try to hide it because the

interval between Francis being activated and the virus being activated was so short.

For several years, Francis consistently attended socialization activities, completed training sessions, and passed assessments as usual. At every annual induction of new developmental subjects, the AI rolled back his timeline. Gerard's Mother initially corrupted the section AI.

"How did she manage that?" Laplace asked.

"Sheer brutality," said Morris. "Thank my lucky stars, I never met her. You know how determined and forthright she had to be to raise your brother in secret, with his disorder. The same traits made her belligerent and intransigent. I gather she was a horrible bully. Her colleagues avoided her, but the AI had nowhere to run. It became her loyal pet.

It managed to trick the investigators at the time. It convinced them that it had come through its ordeal with Gerard's mother unscathed. It never got reprogrammed. It was ready for us to use.

It did all the remote puppetry with simulations of Francis and his mother. It covered the monitors and audio channels when I communicated with Thomas in any way. It also helped with a couple of close calls. The Authority investigators did come back to wrap up their investigation.

The Mother's simulation arrived at the old quarters just in time to steer them away. To guarantee their ongoing disinterest, I had to give them several large payments from the stash that Thomas and I had accumulated. When they gave the signal, I sent Francis's modified reports to the Foundation and the Authority and then called his Mother to the mothballed quarters to help me with a problem involving the stasis pod.

When she arrived, we gave them the highest dose of the standard two-drug regimen I have ever seen administered. We put the pair of them in wheelchairs and rolled them down to the fold chamber.

Augustine remained on the other side the entire time. We were fortunate that no one saw us. We had not asked the AI for cover, but I suppose it determined on its own that we needed help and interfered with the monitors accordingly. With great difficulty, we managed to push them through the fold, and that was that. Until today."

"You said that the quarters that Gerard's mother inhabited

were kept as a potential crime scene?" Laplace asked. "That means that the cache of medicine for my brother is still there?"

"It should be," Morris said, "if the agents of the Authority haven't made off with it. Has he had a flare? You should look for another condition if so, something that causes

systemic inflammation, especially inflammation of the brain and meninges.

The treatments are significantly more effective than we initially thought. They stabilize the condition quite well unless it reawakens in response to a systemic inflammatory condition. You should be aware that subsequent treatments undertaken after initial stabilization are much less reliable."

"What about late-onset cases?" Laplace asked, "nascent disease."

"Oh my. I am so very sorry," said Morris, "nobody knows."

The Director groaned and leaned forward to rest her head on the table. "You are right. Our defenses against the outside world functioned as

planned. Internal vulnerabilities sank us," the Director said. "Welcome," said Laplace with a sardonic smile, "to our world."

Forty-three

Be Seated for the Standoff

At first, the silence was unbearably tense, then it became oppressive, and finally it grew unbearably tedious. Takezo was the only one of the three who did not look ready to chew off a leg to escape. He continued playing his game.

It would have been compelling to watch in other circumstances. His fingers flew over the screen, and his concentration never wavered. Intermittently, the screen would light up with accolades for new accomplishments.

For Anisa and Lucky, the divine presence was too palpable. Their attention was inexorably drawn to every creak and rustle from the other side of the wall. God took advantage of their imperfect discipline by randomly punching the wall in front of them. He did that at intervals ranging from 15 minutes to 2 hours. He laughed whenever the impacts evoked a noise from the other side.

Finally, Anisa had had enough. She jumped out of her chair and stepped over to the wall.

"You rotten bastard!" she yelled at the deity on the other side. "Quit that,

and let's go!"

God laughed. 'It isn't time yet. Ask Takezo if you doubt me."

"It is not time," Takezo volunteered.

"I'm leaving then," she said.

Lucky followed her out of the room to the barricades on the plaza.

"Where are we going?" he asked.

"I have a place I can stay. Nobody knows about it, and I am going to keep it that way," she said.

"He doesn't need us there, does he?" Lucky asked.

"No, he doesn't need us there. He does not need anyone there any more than you do, though the reasons for your exceptional integrity differ," Anisa said.

"Oh?" Lucky said.

"Yes. He has worked for many years to become self-sufficient. You are protected from the consequences of dependency by your limited consciousness," Anisa said.

"Limited consciousness, not lack of consciousness?" said Lucky. "What changed your mind?"

"Because I recognized your dependency on him. It is different than the reflex response to a need that may exist without consciousness. You have invested your attitude towards yourself in him.

When he tells you that you have done well in one of your fencing exercises, you feel happy. When he is in danger, you are afraid. The sensations you have are different from the emotional reflexes that a fly exhibits when it dodges away from the swatter in fear or the happiness it feels when it sops up nutritious residue from the garbage. The flies' feelings don't require intention.

It's the same as the pain traveling through a reflex arc from your finger on the hot stove to your spinal cord and then to the muscles in your arm. Reflexes occur within your person. When you shy away from a hot stove after getting burned, you do so without necessary reference to an identity

or recollection of

a personal experience of pain. When his praise makes you feel happy, your happiness exists within a system that encompasses both of you. The stove that burns your finger can be any old stove. The Takezo that praises you cannot be just any Takezo."

"You make it sound like I might have been better off without it. Consciousness, that is," Lucky said.

"I don't know. That may be giving consciousness too much credit. It only allows you to be worse off. Assuming that a rock is not conscious, a rock can't be better off or worse off.

As a conscious creature, when you regard the world, your experience feels a certain way. That feeling belongs only to you. You can't paint it, speak it, or sculpt it for other people to experience and understand. You will surmise that others experience the same thing, but you can never be sure. That means that there is a hiddenness to other people, and we are prone to fear and doubt what may lurk there."

"I wonder if that is why we see the skin the way we do, especially the eyes and teeth. We are filling a space with our primitive fears—the consequences of consciousness, "Lucky said.

"I wouldn't be surprised," said Anisa, "our oldest problems have their roots in the hiddenness of others: jealousy, resentment, denial, and suspicion."

"You say that like there's no solution for those problems. I have a hard time believing that. We are still here, and consciousness abounds. It seems that we would have long since been relegated to the annals of failed evolutionary experiments if those problems were truly intractable. Haven't we recognized our flaws and responded to them with those attitudes that we call virtue? Magnanimity for jealousy, generosity for resentment, steadfastness for denial, and openness for suspicion," Lucky

said.

"Indeed but consider what those virtues entail. Virtue occurs within the virtuous in response to their own flaws. Virtue is a paradox. It comes in response to the toxicities of our bonds with others, but it only develops in solitude," Anisa said.

"Okay. So, how do you know the difference between solitude and isolation? Retiring to develop one's virtue doesn't look much different than running away from your problems as far as I can tell," Lucky said.

"That's why enlightenment is rare while selfishness and war are common," Anisa said.

Lucky surveyed the crowds still gathered at that late hour, watching the threat in their midst like zebras following a lion.

"Are you still going to kill me?" He asked again.

"No. I've changed my mind; I will not kill you, at least not on purpose," Anisa said.

"You're going to sleep at the Villa tonight, then?" She asked.

"I may go by the Villa," Lucky answered, "but I don't think I will be sleeping tonight."

"Until tomorrow then," said Anisa as she turned and walked off in the direction of the medical center.

"Until tomorrow," said Lucky.

Forty-four

Reconciliation

The test results confirmed what his difficulties operating the abacus had already told Laplace. He consulted with two of the geneticists at the developmental center. They updated him on medical sciences' current understanding of his condition. They told him that it was a vulnerability related to an abnormal non-stop codon that the treatment primarily targeted. They went so far as to guarantee him that he would not develop psychiatric symptoms like his brother had. They sounded nearly as confident when they told him that he would not regain his aptitude for the abacus.

Morris disappeared sometime during his first night of incarceration. The director presented a report to the Authority, describing the security breach and attributing it to vulnerabilities in the culture of the developmental centers as a whole, as well as Morris's actions. The document featured no other persons or factors. The Authority responded quickly, accepting the director's report without question and issuing a death warrant for Morris. At Laplace's request, Araceli and Francis drafted and submitted several grant

requests seeking sponsorship for

research proposals related to restoring the Metizians' genetic sustainability. For a few hours, all of them enjoyed the center's calm and safety, but as those hours rolled into another day, Laplace grew restless. Francis finally approached him.

"Shouldn't we be going?" Francis asked, "I know we haven't heard any news, but things are probably progressing beneath the surface. Plus, I would like to get back to the specialists at the center so they can finally get this virus out of my system and me out of this pressure suit."

FORTY-FOUR

"You're right, but we need to have a brief discussion before we return to the center's activities," said Laplace as he guided Francis into the room containing the permanent fold at the end of the quarantine tunnel.

"Currently," Laplace began, "I am severely impaired. I share a genetic condition with my brother. It has variable penetrance and was active in my brother's case early on. We are twins, so the protocol dictates that one of us would be deleted anyway. It was an easy choice at the time.

The consequences of Gerard's Mother saving him from that fate have led us to this day. The same condition he suffered from has now become active in me. Also, thanks to his Mother, I have treatment available. With the help of the treatment, I won't deteriorate further, but I'm not going to get back what I've lost so far. I may have a way out, thanks to Danilo's hubris, but I will need you to navigate the radiation so I can reach what I need to remedy the situation.

"I can do it, but I don't have an abacus. I will need several nachinaks as well to meet a reasonable safety standard," Francis said in a carefully controlled tone.

"Very good. There is something else I need to tell you," Laplace continued. "The genetic abnormality that troubles my brother and me is also present in your genome. Inflammation is

one factor that can trigger it. They recommend continuing the immunoglobulin treatments, but they have cautioned against further attempts at vaccination for now. For the foreseeable future, you must take precautions, including the use of a pressure suit whenever you're out of an isolation suite."

"That doesn't make me very happy," Francis sighed, "but I've kind of grown accustomed to it by now. Maybe I had a premonition of this moment because I've been working on an improved design. No matter what, I can put up with it."

"Here," said Laplace as he swung his abacus down from its place in front of him and transferred it to the attachment points on the front of Francis's pressure suit, "now you have an abacus, and your abacus has all the nachinaks that you will need."

"Are you sure?" Francis asked.

"Absolutely," Laplace said as he pulled down and secured the outer cover, "let's go."

Forty-five

Listening to the Whiskey

The more Lucky drank, the angrier he became. He made a mistake when he ordered his first round. He was fond of the liquor brand on the wine list, and he ordered two shots on the waiter's first pass. He looked up with a scowl on his face, which he morphed into a grimace mimicking a smile when he noticed Marge at the grill watching him.

He waved to her, and she smiled and waved back. He noted that the cheese-burger he had ordered over half an hour ago was still waiting to go on the coals. The outdoor dining area was busy.

All the customers save for Lucky were members of the Species. Lucky's rough education in Species fashion told him that they were trendy people.

Classic rock

blared over the PA, and six customers stood on the open section of the deck, exhibiting a kind of choreoathetoid movement that was not easily mistaken for dance.

He resolved to leave without his burger. He hadn't meant to come to the old country store in the first place. When he and Anisa parted ways, he did go back to the villa, but he never made it to his room. As he came down the first switch-back, he saw a flickering light in the Valley. He concentrated on being unnotice-able and moved along the trail as quickly as he could.

Soon, he could see the fire consuming the remains of Takezo's workshop.

He also heard voices in the vicinity. He moved as close as he could to the small group of people discussing in front of the burning building. As he approached, Lucky recognized Augustine, Marge, and Dion.

One more person, a calculator, stood beside Augustine, looking very nervous. Lucky took him to be Augustine's assistant, Thomas.

"He must have taken it to the center of excellence. There's no telling where he's hiding in that complex, "said Augustine, "not that it matters, because we can't march in there and take it from him. We need to monitor the excavation to ensure he doesn't show up there while we wait for the representatives from the Authority and the Foundation to arrive.

Without further discussion, the group split up. Lucky turned around and ascended the trail back to the larger path between the center of excellence and the old country store. He stopped to weigh his options briefly, then took a left turn and followed the trail past the end of the sandstone Mesa, through the meadow and the trees to the store.

He hoped Casper escaped the inferno, but it seemed terribly unlikely. He needed a whiskey.

He focused on his growing collection of shot glasses to maintain his composure. Despite his efforts, people around him began to stare. With confused expressions on their faces, they

murmured to the people beside them.

As the wave of puzzlement passed through the crowd and reached Marge at the grill, she slapped the spatula down on the cutting board and began struggling to pass one of the waiters who stood dumbfounded beside the cooler.

"Hey!" Marge yelled in Lucky's direction, "what are you up to over there?" Lucky didn't respond. He was up and across the parking lot before Marge reached the dance floor. He broke into a run and didn't slow down until he was midway across the meadow. He started to walk as he came within visual range of the guard minding the shed at the end of the tunnel to the

cliff dwelling.

The guard didn't look up as Lucky walked calmly through the door. The

shed looked small from the outside, but it held a surprising array of junk in bulk. Lucky's gaze roamed over the crates, boxes, and loose items crowding into the center of the room.

Unfortunately, the few items that he recognized would not help him.

He proceeded past a man seated at a small table reviewing a projected list. He continued up the corridor to the carve outs in the tunnel wall. Those areas had accumulated a buildup of pieces and parts since his last visit. There were two more sizable external power sources parked there, one on either side of the passageway. At the end of the left side carve-out, he saw what he was looking for.

A rack stood there above four large metal boxes. The rack held some unfamiliar and odd devices in addition to a pair of semi-automatic shotguns. The cans below the rack contained a healthy supply of ammunition for the shotguns as well as other loose items. He stuffed the boxes into his pack, taking equal quantities of buckshot and rifled slugs. He looked over the different items.

Most of them were incomprehensible. He refrained from excess handling, given the items' association with familiar weapons. He collected three examples of two items that looked manageable.

One was a green metal ball with a catch on the equator. It had no other features on the surface but carried a block of text in red on the other side of the ball, extending from one pole to the other. The text warned of extreme fire hazard, residual fire hazard in the affected area after use, and a prohibition against the use of the device on human targets, military or Civilian, with penalties up to and including a death warrant.

Without the alcohol on board, Lucky might not have checked, but curiosity prevailed, and he pushed down on the catch. A rectangular segment of the sphere popped open and flipped back to reveal two buttons, one labeled "time" and the other labeled "proximity." The other items that went in his pack were examples of a small baton, fourteen cm long and six cm wide. The batons had a single button on one end and an orange light on the other. Each bore a label with an orange skull printed above a warning that read:

safe for use around most machinery. Avoid use within twenty meters of friendly Biologics, nachinaks, and AI. He loaded one of the shotguns with buckshot and kept it in hand while he slung the other weapon across his back and adjusted his pack straps to fit over it.

Once his load felt stable, he continued past the bend in the tunnel where it sloped down towards the cliff dwelling. Just as the indirect lighting from the carveouts became inadequate, the floor of the tunnel flattened out in the distance, and another light source in the space beyond compensated.

The sounds of construction echoed in the tunnel ahead. Lucky strolled casually into the worksite. The new proprietors had transformed the space since Lucky last visited. The partition wall between the stairwell and the cavern room was gone. A

circular hole, approximately 10 m in

diameter, occupied the floor between the end of the stairs and the adjacent cavern walls. Lucky could not see into the hole, but a silvery light shone from within the space below at an angle suggesting a relatively shallow depth.

A man dressed in the same red garments that Augustine wore stood at a workbench beside the hole, conferring with one of the workers. Two other workers assembled machinery on the workbench while two men in spacesuits fiddled with instruments lining the edge of the hole. Four nachinaks hovered close by. The hole in the outer wall of the cavern was the only remaining familiar feature.

Lucky could make out a pile of detritus stacked on the ledge outside, including skeletal remains mixed with the dirt and branches. As he passed the site, two nachinaks suddenly pivoted toward the end of the tunnel. The two men in spacesuits were on their feet immediately. They ran in pursuit of the two nachinaks, both of which flew to the tunnel entrance and began slowly advancing along the same line that Lucky had taken across the cavern. Lucky clamped his mouth shut on a curse and ran for the ledge outside.

He jettisoned the shotgun in his hand and started up the steep, loose ground where the ledge intersected the boundary of the slick rock and the vegetated canyon wall.

Some light reached him from the breach in the cavern wall and the site of the cliff dwelling above, but he had to climb mostly by feel. The going was difficult. The terrain had changed since he last made the climb. Many of the large, unstable rocks that he had utilized for holds were gone. The angle was less, but there were more dirt patches and exposed roots.

Despite his caution, he had already dislodged several small rocks and clumps of dirt. The light from below dimmed as his pursuers reached the opening to the ledge.

He could not see the men or the nachinaks, but he knew that they would not give up, and eventually, the little machines would

catch up with him. He stopped and reset his focus.

He swung the pack around and fished for one of the batons. Hoping that he was outside of the 20 m radius, he pushed the button and dropped the baton onto the ledge.

He tensed as he heard the weapon bounce twice and saw the small light on one end fall past the ledge. He didn't hear or see anything, but suddenly felt severely short of breath, weak, and lightheaded.

From the top of his head to the tips of his toes, his skin tingled and burned.

He threw his left arm through an exposed root that had formed a loop as it doubled back towards deeper soil in its quest for water. He briefly lost consciousness. His arm hurt where it levered against the root, but he did not fall. He heard something small tumbling down the steep sandstone ramps below. All was silent otherwise.

Despite feeling like he was in the grip of the worst influenza infection of his life, he made it up the rest of the climb to the ledge. He peeked over the lip of the ledge to find that the new proprietors of the cliff and cavern had completely demolished the Adobe structures.

He picked up a rock and threw it as hard as he could towards the cavern's opening. With an eye on the trail at the end of the ledge, he sidled across with both hands, maintaining contact with the wall. He stumbled up the trail for a few meters in the dark.

When he felt safely out of sight, he fished his headlamp out of the pack and turned it on. He listened for a moment, and when he heard no sounds

of pursuit or discovery, he embarked on the march back to God's prison.

Forty-six

The Gauntlet

Laplace struggled with the abacus. If he tried anything too fast and complicated, his filaments would tangle with each other, and the exclusion sphere would begin to drift in the direction of its origin. As a pleasant surprise, however, he found that he had retained his proficiency in inducing and maintaining folds.

That slight advantage became the basis of a successful strategy that supplanted the original, Francis-centered plan within the first dozen calculations into the trip back to the Bilateral Nephrectomy Center of Excellence.

The initial maze, leading from the developmental center back to the Nachinak statue, was crucial. Francis experienced typical initiate problems during the navigation.

During their elective simulations in the developmental center, adolescent aspirants pushed themselves with challenging calculations aimed at completion. Their interaction with the complex world, where all calculations began, aimed at simplifying the complexities as rapidly as possible.

Because millions of others had passed that way before them, the beginners had detailed, yet rote, directions to guide them through. Thus, the adolescents fresh from presentation and loose on the world had relatively mediocre

skills when it came to puzzling their way along the class of dependencies called "lateral aspects."

After the second wrong turn, Laplace called a timeout and took the abacus back. He turned the defenses over to Francis. If Francis had harbored any resentment over the switch, it evaporated during the maneuver constituting the last leg of their return to the labyrinth.

Laplace improvised a tricky formula to avoid the collapsed hallway and landed them one step away from the exclusion sphere generator that formed the mouth of the

nachinak statue. His precision won them a bye on a fight with the large contingent of God's Helping Angels gathered around the statue.

Their exposure only lasted long enough to allow them a smile and a wave as they eased into the next segment of the journey. A few of the helpers pursued them into the radiation, but the effort was pointless.

Since the group had abandoned their race's great project, their familiarity with the radiation had degraded. Laplace didn't even slow down to destroy them. A safe landing at Node 8 was his single purpose.

He took them through an intricate web of aspects, tracing the possibilities of initial events arising in the simplest subvening elements of adjacent dependencies. Even so, it was not enough. They confronted one calculator after the next as they approached the node eight access point.

Laplace maneuvered this way and that to maintain a safe distance, but soon, he could find no way forward in stealth.

"Francis, are you ready?" He asked as they paused to review their checklist, "Start with a surprise. Don't get stuck on your defenses, check with your defensive units at the prescribed intervals. The same is true with the darts and torus generators. If you fall back in this sort of confrontation, you've lost. That goes even if you face someone in the sphere with us. Trust your reflexes when it comes to your role in defense and leave the rest to the little ones. No more than one action, then your attention must be right back out there."

Francis nodded. They checked their equipment, and Laplace handed over the loop of beads sequestered along the rim of his abacus. Francis fed the loop through the isolation access port at the junction of his helmet and suit. As the loop came through the other side of the seal, his filaments took over and wove the loop expertly around the flaps on his chest and abdomen.

The beads began to spin as the loop shifted over and around its supporting flaps. Four nachinaks left a compartment on the side of Laplace's abacus and took up positions at the corners of a rectangle encompassing Laplace and

Francis. Four external power supply accessory nachinaks of the standard variety, along with Laplace's modified unit, stationed themselves around the horizontal equator of the exclusion sphere.

The red and black nachinak rose to a position between Francis and Laplace while the four components of the neutralizing device assembled themselves into a rotating knot overhead. A pair of torus generators occupied each side of an invisible line tracing the vertical equator of the exclusion sphere. A standard nachinak escorted each of the offensive weapons.

Laplace held an open box of darts in his right hand and a dagger in his left. Francis opened his box of darts, holding it in his right hand, and took up the double-headed, black striped nachinak in his left hand. The shimmering gossamer defensive web unfurled between its four supporting nachinaks to encompass them completely.

Laplace looked at Francis. His broad grin accentuated the unsettling effect of his lidless eyes. Without further warning, they began to shift.

Laplace traced a sweeping corkscrew centered on the prominent crease in the brightly tinted, crowded geometry of the radiation. They passed three opponents before anyone reacted.

Clearly annoyed, the three activated their defenses and sent a swarm of nachinaks, several darts, and a green metal ball toward Laplace and Francis. In response, darts swarmed from the box in Laplace's right hand until the supply was depleted.

Laplace's pair of power accessory units intercepted a standard unit from

the first pursuer and a torus generator from the second pursuer. Both of the friendly units managed

to get their mouths around the trunks of their

respective opponents. All of the devices belonging to the first two pursuers froze. The defensive web surrounding each of them disintegrated, freeing the darts sequestered in the material. Both of them slumped, lifeless in their exclusion spheres.

Laplace and Francis' own defensive web sequestered the darts directed at them and absorbed a detonation and persistent flames from the ball of green metal as it struck the web..

Laplace's path drew even with the fold as three more enemies joined the chase from above. Unexpectedly, Laplace and Francis continued to shift along the same vector. The pursuer below them launched another green sphere, this time in the wake of a nachinak with a large pair of legs in front and an accentuated mouth and trunk.

The two friendly accessory units moved to intercept, but as they ap-proached, the sphere began to spin and ejected a tiny sliver of yellow metal toward each of Laplace's attacking nachinaks. Both of the slivers found their mark, and Laplace's units burst into flame.

In the meantime, Laplace lost one of his torus generators to a collision with a unit configured for blunt force from the nearest of their new pursuing trio. The nachinak in front of the green sphere arrived and struck the defensive web around Francis and Laplace.

It continued through the right side of the web, leaving an expanding hole in the material. The sphere reached the middle of the defensive rectangle and ex-ploded just as Laplace stepped through the intact curtain to his left. Francis dropped to a crouch as the sphere burst, and the remains of the web engulfed the explosion.

Laplace altered their course to an arc leading back down to the crease. The single pursuer below shifted to compensate and moved between Laplace and Francis' sphere and the three oncoming enemies. The attacker from below ap-peared behind

Laplace.

Francis sprang to his feet and slapped her in the neck with the black striped nachinak in his left hand. She stopped being behind Laplace and started being behind the closest of the three remaining pursuers. Her eyes turned from side to side in panic, but she was unable to move. The filaments on her chest disgorged another sphere of green metal, which exploded as it emerged, and flames con-sumed everything inside the affected sphere.

Laplace could almost touch the crease. He signaled for Francis to go through. As Francis complied, another salvo of darts came at close range from the next pursuer. The black and red unit belonging to Laplace latched on to a nachinak associated with the enemy, who fired the darts. All of that opponent's nachinaks froze, and the darts stopped tracking, passing wide to Laplace's right.

All of Laplace's remaining nachinaks escaped through the fold behind Francis as the last nearby enemy launched her darts. Laplace swung the abacus off his chest and cast it through the fold as he pushed off to follow. He kept his left leg extended while flexing his left arm, right arm, and right leg as close to his body as possible. The crease in the event radiation was closing quickly.

It appeared uncertain that he would make it through, but there was no way he would avoid the darts. They struck the calf of his left leg as he threw both hands overhead and arched to pass through the fold.

He landed hard on the metal floor of the Node Eight access point. A wisp of pink vapor trailed off the clean cut just below his left knee. He ran his hands quickly around the remainder of his left leg, feeling for a dart that might have gotten through. It was clean.

Francis sat on the floor to his left, looking exhausted. Drusilla knelt beside him on one knee, holding a semi-automatic rifle and scanning the ballroom.

Gerard was across the room on the
right, monitoring one of the instruments associated with the node.

"There are still more out there," he announced, "but they dare not enter the node."

He walked over to Laplace and looked down at the pool of blood slowly spreading out from his severed leg.

"Brother, you are the luckiest person I have ever met or even heard of," he said.

"Little help?" asked Laplace.

They could hear footsteps down the hall as a medical team approached. "Never fear. We are next door to a transplant hospital."

Forty-seven

The Price of Justice

Lucky ambled up the road with a newfound appreciation for obscurity. True to his word, he had not slept at all. He grew tired of walking in the early hours of the morning, so he sat down at the edge of the parking lot behind the medical center and waited for the sun to rise.

In the final dark hours of the morning, a drone flew overhead, but it did not seem to notice him. He felt the urge to move as soon as it got fully light. The top of the solar disk had barely crested the horizon, so he decided to take the long way around to allow Takezo ample opportunity to sleep.

He walked down the road until he reached the entrance to the covered lot where the important people parked. He walked past the attendant nonchalantly. On the other side of the lot, he confronted the marble block of a building where he found Casper.

The sight of the front doors piqued his curiosity. He had learned a great deal since his last visit, and he would not need to engage in any elevator shenanigans this time to take a look inside. He nodded to the guards at the doors.

Neither acknowledged him,
and he went ahead into the building.

There was a small foyer in the middle of a hallway that ran from one side of the building to the other. A pair of wide doors stood directly opposite the entrance. Lucky cracked open one of the doors to have a look inside.

There was one large room beyond the doorway. It contained lines of benches and a few large pieces of equipment that Lucky did not recognize. Only five people were using the facility at that time of day. Lucky closed the door and went down the right-hand hallway.

There were a couple of offices set between the inner and outer walls after the hallway turned left. At the very end of the hall, a stairway led upward from a fire door. The second floor was very similar to the first, although the central room was more crowded with people and equipment. The third floor was a puzzle.

Instead of the large room in the middle, a series of storerooms occupied the perimeter. There were only two perimeter offices, one at the back corner on the southeast and one towards the middle of the opposite side corridor. The stairs ended on that floor, right next to the corner office. Lucky looked inside. It was furnished but did not look like it was occupied.

It was spotless. There were no marks on the chair or the floor, no books on the bookshelves, and no trash in the wastebasket.

The office on the opposite side was very similar, but he could see scuffs on the arms of the chair and the carpet. Both offices had large, tinted windows; on one side, they looked out at the hillside beyond the corner office, and on the other side, they looked out at the medical center and administrative buildings.

Remembering what he found on the fourth floor West, Lucky felt around the edges of the window frames. The frame on the window overlooking the campus buildings was completely smooth. In the corner office, however, he felt a slight irregularity

in the corner of the frame.

He pushed on it, and it flipped open. Underneath hid a small latch, similar to the one on the other fourth-floor window frame. He dug up the latch and felt something give. He looked around the room, but nothing had changed. On a hunch, he went to the stairwell and saw that the inside wall contained a partially sprung one-half by two-meter panel.

Behind the panel, the stairs continued up to the next floor. There were no more fire doors in the stairwell.

The third floor consisted of a narrow walk space between shelving units forming a perimeter with no access to the middle of the building. The shelves contained a variety of supplies, including chemicals, electronic components, structural elements, welding equipment, and hand tools. Lucky only looked through a few of the crates and boxes before moving onto the fourth floor. The fourth floor was not exactly a floor. The stairs ended at a walkway around the top of a space that extended from the second floor to the roof. Stairs at the end of the walkway, located in the middle of the wall to the left of Lucky, provided access to the floor of the space, which was piled high with tools and supplies stacked on workbenches, side shelves, and the floor.

Each wall had a desk built into it with a projector permanently affixed.

Lucky examined the mess up close and found that it contained many nachinaks in various states of repair and construction. He turned on one of the projectors. It brought up an image of a nachinak that he had not seen before.

It was blocky and had a four-part trunk, which gave it a distinctive appearance, as if it were trying to swallow a squid. Over its back, it sprouted an intricate thicket of delicate wire structures joined together at the intersections of wire ends with tiny versions of the carved beads he had seen on the wire loops that some of the Species carried around with them.

He turned it off and scratched

his head. He shrugged in mild disappointment and made his way back down the stairway, carefully restoring the panel and the latch to their proper

positions before exiting the building. By the time Lucky walked into the room behind the amphitheater stage, Takezo was already awake, as Lucky had hoped. Contrary to Lucky's wishes, Takezo was awake somewhere else. All morning, God had refrained from pounding on the walls. As Lucky stood in the narrow space behind the barrier, silent and alone, he began to

panic. He turned to leave, but not in time.

God's fist slammed into the wall. It seemed to Lucky like an especially powerful blow.

"Do you have to start that again?" Lucky asked, "Doesn't it hurt your hands?"

"Yes, my ex-prophet," God replied calmly, "my pain is a down payment on the just punishment that I will bring to all of you when the time comes."

"You do seem committed, and I'll admit that commitment to a cause is admirable, but in this particular case… I don't know how else to say this; I don't see the point," Lucky said.

God did not hold back in response. The three consecutive blows he laid on the barrier were deafening, and the shockwave knocked Lucky off his feet. A gap appeared between the door and the doorframe. God grabbed the edge and pulled, expanding the hole until he could see Lucky's face.

"You've developed enough courage to remain visible before me. Congratulations, it won't help you. What do you mean when you say that you don't see the point? Justice is the point. Fulfilling my inherent duty is the point. I've explained this to you already. I've explained this to all of you a million times already!" God said.

"I appreciate that," said Lucky, "but if you tried for something
a million times, and you have tried to explain it to everybody a million times, and they still haven't understood, and you still find yourself back here in the same position you were in after try number 999,999, then it might be time to reassess."

God cocked his fist. Electricity arced around his hand.

"Listen to the rest, please, "Lucky asked, "You can hit me anytime, right?"

The sparks died down, and God lowered his fist.

"I appreciate the opportunity. Maybe I'm wrong, but this is how it looks to me," Lucky continued. "In a sense, you have seen what success looks like. You have succeeded locally, right? I mean, you have brought some people justice, even when you had to rely on your believers and their little machines to do the actual punishing."

As you have pointed out, though, you have not made incremental gains. To truly have justice served, it must be served in full. Let's say that you can accomplish that. There's a new sinner born every day and they are bound to step on an ant on purpose, give an alcoholic a drink or ignore a call for help – someday they are bound to do something that merits divine punishment, and like you say: If there is a drop of sin in that bucket, the bucket is full."

"Go on," God prompted.

"How does all that look to the sinning public? Like you say, the scale of their crime is incomprehensible to them. Punishment is inevitable. The situation is the same as if an asteroid were headed their way or their house were sitting on a subduction zone. They're going to tell themselves that none of it's their fault and it's going to happen to somebody else, and then they're going to get on with their day," Lucky said.

"And?" God asked.

"I'm sorry," Lucky said,' but don't you think it's futile to seek justice in a world where time evens out the score anyway. Why not just let it?"

God scowled and drew his arm back, then reconsidered.

A very uncomfortable interlude ensued, filled with pacing, muttering, and furniture kicking on God's part, and nervous perspiring on Lucky's part.

"I have to think about this," God announced as he assumed the lotus position, "consider yourself re-anointed prophet, for the time being."

Lucky waited for what he considered a reasonable interval before shuffling slowly over to the door. It was in better shape than it looked from across the room. He grabbed the handle, braced his foot against the doorframe, and pulled. It creaked and popped, but God did not seem to mind. Lucky finally managed to get the door to catch.

As soon as he felt the click, he turned and ran. He was looking back as he turned the corner when he slammed into Anisa. He bounced off of her and landed on the other side of the hall, looking up at Takezo.

"Did he change his mind and start without me?" Takezo asked.

"No, things are copacetic for now," Lucky said.

"Maybe we should give him some space," Anisa suggested.

Lucky nodded in agreement. He got up and brushed himself off. Anisa was already making for the exit. Takezo took a look around the corner and, seeing no signs of pursuit, joined the other two outside the academic building.

"He is waiting for something else," Takezo told them. "I am ready, and he knows it."

"You have convinced yourself beyond a shadow of a doubt that he is God?" Lucky asked.

"No, I don't believe that he is God. I think he is a Kami who cannot find his way back to the tree or stone to which he belongs. I understand him well enough to beat him. We are errant Kami ourselves, aren't we?" Takezo replied.

"Do you know what he's referring to?" Anisa asked Lucky.

"No. What's a Kami?" Lucky asked Takezo.

"Spirits. They play a role in Japanese folklore similar to that of the little people in European tradition. They are more complicated, though. They don't solely inhabit a feature of the landscape; they are the spirit of that feature. From a scientific viewpoint, the spirits explain all the things that we cannot, and they preserve our delusion of control."

For example, ancient farmers did not understand blights that destroyed their crops. Without understanding, they could not do anything to prevent or cure a blight," Takezo continued, "But the Kami who came to live at the shrine next to the field might be able to if the farmer could persuade them." However, Kami is also the peaceful feeling you get when kneeling at the shrine and the sensation you get when you run your hands through the rich

soil in the rice field next to the shrine."

"That does make a little more sense than the hypothesis that he is God, though I would point out that it is his hypothesis," Anisa said. "So, where does he come from, and what does he represent? Can we somehow send him back there?"

Takezo laughed, "Is anything ever that convenient? We are still no better off than the farmers facing rice blight. We still can't control anything, even ourselves. If I decide to do something contrary to my purpose, then my purpose has become acting against my will, and I had already failed before I began. All I can do is be myself and act accordingly."

'Why waste all the time you spent meditating? You're admitting that it won't make a damn bit of difference," said Lucky.

Takezo took the phone out of a pocket inside his kimono and held the screen in front of Lucky's face.

"Through meditation and concentration, all things are possible."

Number one high score," Takezo proclaimed.

317

Anisa and Lucky looked at the phone and then back at Takezo. Lucky regained the power of speech first.

"The game? You've just been playing the video game all this time? You told me that you had a revelation. You told me that you knew how to defeat him," Lucky said.

Takezo's face lost all expression. He dropped the phone on the floor and stepped on it.

"I know that he is not all-powerful despite his expectations. I know that he is uncertain because I have listened to his sermons and seen his response to a dilemma."

Now I know that he has no ground to defend, only his own body, so he will attack, but he will not attack headlong in the face of certain death. His defense will be desperate and without a thought for how it positions him for the next move. No revelations. Through meditation and concentration, I know how to beat him," Takezo told them.

"If we are all errant Kami, then you don't defend any ground either," Anisa said.

"We are different than the others; we defend the ground that supports us," Takezo said.

"What now?" Lucky asked.

"Let's walk," Takezo suggested, "all that meditation has left my legs stiff and my back sore."

In silent agreement, the three of them began walking, following the sidewalk to the hedgerow surrounding the inner Plaza. Usually, two humans, one of them carrying a long metal stake, would attract a few gawkers even at a cosmopolitan academic institution, but no one gave them a second glance. The crowd found events within the encircling hedge more compelling. The iron gates and transparent doors were all locked and guarded.

"We should go the other way," Takezo suggested.

They backtracked to the amphitheater entrance and continued down the sidewalk to the dormitories and lecture halls. Takezo took in the flower beds between the dorms but seemed unimpressed. They had exhausted their entertainment options. Lucky looked up the hill.

"Want to see what else is in there?" he asked, pointing at the Node Eight building.

"No. I already know enough about what's in there: a bunch of stuff I already have and a bunch of people who want to kill me," said Anisa.

"Perfect!" said Takezo, "We can define a threat, send a message, and leave without souvenirs."

To everyone's surprise, Anisa shrugged and began walking up the hill toward the Node 8 building. Takezo and Lucky hurried to keep up and only managed to catch up with her at the door, which she held open for them. Both of them stopped before crossing the threshold.

"Well? Go ahead," Anisa said. "I'm sick of arguing with you people, but I won't be held responsible for what happens when someone recognizes us."

Forty-eight

What Tomorrow May Bring

Inside the doors, a stream of air washed over them from a grate in the floor and exited through a grate in the ceiling. A chime sounded, informing them that they were free of easily transmitted, dangerous, and common infectious diseases. The inner door opened, and they entered the lobby of the node.

A guard wanted to confiscate Lucky's shotgun, but on Takezo's word, the officer allowed Lucky to keep it. A continuous check-in desk followed the arc of the round building's outer wall. Representatives of various businesses offering supplies, information, and services stood at intervals behind the desk.

Prospective sojourners in the radiation of events wandered the floor looking for vital items they had inadvertently left at home and vital items that they didn't know they needed before viewing the goods in the sparkling display cases.

A bank of glass elevators occupied the center of the circular room. They examined the directory beside the lifts. It listed floors devoted to lodging and equipment, storage and repair, minor medical care, the Authority's

offices, the ballroom and lounge, and the deck.

"Let's see the deck," Lucky said. "I got a partial view
from a high point, and it looks like it might be interesting."

Anisa and Takezo agreed that it would be a good place to start, so they took the elevator straight to the top. The deck was a pleasant place. It featured several watercourses, hanging and potted flowering plants, resident amphibians, and many Species of visiting birds. Wicker chairs, glass tables, couches, and a single agent of the Authority furnished the space.

They picked a table with a good vantage point and sat down to watch the people come and go. They were there no longer than 10 minutes when Drusilla stepped from the elevators, glanced at the agent, and then walked directly over to their table.

"To what do we owe the honor?" Anisa asked in greeting. Drusilla pulled up a chair and sat down.

"Now that you ask, I'm trying to sort out what that shit hound over there is up to. He's not going to do anything except what he's doing right now as long as the three of you are here," Drusilla said.

"So, you are kicking us out?" Lucky asked.

"Oh no, on the contrary," said Drusilla cheerfully, "I'm inviting you in."

She went back to the elevators and motioned for them to follow. They complied hesitantly.

"We were having fun. We were just starting to have fun," Lucky said, as the doors closed and the elevator dropped.

Drusilla stared at him and inserted a key in the elevator panel. She gave it an exaggerated twist. The elevator lurched to a stop. A segment of the elevator shaft retracted and slid into the wall, revealing a large conference room. Drusilla held the door as the others stepped across the threshold.

A long, oval table resting on an ornate carpet occupied the center of the space. Smaller square tables, placed at random intervals, took up the rest of the usable floor.

The floor was metal, and the stuffed chairs surrounding

the tables floated on magnets to reduce noise. Projections from surveillance cameras around the campus and beyond, along with reports, algorithms, and datasets, floated over the tabletops, all under scrutiny by Node 8 analysts. Gerard was there, conferring with one of the specialists over an image from a surveillance camera aimed at the juniper forest North of the great square. As soon as he noticed them, he broke away from the consultation to greet his visitors.

"Please come with me," he said. I have some information for you." He went to the conference table and pulled up a report.

"None of us knows how the events tomorrow will play out, but for now and into the foreseeable future, our interests are aligned, so we will coordinate with you as we would with any other ally," Gerard said.

"We?" Anisa asked. "You mean your brother is back? If so, I am out."

Gerard put his hand on her shoulder to keep her from turning away. She struck him in the mouth with her elbow, knocking him to the floor. A few drops of blood landed on the plate beside him. He wiped the drops up with his finger, regarding them with an expression of pleased surprise.

"Liked that, did you?" Anisa asked," Have some more." Takezo stepped between Anisa and Gerard as he rebuffed Drusilla with the flat of his blade.

"Nandayo! Tell us," Takezo said nodding in Gerard's direction, "The rest will sit down and shut up."

Gerard got to his feet and sat down at the table. "Please, everyone, be seated," said Gerard.

The group finally arranged itself around the table. Anisa settled on a position as far away from Gerard as possible. Drusilla seated herself within arm's reach of Anisa.

Gerard paged through the report as if it were a slideshow.

"Let me orient you to the original plan so that you can understand how we arrived at our current situation. My brother is always alert for opportunities to improve his odds of completing a mathematical description

of the universe under the rules governing the dendritic radiation of events. He has made multiple attempts over the years, but none for the last 8 years. He has deferred because he discovered some disconcerting information in the old archives that validated his experience with very close approaches."

There is a problem with the final calculation that lies in the structure of the radiation rather than the operator's abilities. He thinks that the problem is amenable to the action of a nachinak. The design of the device would be unique, and it would be a primary unit requiring 4 to 5 support units," Gerard said.

"Has he seen a psychiatrist since he shared this crazy-ass epiphany with you? It sounds like he may be suicidal," said Anisa.

Gerard ignored her and continued, "The time required to build the necessary devices would be prohibitive, not because the bench work was too difficult, but because the testing and data acquisition were so complicated. He estimated that he could get the nachinak built in his lifetime if he could find a stable patch of gray space."

He returned to the archives with his new question in hand and quickly found an answer: the God phenomenon."

Thus, the contest and the results of our safari currently audible in the amphitheater. My brother presented his idea to the Authority, the local banking consortium, and the governing board of the Centers of Excellence. The response was very positive. He initially sought craftsmen among the Species but found none, and so he had to broaden his search."

Putting the competition

out in the open drew the interest of prominent aspirants to a complete calculation. Augustine was the most enamored, and he approached us with an offer to cosponsor the competition."

We were already facing unanticipated problems – for instance, we had to construct a conduit with associated permanent folds to avoid fatalities among the species that cannot tolerate complete immersion in the radiation.

We also needed to build a workshop and housing to limit trips outside the conduit."

When Augustine also offered to cover the cost of the workshop, we brought him in—the rest, you know better than I.

Representatives of the sponsors are expected to arrive this evening, and the weapon demonstration is scheduled to take place tomorrow morning. We are unsure how to orchestrate the entire chain of events to a satisfactory conclusion."

We have a preferred venue for the harvest. The cliff dwelling, which some of you are familiar with, provides an ideal environment for the gray space. We don't know how we will convince God to travel there. He is loose, do not doubt that. Our barrier is strong, but not strong enough to withstand an all-out assault."

We are not sure what he is waiting for, though his Helping Angels know who we are now, and so they will quickly discover our location. They will show up soon with their zombie nachinaks in tow."

They all sat silently, absorbing what Gerard had told them.

"Are there any more competitors coming tomorrow to demonstrate their weapons?" Takezo asked.

"None," Gerard said. "It appears that Augustine terminated the other sponsorships he was funding as soon as you demonstrated your prototype to him."

"It doesn't seem like we have enough information to form the basis of a strategy," Lucky said, "so do we just arm ourselves to the teeth, show up, and see what happens?"

"Well put, General," said Anisa, "your plan has my vote."

"Your tactics are your strategy?" Drusilla asked, "Not exactly preferred doctrine."

"That approach can succeed," Takezo said, "but only if you do not have

an unspoken strategy at work simultaneously. That goes for the group and its members. Remain bound by your determination to destroy the enemy, and you may succeed. Divert your efforts, and you will fail."

"It will have to do," said Gerard. "There's one more thing: an introduction. Please come with me to the medical center."

They piled into the elevator once again and rode it to the first floor. As they walked across campus to the medical center, all was quiet. Even the atmosphere in the medical center seemed subdued. No one gave them a second look as the odd assortment crossed the lobby and took a key-controlled elevator to the sixth floor. Gerard stopped briefly to check in at the nurses' station, where the banner of text over the front desk proclaimed, "Isolation Ward." He led them to a room just a few doors down the hall, where a young man sat on a stool, tinkering with an exotic brand of EVA suit.

Gerard knocked on the glass to get his attention. He paused and rubbed his eyes. He smiled when he recognized Gerard standing there. He rose from his seat stiffly and walked over to the window.

"This is Francis," said Gerard. "He will be joining our effort tomorrow. I want to be sure that you're able to recognize him and vice versa. He will be wearing that contraption. I also want you to be aware that he is currently infected with an extremely hazardous microorganism."

If that suit is breached or his condition requires you to render aid, you must make contact only under strict isolation precautions, even if that means delaying critical interventions. Francis

is aware of that stipulation and is in complete agreement."

The members of the group introduced themselves to Francis one by one and wished him good luck.

With the last of their joint business concluded, they left the medical center and said their farewells by the pool in the center of the inner Plaza. It was early in the evening, and work crews were still busy preparing for the next day's gathering.

They had already assembled the small stage where the representatives would sit. They were still setting up rows of chairs for guests of lesser distinction. Between the stage and the seating area, a 10 m x 10 m deck stood, raised 0.5 m above the ground.

Takezo eyed the construction with a frown but did not comment further. "I will come out to the main plaza near the first line of stairs just before

sunrise," Takezo said, "then it will be up to God."

Forty-nine

The Fourth Floor

With that, Takezo walked off in the direction of the amphitheater. Drusilla and Gerard turned back toward the medical center. Lucky set off for the west side of the campus, walking quickly. Anisa eyed him skeptically and followed. She caught up with him as he was turning into the front entrance of the square marble building. Seeing his intent, she grabbed him by the elbow and pulled him to the side, out of sight of the building's security personnel.

"What are you doing?" She asked.

"I have a place where I can stay and stay unnoticed. It's inside that building. I'm going in there so I can get some rest for the night. I thought you were off to do the same?" Lucky said, "Unless you're the one who's been sleeping in that vacant fourth-floor office."

"What do you gain from this?" She asked.

"Habitual honesty, I hope," Lucky answered, "and a second opinion."

"About what?" Anisa asked.

"About what else is in that building? Have you seen the other rooms?" Lucky asked.

"Yeah, it's all a bunch of labs, storage spaces, and administrative offices," Anisa said.

"You never found the latch on the window frame," Lucky said. "How have you been getting in and out of the place?"

"What? I've been coming through the basement. I took a key from one of the custodians," Anisa said.

"Lead on," said Lucky.

Anisa turned and walked to the back of the building. She went to one of the stairwells that Lucky had tried during his initial foray before he was forced to resort to the freight elevator. After opening the door at the bottom, she looked both ways to make sure it was all clear.

She started right where the vacant office lay. Lucky tapped her on the shoulder and pointed in the other direction. They followed the hallway to the left until they reached the stairwell on the northeast corner of the building. Her key did not fit the door at the bottom, but there were plenty of tools lying about, and she soon came upon a sturdy crowbar that granted access.

They walked up the stairs cautiously until they came to the dead-end. Lucky brought her into the office and showed her how to work the hidden latch in the window frame.

He led the way up the hidden flights of stairs to the catwalk around the top of the fourth-floor workshop.

In contrast to his previous visit, the area was dark. Anisa activated a flashlight sequestered in the filaments beside each shoulder. As they descended the stairs to the workspace floor, her attention and the light remained fixed on a workbench set into the wall and its contents.

It was the same blocky nachinak, with a blanket of ornate metalwork covering its back. Someone had been working on it since Lucky was there last. The unit now looked complete. As they approached the workbench, the lights came up.

"You like it? It's a new model, one-of-a-kind. It's designed to take you all the way to the end," said Laplace.

Anisa froze. Laplace sat in an office chair on the far side of the room. He had laid his hat to one side, and his left leg was partially extended. Just below the knee on that side, a series of pins in two horizontal rows joined the halves of a circular frame and anchored it to bone underneath. The frame contained bone stimulators in series, housed between the rings. Each displayed a small, flashing green light in the middle.

"Get to the point," Anisa said. "Who are you talking to? Me? I don't give a shit what you have to say. Him?" She asked, gesturing at Lucky. "He's not conscious; he's not even experiencing this exposition. Or are you talking to yourself, to hear yourself talk?"

"Not conscious? Is that what she's been telling you?" Asked Laplace, "Of course, you are conscious. You wouldn't be here if you weren't. The last visit made an impression. There was a certain way that the room presented itself to you, and that quality wove its way through the fabric of your experience. It pulled together the tapestry's image. It's why she is here with you to tie up the loose ends. She's made the error of assuming that something episodic can't be useful or predominant."

"You have one more chance to get to the point," Anisa said," I don't have to listen to your bullshit anymore."

"Because you're free. That's true, as a matter of fact, and now as a matter of principle. I'm calling it off, Anisa, and not just for you. I'm no longer persuaded that there is any justifying rationale for slavery. It is erosive to the personality of anyone who comes into contact with it. We keep it around to avoid the pain of ripping it out of the culture. We cling to the utopian myth for the same reason."

Anisa's breath quickened, and she began to sweat.

"What do you mean by that?" She asked with a note of panic in her voice, "What have you discovered to make you say something like that?"

"I'm saying that it can't be done. It hasn't been done because it can't

be done. The little ones showed me, inadvertently. They only ever see the world as it relates to the impression stamped inside them."

We are no different. We only see an aspect of the event radiation, so even our best descriptions devolve to that aspect. They can never add up to a complete account. We have been wasting our time. We will never control the world. It cannot be a better place."

Anisa began walking toward him.

"You don't know that. You can't know that. There are millions of years of lost records..." She said.

"There are millions of years of intact records after that. None of them record a successful calculation," he said.

"That proves nothing," she said. "How can we be confident that they haven't been using the simulator the entire time? We wouldn't expect them to be able to get word back, and we all know how complex the complete calculation would be. They're likely to be understaffed."

Laplace laughed.

"Does the world look that much better to you? Or does it make more sense that utopia is an illusion?"

She was nearly in front of him, and he stood to meet her. She hit him before he could say anything more. He slipped the punch, grabbed her wrists, and pulled her over to the table.

When they were close enough, he cast her off with a shove and scooped up the ornate nachinak. His hands shook as he held it up to her face.

"A beautiful creature, isn't it?" Laplace asked. "I found the blueprint and a mostly intact example in a collection of

antiquities that was itself quite ancient. It is designed to put you in the position of an ideal observer. It cannot take you back, and there's no way to test it before use. It requires four other nachinaks to control the lateral contingencies and eliminate drift. I possess all of those accessory units. I'm giving this to you if you want it. To be clear: You cannot come back. You will never enjoy your fame. We cannot even begin to guess what you will find. However, I can tell you this: you can verify whether what I told you is correct or not. The device has an orientation protocol to tell it where it's beginning when it launches the description. If it completes its task, it will return to that starting point. What do you say, Anisa?"

"I don't get it," she said as she took the nachinak in her hands and turned it over to examine the workmanship. "Why aren't you doing this yourself?"

"You know about Gerard's condition?" Laplace asked. "I have it as well.

It was never active until recently, when one of my opponents managed to awaken it from its slumber in the noncoding DNA."

"Ha! Danilo! So that's why you are suddenly condemning slavery because one of your slaves finally stuck it to you," said Anisa. "I knew it!"

"Keep thinking that if you must, but give me an answer," said Laplace. "Sure, I'll take it. Do you have the other units? The accessories? "Anisa asked.

"They are in the box next to my chair," he said. "There's one more thing I need to tell you. I will be there tomorrow. My weapons still work, and I can still travel through the radiation locally. You must not deploy your nachinaks before I give you the green light. They must remain dormant until then.

Remind Gerard to inform the others."

Anisa stacked her new arsenal of nachinaks neatly in a box and started up the stairs to the catwalk.

"Don't worry, "said Lucky, "I will remind her to remind them."

"Thank you," said Laplace.

Fifty

Tactical Socks: Check. Tactical Underwear: Check, Tactical
Strategy: Check

Tactical Socks: Check. Tactical Underwear: Check, Tactical Strategy: Check

Lucky did not stay in the marble building that night. He parted ways with Anisa in silence when they reached the bottom of the stairwell. She continued into the basement. He walked out the front doors.

He followed the road westward until it became a double track and then a single track. Traffic was very light, with no solo travelers in sight. No one looked at him for very long, choosing instead to hurry by whispering to one another as they passed. He proceeded down the switchbacks and past the smoldering remains of Takezo's shop to the villa.

Augustine's lackeys had made a mess of the place. He managed to salvage a mattress and blanket. He dragged those out to the table in the middle of the mosaic and slept there for the night. He woke before dawn. He had been using his pack for a pillow. He unfolded it and did a quick inventory. He still had his medications, and he took his morning dose at that time. The machete had gone missing amid the turmoil.

However, he still had his headlamp as well as his keys and wallet. He had managed to keep the weapons that he took from the excavation site. He still had the shotgun. He was a little hungry, but he didn't bother to look around for anything to eat. He started up the trail at a clip that he could maintain all the way back to the center of excellence. He hurried along, making good time in the cool morning air. He was winded by the time he got to the outer Plaza at the top of the stairways. He did not find Takezo there.

Fear gave him a second wind, and he sprinted toward the hedgerow surrounding the inner Plaza. His legs were so tired by the time he arrived that he stumbled and nearly fell as he passed the inner transparent door. Early-bird guests occupied

50% of the chairs. They turned around to see what made the noise as he stumbled in.

In front of the raised deck and below the tables on the stage stood Takezo. He had his welding gear on, with a helmet Lucky had never seen before, shaped like an Oni mask. He wore thicker gauntlets with white plates on the palms and folded articulations at the wrists.

The weapon rested on his right shoulder. Laplace stood on his left. It looked as though Lucky had interrupted an argument between them and the half-dozen people seated at the tables on stage. Lucky waved awkwardly and ambled toward the scrum.

"This is not a sacrifice for the spring festival. There is no place for unprotected noncombatants here. You should not be surprised if they are all wiped out. That is my prediction for the spectators and for you," Takezo said.

"I certainly wish this had been coordinated with the COE administration beforehand," a representative from the local bankers complained. "Perhaps if we moved everyone back to the entrance of the administration building?"

"Shinjinarenai!" Takezo muttered, then, raising his voice, said, "Anyone who wishes to live beyond midmorning should move immediately into the passageways through the hedgerow."

Members of the audience looked from side to side cautiously to see what others were doing. A few people rose to their feet immediately and made for the cover of the hedgerow. As the remainder watched the subsequent smattering of audience members seek shelter, the trickle became a wave, with people shoving their way into the gateways.

The security personnel quickly got a handle on the rush before it turned into a panic. They redistributed the crowd and shut the doors.

Lucky watched the scramble with alarm. He jumped and reached for his shotgun when he felt a hand on his shoulder. He wheeled around to find himself face-to-face plate with Francis.

He was wearing the same pressure suit that he had been working on when they came to visit him in the isolation ward. He carried a shotgun as well and had four cans of darts clipped to a belt slung over his shoulder. Flexible plates like blue water bags made of translucent alligator skin covered the suit. The plates zipped together seamlessly, and small flexible tubes joined them to a reservoir on his back. His left wrist bore a structure resembling a paper fan, made of the same materials. He had a strip of fabric tied around the top of his helmet. It was blue gray with the number 9 printed on either side of a pair of stylized nachinak eyes, the left of which winked at the observer.

"Hey, you're Lucky, aren't you?" said Francis. "I'm Francis, from the hospital, remember?"

"Yes," Lucky replied, "I remember. How are you this morning, Francis?"

"Little nervous," Francis admitted. "I am not a big fan of violence. I guess I'm stuck with it, judging by my family history."

"I have seen what you mean," Lucky agreed, "but you can make adjustments even if you can't completely escape your history. Let's just see if we can make it through today, and then maybe you'll have a chance to change
your direction."

"That sounds good," Francis said. "Say, how about I watch your back, and you watch mine?"

"It's a deal," Lucky replied.

They stood quietly for a few more minutes. Anisa showed up and took a position nearby, to Francis's right. The crowd sequestered in the hedgerow behind them stirred. They saw Drusilla running from person to person inside the Plaza. They watched Laplace and Takezo break off and jog to the administration building.

Drusilla arrived at their position not long after. "Maintain radio silence," she said. "The Helpers are here with their nachinaks. They're approaching from the northeast. So far, they're moving slowly. reposition to the outside of the barrier. Lucky I passed on the
instructions about our nachinaks. Anisa wanted to let you know." Lucky nodded.

They held their position until Drusilla finished conveying the message to the guards from the hospital.

Anisa glanced their way and then trotted off to the doorway that joined the emergency entrance to the medical center. They followed, making up some ground on her. They stopped when they reached their previous position relative to the heart of the hedgerow, but she kept going.

Lucky shouted to get her attention, but she only gave him a quick look over her shoulder before sprinting into the woods north of the large plaza.

"That's not a good way to start the day," Lucky said.

They had scarcely turned to watch the northeast corner of the square when they heard the sound of a horn coming out of the West. Shortly, a series of three side-by-side off-highway vehicles came trundling up the stairs, blowing their horns all the way.

The racket stopped when they arrived at the barrier of vines and trees. They parked about twenty meters out and exited the vehicles. From his vantage point, Lucky could see that it was the crew from the old country store. Dion helped Augustine out of the lead vehicle. Margie and Thomas took positions on either side. All three staff members were armed with rifles.

Augustine stepped forward and unfolded three pieces of paper. Without preamble, he began to read.

"Before the assembled witnesses and representatives of the

governing boards of the Authority and the Foundation, I, Augustine, agent of the Authority, present this report of the findings of the investigation into the conduct of the current director of the Bilateral Nephrectomy Center of Excellence, along with recommendations for further action. Please see the package of evidence, which includes interviews, written statements from the accused and witnesses to the alleged crimes in this report, as well as supporting circumstantial evidence, such as invoices and operating room logs.

We have found ample evidence to publicly accuse the subject of this report with the following violations: murder of forensic psychologist, misuse of allocated funds belonging to the bilateral nephrectomy center of excellence, reckless and negligent use of surgical procedures outside of recognized indications, surgical procedures performed without informed consent, use of experimental interventions without IRB approval..."

As Augustine concluded the litany of accusations, something fell out of the sky and struck him on the forehead. He put his hand to the area of impact and swore when he brought back drops of blood on his fingers. Seconds later, another projectile struck him in the shoulder, and then Margie got hit. The crowd hiding inside the barricade panicked, neutralizing the security personnel. Dion, Margie, Thomas, and Augustine scrambled to their vehicles and sped off in the direction they had come. A single motorcycle rolled out from the back of the administration building in pursuit. Meanwhile, the rain of projectiles continued.

Lucky covered his head with his arms and did his best to hide beneath Francis. All around him, on the ground, he saw the remains of nachinak, and more crashing to the paving stones with each passing second. He heard unfamiliar voices from the northeast side of the barrier. Close behind the voices, a heavily armed group of Gods Helping Angels marched into view.

Abruptly, all of the dozen or so fighters dropped like rag dolls before they had a chance to fire their weapons. Laplace stepped from the hedgerow between the fallen group of helpers and Lucky's position. He was unarmed and unprotected, except for a writhing knot of nachinaks stationed just above his head. He tapped the metal ring clamped to his auditory meatus. Nothing happened for a few seconds and then came a deluge of inert nachinaks falling to the ground all around them.

Another tap on the metal ring, and the group of nachinaks assembled above Laplace retreated to their assigned compartments in the abacus he held in front of him.

At the same time, multiple new units poured out of abacus compartments, filamentary tufts, and pockets in his clothing. Four of them unfurled delicate, transparent webs encompassing Laplace from head to foot. A black and red speckled device hovered directly in front of his face. Two heavier units whose beating legs generated a torus of spatial distortion rose to either side of him. He flipped open a can of darts held in his right hand. From the Southwest came the sound of a detonation. Laplace turned and ran off in the direction that the troop of helpers had come from.

A pair of external power sources burst out of the foliage and followed him. Laplace had not yet laid eyes on the main body of the enemy force when he came to a halt. Someone called out to him from the foliage, and out of the tangled

335

vines stepped Gerard, accompanied by a helper dressed in a pressure suit, supplemented by reactive armor pads that protected his torso and an armored helmet, with its faceplate closed.

"He insisted on speaking with you," the Helper said. Laplace recognized the voice.

"I'm going back with them," said Gerard, "to 538. There is no real place for me here. My last encounter with Augustine

proved that. The Authority will never leave me in peace. Besides, Augustine was right. "

I have concocted an elaborate crust of morally consistent, morally accept-able sweets to hide my bitter core. My motive has always come from the

core, however. My art is the most important thing to me, and I need a place to perfect it. This is not the place."

"I… I understand," said Laplace, "but there has to be somewhere besides

538. There is no art or interest in art among those exiles. Their interest in pain and suffering has no greater context. It is simply a prurient fascination."

"That is why he must go to 538," Luther said, "The time has come for a new sect to arise from the old."

He is the one who knows how to transform the simple fascination that you disparage into a beautiful icon worthy of its own place at the Lord's feet."

"Shut up, Luther!" said Laplace as he directed the torus generator to destroy the helper.

"Here is the Way of the Lord, easily spoken but impossible to desire! You take it first, Luther, if you think it is so redeeming!" Only Gerard's intercession saved Luther.

"No Laplace. I can fix this. Even him," he said as he stepped between Luther and certain death.

"I have made my decision, brother," said Gerard without missing a beat. "I don't want to stay here and be stifled. I think I can transform them. Day and night, they get the message that they are sick and deteriorating, and that is how they come to view themselves. I can teach them otherwise. You have shown me how that can be and how I can make it happen. Thank you. Now, let me go."

Gerard turned his back and walked off to meet the unseen mass of helpers invading the COE. Laplace made a move to go after him, but there was no time.

On the other side of the Plaza, God came pounding around the corner from the amphitheater building, which was now unrecognizable.

In the confusion during the skirmish, Lucky had lost track of Takezo, but

just as God reached the edge of the outer Plaza, Takezo shouted from the top of the first staircase and waved his weapon over his head.

God turned away from the shrinking crowd, trying its best to disappear beneath the vines and trees. In three bounds, he reached the top of the stairs.

He tried to land his last step on Takezo, but Takezo slipped under the blow and stabbed blindly up and slightly behind him, catching God's trailing leg precisely along the course of a human femoral artery.

The world blinked and then came the explosion. It blew God off his feet and vaporized the soft tissue down to the bone. Takezo circled warily in the direction of the injured leg.

"You decided against turning over a new leaf, "Takezo said.

"I decided that I'd better pursue my current methods to the bitter end before abandoning them," said God.

When a batter hits a fastball, he never sees the pitch. The ball crosses the distance between the pitcher and the strike zone faster than the retina's refresh rate.

The only reason that bat and ball ever meet is a batter's talent, accrued over years of practice, for reading the pitch.

He picks up on clues from the pitcher to estimate where the bat needs to be and when. He can swing blindly and still hit the ball.

That talent saved Takezo from divine retribution. He raised his blade in a covering guard and sidestepped as God flew at him with a raised fist. Though the blow did not strike his body, he had to absorb some of the impact with his weapon.

Sparks erupted

from the point of contact, and silver frost feathers bloomed in the dark metal. The residual force was still significant enough to send Takezo tumbling down the next set of stairs.

FIFTY

Lucky moved with Francis to aid Takezo, but a salvo of neurotoxic darts forced Francis to stop and cover Lucky.

"This isn't working," said Lucky, "I'm breaking off. I'll meet you at the bottom of the stairs."

Lucky focused as hard as he could on being uninteresting. He left the protection of the armored pressure suit and ran towards the north side of the outer Plaza. The entire force of helpers had arrived and now marshalled at the top of the hill overlooking the administrative offices and the medical Center.

The Center's security forces held the line so far. An artillery battle began to intensify, with projectiles from two armored vehicles and four towed rocket launchers facing off against kinetic rounds from a radar-guided missile defense system.

As he moved to assault the group of four hundred or so helpers, Lucky turned his head to see what had become of God and Takezo.

Takezo was still down, though he was trying to stand as he groped for his weapon. God dragged his left leg. He, too, was having difficulty getting up, but he was recovering more rapidly than Takezo, and the combatants had landed dangerously close to one another. As he watched the duel, Lucky rummaged through his pack.

He quickly came upon the item he was looking for. He was at least 100 m, if not farther, from the lead element of the helpers, who had begun to move out from their assembly area. He bounced the green metal sphere in his hand as he eyed the distance. He flipped open the latch and pushed the button, activating the sphere's proximity function.

He took a three-step, running start and threw the sphere as hard as he could toward the advancing troops.

The sphere entered the downslope of its flight well before it reached its target. Lucky had begun looking for an alternative in his pack when jets of flame burst from the sides of the sphere, setting the device spinning and arresting its fall.

As it took a flat trajectory towards the greatest concentration of opponents, the small jets fanned out into a disk of flaming particles broadcast in a fifty-meter diameter. Anything that the particles touched got consumed by fire spreading from the point of contact.

Takezo was back on his feet, but he looked unsteady. He had the blade in one hand, and his other hand was behind his back.

From a three-point stance, God jumped at Takezo again. Takezo set the point of his blade on the paving stones and knelt behind it.

The knee on God's good leg came forward to crush Takezo, who adeptly adjusted the angle of his weapon to intercept the blow in line with the direction of force.

The explosion counteracted the divine body's forward momentum, flip-ping God onto his back with his head toward Takezo. The leg flopped to the ground and lay at an unnatural angle.

The impact drove half of Takezo's blade through the paving stone and into the ground. It bowled Takezo over, but this time, he controlled the fall, rolling backward with it and coming out of the roll on his feet.

He was well within reach of the deity, who moved to grab Takezo.

The choice to grab required God to arch his back and extend his neck so that he could see what he was doing. The decision placed him second in the tempo of movement.

As Takezo came to his feet, he spun ninety degrees, and his left hand, holding an oblong black-and-white striped object, came down on God's forehead with a smack. The two of them disappeared.

Lucky slipped his pack over his hands, as he ran to Takezo's blade. He grasped the handle, but it shocked him, and he had to let go. He tried again and was able to apply full force to the embedded weapon, but it would not budge.

"Forget it!" Francis yelled as he came up behind Lucky, "Let's go!"

An external power source screeched to a stop beside Francis with an accessory nachinak hovering above it.

Beneath the outer shell of Francis's breastplate, filaments on his chest were already spinning a loop of beads.

"But how will he…" A sensation of pressure on Lucky's chest and back cut short his objection. His vision blurred, cleared again for a brief glimpse of the radiation's dazzling enormity, and then blurred once more as the pressure returned, and he slipped past the squeeze into a familiar environment. Francis was right behind him.

They stood in the excavated cavern beneath the cliff dwelling. God lay on his back, screaming the same scream that accompanied his rebirth. His legs flopped uselessly as he struggled to arch his neck and dislodge Takezo, who knelt on God's upper chest, trying to achieve a stance steady enough that he could bring the knife in his right hand to bear.

Four nachinaks swung and dipped wildly about God's head as he thrashed his arms to free them from the sticky, gossamer webbing entangling his upper limbs from hand to elbow. Just to their left stood Laplace, emptying a can of darts rapidly into the divine flank.

Takezo managed to stabilize himself and drew back the knife, but instead of stabbing at God, he jabbed the blade into the back of his own calf. He dropped the knife and dug his fingers into the wound with a grimace. He pulled against resistance, and then his hand popped free, emerging from the cut with a bloody nachinak in its grasp.

The Nachinak's body curled and then

arched. Its mouth opened wide, and a torrent of black specks poured out. The cloud of particles swarmed around God as he lay on the cavern floor. They quickly engulfed him and sprouted a pair of eyes whose stalks swiveled, directing their gaze into the eyes of God. The specks rolled across the surface of the eyes and into the pupils, disappearing in the bottomless depths. As the flow of particles into the depths increased, the black grains

replenished their number from God's flesh. "No! That is not the way!" said Takezo.

He crushed the nachinak in his fist, and God and the specks were gone in

a silent, blinding white flash like a view from the interior of a lightning bolt. A shadow passed across the glow from the pit in front of them. A single gray bubble no bigger than a plum rose from the black surface, pinched off

at its base, and floated up as it expanded, stabilizing as the globe reached twelve meters in diameter at a distance of six meters from the surface in the pit.

Laplace was the first to recover his wits. He rushed over to Takezo and helped him lie down on the sandstone floor. Laplace removed the welding mask and helme t as well as the gauntlets, which he placed under Takezo's head as cushions. Despite the improved gloves, Takezo suffered severe burns on the palms of both hands.

Laplace turned sharply to Francis and Lucky.

"Go help Anisa, you two! At the old country store. Use the tunnel," he said.

They sprinted into the tunnel, where they found a side-by-side off-highway vehicle belonging to Augustine parked against the left wall of the passageway. It showed a full battery as they initialized the machine. Lucky exchanged seats with Francis.

"You drive," he told Francis, "I've got to prepare."

They sped off into the passageway while Lucky rummaged through his backpack. He stuffed the three remaining batons under his belt and tucked the last sphere into his shirt. He double-checked the shotgun and filled his pockets with shells. Francis scraped the wall of the tunnel as they made the turn, removing a fender and the door on his side. They didn't slow down for the shed covering the far end of the tunnel. A guard remained in the room. He knelt by a window on the right and aimed a rifle toward something in the woods beyond the meadow. He tried to turn as they rolled by, but Francis had already sent a dart his way.

The vehicle smashed the door off its hinges and rolled into the meadow. They skidded to a stop beside the trail and jumped out, using the car for cover while they sorted out the situation. Lucky motioned for Francis to remain with the vehicle. Lucky became unnoticeable and trotted into the woods surrounding the store. A high-pitched buzz bordering on a whistle

grew louder as he approached.

The constant undertone was punctuated by gunshots from the southeast side of the store, the large tree by the dumpster, and the underbrush near the driveway.

He started his foray closest to the position in the underbrush, so he chose to visit it first. He found Drusilla there.

He placed a hand over her rifle's bolt before transitioning to a noticeable state. She nearly managed to wheel around and shoot him anyway. After she recognized him and relaxed, he noted a bullet wound in her lower right abdomen and another in her left forearm, rendering her unable to use her left hand.

"Augustine is on the other side of the building," Drusilla informed him. "One of his lackeys is with him over there; Dion is the guy's name, I think. Augustine has his best offensive weapon deployed, and the pair of them have Anisa pinned down behind the big tree."

341

"Squeeze off a couple of rounds and retreat further back in the woods," Lucky said. She started to move off, and then he remembered.

"Here," he said, pulling the green metal globe from his shirt, "for emergency use." He returned to obscurity and moved to the side wall of the building. Marge was hunkered down behind the grill, aiming her rifle in Drusilla's direction.

She ducked as Drusilla fired off her prescribed shots. Marge looked both ways after she ducked and spotted Lucky immediately. He scrambled to get his shotgun lined up, but she was already aiming.

Before she could squeeze the trigger, another shot came from her direction, and blood erupted from her chest.

Lucky ceased concentrating on his own obscurity. Thomas stood behind the propane tank with his rifle still leveled at Marge's last position. He dropped his gun and held up both hands. Lucky held up his palm in Drusilla's direction, hoping that she would see it and understand. With his other hand, he motioned Thomas over and indicated that he should stay low.

As soon as Thomas was close enough to hear, Lucky instructed him, "Stroll and keep your hands up until you reach the young man in the spacesuit behind the side-by-side. Tell him that I said to stay where he is, then keep going as far away from here as you can get."

Thomas nodded his understanding and moved quickly off into the woods. Lucky focused on keeping a low profile once more and crept over to the side of the building where Dion and Augustine were positioned.

They held the corner of the cinderblock extension to the building as well as the office. Augustine stood behind the corner, surrounded by a swirl of glass shards. Dion aimed out the office window. The arrangement allowed them a slight crossfire. Augustine stepped out from the corner and

directed the tornado of glass shards toward the tree and the dumpster. The shards ripped into the tree's bark and shredded two of the lower limbs. Sparks flew off the dumpster as the side of the metal bin eroded into powder.

Returning fire forced him back around the corner.

Lucky tried to estimate the distances in his head but couldn't do better than a wild guess. He could see no other option, though. He retreated to the middle of the side wall, pulled one of the batons from his belt, and set it according to the directions printed on the casing. He backed up against the wall and then slowly sidestepped until he was able to see Augustine hiding behind the corner of the cinder block addition.

He aimed the shotgun and fired a slug at Augustine. He was relatively far away by then, and the slug missed high and to the left, hitting the corner of the roof. It startled Augustine, and he turned around to look for the source of the gunfire.

Lucky fired again, and then one more time to be sure that both of them were aware of his position. Lucky could see now that the whirlwind of glass was under the direction of a nachinak floating in the eye of the storm.

Augustine sent it Lucky's way while Dion appeared at the screen door on the side of the addition and started looking for his target. Lucky ducked around the tree trunk and started running up the hill at an angle calculated to keep

the tree between him and his pursuers. The Glass tornado had difficulty maneuvering through the woods, and he outpaced it for a while.

It had almost caught up with him by the time he got to the border of the meadow.

Suddenly, it dropped. Lucky felt no effect, which brought him no relief. He turned immediately and ran to the trail that led to the parking lot. He swung around the tree next to the defunct dumpster and found Anisa lying there.

He wasn't sure that she was breathing, and he tried to feel for a pulse, but lacking any knowledge of the species' vascular anatomy in the neck, he couldn't be sure whether or not a pulse was present.

He turned her on her side, and she took a deep gasp of air. He sat down next to her and waited. Francis soon rolled up with Drusilla in the other seat. Anisa blinked and then sat up. Lucky helped her to her feet and began escorting her to a vehicle in the parking lot.

She stopped and disengaged his hand from her elbow. "Wait, not yet," she said, "stay here."

She walked around the end of the cinder block addition and was gone for several minutes. When she returned, she was lugging an oversized abacus on her right shoulder.

FIFTY

She dumped it in the cargo area of the closest OHV in the parking area. She sat down behind the wheel as Lucky settled into the passenger seat.

"No use in leaving without the point of this whole thing anyway," she remarked.

Fifty-one

At the End of the Rainbow, There Is Hawking Radiation

As they pulled into the cavern, Takezo still lay on the floor with Laplace beside him. While they were gone, his condition had deteriorated. They gathered around him, and Laplace explained.

"Look at the shadow his neck casts on the floor. That reddish sheen is a sign that the extraction has failed. His situation is unique, so I cannot predict how long he will last, but it will not be long. We should stay here until he's gone."

"Must you speak that way in front of him?" Drusilla whispered.

"I wouldn't insult anyone of his stature with patronizing lies and omissions," Laplace said. "Go, you needn't witness this, "he added in a softer tone, "and you need treatment for your injuries."

Drusilla frowned.

"Where's Gerard?" she asked. "Has there been any change in the situation at the COE?"

"Gerard has chosen to leave us. He will return with the contingent of troops sent against the COE." said Laplace.

"I will bring him back," Drusilla said.

"He has chosen, for the second time," Laplace said. "He won't come back. I was wrong about him, too. I thought that his preoccupation with pain and death was an externality that the Helpers indulged and promoted. I thought that they put that preoccupation in charge of his true personality.

His preoccupation is part of his true personality. We can't displace it without wrecking everything else. I find it horrifying. I could never accept it, but I have no more right to condemn him than I have the right to condemn a tiger for its carnivorous habits."

Drusilla spat on the floor in front of Laplace as she passed him on her way out of the cavern.

"Stable gray space," Anisa said, staring at the sphere in disbelief. "What is in the well?"

"I don't know," said Laplace, "the negative pole? The sphere is what matters. You're looking at the radiation's entire data set, which compiles constantly until the heat death of the universe.

"Lucky," Takezo called out.

Lucky hurried over to him. A pinkish vapor condensed around his body, dissipating as it flowed away from him across the floor.

"I understand what the slaves mean when they speak of erasure. It is happening to me," said Takezo," I would not have agreed to the design competition or any of the rest of it if I knew this was how it might end."

Every reference is carried away on the wind, thinned out to nothing. You are different, Lucky, so maybe there's a chance that you can recall what others don't. I ask you to remember."

"I will," said Lucky, but when he tried to lay a hand on Takezo's shoulder, he only found mist.

He pulled his hand back in confusion. Still

kneeling, he turned to Laplace.

"Do you recall what I was doing down here?" Lucky asked. "No. I mean, it was something. No, I'm not sure," Laplace said.

Lucky looked down again at a pair of gauntlets lying on the floor. He picked them up and turned them over in his hands as if looking for a clue to their origins. He shook his head, shrugged, and tucked the gloves into his belt.

Lucky looked up again to see Anisa, Laplace, and Francis gathered around the sphere of gray space.

Five nachinaks lay on the floor in front of them. They were all of a blocky construction, each about the size of a miniature poodle, with the central unit being slightly larger than the others.

Lucky recognized the central nachinak as the device that Laplace was working on in the lab, in the marble building. The others were similar to each other, each with a single trunk, multiple eyes covering their bodies, and a red polka-dot pattern on their skin. The legs were small, even vestigial.

"You don't have to do this," Laplace told Anisa. "In fact, I think you shouldn't. I'm sure of less and less with each passing day, but I'm still certain that something is wrong. We have misunderstood something. Something other than utopia awaits us at the end of a complete description of events. I have advised you poorly all along. I want to begin to correct that history. Please don't try it."

"Is that supposed to be an argument for or against? "Anisa asked," I'm persuaded not to take your advice any longer. I made that determination long before you developed a neurologic condition that puts your judgment further in doubt. If you want to start changing things between us, then step aside."

Laplace turned away, walked over to the stairs, and sat down.

Anisa selected the central nachinak and affixed a carrier nachinak on either side of the rectangular body. She attached a wire to a hidden aperture on

the tail end of the central unit and observed as the carrier devices bore their passenger into the sphere of gray space.

They passed entirely into the interior rather than skimming the surface as usual. There were no tugs or buffets while they worked. She arranged the abacus that she had taken from Augustine's body and found the compartment holding the spray bottle with ammonium. She fired a drop at the gray space, and it penetrated the surface with no reaction.

She raised the glass rectangle to her eyes and waited. The green dot finally appeared, and she reeled in the trio of devices. After disconnecting them, she examined the central unit for its small vial of glowing fluid. She found it and fed it into an aperture between the four branching trunks. The entire unit vibrated momentarily and then stood ready. She attached the other four to each of the central unit's four branching trunks.

"Laplace! Come here," she called. "I'm ready for you to open the fold."

Laplace rose from the step wearily and collected his two external power sources. "Please reconsider," he asked one last time.

"Open the fold," she said.

Laplace complied. Anisa stepped through with no hesitation. Laplace walked away before the fold disappeared and knelt beside the well beneath the sphere of gray space and stared at the black surface.

Five minutes passed, then ten. A small slit in the air appeared, and the nachinak with the four-part trunk fell out of it onto the floor of the cavern. They all stood up, and Laplace stooped down to pick up the nachinak.

On the backside, in the upper half of the body, along the midline, a small metal disk

with a raised edge on its upper margin was attached to the body by a rivet. Laplace flipped the disc up and peered into a small screen beneath. He stared intently, as if turned to stone. At last, he blinked and slowly lowered the nachinak.

"How could we have been so wrong?"

He hugged the nachinak to his chest briefly and then set it down beside the well.

"Let them see it," Laplace asked, "if even some of them can admit to what that image shows, it will make up a little bit for my participation in this fool's errand."

He slowly backed over to the well and stepped in. He began to sink slowly. He closed his eyes and leaned his head back. Francis ran to the side of the pool, with Lucky close behind.

"No, Laplace," Francis begged, "please don't leave me."

He grabbed Laplace by the arm, but he was unable to arrest the descent. Lucky held Francis's other hand.

"Don't let go, we have to save him!" Francis implored, as the pool drew him in as well.

Lucky hesitated but then firmed up his grip and held on with all his might. The traction was slow but irresistible. His hand began to slip into the featureless black surface with Francis. He suddenly felt tired.

The substance in the well felt smooth. It wasn't warm or cold. It didn't resist his fingers' motion. The fatigue was overwhelming, and despite his best efforts, his hand slipped off Francis's glove, causing him to sit down hard on the sandstone floor.

Francis spoke again into Lucky's left ear.

"Where are you, Lucky? Help me save him," Francis begged. "I'm here, Francis. I'm coming," Lucky promised.

Lucky took off his pack and dumped it out. He scratched his right leg. A pair of small white feet shuffled into his visual field.

He looked up with a start. Casper stood before him, bearing a few scrapes but otherwise intact. He smiled and turned his attention back to the pack.

He noticed that, somehow, he had picked up a pair of gloves. They were tucked in his belt and promised not to be in the way. He should have removed

them and left them in the cavern, but he didn't. He tucked his headlamp into a shirt pocket. He left everything else.

Something bit him on his right leg, below the knee, at the top of the calf. He slapped at whatever sank its teeth into him, and a nachinak stained with blood fell out of his pant leg. Trailing it came a stream of small black particles like a swarm of insects.

The nachinak arched its back and began to twitch, sending the particles into a frenzy. Lucky scrambled to put distance between himself and it. Casper walked past into the cloud of specks. He reached down, picked up the nachinak, and stuffed it in his mouth.

Specks poured out between his lips. Somehow, he managed to swallow the nachinak. The swarm coalesced around him in its familiar animal form. It looked at Lucky. The eyes were bottomless, and a stream of black particles fell into the pupils perpetually. Lucky didn't feel it threatening to bite this time.

Though he couldn't account for the difference, it seemed to Lucky that the specks acted of their own accord, seeking shelter instead of helplessly succumbing to a dark, ravenous vacuum.

It touched Lucky's hand briefly, and its tall, pointed ears lay back close to its head. "You.   Alone,"   it   said,   "You.   Alone."

It reached down and picked up Lucky's backpack, restoring its contents to the bottom. With one more glance at Lucky, it turned and walked out of the cavern, pausing at the edge of the hole blasted through the outer wall to gather the bones remaining there and stack them carefully in the pack.

"Are you still there, Lucky?" Francis spoke faintly into Lucky's left ear, "Hurry, please, I'm getting so tired."

Lucky examined his skin for any hint of reddish fluorescence.

It was the same old skin, brown, sun-damaged, and not glowing. "On my way," he promised as he stepped into the pool and slipped beneath the black surface.

In the Nachinak's lens, there was a lone still image documenting the completion of a mathematical description of the universe. Anisa was the central figure, but she was not alone. She floated in a column of glass, like a fly preserved in amber, above thousands like her, immobile and facing the same point below them in the distance, where they beheld the ideal observer's portal.

The portal revealed the dendritic radiation of events for the maelstrom that it was: a pointless transformation with no symmetry, solidity, or memory. No one belonged on the other side of the ideal observer's portal, where being and doing went their separate ways. The Masters of the abacus, suspended in amber as they were, had no limits.

They didn't age. They didn't become weak or demented. They saw everything in perfect detail. From their vantage point in the center of everything, they could appreciate the inevitability and perfect rationality of all events, as well as the unintelligibility of agency. That's how their thoughts ran, evolving along the same lines, mimicking the trajectory of actual existence until they all reached the same conclusion.

They concluded that they hadn't been wrong at all. The glass column was a utopia. It was the world perfected. Within it, one endured. Looking down into the dendritic radiation of events at the undistorted outcome ended all thoughts of justice, permanence, purpose, freedom, and all the sorrows those things entailed.

The relief they got from the penultimate thought, concluding that they had not been wrong from the beginning, on the contrary, that they had been right, that they had done what

they set out to do and established a utopia even though it was a utopia for the few, bound in amber, reverberated through them for ages before dying out in deference to the last thought.

The final thought came to them all as they observed the last of the black holes spit out a positron and boil away, leaving an undifferentiated fizz of tiny particles winking in and out of existence for no reason whatsoever.

We were the lucky ones. For an instant, we made it all make sense in the only instant where it could make sense. For an instant only, but the rest, for all its dizzying expanse, was nothing more than the orchestra warming up and the dark symphony hall in the aftermath. It all mattered in a flash, and we missed it. It is not fair. We tried the hardest to possess our time. Why can't we have it back?

www.ingramcontent.com/pod-product-compliance
Lightning Source LLC
Chambersburg PA
CBHW072341020726
47506CB00004B/962